Field Two

SIMON
WINSTANLEY

www.futurewords.uk

First Edition

ISBN-13: 9781539127680
ISBN: 1539127680
Library of Congress Control Number: 2016916624
CreateSpace Independent Publishing Platform
North Charleston, South Carolina

For Janet, Ben and Joseph,
my constants in the great equation.

PROLOGUE

At first glance, the events appeared to be out of order.
Like a neatly ordered deck of cards had been shuffled.

There was obviously a definite structure at work, but the pattern seemed to defy immediate analysis. Some of the elements were recognisable, but it appeared there were deeper, underlying connections that added new layers of complexity.

When observed this way, there seemed to be no merit in maintaining the concept of layering events in a linear fashion.

She would need to adjust to the new frame of reference.

It would just take a little time.

TRANQUILLITY

29th December 2013

Earth's longest orbiting companion was decimated. The focus and inspiration for countless millennia of human worship, study, love songs and brief exploration now lay in ruins.

In its death throes, the Moon had birthed thousands of fragments of varying magnitudes. With gravitational generosity, Earth had reached out and pulled the lethal shards towards itself.

Despite human civilisation on Earth drawing to a close, the larger of the super-fragments were documented and named according to their lunar origin; the hope being that one day the information would be rediscovered.

Copernicus and *Stadius* had struck only the Pacific Ocean, but during their arrival they had converted the satellite networks into a mere expanding cloud of orbiting wreckage.

Sinus had struck ground, removing Malaysia and Singapore from the map, and had initiated major tectonic shifts and tsunamis. The Himalayan mountain range in Nepal had shivered avalanches of snow into the newly formed sea at its base.

The super-cluster of *Palla*, *Hyginus* and *Agrippa* tore a deep, fiery canyon through Africa, reaching from the Gulf of Aden to Nigeria. The fires were quenched within hours as the tidal displacement created by *Sinus* drowned the gaping wound.

Throughout the onslaught, the uncharted smaller fragments continued to rain down on the terrified and dwindling population, ensuring their final hours knew no peace.

When the largest and final super-fragment *Tranquillity* struck, Venezuela was converted into a new Gulf of Colombia; beginning a chain reaction of earthquakes as the tectonic stresses equalised across four major tectonic plates. Shockwaves and tsunamis radiated out and travelled north along the Mid-Atlantic Ridge line towards the Arctic Circle.

After the tremors had pummelled Iceland's volcanic terrain, the tsunami ran inland. When it reached the centre of Öskjuvatn Lake it encountered an artificial bubble of space-time clinging to the surface, and folded it beneath the waves.

HIVE

27th December 2013

The jeep smashed through the security barrier, prompting a swift reply of machine-gun fire. The first burst peppered the rear of the vehicle with thumbnail-sized holes, the second exploded the rear windshield into a shower of glass crumbs. Instinctively, Lars hunched lower in his seat to avoid the gunfire but his low viewpoint was now obscured by the broken yellow-black barrier wedged across the front windscreen. The problem was soon resolved when the glass in front of him disintegrated as another burst of gunfire crackled from behind. Punching his hand through the shattered glass, he yanked the obstruction from his view and was immediately confronted with the sight of the main hangar's concrete wall ahead of him. Hauling hard on the steering wheel, he skidded the jeep sideways and avoided the impact. The hangar door was ahead on the left and currently unguarded; exactly as he had been told.

The cell phone on the passenger seat next to him was still actively displaying both the phone call and a countdown timer; he could see there were only thirty-two seconds remaining.

"I'm at the Hive," he shouted towards the phone, "Do you hear me? I'm doing it! I'm doing it!"

He slammed on the brakes, arriving directly outside the hangar's entrance. As he unclipped the seatbelt he pulled on the jeep's door handle but the door wouldn't open. He pulled up on the central locking button, but the result was the same; the locking mechanism had been too badly damaged during his forced entry to the base. As he climbed over into the passenger seat his jacket pocket snagged on the handbrake and he fell back again. His second hasty attempt was successful and he managed to swipe up the phone as he threw the opposite door open. As he emerged from the badly scarred jeep he could hear voices and footsteps converging from the direction of the gatehouse.

"Can you hear me?!" he yelled into the phone, "I'm doing it now!"

As he ran to the access panel, another sound reached him from the other side of the armoured hangar door, an incessant droning noise.

He reached the panel and inserted his small brass key into it. He turned it to the right and began entering digits into the panel's number pad. At the same moment, the heavily armed guards rounded the corner behind him and opened fire. The first few shots went wide and ricocheted off the jeep's front grill, then one found its mark, impacting him in the upper arm. He fell forward to the ground, still clutching the phone.

"It's done!" he yelled in pain, "I've done what you asked! I can still be useful to you. Please!"

As he spoke, the thick armour-plated door began to slide open and the droning noise increased in pitch and volume.

"Please!" he yelled over the rising noise.

"Drop the phone and stay down!" came an urgent voice, advancing on him from a few yards away.

"Please!" he yelled again.

The door reached its halfway point.

"Your Lifeboat Pass is now safe, Dr. Helgasenn," came the voice from the cell phone, then the call disconnected, leaving only the timer counting off the last four seconds.

As the doorway continued to widen, he began to see a seething mass of random-looking motion within the hangar. Suddenly the door seemed to pass a critical point and a fast, agile swarm of hovering, weaponized drones erupted through the opening. As he lay cradling his injured arm, the stream of rapidly departing drones swelled and thickened the air above him. Almost as one, they turned and headed northeast.

ANOMALY

17th August 2009

The seals were airtight and she was confident that she'd made all the necessary exit checks. She switched comms channel and reported back to the Drum:

"Suit and airlock checks complete. Proceeding to surface."

"Confirmed. Safe trip," came the reply.

She placed her hand on the actuation panel and, after taking a slightly deeper breath than usual, pushed. Immediately she could hear the faint hiss of the Chamber 1 airlock cycling, and the display in front of her changed to read:

'Pressure:0.0 - Exit.'

As the door opened she became more aware of her own breathing, which seemed amplified within the confines of the claustrophobic helmet. She bent slightly to pick up the handle of the case and felt the suit's stiff material resisting her mobility. Even under this gravity the case felt heavy and its large bulk made manoeuvrability an issue.

She stepped aside and allowed the airlock door to close behind her, leaving her standing on the rough, grey regolith.

She set her eyes on the horizon; from here the Sun was a distant point source of light in a velvet-black sky. Although the suit was insulated she could feel its warmth through the glass face plate.

"In transit to Chamber 2 airlock," she reported.

"Acknowledged."

An unknown fault inside Chamber 2 had forced the internal airlock to protect the central Drum of the Floyd Lunar Complex, denying all access from the inside. Using the new tools, it would be her job to enter from the outside and assess the level of damage. If she could find the fault, then the crew would regain access to their dormitory.

At present, the FLC crew had been forced to take up residence around the circumference of the upper levels of the Drum; makeshift bunks situated directly below the Observatory and Prism. What little privacy the crew had enjoyed in the dormitory was now virtually non-existent and, whilst she knew the crew were probably accustomed to each other, the close confines would inevitably lead to tension.

At the moment though, all she had to concern herself with was the issue of regaining external access. She continued to make her way across the dust-grey surface between the micro-craters.

It was then that she saw it.

Two parallel grooves in the regolith were leading into one of the craters.

The tracks were too close together to have been made by any of the FLC's wheeled equipment, so she changed direction and headed away from the central complex, in order to gain a better look.

From the corner of her eye, she thought she saw a movement.

She was the only one scheduled to be on the surface; there should be no-one else out here.

As she moved slowly closer, she could see that the parallel tracks had a ragged, weaving quality to them. She could also see that on either side of the tracks were rough hand-prints heading into the sloping, shallow crater.

EYE WITNESS

15th March 2013

From his elevated position inside one of the London Eye's glass capsules, Maxwell Troye could see all of the city. Far below him ran the River Thames, a thick transportation artery that wound its way through the heart of commercial London. In the distance, to his right, he could make out the curved roof above Charing Cross station, its glass panels reflecting the insipid, grey sunlight. Whilst to his left lay Westminster Bridge and the Houses of Parliament.

A round trip on this oversized Ferris wheel took around thirty minutes, but the power had gone out barely three minutes after he had passed the apex. He knew that it was just a matter of time before someone spotted the problem, but he felt a slight rise in anxiety. He twisted the cap off his bottled water and took a small sip; he didn't know how long he'd have to make it last, but there seemed little point compounding any discomfort by adding a full bladder.

The neighbouring capsules of the wheel seemed overcrowded in comparison to his own. He could see people with cell phones pressed against their ears, no doubt rearranging their busy tourist schedules, confident of their imminent rescue. He was glad that he'd paid the extra fee to buy out the whole capsule; he was also glad that he didn't have to listen to their incessant babble. He took another sip and re-capped the bottle.

Where the wheel had come to rest he had a direct view of Richmond Terrace and, beyond that, Downing Street. At this distance it was quite apparent that there was a huge crowd gathered at the gates; a single police car, blue lights flashing passively, stood nearby.

In the relative quiet, his cell phone vibrated and displayed a message: '10'.

He returned his attention to the distant Downing Street and raised his binoculars.

Most of the street was in shadow but he could see the flashes of reporters' cameras; it was almost time.

Following the immediate financial turmoil surrounding the Siva news, Archive had promised a flow of funds and relief to the United Kingdom. Neville Asquith, who had one of the worst approval ratings of any British Prime Minister, had been given Archive's permission to deliver the good news to an unbriefed press. By all accounts he was relishing the opportunity and was seeing the media event as the chance to reinvent his waning political persona.

From the centre of Downing Street, a sudden and blinding flash of light erupted, lasting a whole second. It was only then that the sound of the explosion reached him; arriving at the glass capsule as a dull thud. Almost automatically he found himself thinking 'For the good of Mankind', before correcting himself:

"Exordi Nova."

He was very much aware of his own recent reprogramming and the chemical reinforcement of the metathene compound bolstering his cold intellect, but the words had the desired effect and he felt his mild anxiety fade.

He lowered the binoculars and witnessed the unfolding events with his own eyes.

In the immediate aftermath of Number 10's destruction, people fled east towards the Thames; exactly as planned. The emergency services had responded slightly faster than he'd anticipated though; in his elevated position he could see several police cars screaming along Whitehall, converging on the Downing Street crater. Not that their presence could in any way prevent what was yet to come. In fact, it would only help him; by effectively drawing the emergency resources away from the London Eye, it would be much longer before his sabotage of the popular London attraction was discovered. If at all.

He knew that, in response to an act of terrorism, the transport networks would shut down next. The security services would begin their pedestrian attempt to cauterise the wound and, in the process, thousands of people would be ejected onto the already crowded streets. Later, those same people would turn to their cell phones, eager to capture and then virally share the act he was yet to commit.

As it had been pointed out to him, the death of a Prime Minister and the destruction of a historic building would soon be yesterday's news. What was needed was an enduring symbol, something that would provoke fear in all who saw it. His patient associate at Number 10 had sacrificed himself as a catalyst; now he must complete the process, ensuring the timing and clarity of the symbol.

As predicted, he could see that people had begun to pour out of Westminster Station next to Big Ben. The iconic clock tower, still doing its best to project an air of authority, cast a weak shadow over the confused crowd gathering around its base.

One of the few aspects beyond his control was the weather, but even this appeared cooperative today. It was overcast and dull; the dark sky itself a perfect backdrop for the day's main event.

He knew he could not afford any mental distraction in the minutes ahead so he retrieved a small silver case from his jacket's inner pocket. He opened it, exposing a single vial of whiskey-coloured liquid and a groove in which to rest his finger. Ordinarily, the small mechanism in the case would prick his finger and measure the levels of metathene in his blood, but he knew the levels no longer mattered; this would be his last dose.

He loaded the last vial into the case's injector mount, pressed the flat side of the case against his thigh, and without hesitation he pressed the injector button. The thin needle efficiently stabbed between the fibres of his trousers and into his flesh. While the compound got to work, he tied back his hair into a ponytail, unpacked the components from his backpack and began assembly.

As he worked, he could feel the cold guiding hand of the drug reinforcing his mental faculties. As an ego-morph he was accustomed to his heightened sense of perception, both in terms of how he viewed the world and how he regulated his own mind, but just on the periphery of his thoughts he became aware of something genuinely new.

Perhaps it was down to the combination of the metathene and the abnormally high levels of adrenaline that were flooding his veins, but he knew the signs well enough to realise that the thought was not a stray one; it was uncomfortably persistent, demanded attention and, as far as he could tell, the voice appeared rational.

By the time he had finished rigging the capsule's interior, a few minutes later, he had absorbed the tangential voice and arrived at a new personal directive. With a subtle alteration, Archive's spectacular launch of Exordi Nova onto the world's political stage would continue as planned. As another method of control, fear itself would now be used for the good of mankind.

Maxwell knew he would make Archive proud.

In time, even Archive would fear Exordi Nova's symbol.

He twisted the cap off his bottled water and drank the contents; the plan no longer required his own sacrifice.

A little over ten minutes later, people lining the banks of the Thames watched in terrified awe as the London Eye ignited. Livid, red flames swept upwards around its chemical-soaked circular framework to meet at the apex; then one of the capsules, in the upper right of the fiery circumference, detonated. It burned more intensely than the weak afternoon sun.

Against the darkening London skies, the massive ring of fire, joined in one place by a smaller circular inferno, defiantly faced the direction of Downing Street. Almost as one, the crowd raised their phones and relayed Exordi Nova's symbol of fear around the globe.

Many diligently continued to record as the secondary detonations cut through the high tension support cables. The wheel lurched forwards under its own weight, crushing the lower capsules instantly and sinking the bottom of the structure into the river. The combination of sudden, intense heat and water ejected plumes of thick steam upwards through the metal spokes. As it hit the flames above, the super-heated vapour flashed into a deep orange and black fireball which rolled skyward.

Exordi Nova's birth cry was the ear-splitting shriek of metal as the wheel sheared itself from the central hub. The fiery symbol of fear began its slow fall across the width of the Thames, trailing a perfect arc of black smoke. In its final seconds, the mass of burning steel crushed and drowned the boats below it, before slicing London's artery permanently in two.

SYMBOLS

8th February 2010

The realisation that the FLC had suffered a minor targeting error during its first firing had only been confirmed the day before. The minor error had an unforeseen consequence. A smaller shard, that Archive had named Tenca, had been split from Siva sending it on an alternative trajectory; one that would reach Earth two years before Siva.

Whilst the impact would not be devastating to the planet itself, it would be devastating to Archive who depended on the public's ignorance of Siva's potential collision. Even with all of Archive's resources, their complex veil of secrecy must ultimately fall. Unless planned for, what would follow next would be public panic and a destabilising of the very systems that Archive depended on.

Andersen Air Force Base had been the perfect choice as the summit location. With at least a thousand miles of Pacific Ocean surrounding it in every direction, it was remote enough to ensure the level of privacy that Archive required.

Having collated all of the feedback from the previous day's Think Tank, Alfred Barnes had absorbed the contents of a classified folder of Archive's history. It was his responsibility to make the recommendations and propose a system of social control. In a state of exhaustion, he had finally succumbed to sleep and been plagued by a bizarre nightmare - a Minotaur had chased him through a maze of multiple choices. When he had tripped over his own tangled thread of choices he had awoken with the nucleus of an idea; one that quickly became a fully developed solution framework on how to deal with a time after Archive's 'Fallen Veil' of secrecy.

After following General Napier into the briefing room, he had begun to outline his proposed method of enforcing a new, controllable, social order when the appropriate time came.

"After Tenca makes its demonstration in 2013, our enemy will become Siva," Alfred continued, "But even then it will be more than two years away from a *possible* impact. It's too distant, too intangible, to ignite action. We'll need to give the world something real to fear, something that will be happening *right now* for them, something to unite *against*."

He walked to the front of the room again and deliberately pushed his spectacles back into place. It was a subtle action, but it conferred on him an air of authority and he knew he needed to maintain their confidence before continuing.

"The anatomy of fear has its roots based in a breakdown of perceived order. We should not be seeking to create a system of social order," he summarised, "if we want true control, true fear, we should be imposing social *dis*-order, by creating our own foe."

He paused just long enough before allowing them the mental relief of a simplified summary.

"We need our own terrorist group."

Objections immediately flew around the room, but he knew this procrastination was to be expected. When he had brought the situation back under his guidance he turned to visual metaphor to assist him.

"When people are trapped in a maze of choices, where no single choice is any more valid than another, having more choices *impedes* escape. Options become *less* clear. So the more avenues we can give people to exert their 'free will' the better. For them, the focus of the primitive drive becomes about out-surviving an unseen foe inside the maze, rather than escaping the maze itself. It will occupy their attention completely, while they labour for the benevolent Archive who are trying to save them."

"Benevolent?" Bradley Pittman snorted.

"Benevolent by comparison," Alfred smiled, "and that's the key. We'll be telling the public how we've been trying to help them all along, but by creating an enemy that seems to be attacking that very help, we get public sympathy, support and willingness to cooperate…"

"And maintain constant state of fear," Alexey Yakovna completed, "Maskirovka."

Alfred bowed his head slightly and smiled, "Exactly."

"Well I'll be..." drawled Bradley, "While they're trying to fathom who's hitting 'em, we're handing out the bandages and the sticks."

"I assume you have the basis of how we'll achieve this objective?" said General Napier directly.

"I do," Alfred glanced around the room hesitantly, "but I'm unsure if I'm permitted to outline it..."

Without a word, Sarah Pittman and Chandra Patil started to gather their things.

"Sorry Sally," Bradley mock-consoled.

"It's fine Dad. Anyway, I ought to get started formulating the Debris Cascade Protection system with Dr. Patil."

"D. C. P." Chandra sighed, "Great. Another abbreviation to add to the book."

The pair left the room and closed the door behind them. There was some noticeable shuffling in seats, which Alfred correctly read as their physical preparation for a new phase in the discussion.

"Ego-morphs," began Alfred, "Scary stuff."

"You're damn straight they are," Bradley shook his head.

"Willing to kill for an authority figure while simultaneously persuading themselves that they're doing it for the good of humanity," Alfred summarised more for his own benefit, "And, have no vested interest in their own long-term survival. That psychological subset of humanity should be empty, but..."

"But here we are," General Napier stared back at him.

"On the day we lose containment of the knowledge of Siva, on the day that Archive's veil of secrecy actually falls, our ego-morphs will have no function."

"I am not understand, Dr. Barnes," said Alexey Yakovna, "they will still have function to protect Archive knowledge, yes?"

"Yes, but by the time we reach 'Fallen Veil', Archive's knowledge will become largely redundant. There will be so much Archive knowledge out there in the public domain that they won't be able to filter who represents a threat to us. They will still be driven to protect Archive, but that drive needs retargeting."

"Sweet mother o' mercy, you're talking 'bout reprogramming," Bradley leaned forward in his chair.

Alfred nodded, it seemed that Bradley had got there quicker than he'd anticipated.

"Dorothy Pittman pioneered the technique," Alfred followed up, pointing loosely in the direction of the Siva folder on the table.

"God rest her, if my mom could hear you talk…" Bradley trailed off.

"With a small alteration, it can be made to work."

"You've never met an ego-morph," General Napier stated, "I have. They anticipate, they're logical…"

"I'm depending on it," agreed Alfred, "Just as they are dependent on us."

"The metathene drug?" Dr. Chen spoke up.

"They can only get it from one place," continued Alfred, "We'll need to adjust their metathene compound to increase dependency, and then reprogram a percentage."

"Do you have any idea of the cost that…" began Napier, "…never mind. Anything else Dr. Barnes?"

"Yes, we'll need our terrorist organisation to be in place and making noise before Tenca hits."

"Why?"

"We need to establish their credibility and visibility before panic sets in, not during. The idea of the threat has to have time to grow. It has to have time to embed itself in the subconscious, so that by the time of their first act, the fear response will be automatic."

"I can set back-channels for communication with Alexey," confirmed Napier, "but best if we leave the Brits out of the loop, I don't know how much of our chatter will be picked up…"

"The fly in the ointment," Bradley noticeably clenched his fists on the table.

"Excuse me?" asked Alfred.

"Monica Walker," Napier replied, "she has an annoying habit of discovering things. There are… reasons… we can't act against her, but I'd rather limit her potential access to any new information."

"Excluding the British could work in our favour," Alfred nodded, scribbling down some notes, "They have experience of politically motivated terrorism. With a suitable high-level act, we may be able to key into pre-existing fear responses."

"Yǔyán zhàng'ài," came Dr. Chen's voice.

"Say what now?" Bradley paraphrased the others' thoughts.

"I said 'language barrier'," Dr. Chen smiled, "How do you ensure your state of fear translates globally, Dr. Barnes?"

Alfred was now openly smiling; he found Dr. Chen's succinct demonstration quite timely.

"People fear the unknown, the new," he replied, "so we give them both, and back it up with a symbol. Where language fails, symbology remains powerful. Just look at the effect of the swastika, you didn't need to understand German to understand the fear."

He turned the overhead projector on and, taking a pen, drew on the bright surface so that everyone could see his proposed symbol.

It was a circle, its circumference broken in one place by a smaller dot.

"This is the symbol of our terrorist organisation," he told them.

"It don't look that terrifying to me," chuckled Bradley, leaning back in his seat and looking around at the others.

"Shouldn't it be more," hesitated Napier through a thick frown, "aggressive? I don't understand it."

"Good," Alfred concluded, "You're not supposed to understand it. The most important aspect of the symbol is that it is open to interpretation. Once atrocities are committed in its name, people will begin to assign all sorts of rationale to it."

"I see a Zero," Alexey offered.

"Good! It taps right into nihilism. Perfect!"

"A new beginning," offered Dr. Chen, tilting his head a little and making cyclical motions with his finger.

Alfred froze, "Now that, is very good. People fear new beginnings, they want the familiar."

Alfred began scribbling notes again, during which Bradley voiced his opinion.

"I see a big ol' space rock smackin' into the planet," he thumped the table for extra emphasis.

"All good interpretations," Alfred walked back to the projector, "you begin to see the point?"

There were noises of assent and Alfred took the opportunity to follow up.

"I'm expanding on Dr. Chen's suggestion here, but I'm translating it into a more arcane language," he began writing on the projector again, underneath the symbol, "it will lend a good deal of weight to the perceived age of the organisation… plus we can track internet searches for the term, which could be useful."

He stood back from the projector and allowed them to see the words:

'Exordi Nova'

"It's Latin," Alfred explained, "it means- "

"New Beginnings," General Napier completed, much to Alfred's surprise.

They coordinated with each other to arrange the next meeting and where it should be held in the event of unforeseen circumstances, then they began to depart from the room.

Alfred caught Bradley's eye and asked, "Have you got a moment?"

Bradley nodded and held a finger up, indicating to Alfred that he needed to finish his conversation with General Napier. While waiting, Alfred gathered the last of his things.

"Dr. Barnes," said Dr. Chen pushing himself forwards in his wheelchair and extending up his hand, "thank you. It has been a most insightful meeting."

Alfred bent over slightly to shake his hand, "Thank you too, Sir."

General Napier assisted Dr. Chen in navigating through the narrow doorway, leaving Alfred and Bradley in the room. Alfred's analysis of the Siva file had left more than a few questions unanswered, but he knew he wouldn't be able to dig any deeper without assistance. He also knew he couldn't ask for that assistance; he would have to make it someone else's idea to involve him. Alfred cleared his throat and lowered his tone before talking with Bradley.

"Dr. Walker doesn't know his family's alive, does he?" he said, patting the Siva folder.

"No, and it stays that way," Bradley fixed him with a stare, "We need him focussed on the Node."

"Of course, of course," Alfred nodded deferentially, "But Walker's parents, er…"

"Howard and Betty?"

"Yes, thank you. Were they ever part of the cortical enhancement program?"

"I… No," Bradley frowned.

"No. Of course not, sorry. It's just that I assumed that because Douglas himself is, well, er..."

"A genius?" laughed Bradley, "No that's all him, hundred percent genius. No artificial sweeteners!"

Alfred laughed along too, but noticed a slight deflection in the gaze of Bradley's pupils; he knew that Bradley had just made the necessary mental note.

Now he had to wait.

VISITORS

10th October 1957

Howard and Elizabeth Walker lived in Atlanta, about five miles west of the Bradley Observatory where Howard conducted his practical work. Their house was a fairly modest single storey home, with a small veranda skirting the front to provide shade during the warm summers. In their compact living room, they were playing with their son who was busy trying to taste the shapes of various coloured wooden blocks and squealing delightedly to his parents' smiles.

"Blue," Howard said, holding the rectangular block for his son to see, "Blue. Cuboid."

He placed it down on the thick rug in front of him.

"Douglas?" said Elizabeth, miming 'where' with a puzzled expression, "Blue, sphere?"

Douglas immediately grabbed the blue ball that had been placed on the rug earlier in the game, and began biting it.

"Good boy, Dougie!" clapped his parents.

The front door bell chimed.

"Think he's going to be bright," Elizabeth gave her husband a peck on the cheek and headed towards the door.

"Going to be?" he half laughed, beaming at his son, "I'd say he's well on the way!"

"You're biased, remember your academic rigour…" she teased.

She opened the door to find two men standing a few feet away, wearing identical grey suits.

"Mrs. Walker? Sorry to disturb you, is your husband home?" said one of them.

"Sure, hold on one second," she said then called to Howard, "There's someone to see you, honey."

She watched him scoop Douglas up from the rug and, half skidding on some home-made flashcards, he made his way over to her.

"Here, take Dougie will you?" he said, tapping his son gently on the nose, "There you go little fella, thanks Betty."

She walked back to the living room and set Douglas down on the rug. While her husband talked with the men, she gathered the flashcards from the floor and carried them to the nearby kitchen table. She picked up the bottle she'd been warming and walked back to the living room sofa. She collected Douglas from the rug and settled on the sofa, ready to begin feeding him. She was just checking the milk's temperature, when a voice came from the direction of the front door.

"Mrs. Walker?" called one of the men.

She shuffled forwards on the sofa in order to stand up but was interrupted.

"No, please don't get up, I can see you're busy with baby Dougie!"

Although she and Howard used the diminutive form of their son's name all the time, she disliked it when it was used by people she didn't know. It put her a little on edge, mostly because the man was continuing to smile cheerfully as he visibly leaned around her husband to talk to her.

"It seems that someone broke in at the observatory," he smiled with a shrug, "so Howard's going to come with us and secure the premises. I'm sorry for the inconvenience, I truly am."

Something didn't seem right to her.

"Howard…?" she called, hoping that he would pick up on her sense of unease.

Howard turned around and faced her, his expression blank.

"It's OK honey," he called, "I'll be back before Dougie's next bottle."

She had only just begun feeding him, which presumably Howard could see. The next bottle wouldn't be for several hours, which Howard must have known. The observatory was only a few miles away so she couldn't understand why he would possibly be gone for several hours.

"OK, look, call me when you get there?"

She watched as her husband pulled on his coat and beamed a smile at her. As he was closing the door she heard him reply, "You know me!"

She did know him, very well. It appeared that he had no control over what had just happened.

She carefully pulled the bottle from Douglas' mouth and placed him back down on the rug. She swiftly crossed the living room to arrive at the window next to the front door. Douglas was making the first attempts at starting to cry, but she knew she had to see what was happening outside.

Through the window she could see that the shorter man had opened the rear door of a car. Meanwhile, Douglas had moved onto the more urgent bleat-like crying and she knew it wouldn't be long before this graduated into a full communication of hunger.

The man was gesturing for Howard to get into the back of the car and it seemed that her husband was complying. To her eyes, they didn't look like plain clothes police officers, and she doubted that the observatory was their real destination.

Douglas began to cry with full force now.

"Mommy's coming, Dougie!" she called out, but felt compelled to watch the scene outside and did not move from the spot.

Even after the two men closed their front doors, there were several long seconds before the car engine started. She tried to take in as much information as possible but found that, in addition to the car having no licence plates, it was completely black. It also did not appear to have either a make or model number anywhere on its body. She tried to recall the appearance of the men, but all that came to mind was their minor height difference and the fact that they wore the same dark grey suits.

The black car drove away, leaving the quiet street filled only with the sound of crickets. Everything was as quiet as it had been before the visitors had rung the doorbell.

It was at that point that she realised the lack of noise was within the house too. She couldn't tell when it had happened but Douglas had stopped crying. Somehow doubting her own senses, she cautiously turned and began to move quietly and slowly back through the living room. If he was asleep then she didn't want to wake him, but then the thought occurred that there may be a more worrying reason for his silence and she started to increase the length of her steps.

It only took a few seconds to reach him, but when she arrived she saw that Douglas was sitting upright on the rug's edge. With the memory of Howard being driven away still distracting her, she absent-mindedly started to praise Douglas.

"Oh! Well done, Dou-" she stopped dead in her tracks and felt a chill run through her.

The colourful band that ran around the circumference of the rug was broken in one place by the presence of her son, who was sitting bolt-upright. But it was not his posture that had caused her to stop.

Her seven month old had arranged each of the wooden blocks into geometric types, that were further sorted into neat rows of red, green and blue. From his sitting position he was looking at her, quietly.

No, she thought, 'looking' was too passive a word.

He was watching her.

As she looked back at him she saw his focus suddenly slide away; his previously well controlled head suddenly seemed too heavy for him and it resumed the slight bob and weave she'd become accustomed to. Now lacking his former precision, he turned to look in her general direction.

In the silent living room, Douglas suddenly continued screaming.

SYNC

27th December 2013, 8 p.m.

Douglas pushed his daughter into the airlock as hard as he could, slammed the 'close' button, and stepped outside as the door hissed shut. The Node's insulation was far too efficient to let sound escape but he could still see his daughter through the airlock window; she was already back on her feet and pounding at the glass.

The only sound reaching him now was that of the panicked crowd still attempting to escape the fiery remains of the bridge which, until a few seconds ago, had connected the Node's island to the bank of Öskjuvatn Lake. Above the cries he could now hear the distant throb of helicopter blades too, receding from the Node.

All that mattered now was that Kate was safe inside the Node wearing his Biomag. In the rush to reach one of the Node's airlocks, Kate had fallen and smashed her Biomag; he had acted quickly to ensure her safety by forcing his own functional one around her neck.

In less than thirty seconds the Field would activate. Without the protection of a functional Biomag, Douglas knew he would need to get clear of the spherical field that would shortly surround the Node, or risk being torn apart.

He turned away from her and pulled on his rucksack. After clipping the belt around his waist, he checked his watch; perhaps twenty seconds remained. He knew he could not afford to look back, even once, to see his daughter; it would be too painful and he would need every second to get clear in time. Steeling himself, he looked skyward then set off swiftly in the direction of the island's main lab.

The heat from the bridge fire had somehow grown more intense, as the materials within it began to be consumed. A sharp snap and retort of gunfire rang out from the middle of the distant crowd. Even now, people were still fighting for any conceivable vantage point over their fellow human beings. The reality was that there would be very few safe places once the lunar fragments hit. As he ran back towards the lab, the thought of Monica and the underground Dover facility pushed into his mind. The deep, warren-like tunnels were airtight at the entrances; perhaps his wife could still survive.

He felt a deep rumbling sensation underfoot and knew the Node must nearly be at sync; a fresh burst of adrenaline forced him onwards. Although he was now clear of the Node's circular footprint, the plan had always been to make the diameter of the spherical Field much larger than the Node, so that a large volume of breathable air could be taken along with them. He had no choice but to keep going. He was no longer an agile man, and his chest began to burn with the continued effort of running. Ahead lay a safety marker, one of twelve crude concrete slabs surrounding the circumference of the intended Field. He pushed on against his body's protest, and only when he had passed the marker by several yards did he allow himself a controlled collapse to the ground.

From behind him, there came a high-pitched sound followed by an immediate, and total, silence.

He rolled into a sitting position and, still breathing hard, turned to look up at the Node.

The Node was just as imposing as it had been a moment ago, except the entire hemispherical structure appeared to be perfectly muted. In the moment that the Field had been established, a thin sliver of the crowd's chaotic noise, echoing off the Node's structure, had also been captured within the Field; never to be returned. The result was a bizarre discontinuity of sound. Even the Icelandic wind was having to find an alternative way around the Node's impermeable Field.

The Node was also beginning to exert its presence in other ways; in the night sky Douglas could see that the intense magnetic field was inducing an aurora. But as with its much smaller predecessors, the Mark IV Field itself was not directly visible. Only a soap-bubble-thin shimmer betrayed the perfectly spherical fracture between two states of time.

He levered himself up on one elbow and looked up at the orb-like structure, dominating the island.

"Well Monica, I did it," he wheezed, allowing himself a moment of pride, "Our daughter's safe."

The thick black smoke continued to stream upwards from the moat behind him. From his position at the safety marker, Douglas could see that the Node's island was effectively cut off from Öskjuvatn Lake's shoreline a hundred yards away. No-one would be able to reach the Node. However, this also meant he wouldn't be able to leave.

ATKA

2nd January 7142

Long ago the forefathers had repaired the bridge, allowing the Elders to reach the wooded island beyond. It was at the heart of this island that the Orb sat; but even from here its cold, ethereal dome was visible above the small trees.

The most senior Elder called forth Atka alone and together the pair began to walk across the long, wood and vine bridge. In the spaces between the wooden branches below his feet, he could see the chasm below and the still waters that ran deep and dark. He could see the strange jagged shapes, from a long-departed era, jutting out from the mirror-like surface.

They reached the end of the bridge and stepped onto more solid ground. As was the custom, they touched the fractured, ancient carved stone that bore the inscription 'ARK IV'. Then they moved towards the Orb's light.

They knew not to tread too close to the impenetrable field surrounding The Guardians' domain, and stopped many footfalls short. But even at this distance Atka could feel its powerful force tugging at him. He was about to bow in reverence, but the senior Elder bade him stand.

Kneeling beside the cooling remains of Atka's campfire, the Elder scooped up a handful of the warm ash and then returned to Atka's side. Lifting his hand to his mouth he dropped a small amount of spittle into the ash and then invited Atka to do the same.

As the Elder mixed their spittle and ashes into a paste, Atka looked around at the perfect night; the bright stars and rings, the Orb and even the Sky-Spirits were here to witness his initiation. He became aware of his place within the long chain of his ancestors and their dedication to preserving this place.

Atka turned to face the Elder as he began the ritual.

Although the words themselves had lost their meaning to the depths of time, they knew the importance of saying them aloud.

"Arkiv," said the Elder raising the ashes.

"Exordi Nova," replied Atka, brushing the hair away from his forehead.

Dipping his thumb into the black paste, the Elder marked a circle on Atka's forehead then placed a wide dot to intersect the circumference.

The exact origin of the symbol was long-forgotten knowledge, but Atka believed in what it represented now: the circle meaning the unbroken renewal of life and the dot depicting the Orb watching over each new beginning.

Atka felt the hairs on his arms stand upright, but it was not in reaction to the symbol being placed.

He turned towards the Orb and saw that within, a Guardian had appeared.

She was pointing at him.

He recalled the night, many suns ago, when he had seen his first Guardian standing motionless within the Orb. He had fallen to his knees and bowed in reverence, averting his eyes. But now he found he was unable to look away.

Her face was aglow and her floating hair was the colour of a fiery, crimson sunset. Her outstretched arm trailed a garment that appeared to be woven from light itself; its folds sparkling like the sun reflecting from the surface of the sea. The precious stone on the Guardian's chest was like the one that the Elder wore tied to a necklace, but it appeared that her stone was not held by a ring of gleaming metal.

"Atka?" the Elder now called for his attention.

He forced himself to look away from the Orb's radiance and the watchful gaze of the Guardian, all else now seemed dim by comparison.

The Elder untied the ring of metal from his vine-weaved necklace and held it; all five of his fingers touching the smooth, shiny, palm-sized circle. He held it out towards Atka, then spoke the word of guidance:

"Ekwayta."

Atka stared at the precious stone set within the unbroken loop of shining metal. Its form was like that of the ash symbol upon his forehead, but it appeared to gleam in the light of the nearby Orb. He desperately wanted to turn again to bathe his face in its light, but he knew that the Sky-Spirits must be watching his every action. He placed his forefinger on the sparkling stone, and the Elder nodded for him to continue.

"Fine-dus," Atka traced his fingertip around the metal circle until it returned to the stone once more, "Eridanus."

The Elder now brought forth a small pale-coloured box. The size was such that he could hold it in one hand, yet he held it in both, cradling it with care. Gently he prised open the box, dividing it in two.

One part held green-coloured metallic veins frozen into a flat surface that was covered with tiny, spider-like, boxes; the other part contained a hole and a circular indentation.

Until Atka could fashion his own necklace, he knew that he must place the metal ring into the box. He carefully turned the ring and placed it into the circular groove so that the precious stone sat safely within the hole.

The Elder joined both pieces of the box together again, then placed it into Atka's waiting hands.

Its time-worn surfaces were hard, and pebble-like, yet it weighed as little as tree bark. He ran his fingers over the surface, feeling the scratches and bruises that the box had endured on its long ancestral journey. Next to the precious stone, now visible in its surface, was a small grey patch that looked as smooth and as clear as ice, but was not cold to the touch.

Low thunder suddenly grumbled from the ground under his feet, as it had done earlier that night. But instead of running in fear he looked to the sky. As he did so, he saw the Sky-Spirits become weaker and thinner. The ground thunder grew a little stronger but now a new noise reached his ears.

A sickly, quiet wail was coming from the box within his hands. At the same time, light came from within the warm ice; it was as pale as the light before dawn and, as Atka watched, the light quickly spread through its surface, leaving darker patches of shadow.

The shadows seemed to form shapes; some of which he had seen before on the ancient carved 'ARK IV' stone. He had no sense of the meaning of the shapes but he saw the shadows take the form of '2400'. The shadows swiftly flowed like black water to form '1200', then the quiet wailing sound died and the ice became inert and dark again.

He felt the hairs on his arms tingle as they had done a few moments ago and there was a sudden, unnatural quiet.

2974

11th March 2013

Benton took a moment to assess the man at the ATM across the street. Twenty minutes ago Kate Walker's credit card had been used and it appeared that it was happening again now. He'd been alerted to the card's use and was watching the man carefully, but even at this distance he could tell that it wasn't Blackbox. This man was obviously homeless and for a moment Benton felt a flash of pity, but he pushed the thought aside with the assurance that he was operating with Archive's authority.

This sort of situation had genuinely not arisen before.

Normally his targets were in possession of something with abstract value. His threats were normally constructed around what his target would lose by not complying. If the person had already lost everything, he thought, how could he possibly threaten him?

In the few short strides from his car, he quickly assessed his target.

The dishevelled figure wore several layers of clothing, making him look larger, but from the folds and creases in the stained materials he could tell that there were no well-developed muscle groups likely to be of any resistance. Although the man's shoes were heavily soiled and degenerated, the laces were wrapped and tied around his ankles; at some time in the past, this man's shoes had been stolen from him while he slept, so he was obviously taking no chances.

The man did not see his approach, not because Benton had been particularly stealthy, but because the man was crouched over at the ATM keypad and focussed on the cash it was dispensing. The man hadn't seen him but, almost on autopilot, he'd hidden the number pad from view. To Benton, this spoke volumes; this was someone who had once had a credit card and all the modern trappings, but had then lost it.

Benton checked the street and was glad it was empty, there would be fewer variables to track. He much preferred remote locations. Isolated. Controllable.

"Are you going to be long?" Benton called to the man.

It had the desired effect. The man twisted around and froze in place, staring at him.

"You're not in trouble, yet," Benton stepped a little closer. Almost theatrically, and mostly for the benefit of the man, he checked around the dark street. In stressful situations such as this, ordinary people were less attuned to nuance and should be given clear indications of what the threat is, in order to leverage their responses effectively.

"Where did you get the card?"

It took a few seconds for the man to find his voice.

"I found it."

"Did you also find the PIN code?" Benton followed up, stepping a little nearer.

"I..." he stammered.

Benton had his suspicions confirmed in that moment. The man's repeated use of the credit card was a distraction, arranged by Blackbox. He found himself almost admiring Blackbox's behaviour, whilst simultaneously relishing the possibility of a long conversation with him under circumstances that were more under Benton's control.

"I'm going to ask you the same question again," Benton stopped a yard away from the man, "and you are going to tell me the truth. Or, I'll be taking the cash and your shoes. It looks like they're tied pretty tight, so you'd have to be unconscious for me to get them. Nod if you understand."

The man nodded.

"Good," said Benton, then paused before asking the question again, "Where did you get the card?"

The man pointed back along the High Street, "They gave it me, up there."

"Good. Who gave it to you?"

"Some guy and 'is girlfriend," the man complied, "I let them borrow me shopping trolley, and they gave me the card."

"And they gave you the PIN code?"

"2974," the man replied immediately.

Benton hadn't asked for the PIN number, he'd asked whether the couple had *given* him the PIN number. The man was obviously doing his best to comply.

"Good. Now," he changed tone, "which way did they go?"

The man pointed towards the opposite end of the High Street.

"They turned left," said the man, then qualified it, "I think."

The man seemed genuinely helpful and therefore possibly useful.

Benton was about to demand the card from him when a thought crossed his mind. Blackbox had obviously been intelligent enough to set this diversion, but Benton had no way of knowing if Blackbox was also monitoring the card's use. If he confiscated the card now, it would interrupt its continued use and this might alert Blackbox to Benton's progress.

"What's your name?" said Benton.

"Terry," he managed.

Before he could say any more, Benton turned and waved his hand to a building at the other end of the street. He raised a forefinger towards his ear and spoke into his sleeve.

"Control? Suspect's name is Terry. He's in possession of the stolen card."

Terry turned, trying to see who Benton was talking to, but unsurprisingly there were too many windows. After a pause Benton spoke again.

"OK, you come down here then," he took his finger away from his ear and addressed Terry, "Did Blackbox and Walker give you any instructions?"

As Terry searched his memory, Benton considered his own. There had been no reason to mention Blackbox or Walker by name, it had been a mental slip; crosstalk between the facts and the fictitious scenario he was concocting for the homeless man. He made a mental note to check on his metathene level when he was in a more secluded space.

"They just told me to keep putting in 2974 and take fifty quid each time," Terry replied.

"Each time?"

"Every twenty minutes," he said pointing to the High Street's clock.

Benton put his finger to his ear again and resumed his fictitious conversation.

"2974," he continued to stare at Terry, "Understood."

Benton pointed to the building at the other end of the street. At the same moment a distant police car siren reached them. From its pitch Benton knew it was heading away, but he used the auditory presence to his advantage.

"My colleague, watching you up there, wants you to keep taking the cash out, so that we can apprehend the two criminals."

"But the money?" Terry asked hesitantly.

"Keep it. Where they're going, they won't need it," Benton summarised, "Do you understand your part?"

Terry nodded and carefully leaned back against the ATM.

"Good. My colleague will be down here shortly," Benton lied, "Thank you, Terry."

As Benton walked away, he stuck a finger to his ear again and spoke so that Terry could overhear him.

"Do not shoot him."

Aside from knowing the direction that Blackbox had gone, he was virtually no closer to catching him. However, he had potentially sidestepped Blackbox and Walker's card trap and had depleted their cash reserves whilst helping someone in need. A distant part of Benton recalled that he liked it when he could help others.

MINUTE ONE

T-09:12:00

The slightly nauseous feeling passed as the Node transitioned into the decelerated time-frame, then Colonel Beck came back to his senses. A tremor ran through the control room as the seismic shifts of the tectonic plates beneath it registered feebly against the Field. Ahead, he could see the approach of a tsunami as it ran inland. The accelerated time-frame beyond the window meant that events were now unfolding at a disturbingly fast rate. He knew that, in theory, the wavefront's impact should have no effect on the Field, but he still felt the primitive need to brace himself for the event. There was no time to warn everyone aboard the Node; there was barely the time to warn those in the room.

"Brace!" he yelled.

The scale of the surrounding Icelandic landscape, combined with the false motion cues of nature itself, gave a surreal quality to the tsunami. To his eye, distances seemed compressed and the wavefront covered the apparent ten miles in under a second. The wall of water hit the spherical Field and swept overhead.

There was a flash of light, as the hydrogen and oxygen within the water attempted to travel through the impenetrable Field, then light levels dropped within the Node as it became submerged. The Node itself shuddered only slightly as the Field passed through the local variation in gravity caused by the seawater; but otherwise it remained isolated from the effects.

There were almost subliminal moments of large objects hitting the Field before vanishing from view; ships, military jeeps and even small aircraft, registering only momentarily on the eye before being deflected away. Then, just as suddenly, the water drained away in an instant.

Colonel Beck looked out at the devastation.

Öskjuvatn Lake, normally the home to relatively shallow melt-water, had been inundated by the combined swell of the Atlantic Ocean and Norwegian Sea pushing inland. The waters would recede in time, but already the landscape seemed part of a different epoch.

The Node's surrounding base and bridge were now mostly washed away, the only evidence of their former existence being the jagged tips of observation towers drowning in the time-smoothed, mirror-like water.

He pulled his eyes away from the sight.

"All stations report in," he commanded, "Mission order."

While each station reported in, he considered what lay ahead.

"Structural, intact!"

They would mourn the loss of a civilisation…

"Power, ninety-eight percent, holding!"

They would rebuild their lives and the world beyond…

"Field, twelve-hundred to one gradient, stable!"

Out of the fires of the old, they would begin again…

"Gravitational tether, fifty-nine milligals, steady."

On hearing the final station report, Beck lifted the Main Circuit public address handset.

"All hands, this is Colonel Beck. We are underway, report for roll call at duty stations."

He hung up the handset and returned to his own workstation.

Originally the Node had only been scheduled for its departure through time in the event that Siva could not be stopped. The destruction of the FLC meant that Siva's arrival was now guaranteed. However, that still left fifteen months of preparation time before the April 1st 2015 deadline. The cascade fusion event that had torn the Moon apart had brought a more immediate problem - the arrival of the lunar fragments thrown towards Earth; the premature departure of the Node had suddenly become a necessity.

Colonel Beck's workstation screen was blank.

Mere minutes ago, before their departure, the Node had come under threat from two different sources. The ten-mile mark defence stations surrounding the Node had begun firing on multiple airspace incursions; judging by the sheer number of missiles that the defence station was depleting, Beck knew it was a coordinated attack.

The second threat had been immediately outside the Node itself. The electrified perimeter fence had somehow been breached by the thousands of people making camp beyond. All were desperately seeking shelter within what they saw as a fortified military installation; but Beck knew that without the appropriate isotope protection, none of them could survive the Field's departure.

To deal with the local threat, it had been his decision to destroy the bridge that connected the shore to the Node's island. He could understand the panicked local attempt for people to seek shelter, but he could not understand the sustained attack of the ten-mile perimeter. It was an aggressive action with, he presumed, the hostile end goal of either capturing or destroying the Node. When the lunar fragments had been due to impact Earth in a matter of hours, he thought, who could possibly have benefited from the destruction of the Node?

His workstation no longer emitted any warning tones. The ten-mile mark defence stations were no longer relaying any missile telemetry; radio frequencies had never worked through the Field.

He looked out at the Node-induced, purple-green aurora and the rising, but utterly destroyed, Moon. The fragments that were still in orbit had already begun to string out in a thin line.

Before their departure he'd overheard that the lunar fragments may possibly fall into orbit around the planet, giving the Earth a Saturn-like system of rings. Now it seemed that this would become a certainty.

He realised that the Node's aggressor no longer mattered; whoever they were, they belonged to an already vanished world. His thoughts of the past were dispelled when Roy Carter's voice called him from across the control room.

"Sir. The Siva clock stands at four hundred and sixty days."

Siva's inexorable course to Earth had not been swayed by the lunar events; they now had to prepare for its actual arrival, just over a year away. No, Beck thought, it was a year away outside the Field.

"Internal Clock?" he shot at Carter.

Carter inhaled deeply before replying.

"In here, Sir, that's nine hours, twelve minutes."

The plan had always been for General Napier to oversee the journey, but for some reason his flight hadn't arrived at the base before the Node's departure; a departure Beck himself had instigated. In just nine hours Siva would, in all probability, usher in a new ice age, so the prospect of commanding this journey seemed daunting to him. Military and civilians alike would look to him now for answers and leadership.

At the entrance to the control room a sudden commotion broke out, a young woman was pushing her way in.

"General Napier," she was gasping, "I need to speak with -"

"Wait! Let her through, it's Walker's daughter," said Beck, recognising her and crossing the room to meet her, "Miss

Walker? I'm afraid General Napier didn't... wait, where's your father?"

She just shook her head.

Beck shot an angry glance across the room at Scott Dexter; a minute ago Scott had confirmed that Douglas Walker's Biomag had safely entered Airlock 2. Scott's face fell; although the system had verified who the Biomag had been assigned to, he hadn't checked to see who was actually wearing it.

Still clasping her father's Biomag, Kate Walker simply said: "He's not coming."

Each section of Field Control knew their own roles within the narrow operational parameters of their own contribution, but the absence of the Field's creator was a loss that none were prepared for. Colonel Beck ran his fingers through his hair.

"This is *not* part of the plan," he muttered mostly for his own benefit.

He looked back over at Kate who was smiling through tears.

"No, it's not," she said, "but *this* is."

She was holding up a pair of digital recording binoculars.

"My Dad sent me a message."

Beck knew that she was clearly traumatised by the loss of her father, but he knew he had to prioritise. He had nine hours to prepare for whatever Siva threw at them.

"Miss Walker," he began, "You have our deepest condolences for your father, he was a great man. Doubtless we all owe our lives to him. We have a short time to prepare for Siva's arrival but, assuming we get past that, I will make resources available to you so that you can watch your father's message -"

"Damn it, Beck!" Kate stopped him mid-sentence.

Colonel Beck was not used to being interrupted, but he had to remind himself that this was a civilian who would not necessarily have respect for the chain of command. Given the mix of personnel now inside the Node, this was an issue he would have to deal with more often.

Taking advantage of the temporary shocked silence, Kate strode across the room and continued:

"This is not some simple 'Goodbye Sweetie' video call! It's important! There's hundreds of pages, he stood there for hours -" her voice faltered, but she gritted her teeth and pushed on, "he stood there, knowing the world was ending all around him, just to get this message to us!"

She pushed the binoculars into Colonel Beck's chest and held them there.

"You make this happen," her bottom lip trembled, but her eyes remained fiercely locked onto his.

He knew in this moment he had to make a choice. It would set a dangerous precedent to allow a civilian to override his authority, so here was not the place to make that choice.

"Miss Walker," he lowered his tone, "My office."

He turned away from her and walked the few steps to a small office built into a segment of the control room. He opened the door and, after Kate had entered, he followed her in. He was about to close the door when a thought struck him.

In full view of the quiet and startled occupants of the control room, he slid the 'Gen. Napier' nameplate out of its holder on the door. He dropped it into an open drawer of a nearby filing cabinet, and then quietly closed the office door.

BLACKBOX

4th July 2013

"It's getting worse," Kate sighed, looking out through the passenger window.

"Yeah," Marcus replied, watching the checkpoint recede in his rear-view mirror, "Archive bloody checkpoints, they got us living in fear, twenty-four seven."

"I meant the rain," she gestured outside, "Can the plane even land in this weather?"

"Hope so," Marcus shrugged, "Your mum says he's done it before."

They drove on through the night's downpour.

After leaving Monica Walker's underground facility beneath Samphire Hoe, they had encountered a security checkpoint, one of several now dotted around Dover. It was not an uncommon sight; similar Archive checkpoints had recently sprung up around ports and towns all over Britain.

The public had been advised that checkpoints had been put in place for their protection and to reduce the risk of Exordi Nova terror attacks. Following the events in London on March 15th, daily life began to be dominated by multiple levels of fear. Understandably, most people had the fear that Archive's efforts may fail to stop Siva's advance. In counterpoint, they also feared that Exordi Nova may strike at Archive's humanitarian efforts. At the intersection of these perfectly orchestrated fears was Archive's sympathiser hook; fear of being labelled a 'Novaphile' by failing to report someone you suspected.

The need for vigilance quickly twisted into the creation of vigilante groups, who metered out barbaric justice to those they deemed were guilty. While some groups would simply execute Novaphiles, others would cattle-brand their victims with the circle and dot symbol, then return them as a warning to others. Of course, the presence of a branded person within an already fearful community only raised tensions further.

A cycle of tension persisted, feeding on the abundant fear. All the while, Archive very publicly empowered the people by arming them with rations and shovels; encouraging people to dig their own deep tunnels and bunkers in the dirt. The reappearance of posters proclaiming 'Dig for Victory' and the decision to save power by extinguishing street lighting at night, contributed to a wartime air of caution.

The windscreen wipers beat back and forth across his field of view. As swiftly as one arc of rain was swept from the screen, another would flood in to take its place. Marcus idly wondered if any of their actions tonight would have any effect at all, or whether they were simply thrashing at an unstoppable foe.

After another mile the rain subsided and, passing a vandalised road sign, Marcus pulled the car in at the side of the road. He turned off the headlights and the windscreen wipers, leaving only the sound of the light rain drumming at the roof.

"This is it," he pointed to the entrance gate of the RAF Manston airfield, a hundred yards ahead.

"You sure?" Kate leaned forward to peer through the windscreen, "Looks derelict."

Miles Benton, who had said nothing during their entire trip, chose that moment to offer his own unique perspective.

"*Looks* derelict," he said, highlighting the deceptive nature of appearances. Without another word he got out of the car, taking his rucksack with him. Marcus and Kate exchanged a look in the rear-view mirror.

"I'm coming in with you," Marcus insisted.

"That's not the plan," she began, "Benton and -".

Marcus had already left the car.

Before the news of Siva had become common knowledge, Miles Benton had discovered that Kate had unwittingly come into the possession of some sensitive Archive data. As an ego-morph, his cold logic and adept manner of silencing leaks had come dangerously close to silencing Kate; had Marcus not intervened, she would not be here today. Over the past months, Marcus and Kate had watched the progress of Benton's reprogramming and had seen him reduce his dependence on metathene, but his detached intellect had remained. Despite it being useful, it was a trait that Marcus found unnerving and difficult to trust.

In the thin sliver of moonlight, they could make out a dishevelled-looking Spitfire aircraft, impotently guarding the entrance to the airfield. Its RAF roundel had been graffitied with an additional dot in the outer circle; a sign that, in some way, the area had suffered contact with Exordi Nova.

Using only their torches to guide them through the darkness and rain, they walked the few hundred yards to the side of the runway and waited by a triangular orange flag. When Marcus heard the sound of an engine, he couldn't be sure where the noise was coming from, so he instructed them to turn off their torches.

As the noise became louder, Marcus turned his head in the general direction of the sound. Through the continuous drizzle he could just see the approach of a dimly pulsing red light. Then, without warning, dozens of high-powered LED light clusters lit up along the edges of the runway. Spaced every fifty feet or so, they defined a long illuminated landing corridor in an otherwise pitch-black landscape.

Moments later a single propeller Cessna 172 emerged through the rain and shot past them. With a squeal of rubber, the aircraft made a swift touchdown and they could hear the engine throttle back.

"OK," Marcus said, turning Kate around to access her backpack, "Your mum said to give you this."

He pushed a letter from Monica into one of the pockets and zipped it closed, "She said you'd understand when you open it. Don't ask me, I dunno. You take care of yourself, you get me?"

"I get you," she nodded with a significant glance at Miles, who was busy watching the aircraft.

"OK then," shrugged Marcus.

"Thank you, Marcus. I -"

"Oh shut up," he exhaled, not knowing how to deal with the moment, "Just get back with your dad before the space rock does. Shouldn't be hard, you got, like, a year and a half."

The aircraft had turned around on the runway and was now making its way back to them.

"Benton? You take care of her," Marcus stared directly at him, "and just so's we're clear, I don't mean in the way that you would 'Take care of a problem', d'you know what I'm sayin'?"

"Marcus," Miles shook his head, "the man who pursued 'Blackbox' is gone. I remember him, and all of his... experiences... but he's not me."

It had been months since Marcus had heard his old alias spoken aloud and the moment caught him off guard. In reply he simply narrowed his eyes slightly and nodded.

The plane drew to a halt a few feet from them, its propeller idling at a low speed. Inside they could see the pilot and one passenger.

Marcus straightened his jacket, "That'll be the new guest."

They watched as the man climbed awkwardly out of the small doorway holding a bulky suitcase. He checked the case and then walked towards them.

Marcus stepped forwards, pointing at the suitcase, "Is that it?"

The man only nodded, evidently he was not sure who he should be talking to.

"Good," Marcus directed him towards the orange flag, "Wait over there."

It seemed that Miles was keen to be underway, he was already settling himself aboard, leaving Marcus and Kate behind.

"Send word before you leave the Faroe Islands, yeah?"

The limited range of the light aircraft meant refuelling along the way, but the plan was to reach Reykjavik. Once there, they would switch to some form of ground transport in order to reach the Node.

"Will do," Kate replied, "Look after Mum?"

Marcus nodded and smiled, not sure what else to say.

"Any chance of us shiftin' a wee bit faster there?" came the thick, Scottish accent of the pilot, shouting over the propeller noise, "We're lit up like a bloody Christmas tree out here!"

Kate's smile cracked into a grin.

Marcus could feel time dragging him, too quickly, towards the moment of her departure. Over the past few months they had been through a lot together and he knew he'd miss her while she was away.

"Look, er, I -" he began.

"Shut up!" she continued to grin, then leaned forward and kissed him on the cheek.

Before he could say anything more, she had started climbing aboard the plane.

"What was that for?" he smiled, reaching up to touch his face.

"Merry Christmas!" she pointed at the runway lights that the pilot disliked so much, then she closed the door.

The engine noise raised in pitch immediately and the light aircraft began to taxi away. He watched as the Cessna took off heading north. With the aircraft's transponder now out of range, the covert runway lighting deactivated again, leaving Marcus and his guest in the dark once more.

He stood for a moment in the darkness and drew a quiet breath; now he had to put his trust in Miles to return Kate safely.

Behind him, the man gave a discreet cough.

"Somethin' wrong with your throat?" said Marcus, deciding to externalise his internal angst in the direction of the nearest person. Marcus clicked on his torch and turned to face him.

The man was holding his passport out towards him at arm's length, raindrops occasionally splashing over both the open pages and his slightly shaky hand. Marcus took the proffered document without comment and looked at the details, then he spoke the first line of a passphrase that Monica had arranged in advance.

"Happy Fourth of July, welcome to sunny Britain."

The man cleared his throat again to speak the appropriate counter phrase but from the look of disdain on his face,

Marcus could tell that the words he was about to speak were far from his actual belief.

"Independence Day was a mistake," came the American's unenthusiastic response, "Rule Britannia."

Despite the rain, Marcus smirked. Having received the correct security response, he took advantage of the situation for his own amusement.

"One more time," he beckoned, then cupped his hand around one ear.

The American drew breath to state the phrase again, but spotting the look of delight creeping across Marcus' face, it had the effect of diffusing the situation's tension.

"Here, let me turn it up a little," he made a loose fist with his left hand, then raised his middle finger.

Against the sibilant patter of rain on the runway tarmac, they both heard each other suppress a laugh.

"Nathan," he introduced himself, offering his hand to Marcus.

"Yeah, I can read," said Marcus, handing his passport back then shaking his hand.

"What do I call you?" said Nathan, picking up the suitcase again.

Although he had only met him a minute ago, Marcus thought he seemed decent enough. However, distrust had been Marcus' guide for longer, it had kept him alive.

"For now," Marcus replied with a smile, "you can call me Blackbox."

UNUM

11th March 2013

*T*he feeling of falling was going away now. He felt warm and comfortable. He could hear a voice calling to him, as though someone was trying to wake him, except he was already awake, or at least that's how it felt.

"Hello Miles, we have spoken before, do you remember me?"

It was still dark and he couldn't tell where the voice was coming from but, when he thought hard enough, he was sure he recognised it.

"Is that you Aunty Dot?" he liked Aunty Dot and she liked him.

"Yes, Miles," said Aunty Dot's voice, "You're still very special to me, but do you remember why?"

"You gave me a special coin," he smiled proudly, thinking of the silver dollar she had given to him, "It said 'E Pluribus Unum' on it, which means -"

"Out of many, one," she completed, "That's right. Do you still remember when I gave it to you?"

Miles thought of his fourth birthday party, and Aunty Dot crouching at his side handing him a small, bright red parcel.

"It was at my fourth birthday party, Aunty Dot."

He could picture the scene clearly; the buzz of conversation in the air and people laughing. He also remembered a girl with a splinter in her finger, and the upsetting feeling it had given him when he knew that he couldn't help. For some reason he felt a rising sense of panic, but Aunty Dot must have seen his discomfort somehow.

"It's OK, Miles," her voice reassured him.

He remembered how, back then, Aunty Dot had put her arm around him to comfort him. He felt this same warmth again now as she continued to talk.

"Do you remember why I gave it to you?"

He remembered that she had not let go of the small red parcel until she had told him something. She had looked at him when she had said it, but he had to concentrate really hard to remember it. He pictured her saying the words.

"For helping others," he smiled, pleased that he had remembered what Aunty Dot needed to know. He liked it when he could help others.

"That's right, Miles. Will you help me, Miles?"

"Of course Aunty Dot," he beamed, "I like to help."

He remembered unwrapping her present and looking at the silver dollar. He remembered his fascination with the two dates, representing two hundred years of liberty. He pictured the coin in front of him now, and imagined running his fingers over the familiar embossed surface. He could see the Liberty Bell and the Latin inscription to its right. But above the inscription there was just empty space. Something was missing.

Or, he thought, he was missing something.

"Something's wrong," he heard himself say, and suddenly he felt cold.

"We'll speak again," came the voice from the darkness.

Then he was falling again.

FORECAST

22nd March 1989

"The chalk marl is pretty fault riddled, but really," Monica shrugged, topping up her glass of orange juice, "what're you gonna do, we're stuck with it. We can't control strata that was put there thousands of years ago, we've just got to -"

"Embrace the chaos?" Douglas completed her oft used phrase.

"Exactly," she smiled, nodding to the stairs, "Speaking of which…"

"Good morning, honey," they both called in the direction of feet completing their run down the stairs and into the kitchen.

"Morning Mummy!" Kate ran to Monica and hugged her and then did the same to Douglas, "Morning Daddy!"

"Wednesday, so, toast?" Monica checked.

Kate nodded and sat down at the kitchen table, "Mummy?"

"Yes, Katie," she replied, loading slices of bread into the toaster.

"What type of animal is a Chalk Mole?"

It took Monica and Douglas a moment to realise that their daughter had wrongly heard, or rather wrongly overheard, part of their conversation.

"Ah, no, I said chalk marl," she smiled at her, then flashed some raised eyebrows at Douglas; they would have to be more careful with their conversations, "It's just a type of rock layer that we're digging the Channel Tunnel through... but I think I like the sound of a Chalk Mole, all soft and furry... Juice?"

"Yes please," Kate pushed her glass forward, "but I don't think it would be furry. It would have a hard nose and strong armour, like a knight, so that it could dig and not get squished."

"That's very logical," Douglas admitted and sipped at his coffee. Since moving to England, he'd never adopted or even understood the fascination with morning tea; he also preferred to simplify his morning decisions by drinking his coffee black.

In Florida he'd had no local friends, so following the death of his mother it made more sense to conduct his research at the Archive facilities in the UK, where he could be closer to Monica.

"Are you growing pink flowers at work, Daddy?" Kate asked, looking at the photos he'd spread out over the table.

Douglas glanced over towards Monica who was staring out of the window at the clear skies over the Dover Strait.

"Yes, honey," he whispered, shuffling the photos into a pile, "I'm trying to make them grow quicker."

Kate now stole a brief look in the direction of her mother too, before leaning closer to her father.

"Lucky Mummy!" she whispered with a grin.

The telephone rang and Kate jumped down from her chair, dashing across the tiled floor shouting, "I'll get it!"

"Be polite!" Monica smiled.

Kate lifted the heavy handset from above the rotary dial and although the ringing stopped, it took a few moments for the bells inside to stop reverberating.

"Walker residence," Kate put on her most polite sounding voice, "Katherine speaking…"

Monica pulled a plate from the cupboard and set it in front of the toaster. She turned and placed a hand on her husband's shoulder and dropped her voice slightly.

"Little Miss Radar, eh? I think we'll have to watch our mouths," she poked at the photos on table, "How's it going?"

"Three to one temporal ratio's stable," Douglas replied, equally quietly, "We're all set for the mouse test next week."

Kate hung up the phone and returned to the table with a grin on her face. Both Monica and Douglas looked at her puzzled; on a few occasions they had allowed her to answer the telephone, but she had always handed over the receiver to them.

"Who was it, honey?" Douglas studied her.

"It was a silly man!" Kate giggled.

"You know that you should pass the phone to either Daddy or me, don't you?" said Monica.

"I'm sorry, Mummy," said Kate, obviously still amused, "He put his phone down before I could pass it to you."

"That's alright," Monica walked over to her and crouched at her side, "Now, what did he say?"

"He said," Kate placed her hands on her hips and adopted a pouting, frowning expression, which presumably reflected her mental picture of the man, and then spoke in the deepest voice she could manage, *The world forecast is for heavy rain. I repeat. The world forecast is for heavy rain. Message ends.*

Her manly impression ended and she added with a giggle, "Silly man - he got it wrong, didn't he Mummy? It's sunny today."

Still crouched at Kate's side, Monica shot a quick wide-eyed stare at Douglas, whose eyes were frantically darting left and right in calculation. Suddenly he returned Monica's stare.

"Katherine," Douglas asked, "Are you absolutely sure he said Heavy Rain?"

Kate's smile waned slightly, her father hardly ever used that version of her name.

In the quiet of the kitchen, the toaster's release lever popped up sharply.

"Did I do something wrong, Daddy?"

"Oh, no no, Katie darling!" Monica hugged her, "We just need to be sure, that's all. Are you sure that's what the silly man said?"

"Yes," replied Kate, biting her lip, "Heavy rain."

"Good girl! Thank you darling," Monica kissed her forehead and stood immediately to face Douglas, "Go?"

Adapting to a scenario for which he had prepared a decision-tree, Douglas knew exactly what had to happen next.

"Go," said Douglas, picking up the kitchen timer and setting its dial, "Twelve minutes."

DEEP END

25th December 2013

On March 11th, the news of Siva's presence in the solar system had triggered an almost immediate stock market crash. Despite attempts to prop it up, digital currencies stored in banks were rendered useless. Governments compensated people in proportion to their former financial wealth using a newly formed, but equally arbitrary, physical currency. The value of a single Habitation token was supposed to be equal in value to that of feeding and housing one person for one day. In reality though, the exact worth varied dependent on location and status; so a system dependent on the inequality of wealth persisted, as it always had.

Within days there followed a worldwide cessation of all large-scale housing construction projects. Multi-storey luxury apartments, in their closing stages of development, became instant targets for thousands of people keen to take advantage of the sudden legal grey area.

Robbed of their bright future and with no stable present to build on, youths in the vicinity of these forsaken structures banded together in a desperate attempt to find reassurance and social inclusion. At its worst, small variances in the home-spun ideologies of the nihilistic youth had erupted into bitter turf wars. Following the failure of Archive to maintain security checkpoints, some formerly affluent regions of London had become no-go areas in a matter of weeks. At its best, a cautious sense of community surrounded some of these demi-buildings, with locals doing what they could to stem the flow of rising desperation. Most towns were a mix of the two extremes; a complex web of tensions holding the streets in a socially precarious balance.

Danny Smith ducked through the hole in the chain link fence, made his way across the frozen scrubland and down towards the emergency exit of the boarded up building. The more reputable London clubs, despite the current austerity, had sought to maintain the decorative sensibilities of the time before the great collapse. The same was not true of The Gene Pool; born in this new era, it was a cultural orphan with no heritage to build on.

The Gene Pool had evolved in the basement of a large, abandoned hotel construction project. The basement itself contained an unfilled luxury swimming pool and was largely responsible for giving the club its name.

Danny dragged his fingers through his hair, pulling it down over his forehead, then made his way forward to the rough entrance. Even through the closed door he could feel the throb of the place. He took a deep breath and banged hard on the door. After a few seconds, a slot in the door slid open briefly before closing again; the check was always cursory but he knew what they were looking out for. He heard the bolt unfasten and then the door was pushed open. The sounds from within instantly grew louder and a haze of cigarette smoke appeared to flee through the emergency exit.

"Evening, Daniel."

"Evening, Mrs. Jackson," Danny replied, raising his arms so that he could be checked for weapons. Practically, he knew it was impossible to adequately check for that sort of thing; there were so many holes in the building that any sufficiently motivated person could easily bring anything they wanted to into the club. But in terms of maintaining the appearance of safety everyone always submitted to the procedure.

"You got nowhere else better to be on Christmas Day?"

Danny shrugged and averted his eyes, dropping his arms to his sides again.

"Course you don't," she sighed, dragging heavily on her stubby cigarette, "who does?"

Danny knew that the 'comforters', as she called them, were now an expensive vice. She would be paying heavily to feed her habit; he had his suspicions how she was affording it, but was too afraid to ask. She bent down and appeared to pick something up from the floor.

"Here, you dropped this."

She pushed a Hab token into his hand and fixed him with a knowing stare; evidently he was not to react to her gift. Things had been a little tight recently, but he would now be able to eat properly for the next day.

"Thanks Mrs. J," he managed.

"Listen, you be careful, OK? There's a lot of new faces in there tonight."

Danny nodded and walked along the short corridor into the main pool area.

From a position overlooking the deep end of the pool, 'Sonic Desolation', an angry thrashing collective of loud instrument players, filled the entire concrete-clad space with reverberating noise. The lead singer spat tortured lyrics at the enthusiastic, heaving crowd in the pool below her.

As usual, the sheer number of people crammed into the basement pool level had pushed the heat and humidity so high that a mixture of condensation and sweat ran freely down the smooth concrete walls; walls that he couldn't avoid touching as he painstakingly pushed his way past the jostling crowd. Eventually he came to the place where he knew he would have to cross through the room itself and, bracing himself, he turned and walked along the shallow end of the pool.

He remembered when the club had first started. Initially the failed luxury spa venue had become a youth club commandeered by ambitious parents in the area, who wanted to do something positive for their children and the community. In the early days Mrs. Jackson and the other parents had organised it so that the shallow end of the empty pool had been used for conversation and games for younger children. The deep end had been used for thoughtful debate, discussion and even poetry on the new social order; typically this attracted the twenty-somethings, of which he had been one.

However, the last few months had seen the influx of a more rebellious, profiteering element. The Gene Pool now fully embraced the oppressive times and used it to turn existential angst into a venue for easy trade. When he looked at the pool now it was unrecognisable; it was filled to capacity with a crowd that appeared to move as one. In the shallow end, young teens frenetically explored each other's lips, while the deep end now played host to wilder acts of carnal abandon. About half way between those two crowded extremes, Danny noticed a girl staring out at him from a sea of strangers. Her back pressing rhythmically against the damp pool wall, she undulated up and down with everyone else. It took him a moment to realise that she wasn't actually looking at him; rather she was looking through him, caught in the moment of a pleasurable peak. He felt his cheeks flush and he looked away.

That was the second reason people called it The Gene Pool.

Not that he was prudish, he would have welcomed the heat of intimacy; but here he felt it was a little forced. But maybe that was the point, he thought as he neared the other side, if the human race could be about to suffer the same fate as the dinosaurs, what better way to ensure their number than to procreate as fast as possible with as many as possible.

He remembered the day they'd been told about the plan to save the planet using a moon laser. To him and several of the others gathered here tonight it had seemed incredulous; it wouldn't be the first time that a government had lied to its people.

He walked swiftly down the corridor containing the changing rooms which, by the sound of it, were now little more than overflow rooms for the deep end of the pool, then made his way to the stairs. As with most of the flooring within the complex, the steps were still untiled and his scuffing footsteps echoed off the bare concrete stairwell as he proceeded upwards. He could hear voices some way above him and picked up his pace.

The ground floor was understandably colder; lacking the body heat of hundreds of people, the floor also had windows which, although boarded up, still let in the cold night wind. He knew there would be dealers on this floor and he could see the signs of chemical abuse littering the floor; evidently the desperate purchasers could not even wait to escape the building before escaping reality altogether. No doubt the ground floor had been chosen to conduct business because when a raid happened it offered swifter escape routes than the upper floors; most of the window boards, he thought, must have bolts on the inside specifically for this purpose.

Hearing voices nearby he picked up the pace and climbed another three flights of stairs, the last of which were merely exposed steel work that had been denied their concrete coating. He exited the stairwell and gave a wide berth to the open elevator shaft.

"We were beginning to think you weren't coming," a voice called out to him.

After an initial start, he relaxed slightly.

"Hi Sophie," he smiled, straightening the hair over his forehead, "got delayed."

"Come on," she returned his smile, pushing her bright pink hair out of her eyes, "Jake says he's got coffee!"

"No way!" Danny almost laughed and doubled his walking speed.

After the collapse, coffee had been among the first food resources to become rare; Danny knew that if you had coffee you were either rich or you were underground trading.

Danny and Sophie walked into the small, warm, unfinished sauna room. Luxury white aspen wood cladding would never line the concrete walls of this abandoned hotel suite, but the metal grate and vent-work that had been completed kept the small fire alight in the corner of the room. The same familiar group were here as usual.

"Soph' says you've got coffee?" Danny began, sitting down in front of the fire.

"And a merry bloody Christmas to you too Danny," Jake said in mock offence.

Danny laughed along with everyone else at the bizarre situation; he couldn't remember when he'd last laughed out loud, but it was probably the last time they had met.

"Yep. Grab a cup, everyone," Jake smiled and handed out a stack of empty plastic cups.

"Where the hell did you get coffee?" said Oliver, taking a cup and passing the stack around.

"Did you rip it off?" beamed Sophie, the fire reflecting in her eyes, "I bet you did, didn't you?"

"Ain't asking no questions…" said Terry, their oldest member.

"Come on, Jake, where'd you get it?" Danny pushed, passing the last cup to Megan.

"Yeah, spill the coffee beans!" Megan punned.

Jake paused for effect and raised an aloof eyebrow.

"It's mine. I saved it. For today," Jake pulled a tiny jar of instant coffee out of his rucksack. The action earned him a few wolf whistles, "Merry Christmas guys!"

Together they boiled the water in a camping pan over the sauna's fire then Jake carefully added six spoonfuls of the freeze-dried granules to the steaming liquid, before decanting the precious liquid into each of their cups.

"Got any milk 'n' sugar?" Megan piped up, causing them all to laugh out loud. Those commodities were even harder to come by.

There were appreciative whispers of thanks to Jake and then they sat quietly, savouring every sip. After a few moments, Terry cleared his throat. He'd known hard times even before the great collapse and had been one of the first to attempt residence in the building.

"I pity you youngsters," Terry started, looking into the fire, "None of you asked for any of this…"

Everyone continued to sip at their coffee, they didn't need to agree, it had all been said before.

"Whole world's gone nuts," Terry shook his head, "This one time, right, a couple paid me -"

"We know, Terry, you told us," sighed Jake, "They paid you fifty quid to borrow your trolley full of metal cans for half an hour -"

"And gave me a credit card," Terry went on, "What sort of nut does that?"

"One that wants you to get caught using it…" Oliver chipped in.

"They even gave me the PIN code -"

"I rest my case…" Oliver murmured, looking around at the others. It wasn't the first time they'd heard this story, but they knew it would have to run its course now.

"I waited, like they told me to, then put the card into the machine, 2974," Terry mimed the entering of the digits, then shook his head in recalled disbelief, "Never had so much cash. A day later - it's all just worthless bits of paper again."

"Don't forget the man in the black tie…" said Megan, spotting an opportunity to shortcut Terry's trip down memory lane.

"He was a freak…" Terry pulled at the laces on his ragged shoes, "He says he'll take me shoes if I don't tell him where-"

"Blackbox and Walker went," Jake, Megan and Oliver chorused quietly along with Terry.

"Have I told you this before then?" Terry looked confused.

"Just the once," Sophie lied, patting him gently on the forearm.

"All so's his lady-friend can go for a ride in me shopping trolley," Terry muttered to himself, "Nuts, absolutely nuts. I've got a better roof over me head now than I did back then, too. Whole world's upside-down."

Jake raised his precious cup in a toast, "To our bottoms-up world!"

Danny, who always listened more than he contributed, now joined the others.

"Bottoms up."

Danny drank the last of his coffee and discreetly massaged his forehead; sitting so close to the fire had made the wound start to sting again. He flattened the hair into place and shuffled a little further back from the fire.

EFFECT CAUSE

By influencing the random event that had originally produced the PIN code, it had produced a ripple.

She watched as the effects spread out and triggered minor sub-causalities, then the ripple returned to its origin. The fact that it had returned to *her* was significant.

The exact number she had chosen to influence the PIN code event, had returned to her as the very cause of her own choice. By influencing those numbers, she realised a causal loop had been closed.

She could visualise both Cause and Effect appearing as a single event within an otherwise unbroken circle.

The symbol was familiar, but now she began to question the exact causality of that familiarity. That aside, the loop highlighted the fact that even a small influence could have a tangential consequence.

She would have to proceed with more care.

TRIP

22nd March 1989

By the time the kitchen timer started ringing, the Walkers were already on the road and heading north towards London. With her mother's help, Kate had hurriedly packed some of her best clothes and toys into her bright pink suitcase, and she seemed caught up in the sense of adventure surrounding their sudden trip to the capital city.

"But what about school, Mummy?" she asked from the back of the car.

Monica turned around in her seat and faced her with a smile.

"We've already told Mrs. Jenkins that you'll be away," Monica knew that today there was more at stake than finger-painting and role play, so the lie came easily to her.

"But when I said goodbye to Mrs. Jenkins yesterday," came Kate's puzzled reply, "she said that she would see me tomorrow."

"She was just helping to keep our trip a secret!" Monica grinned, then turned to face the front again. Already, as with so many other things within Archive, another insignificant lie had begun to multiply.

"I can't wait to tell her when we get back!" Kate enthused.

Monica closed her eyes and hoped deeply that circumstances would permit them all to return. She turned to Douglas to seek a similar reaction, but his eyes were resolutely set on the road ahead.

The remainder of the journey took a further two hours, during which Monica and Douglas could discuss very little in Kate's presence. Despite this, they kept up the pretence of a happy family trip, encouraging Kate to make the most of seeing the green countryside flying by at great speed outside her window.

When they reached the capital, they got as far as Trafalgar Square before having to leave their car behind. Douglas opened his door, allowing the noise and mild bus-diesel fumes into the car.

"Mummy! Look at the lions!" said Kate, her wide eyes drinking in the view of the bronze sculptures at the base of Nelson's Column.

"I'll get the case," Douglas told Monica, before heading to the back of the car.

Monica speedily exited and opened the rear passenger door for Kate.

"Wow!" grinned Kate, jumping out, "Look at all the pigeons!"

Monica was surprised that Kate would comment on the thousands of birds strutting and flocking around the square before spotting the more obvious towering spectacle of Nelson's Column standing at its centre. But spot it she soon did.

"Can we go to the top?" she asked excitedly, and turned to her father, "Please!"

Douglas closed the boot and, carrying Kate's little pink suitcase along with their more sombre looking one, he walked towards Kate wearing one of his best smiles.

"I'm afraid not, honey, there aren't any steps. But," he bent down so that she could hear his voice above the noisy street bustle, "how would you like to go underneath it?"

It didn't seem possible but her eyes widened even further.

"You can't park that here, sir," came a policeman's voice from behind him, "You'll have to move it."

Monica was the first to realise that it was entirely possible the policeman knew nothing of the emergency procedures that were already underway. She looked at her watch and knew they could not afford to be having this conversation. She stepped between Douglas and the policeman.

"I'll just be over there with Katherine," Monica winked at Douglas and covertly pulled the car keys from his hand.

Douglas played along, watching her take Kate by the hand and hurry away. Whatever she was doing he knew to trust that it would only help.

"Are we not allowed to park here then, Officer?"

"American?" he said, noticing the mild accent, "Figures. No, you can't park here."

"It's only for a few minutes," Douglas said, turning towards Nelson's Column and desperately trying to recall any facts he could, "Did you know that it's almost one hundred and seventy feet tall?"

The policeman wasn't prepared for an architectural response to his last statement and he simply resorted to frowning for a few seconds.

"Fascinating, I'm sure."

"But," Douglas raised a lecturer's finger, "Hitler's plan to move it to Berlin failed."

The policeman opened his mouth to speak but then closed it again. The combination of the two disparate pieces of information, along with the slightly odd way that Douglas had connected them, had ruined his train of thought.

Although Douglas had bought a few more valuable seconds, he didn't know how long he would be tolerated, so it was with some relief that he saw Monica was making her way back through the crowded square. It was difficult to tell from his current perspective, but the crowd behind her appeared to be clearing in her wake. However, he was forced to turn away; the policeman had come to his senses and was talking to him again.

"You either move your vehicle. Now. Or I call for backup."

In the States, Douglas had become used to the fact that officers carried guns, but over here they didn't. Even a call for backup would not bring an armed response, something he felt sure that Monica would be aware of.

"I'll take it from here," said Monica, authoritatively.

Douglas turned again on the spot and saw that behind Monica, stretching perhaps twenty yards along the paving stones of Trafalgar Square, was a thick line of pigeons, hungrily pecking at a trail of birdseed that she'd left behind.

Using only her eyes she motioned Douglas to where Kate was standing, just to her left. Douglas gave a miniscule nod and in return, signalled that he was still holding both suitcases.

"It won't be a problem," she replied to Douglas whilst apparently still addressing the policeman.

The policeman raised one hand and put it on his two-way radio. Douglas carefully placed both suitcases on the ground.

"It's OK, Officer," she took a step forward, holding a dozen cups full of birdseed, "Let me explain."

Douglas lunged forward and scooped Kate up; at the same time, Monica tossed a cup of birdseed at the policeman's chest and let the other cups fall to the floor at his feet.

As the hungry pigeons of Trafalgar Square swooped and rushed at the new abundant source of food on and around the policeman, Monica grabbed the suitcases. Following her husband, she sprinted through the long line of pigeons that she'd set up a few moments before. The birds along the length of the line scattered in front of the sprinting family, sending a wave of flapping chaos into the air. As people instinctively dashed away from the fleeing birds, it cleared an escape path for the Walkers. The birds swooped and wheeled chaotically around the square, which then had the effect of zipping the crowd closed behind them.

They reached the iron railings of the Trafalgar Square subway entrance and continued their run down the curved steps into the London Underground system. Bypassing those queueing for tickets, Douglas slowed to a less suspicious pace and headed across the small ticket hall to the opposite side. Monica caught up with him a few seconds later at a plain grey door marked *'Personnel Only'*.

"Mummy, I'm frightened," Kate said quietly over her father's shoulder.

"Sorry darling, just a little further," Monica ran her hand over Kate's hair, "We don't want to be late."

Douglas entered the four-digit code on the mechanical push-button door lock and twisted the handle. The door clicked open and all three of them hurried through. They slammed it shut behind them and took a breath.

"Less than five minutes," Monica reported, her voicing echoing off the hard, tiled narrow corridor. She adjusted her grip on the cases and after taking a few strides began to hurry down a flight of polished concrete steps. Douglas hitched Kate up to get a more secure grip.

"Nearly there, Katie," he kissed her forehead, then followed Monica at pace down the hard steps.

At the base of the stairs they turned a corner and were met with the sight of a second straight staircase descending to their right and, to the left, a spiral staircase behind a metal gate.

"This way!" Monica yelled and headed off down the straight stairs.

"Stop!" called Douglas.

Lining the walls of the staircase ahead and the one they had just descended, were small green 'Emergency Exit' signs that pointed back up to the surface. The facility they were heading for had taken advantage of the pre-existing London Underground infrastructure; the straight stairs were simply one of several emergency exit routes for the lower levels. If they continued on this route they would only reach the platforms, not the facility.

He quickly backtracked to the metal gate. The sign on it had been designed to be consistent with other London Underground signs, but the power rating was too specific, it read:

'Risk of electric shock: 1951 VA'

He recognised Siva's original alphanumeric designation immediately and shouted for Monica to follow him. Evidently this change to the routing plan was so recent that there had not even been time to send a memo. Douglas pulled the gate open and immediately fluorescent tubes stuttered to life, lighting the way down the metallic spiral stairs. He set Kate down next to him.

"It's too narrow for me to carry you - I'll be right behind you but I want you to hold the handrail and get to the bottom as fast as you can," he ran his hand over her hair, "Can you do that for me?"

Kate said that she could, then the three of them set off down the narrow metal steps. Some way behind them, at the top of the first flight of stairs, they could hear panicked sounding voices and hurried footsteps descending; it appeared they were not the only late arrivals.

The spiral steps emerged into a wide, empty corridor. In contrast to the surrounding architecture of tunnels and passageways, this was brightly lit by a series of lamps lining the wall every few feet. At the far end of the corridor, an elevator door stood open and ready to receive passengers.

The wide corridor had been designed for the possibility of holding a large number of people while they waited to use the elevator. For Monica and Douglas, it was both a relief and a source of instant concern; there were no crowds to slow their sprint, but the lack of people here meant they were among the last to arrive. They ran into the elevator and Monica set down the cases, breathing hard.

"Three minutes!" she gasped.

Douglas set Kate down and instructed her to hold onto the handrail that ran around the wall of the elevator. He could hear the clatter of feet making their way down the spiral steps, they were perhaps only twenty seconds away.

Douglas reached out to a numerical keypad in the elevator wall.

Above the keypad a small notice read:

'Enter code. Transit time 60 seconds. Have passport ready.'

The footsteps were getting closer.

Douglas did the quick sum; one minute down, one for its return to this level, one for a second descent. If the elevator departed now, then the people hurrying down the stairs probably wouldn't make it.

"We have to wait," Douglas pointed back in the direction of the spiral stairs.

At that moment two people burst into the wide corridor and, seeing the elevator was occupied, they shouted, "Wait!"

"Come on!" Monica bellowed, beckoning them on with frantic arm movements.

Poising his fingers over the keypad, Douglas turned to Kate.

"Honey, hold on tight to the rail!" he forced a smile, "This next bit is a little like…"

"A fairground ride!" Monica cut in, noticing her daughter's wide-eyed stare. Monica dashed the few steps across the floor, held onto the handrail and knelt at Kate's side, "Like one of those rides that give you butterflies in your tummy!"

Kate's reaction smile was fleeting; with one hand still on the rail she placed the other in her mother's firm grip.

Douglas knew the elevator would only leave when the full departure code had been entered, so he started pushing the digits. If he timed it correctly, the elevator could depart as soon as the sprinting couple were aboard.

'1'

The keypad reacted with a weak sounding beep, only just audible over the footsteps converging on the elevator.

'9'

The couple continued their frantic sprint. The person furthest away lost their footing and tripped, but managed to regain their balance. Douglas re-estimated their combined arrival time and paused slightly before entering the next digit.

'5'

The first person cleared the threshold at speed and almost instantly collided with the elevator's rear wall. The second person flew in behind and Douglas instantly punched the last digit.

'1'

The panel beeped and simultaneously a bell sounded.

'Doors closing,' said a calm recorded voice from a speaker, *'please stand clear, and hold the handrail.'*

The doors started to close at a painfully slow rate, presumably to allow a far greater number of people the time to squash into place. Douglas realised he'd been holding his breath and let it go suddenly. The fact that the door closure was so slow in comparison to the general haste of the situation mildly amused him. Then, above the panting breaths of the elevator's occupants, they all became aware of a new sound; distant new footsteps were clattering down the spiral metallic steps, accompanied by the sound of yelling voices.

The doors continued to close.

His moment of levity instantly evaporated and Douglas looked at the cancel button, then down at Monica. She closed her eyes and shook her head slightly. He knew she was right, it was already too late.

The doors finally forced themselves closed, then the elevator dropped like a stone.

DESCENT

25th December 2013

Ross Crandall stared at the screen capture displayed on the far wall at Houston Mission Control. A moment ago a low-ranking data analyst had silenced the busy room by deciphering a Morse code message buried in the FLC's power output. The message read:

'SOS FLC SOS GO ANALOG SOS DRUM GRAY HOSTILE SOS MOON'.

The room was still in stunned silence, looking to Ross for instruction.

Above his own pounding pulse, he heard the analyst's voice telling him that the message repeated.

It seemed impossible. Unthinkable. There was only one thing he could do.

He turned his back on the expectant room and picked up the receiver of a red wall-phone.

After a few seconds there was no reply.

"Doesn't anything work in this damn place?" he shouted, slamming the receiver back in its cradle. There was another direct communication phone but he knew it wasn't on this level. He turned back to the room.

"Man your stations. My team, with me. You," he said, frowning and clicking his fingers at the analyst who had made the discovery.

"Larry Clark, Sir," Lawrence said by way of reply.

"Fine, Larry, with me," he beckoned him over, "you're useful."

Since the great collapse, the general conditions around Mission Control had inevitably suffered. People slept in whatever space they could find, but generally the habitation was in a poor state of repair. Those who had been sleeping in the corridors were now fully awake and upright; they stood bolt upright against the walls while Ross and his team swept towards the elevators.

Earlier, Ross had dispatched a sergeant to bring back Larry's immediate supervisor, Todd Baker. Ross knew of Todd's vices and abuse of the so-called 'Hab token' currency but, until this point, Todd had been useful for keeping people in check. The problem wasn't that the Morse code message had been discovered by an analyst, the problem was that valuable time had been lost. Todd's untimely indiscretion was now unforgivable. As they approached the end of the corridor, Ross saw that the sergeant had returned with the half-dressed and babbling supervisor. Ross inserted a key into a wall slot, immediately summoning two elevators to their floor.

"Here he is, Sir," said the sergeant, pushing Todd forwards.

Ross just stared at Todd, whose obviously drug-addled brain was failing to keep up with the situation. Wordlessly, Ross ripped the Lifeboat Pass card from the thin chain around Todd's neck, then handed it to Lawrence. The elevator bell sounded above Todd's incomprehensible sounds of confusion, and then the doors to both elevators opened.

"Sergeant," said Ross, pointing to the elevator on the left, "kick him out on the surface."

A little too late, Todd realised what was going on, but his protestations were drowned out by the louder jeers of approval from his former subordinates still lining the corridor. Ross gestured the team, along with Larry, into the other elevator, and then followed them in; he'd need to be the first one out when they reached the bottom. The doors closed and Todd's screams for mercy were quietened.

During the short but swift descent, Ross saw Lawrence staring at his newly acquired Lifeboat Pass.

"Well played," said Ross without making eye contact. This wasn't the first time he'd seen a play for power, "it's yours for now. But screw this up, and you'll ride this elevator all the way to the top. Am I clear?"

"Crystal," Lawrence managed, still somewhat shocked at the speed of Todd's unceremonious departure.

Lawrence hadn't plotted for Todd's downfall, in fact he'd tried to bring the SOS message to his attention. But when Todd had chosen to continue his debauchery rather than listen to him, Lawrence had seized the opportunity to better his own living circumstances. He'd angrily fantasised about taking Todd's Lifeboat Pass but expected that, at best, his actual reward may be a private shower token or a few extra Habs. He'd never envisioned that Todd would be so brutally kicked out, wearing literally only the shirt on his back.

What bothered him more was the fact that, by taking Todd's Lifeboat Pass, he had assumed a position of seniority; a position that would carry a similar penalty should he fail in anything that was now asked of him.

The elevator jolted to a stop and the doors sprang open.

Lawrence followed Ross out of the elevator and felt the others push past him into a cold, dark room. Their quick footsteps appeared to echo off distant, unseen walls; they were obviously in a large space, but having never been here before he remained routed to the spot on what felt like metal deck plates.

It seemed that Ross had been here before because, despite it being pitch black, he had found the phone line he needed. Above the background noise of feet running on metallic steps, Lawrence could hear him delivering a long string of authentication words.

In quick succession, small patches of light started to come on throughout the space and Lawrence could start to make sense of the environment around him.

Although they had descended to reach this location, a great deal more of the room lay beneath him than above him. He was standing on a wide, metal-plate gantry, bounded by a safety hand rail five feet away, beyond which he could see lights on a distant, black wall. He walked cautiously to the handrail, his own footsteps echoing off the plating and mixing with voices calling to each other from below. He took hold of the hand rail and the space below him opened out dizzyingly.

Below him lights were still coming on, but he could recognise what he was looking at. The regolith that should bury the structure was missing, of course, but the characteristic starfish-like layout was unmistakable. Four storeys below him, on a sandy-grey surface, sat a full scale replica of the Floyd Lunar Complex.

GIFTED

22nd March 1989

At some point prior to 1951, Siva had been captured by the Solar System's gravity. It had begun looping around the Sun, cutting across the orbits of the inner planets. With each successive loop the Sun's gravity pulled it ever closer. On April 1st 2015, Siva's collapsing ellipse and the Earth's orbit would coincide, but before then there would be a series of near passes. Although today's near pass had been anticipated, the panic-inducing automated message advising of an imminent and devastating meteor strike was not.

General Broxbourne stood before several Archive members in the cramped, warm briefing room of the Whitehall Bunker, attempting to summarise what they knew about the false alarm.

"Siva was always due for this near pass, and we were ready for it," he continued, "As planned, the global radio telescope network was focussed on Siva, attempting to gather data as it flew past."

He stopped and held up a large green circuit board, covered with copper tracks, resistors and transistors.

"We think that during the intense capturing of data, a triangulation unit like this one, blew out. It wasn't noticed at the time, but the other radio telescopes in the network interpreted the sudden lack of position data as a Siva course change. As a precaution, the network triggered the *Heavy Rain* automated dial out. As you know, once started it can't be terminated," he dropped the board loudly on the table, "Considering the rush to reach safety, we were lucky not to have had greater casualties. So, damage control?"

At the other side of the room, Robert Wild leaned forward.

"The radio telescope data was apparently secured -"

"Wait a minute, Wild, 'Apparently'?" cut in General Broxbourne.

Robert returned a relaxed smile.

"Until we leave this bunker we won't know for sure. But I've already arranged for the planting of astronomy records that point the finger at, er," he poked at his notes, "4581 Asclepius. It's the closest fit. There's enough X-number-of-football-field stats to scare, but not enough for the public to care."

"You can make the details stand up to scrutiny?" said Broxbourne.

"This plate's a little bigger than usual," Robert flashed a confident smile, "but I can still spin it."

General Broxbourne studied him. There was no doubting that his track record in dealing with unwanted attention was superb; although he could never be sure if the success of Robert Wild was down to naive enthusiasm, genuine ability or a mercurial mix of both.

"We could even shine a light on it," Robert followed up, "use back-channels to push it to the press, pre-packaged. They get a nice juicy story, and after a few days nobody's interested 'cause everybody's heard all about it."

General Broxbourne nodded.

Perry Baker's incredulous and half-barked laugh cut across the table.

"Seriously?" said Perry, gesturing in Robert's direction "With something this big, you're going to play the 'Wild' card?"

"One person," Robert held up a single finger, "That's all it would take. One person to whisper 'cover-up' and a conspiracy theory begins. It may even have happened already. So, yeah Perry, with something 'this big' we need to get it into the bright lights as soon as possible."

Perry shook his head, "Your call, General."

"Yes, Baker," Broxbourne stared at him for slightly longer than was really necessary, "it is. Wild, I want to see the package intel before you leak it."

The discussions turned to the fact that not all of those who had received the Heavy Rain message had reached the various worldwide bunkers in time. It highlighted the cold fact that a broader view needed to be taken.

Archive's scope shifted from ensuring the survival of the human population, to ensuring the survival of the human species.

The change in scope moved the conversation towards the need to establish an archive for genetic material, one that could be used to rebuild a civilisation of people, flora and fauna.

The nature of the Underground Survival Villages was reassessed too. Assuming the worst case outcome that Siva succeeded in reaching Earth, then these villages would need to be larger and focussed on adapting people to life after impact.

Assuming a best case outcome where Siva was defeated by the currently unfinished FLC, the conversation suddenly took a more optimistic turn.

"I want to revisit the idea of Lunar Colony 1."

Before its re-designation, the Floyd Lunar Complex had been named 'Lunar Colony 1', an optimistic title that had encompassed the pioneering spirit of the era.

"We've been through this, Tom!" Perry called out.

Having been shot down by General Broxbourne earlier, Perry's frustration now needed a new vent.

"The concept died in '76," Perry continued, "No matter how many glassy-looking pods you want to build up there, we know the Moon can't independently support life."

The original airbrushed, glossy images of honeycomb-glazed lunar domes containing tropical oases were difficult to forget. Once an inspiration, they were now the object of derision.

"For crying out loud!" Thomas flared, "No-one's talking about making it independent, or building any glass pods! Look, I'd be the first to admit it, we've got some pretty way-out-there projects going on, both down here and up there. But it's because we don't know which one's going to end up being the one that works! All I'm saying is that once we perfect the Helium-3 generator and the..." he hesitated too long.

"Say it," Perry cut in with a chuckle, "I wanna hear the sci-fi words coming out of your mouth."

"Tractor beam," Thomas determinedly continued talking through the smattering of laughter, "If we perfect both of these and remove Siva's threat, then Earth is in the clear."

He waited for the laughter to subside.

"Yeah, it's all very funny. But assuming for a second that some of us have a bit more confidence in our scientific ability," he looked pointedly at Perry, "and that we don't want to just crawl into a deep hole..."

"Watch it, Tommy, my emergency bunkers just hypothetically saved..."

"Yes and hypo-thanks for that," he retorted, "But you've got to listen! Assuming that the FLC, one day, successfully destroys or moves Siva out of the way, then we'll have an operational base up there that can be colonised and expanded. We need to think of what comes after the FLC. Eggs in baskets, right Mrs. Pittman?"

Dorothy Pittman, now approaching sixty, had been with Archive almost from day one. Her husband William, among several other billionaires, had helped to financially sway the course of industrial development during the early days. Her opinions, along with her business fortune, still carried great weight.

"My Bill would always use that exact phrase," she confirmed, "He said, when it came down to the human race, we shouldn't carry all our eggs in one basket."

Thomas smiled back at her, feeling somewhat vindicated that she had shown him support.

"Bill was fond of saying *'Dot, we gotta get off this ball o' rock'*..." Dorothy continued, "We didn't always see eye to eye, but I think he was right on that particular point. We're too fragile and we're all in one basket here on Earth. I can't pretend to understand even one percent of the scientific advances we're making these days, but I do know that we need to be open to them. If we have the chance to get off this rock, we should take it seriously. One day, hopefully, our sons and daughters will praise us. They will continue long after we finish."

She now turned to address Thomas individually.

"How old is your daughter, Dr. Gray?"

"Eva?" he replied, "She's nearly eleven,"

"She's at the Pittman Academy here in London?"

"Not yet," he smiled, "she's studying hard. I hope next year."

"Before returning to the surface, I should very much like to meet her."

After the meeting had concluded, true to her word, Dorothy asked Thomas to escort her to the arrivals room. As they walked the narrow corridors he continued to tell her about his daughter.

"And of course she's doing well in maths too."

Dorothy just continued to listen.

"But you know this already, don't you?" said Thomas, realising that perhaps he'd been speaking too much.

"Of course," she said, "I see all the children's reports, but there's a difference between knowing the statistics and knowing the child. Sometimes I like to meet them in person."

Dorothy stopped walking as they reached a bright orange door and Thomas opened it for her.

"Please, after you."

"Thank you, Thomas," she smiled, and entered the lively room beyond.

The arrivals room mimicked a children's party, with multi-coloured walls, helium balloons and pop music; there were even entertainers shaping long balloons and painting the faces of the younger arrivals. The entertainers had been preselected from the permanent personnel and wore garish clothing. Their bright, friendly make-up was partly to appear clown-like, but mostly it was to disguise their own anxiety.

The brainchild of Dorothy herself, the arrivals room had been created specifically with the purpose of distracting the children in the moments following their arrival at the bunker. The vast array of activities allowed the children to dump any excess adrenalin and bond with other children. Had today's events turned out differently they may have been forced to spend their entire lives together, so Dorothy had reasoned that it was important to have the right environment. Every child had been given a wrapped gift, which further contributed to the party-like ambience, and the abundance of food and soft drinks completed the illusion.

"There's my girl!" Thomas called as his daughter ran over.

"Hi, Dad," Eva beamed and hugged him.

"What have you got there?" Thomas smiled down at her.

A little embarrassed, Eva held up a frilly looking baby doll.

"May I take a look?" Dorothy asked, spotting Eva's less than enthusiastic expression.

Without question, Eva handed over her baby to Dorothy.

"Hmm," Dorothy pretended to study the doll, "lovely. Was this the gift you got when you arrived, Eva?"

"Yes, Mrs. Pittman."

"Well it certainly is a lovely dolly," Dorothy patted the cheap polyester garments, "but I think we can do a little better for you. Your father tells me that you like to study rocks?"

"Yes, I like geology," Eva replied.

"Excellent, excellent," Dorothy said, holding out her bracelet for Eva to inspect.

On the bracelet were several small charms; some were solid gold or silver, but there were a few that appeared to hold tiny stones within delicate wire cages.

"Eva, can you tell me what type of rock this is?" she pointed to a grey rock, held in place by fine filaments of silver.

Eva studied the miniscule rock, but could find little within her knowledge that would help to identify it.

"I'm not sure," she concluded, a little disappointed, "But although it's small, it's extremely valuable."

"Why is it valuable?" Dorothy frowned.

Eva looked a little sheepish, as though she had somehow been caught cheating, "You wear it on your gold bracelet next to the diamond, sapphire and ruby charms, so…"

Dorothy's frown melted into a smile.

"Very good, Eva. It is very valuable. You cannot find this rock anywhere on Earth. This…" she unclipped the tiny grey charm and handed it to Eva, "… is a piece of lunar rock."

"Wow!" Eva studied the tiny fragment with renewed enthusiasm, "You own a piece of Moon rock?"

"No," Dorothy closed Eva's fingers around the charm, "It's yours now."

Both Eva and her father looked at her in disbelief.

"Really?" they both said.

Dorothy nodded and looked at Eva, "It will mean far more to you than it will to me, just hanging around my wrist."

"Thank you so much Mrs. Pittman!"

"Oh, please! I insist, call me Aunty Dot."

"Thank you, Aunty Dot," said Eva, beaming.

"You're very welcome. Now," she said, straightening slightly, "would it be alright if I talk privately with your father for a moment? There's a bright light over in that corner of the room, why not study it over there?"

"Thank you!" Eva said again, her attention now absorbed in the fragment as she walked away.

The cheerful music continued to play and somewhere a balloon popped, causing a ripple of childish laughter. Still watching the scene, Dorothy spoke to Thomas.

"Eva's very gifted," she appeared to mull something over, "in fact I can see the day when you and your daughter are working on the same project."

"Yes, wouldn't that be something!" he replied almost dismissively.

"I'm serious Dr. Gray," Dorothy addressed him formally, "I'm going to double the funding of your deflector research and I'd like you to enrol Eva at the Academy, right now."

Thomas was lost for words, but his agog expression was all she needed to see.

"Thomas, I think that family is so important," Dorothy then spoke in a lower tone, "but you're not appreciated by some people here, so I'd like to move you and Eva to the States, where I can look after you both."

"Not the London Acad... You mean the... Eva?" he struggled.

"No, not the Academy here. Yes, I mean the U.S. Academy," she smiled, "Your research will be much better equipped and I think she'll thrive. She's going to be very bright, Thomas. I think with suitable training, she'll be out of this world."

Dorothy placed a hand on his shoulder before continuing.

"Assuming that your proposed deflection system is the one that allows the FLC to rid us of Siva, then it only seems right. Your daughter should be the first of her generation to benefit from any lunar colony that follows. Her mother would have been proud."

At the mention of his wife, his eyes began to well up, "I don't know what to say…"

"Just say yes," she smiled.

At the other side of the music filled room, Monica and Douglas Walker were engaged in their own musings. Each trying to impose some sense of order on the stress of the day.

"If the facilities in Dover had been ready," Monica looked out over the party floor, "we wouldn't have had this ridiculous trip. Complete waste of time."

Sitting next to her, one hand on his suitcase, Douglas countered.

"But it's a real wake-up call. Things will be different now."

"Everyone will be more determined," agreed Monica, "and more… desperate. The sad thing is that we'll have to adapt."

Monica lapsed back into silence, watching the children play. She saw Dorothy Pittman moving through the party, smiling and greeting people. To the very young, Dorothy was like a kindly aunt, whilst to others she had acquired an almost regal status. Monica spotted that she was moving towards them.

"Incoming," she said quietly to Douglas.

Instinctively they both stood to greet her.

"So glad you made it!" Dorothy smiled at them both, "Have you only just arrived?"

"Car trouble," Monica improvised, "Nice to see you again, Dorothy."

Monica kissed her on both cheeks.

"How European!" Dorothy reacted.

"I think we'll all be doing it soon," Monica smiled, "if my weekly meetings with the French team are anything to go by."

"Of course! How's the tunnelling?"

"Ugh - small setback with a flooding section, but we're all patched up again. Since January we've been *back on track*," Monica smiled to emphasise the wordplay.

Dorothy laughed appreciatively.

"By '93 we should be there," Monica continued, "then the real construction work begins!"

The three of them shared a laugh, for the more daunting task after the completion of the Channel Tunnel would be the Underground Survival Villages at either end of it; one in Dover, the other in Calais. At the English end, the scale of the proposed operation meant that the billions of tonnes of excavated material would be deposited directly in front of the Dover cliffs. The coastline itself would change. By comparison, the Whitehall Bunker they were standing in was a mere hole in the ground.

Dorothy turned to Douglas, during the whole conversation he had kept a tight grip on the suitcase in his hand.

"Is that it?" she asked in a lowered tone.

"It was a rough ride here," Douglas nodded, "So I don't know what state it's going to be in."

"Schrödinger's suitcase?" Dorothy offered.

Monica was momentarily impressed, but then remembered that this was Dorothy Pittman. Despite the image she projected, she was still as sharp as a knife.

"Ha ha! Yes," Douglas agreed, seeing the parallel, "until I open the box, the Mark 1 is both alive and dead."

"The Mark 1?" Dorothy's eyebrows furrowed. The implied existence of a second Chronomagnetic Field generator was not information she was aware of.

Douglas spotted her slight look of alarm and corrected her.

"Sorry. In my mind," he tapped his forehead, "I know that we'll need to move to larger versions eventually, so I've already started differentiating. I'll need to talk with Bradley about the power source for the next test, have you heard from him?"

"Oh my son hardly ever calls me," she feigned outrage, rolling her eyes, "but he made it to the Cheyenne bunker with Suzanne and Sarah. I can't believe Sarah's crawling already, where did that time go? Speaking of which, where's your little darling?"

Monica pointed across the room to a small group of children holding hands and dancing around in a circle in time to the pop music.

"She's over there," Monica shook her head at the bizarre juxtaposition of Kate and the other children dancing in a retrofitted nuclear bunker, "Will she even remember this?"

Dorothy knew that the propranolol compound included in the children's fruit juice would make the recall of fear less likely, but this was not information she wished to share.

"She's still very young, Monica," she sighed, "Maybe she'll only remember the happier part. Please would you give this to her for me?"

"Of course," said Monica, cheerfully accepting the frilly baby doll that Dorothy was trying to rid herself of.

"I'll see you again soon," Dorothy smiled, then after giving them a little wave, she moved off again to tour the other guests. Once Dorothy was safely out of earshot, Monica dumped the dolly behind a stack of chairs.

"We need to get out," she said plainly to Douglas.

He knew that she wasn't referring to the Whitehall Bunker.

"Yeah," he nodded in Kate's direction, "but we can't just leave, can we? Nobody just leaves."

Monica stepped closer to him, put an arm around his waist and rested her head on his chest. It was a comfort, but also an effective way of concealing what she was about to say.

"I've been thinking it over," she said, "We can get out of Archive, but it would take time."

"Time," Douglas wiggled the suitcase slightly, "is something I literally have bags of."

He couldn't hear it above the party noise, but he felt her laugh.

She looked up at him wearing the mischievous grin he'd fallen in love with.

"Good," she said, "I want to make some alterations to the kitchen."

"You can tell me all about it in the car."

"About that…" she patted his chest, "You know how we were in a terrible rush to get here?"

"Yes…"

"And we needed a distraction, desperately…?"

"Yes…" he said hesitantly.

"Well I didn't think we'd be needing the car again so, well…"

"What, Monny?"

"I swapped our car keys, for a whole load of birdseed."

SAMPHIRE HOE

5th July 2013

Their drive from RAF Manston to Samphire Hoe had been, for the most part, uneventful. Along the way Marcus had resorted to bribing the midnight shift checkpoint guard to allow them back through the security barrier without a passport check.

He could foresee a day soon when Archive would lose their grip on these security outposts as people resorted to the time-honoured tradition of resource bartering. The Archive-issued Hab tokens that people used for food and water rations would still be used, but only as a supplement to the richer rewards of physical goods. Goods like the box of two hundred cigarettes he'd just given up to allow them safe passage. In their brief negotiation, Marcus had learned that although the guard didn't smoke, he knew their street value all too well. Archive's tenuous hold on the masses would soon suffer even greater corruption.

Marcus and Nathan had only exchanged pleasantries during the journey, each being aware that neither of them should talk about anything related to their past. So when they arrived at Samphire Hoe's coastal path it was something of a relief to exit the car.

After following the path on foot they eventually came to Samphire Cottage, perched on the cliff overlooking the Dover Strait. Like Monica herself, Marcus thought, it was a statement of defiance.

"This way," he called to Nathan.

He inserted the key into the lock then, to avoid one of Monica's intrusion countermeasures, raised the ring-shaped brass handle before turning the key. With the relief that he hadn't been electrocuted, he opened the door and stepped into the hallway.

It had been almost four months since he had first seen this place. He had first come here following Kate's insistence that they should contact her mother. Benton hadn't been far behind in tracing them - only through Monica's ability to plan ahead had they managed to stop him. It had been in this very room that, between them, they had managed to piece together some of Archive's intentions.

Most of Monica's pictures and possessions had been transferred underground within a day of Archive's Siva announcement, but some items had been left behind in order to give the outward appearance that the cottage was occupied.

In contrast to his mental picture of the room, the fireplace was empty and grey. In the absence of its heat, a deep chill had permeated the whole structure and the walls appeared to echo sound more readily. However, the continuous buffeting of the wind had never changed, it still rattled at the shutters framing the windows.

He walked through to the kitchen and dropped his keys onto the table. Nathan followed him a few seconds later, still a little out of breath following the walk.

"So, what? Is this some sort of safe house?" Nathan asked, "Will she be coming here, or do we have to move again?"

Glancing at the kitchen floor, Marcus recalled his previous high-speed, vomit inducing journey from the cottage down to the facility below. He almost pitied Nathan for what lay ahead.

"Yeah we'll move out again soon," he pointed towards the stairs, "You might wanna empty your bladder first. I'll stay with the case."

"Thanks but the case stays with me," said Nathan, patting it.

"Suit yourself," Marcus replied, walking towards the kitchen's telephone, "but the, er, transport has tight, er, compartments, so you and your case'll have to travel separately soon anyway."

Marcus lifted the receiver of the old fashioned telephone and stuck his finger in the rotary dial. He dialled a zero, his finger tracing a long circular arc around the dial, but instead of letting go, he held it there for a few seconds.

"This is Blackbox. Open the guest bedroom," Marcus said quietly into the handset, then he hung up.

Nathan felt a thump from under the floor and a moment later a tile in the kitchen floor popped up exposing a handle. He watched as Marcus pushed aside the kitchen table and pulled on the handle. The tiles remained stuck to the surface of the door which opened up in the middle of the kitchen floor.

"You gotta be shittin' me?" said Nathan incredulously, seeing that an entire room lay below.

"Nope," again Marcus remembered what lay ahead, "you'll do that all by yourself."

Their discussions were halted by a repetitive rapping on the kitchen windows. It took Marcus a moment to realise that it was machine-gun fire, coming from a black helicopter hovering fifty yards from the cliff edge. He knew the metallic filaments within the toughened glass windows would not hold back the bullets indefinitely and yelled at Nathan to get into the lower room. Nathan did not need to be told twice and was already dashing down the steps, dragging his case awkwardly behind him.

"Ditch the case!" Marcus pushed him.

"It's what they're after!" Nathan yelled back, tightening his grip.

As the glass gave way in the kitchen windows, the opposite wall was thrashed to a pulp by hundreds of bullets ripping into the wallpaper and plaster.

Still at the top of the steps, Marcus cowered behind the kitchen's newly opened trapdoor. He could hear the tiles on the opposite side disintegrating under the continuous assault and knew that the trapdoor wouldn't protect him for much longer. Nathan cleared the bottom of the short steps which then gave Marcus the space to follow. He hit the close button and the trapdoor began to slowly close behind him.

A few seconds later, when the trapdoor was only half closed, the machine gun fire stopped and it seemed that the attack was over. Above them, the sound of the sea and of the helicopter's rotor blades were audible through the former kitchen window.

The trapdoor continued its slow close, but when Marcus realised that the helicopter noise hadn't changed, he knew the attack was far from over.

"No no no!" he murmured and roughly hauled Nathan away from the base of the steps. The machine-gun fire, he realised, was never intended to kill them; it was only intended to breach the bulletproof exterior. Only then could larger munitions reach their target. Presumably the intention of the attackers was to cook their target within a bulletproof container.

The trapdoor was almost closed when they heard a rapid succession of metallic thuds pile into the kitchen wall and fall to the ground. Marcus pressed his fingers into his ears, closed his eyes and turned his back; Nathan even let go of his case to do likewise.

Fifty yards offshore and with incredible precision, the helicopter fired another volley of grenades through the small ragged hole in the cottage window. The first round of explosions blew out all the remaining ground floor windows and sent a spur of flame erupting through the chimney. The second round demolished the remaining internal structure, sending the upper floors and roof crumpling into the broiling fire below.

The helicopter hovered in place for one minute and during that time no-one walked away from the wreckage of Samphire Cottage. Then the power supplying the helicopter tail rotor stopped and it began to spin out of control. The main rotors powered down and it plunged headfirst into the shallow sea, where the waves and its own momentum tore it to shreds on the rocks.

GLAUCUS

10th April 1989

Although the Westhouse company had been founded by Sebastian's great-grandfather, the business still bore some resemblance to its humble origin. Sebastian was aware of the almost symbiotic relationship that his business had with the local community, so during these better times he'd expanded the local site, rather than move to a larger dockyard.

In recent times Westhouse had diversified into the more profitable luxury sea vessel market; there seemed to be no end to the number of stock market millionaires with deep pockets and shallow outlook. He was happy to conduct business with them and, to cover the shortfall in their seafaring knowledge, he also offered a resident crew service for the larger vessels. Invariably these crews were drawn from the local residents who had a lifetime of experience; experience his richer clients lacked and a convenience that they were willing to pay for.

Often, he would have to translate the wishes of his more eccentric clients into practicality; something that seemed to go hand in hand with his sense of innovation. From a very early age he'd shown an uncommon aptitude for practical problem solving, a family trait that seemed to show no signs of waning. The covered slipway had been the latest addition to the business.

The construction of all Westhouse vessels could now be conducted inside an enclosed, weatherproof, hangar-like building. In addition to providing year-round construction time, it also afforded a certain amount of anonymity for his clients during the building process. When ready, the slipway doors could be opened and the finished vessel launched down the sloping ramp to the dock beyond; normally to the cheers of spectators.

Inside the covered slipway, still several months away from such a launch, Sebastian Westhouse was lying on his back, staring up at the underside of an incomplete hull.

"Can you see it?" he called out, "It should be hole I-7?"

He could hear movement above him from the interior of the hull, followed by the sound of a toolbox being dragged.

"Yep, got it," a muted voice replied, "This one?"

A thin steel bar pushed through a hole above him and waggled around in a circle.

"Yeah that's the one," Sebastian waited for the steel to be retracted and then pushed a bolt through the same hole, "Got it?"

"Yep," the bolt was pulled upwards.

He turned to his right to pick up another bolt and saw a pair of feet arrive.

"Sea-bass!" came a voice from above.

Sebastian permitted very few people to use his old school nickname, but Moira Jones was one of them.

"Down here, Moy," he called out.

"Someone's in reception for you."

"Alright, thanks," Sebastian raised his voice above the hammering that had started up in another area, "can you ask them to wait, er, five minutes?"

"This one's got a suit and a briefcase," she prompted.

Sebastian knew that, in general, suits meant new business.

"Henry?" he banged on the hull, "I've gotta go. I'll ask Luke to take over, OK?"

"OK!"

Sebastian pulled himself out from the slipway's channel and climbed up the service ladder.

"Did they say who they're representing?"

"He's not said a thing," Moira met him at the top of the ladder and handed him a clean rag.

"Thanks," he wiped his hands, but it just seemed to spread the grease further, "We didn't have this meeting in the diary did we?"

Moira tilted her head and pursed her lips, which conveyed the fact that she had not missed a thing.

"Go get cleared up," she pointed to his hands and the ineffective rag, "I'll stall him with coffee."

When Sebastian arrived a few minutes later, he could see that his guest was patiently waiting in reception, reading through one of their magazines.

"My apologies for the delay," he said by way of announcing his presence.

"Mr. Westhouse?" the man replied, standing.

"Seb, please," he offered out his hand.

"Jim Cole," the man gave a firm handshake, "Thanks for seeing me."

"Not at all, Jim, please come through to my office," he said leading the way down a short corridor, "Has Moira offered you refreshments?"

"Yes, but no thanks."

Sebastian opened the door and allowed Jim to enter before him. It was a polite gesture but it also forced any prospective client to encounter the scale model yacht display at the centre of the office.

"Impressive," Jim nodded and walked forward to peer through the thick-walled glass case.

"Thank you," said Sebastian, closing the door and walking to stand alongside him.

"I've seen vessel model displays before but not ones with actual water in them," Jim tapped the glass, sending minor ripples over the water's surface.

Sebastian smiled. The centrepiece never failed to impress clients. The fairly minor investment he'd made in its creation had more than paid for the reaction it provoked. He patted the tank fondly.

"It demonstrates a feature that many of our clients choose to include in their optional extras. So it was important to include the water in the model."

"I've read your base specification brochure," Jim replied, looking eagerly at the mechanism that the tank also contained, "but this looks intriguing. I'd be more than happy to take any recommendations back to my... would it be possible to see it now?"

The model was worth every cent, Sebastian thought, "Of course."

He walked to the shortest side of the tank where a small wheel was situated. Attached to the wheel, running through the glass, was an axle that ran the full length of the tank. The water level in the tank was just high enough to touch the axle, and the axle itself appeared to skewer the model yacht from stem to stern.

"We're happy that our powered yachts have the best capsize ratios but, out there, it's a chaotic place."

Sebastian turned the wheel slightly from left to right. The model yacht, fixed to the axle also rolled from left to right, sending minor waves splashing about inside the tank.

"What we like to give our clients is security, against the worst event."

He turned the wheel through a half-turn and the model yacht capsized, sending small waves crashing against the glass.

"Now," Sebastian reached into the tank and tapped a small circular area, protruding from the upside-down hull, "This is our patented Glaucus Docking Ring system. Inside this airlocked assembly is a rescue pod. In a capsize event, the insulated rescue pod is now on top. Filled with emergency supplies, the crew can survive in safety and await rescue."

"And if the yacht sinks?" Jim appeared to spot a flaw.

Sebastian gave a simple twist to the circular cover and the cylindrical, round ended, rescue pod popped up from within the model hull.

"Positive buoyancy," he smiled, "The rescue pod ejects itself and the GPS locator beacon inside is automatically triggered when the pod is occupied."

Jim nodded appreciatively, "As I thought, it's all very impressive... is Glaucus an acronym?"

"No," Sebastian smiled again, glancing at the photo of his father on the office wall, "It's a mythology thing I got from my dad. Glaucus was apparently a sea-god who would come to the rescue of sailors and fishermen. On the day we lost my dad, Glaucus must have taken the day off."

"Ah. My condolences," Jim replied.

"The system has already saved one crew already," Sebastian recovered, "now please take a seat and we can talk through your requirements."

Sebastian took his seat on one side of his desk and guided Jim to sit on the opposite side. While Jim settled into his seat and retrieved paperwork from his briefcase, Sebastian tidied away his own paperwork. Eventually, both were ready to proceed.

"Was there a particular model you were thinking of, as a hull base?" Sebastian laid out three different hull configuration plans and turned them to favour his client's point of view, "The hydrodynamics of each will be -"

"I'm not here to buy, Mr. Westhouse," Jim interrupted, quietly placing a photocopied document on the desk between them, "The people I represent came across your recent patent filing and we think it might be useful."

"I see," Sebastian swiftly re-gathered his hull plans.

"No, there's no possible way you *could* see. But I think this might explain things a little clearer."

Jim reached into his jacket and removed what appeared to be a small black wallet. He placed it on the table and pushed it over for Sebastian to examine.

The wallet contained an ID card. The text under the passport photo declared that 'General J. Broxbourne' was the actual identity of the man in front of him.

"General?" Sebastian closed the wallet and pushed it back, whilst trying to maintain his composure, "Military. OK. Do I need a lawyer?"

"We most definitely do not need lawyers getting involved."

"Then, am I in some kind of trouble?" Sebastian folded his arms, eyeing the telephone on his desk.

"As I've said, quite the opposite. You have a dozen different patents under the Westhouse name, but we think that your existing Glaucus research and development might prove very useful to our project."

Sebastian unfolded his arms and leaned forwards on the desk, "And what project is that exactly?"

"It's a," the General seemed to hesitate, "it's a long duration engineering project involving various disciplines, for the good of mankind."

"I guess that was stupid," Sebastian shook his head, "expecting an actual answer."

"No, Mr. Westhouse, it's just that I can't answer your question here," he returned the patent copies to his briefcase and clipped it closed, "It's something that will require a... non-disclosure agreement, of sorts."

"I've signed NDA's before -" Sebastian began.

"Not like this one, I can assure you," the General stood.

Sebastian took this to mean that their meeting was over, so he stood too.

"So, *General Jim*. What? You'll be in touch?"

"No, Mr. Westhouse, now we leave."

"Oh really?" Sebastian smiled, but he found his expression was not mirrored by the man in front of him.

"We'll take my vehicle," the General now gestured towards the office door with his arm.

Sebastian noticed that only his arm had moved, the rest of him had remained as steady and immovable as stone. This was not an invitation.

"OK," said Sebastian, feeling the situation begin to drift out of his direct control, "But, my son... I'll need to let the school know that I'll be late collecting Tristan."

Sebastian lifted the phone's handset and began to dial.

With his hand and arm still outstretched, the General moved it downwards and pushed the telephone's exposed cradle buttons, cutting off the call.

"We already have your son."

DOMINANT

11th December 2013

Maxwell Troye made his way through the dim and empty supermarket. Food resources had long since been looted and even the massive carcasses of the shelves had been ravaged for valuable scrap metal, leaving only skeletal portions of framework behind. In time, he thought, even these would be salvaged by people trying to prop up their futile tunnels in the dirt.

In several places, under the dust covering the chequered floor, were dried patches of blood; markers of past battles for trivial resources. He idly kicked aside a long-faded sign proclaiming *'March Madness! 2for1 on all green-labels'*. People had fought for this, he thought, none of them realising that their stockpiles could never be enough. Maxwell pitied their intellect, but lacking any emotional engagement he felt nothing for them.

He made his way through the formerly refrigerated stock rooms towards a door that had been daubed with the Exordi Nova circular symbol. Globally the symbol inspired such fear, that it probably explained why the whole supermarket had remained uninhabited. The fact that it was still deserted gave his cell the privacy it needed.

The symbol he'd initiated on the banks of the Thames all those months ago was a complete success.

'Archive would be proud,' the tiny voice in his head nagged.

He shook his head to clear the unwelcome words from another life, he was not the same person now.

He pushed open the door and walked down the narrow steps.

Personally, the symbol was significant for another reason. Shortly before his scheduled suicide in the glass capsule above London, he had experienced a dawning epiphany that seemed to solve a greater problem. In that moment, the hardwired primitive genetic drive to preserve the self was given voice. Designed to override logical thought but disguising itself as timely inspiration, everything that had followed was rationalisation not reason.

The process of eroding the ego-morph's dominance began.

The fact that the primitive drive had any voice at all was perhaps due to the hubris of Archive's own hasty reprogramming. He and others like him had been tasked with creating a controlled chaos that would direct people's attention where Archive needed it. As he understood it, the revised instruction had been to instill fear in the population so that Archive could be seen as a force for good.

In his mind, Archive's authorised destruction of both Downing Street and the London Eye were still 'For the good of Mankind'; it was just a different deployment of the same ethos. But longer term he believed there was a problem; thankfully he also believed he could fix it.

Back then, the small voice within him rationalised that Archive's proposed level of fear could never be truly genuine if Archive themselves did not fear it. After all, what possible motivation would Archive have to continue saving humanity if they did not fear the consequences of failure?

When Maxwell had explained his reasoning to other re-tasked ego-morphs, they had also had similar thoughts. They realised that to deliver the 'New Beginning' that they had promised Archive, 'Exordi Nova' could no longer answer to Archive.

The small voice within him grew more dominant.

To bolster their small numbers, the former ego-morphs recruited the weak-minded, plying them with easily obtainable drugs to ensure a method of control; it was an efficient technique that they were familiar with, having received the same treatment from their former masters.

The method had worked so well that Exordi Nova cells had even begun to spring up in places where there were no ego-morph leaders. Spontaneous and autonomous cells all working to ensure that Archive's endeavours were continually challenged; just as Archive had instructed.

Ahead now he could see the entrance to the basement room, a faint orange glow flickering on the concrete walls told him that they had lit the fire in preparation for his arrival. He purposefully emphasised his own footsteps and a murmur of hushed conversation echoed quietly along the corridor towards him.

As Maxwell's personal supplies of metathene had dwindled, he found that the ego-morph's level of control had almost completely deteriorated, leaving him as the dominant personality. There would be flashes of control, when Maxwell would be forced once again into being a mere passenger, but the instances were getting fewer and further between. He had adopted a personal mantra that aided in keeping the Archive-loving alter-ego at bay. It was a mantra that had even been adopted by his small group of chemically dependent followers, which only served to enhance the control he had on them.

"Exordi Nova," he greeted them as he entered the room.

"The New Beginning," they replied and stood, their voices easily filling the small space.

"We move separately," he intoned.

"But as one," they replied as one.

He motioned for them to sit around the fire, and they complied easily.

Through his network of contacts, he had received word of a heavily defended Archive facility in Iceland. It would require his direct and personal attention.

"Siva must complete its path," he looked around at them earnestly.

"Our self-sacrifice is just," they returned with equal intensity.

"Yes, our sacrifice is just and Siva must complete its path, but now I must say this to you," he looked around at those eagerly awaiting his words, "My destiny lies upon a different path - a path I must walk alone."

There was a look of confusion on some of the faces, but others appeared to nod sagely.

"I must travel to strike at Archive's heart. I will be absent for many weeks," Maxwell clarified.

In truth he suspected that he may not return from Öskjuvatn Lake, but that would not be important. The important point was that his followers should continue to disseminate the disruption he had begun.

"But Troye," a teenager to his right began, "who do we, you know, like, trust while you're gone?"

"Archive," Maxwell's immediate reply surprised himself as much as his followers. He knew the response had come from the deeply buried ego-morph, still struggling to protect Archive. His followers were not as quick witted and he recovered without any notable drop in composure, "Archive will seek to lead you astray, but you must now trust only in yourselves."

"Troye," another, older, man stood up above the others to address Maxwell at eye level, "I will lead us in your absence."

It didn't surprise Maxwell in the least that Shane would wrongly assume there was a hierarchy below his own leadership. Shane's show of intent was timely and one that Maxwell could make an example of. He knew that Shane had been trading resources to secure himself a material advantage in the area. Over the next second, Maxwell assessed him.

Despite the austerity of the times, Shane was lacking the pallor of the others in the room. Maxwell glanced at his belt and noted that fresh holes had been added to accommodate his increased weight. His fingernails did not have the characteristic line of ingrained grime that beset everyone else, instead they were stained a nicotine yellow. Whilst not illegal, tobacco was only obtainable now on the black market, as were the breath mints he was using to try to conceal the fact. His shirt, open to the chest, allowed Maxwell to see a necklace. On a thin leather strap hung an outlawed, metallic Exordi Nova symbol: a ring of polished steel about one inch in diameter, intersected at one point by a ball-bearing. He had seen this type of defiant fashion wear before; the simple circular design was easy to duplicate, and perhaps accounted for its widespread notoriety. Maxwell cleared his throat and pointed at the necklace.

"The symbol of the Exordi Nova is not one to be worn as a piece of jewellery, displayed for all to see as a trinket and removed just as easily. It is a symbol of our hope and of their fear," Maxwell pointed loosely in the direction of the surface, "Give it to me."

Hesitantly, Shane unhooked the necklace and handed it to Maxwell who turned it over in his gloved hands. Gently, he laid the metallic symbol in the fire grate, the thin leather strap began to steam slightly.

"Siva's glorious arrival will cleanse the Earth of those seeking to enslave humanity," he continued his rhetoric, "The new beginning will wipe away all war, corruption and greed, all overpopulation and hunger. It is only we that can destroy those who seek to stop Siva's deliverance. Siva must fulfil its destiny. Siva must complete its path!"

"Our self-sacrifice is just!" they shouted with fervour, but Shane's response was less vocal now and arrived slightly late. The leather strap had shrivelled to a brittle, crispy strand.

"We have spoken often about our calling and I believe we are approaching a time of great upheaval. Each of you will be tested," Maxwell looked around at all of them, before his eyes came to rest on Shane, "and we must demonstrate our devotion."

Maxwell looked into the fire before addressing him.

"Shane, you would seek to lead? You are willing to display your devotion?"

The leather strap had fallen into the fire, leaving only the detached metallic symbol behind. An oily blue line of heat discolouration was working its way through the metal's thickness.

Shane nodded indistinctly and murmured noises of vague assent.

"Then remove the symbol from the fire," Maxwell said simply.

Shane looked from Maxwell to the fire and back again, as though expecting this to be another metaphorical lesson, but Maxwell merely held his stare. Stepping closer to the fire Shane tentatively reached out his hand. The others watched in fearful fascination, neither able to object nor avert their eyes from the spectacle. Shane's reach stopped a few inches above the fire, his fingers forming grasp-like intentions but proceeding no further. Maxwell interrupted:

"Shane, stop. It is one thing to wish to lead others," he gently pulled his hand away from the fire, "It is quite another to demonstrate the sacrifice it requires."

Maxwell offered out his right hand to Shane who, with a smile of relief, grasped it and shook it firmly. The others saw Shane's smile quickly fade as Maxwell's grip tightened. With his other gloved hand, Maxwell scooped up the searing hot metal symbol from the fire and clapped it into the back of Shane's right hand. There was an audible hiss as the metal seared into the flesh. His attempt to pull his hand from Maxwell's vice-like grip was futile, but that did not stop him screaming and desperately trying to free himself.

Maxwell released him and Shane fell backwards, the symbol still stuck to the back of his hand. After frantically shaking his hand the metal ring fell to the floor with a muted ping.

Maxwell stared down at Shane, but addressed the room, "Many will not share our vision and will resist or impede you. You are not to kill them, instead place our mark upon them. They will either become the tool to spread our message, or return to suffer the hatred of their own community."

He crouched at Shane's side and placed a hand on his shoulder.

"Shane you now carry our proud symbol closer to your skin than any necklace, you will be welcome everywhere you see our sign."

Maxwell knew that the converse was also true, Shane was now an outcast everywhere else. He would live out his days wearing gloves, or be dependent on the members of the cell he had just sought to control.

The branding of 'Novaphiles' was a practice that Maxwell had heard about months ago. Normally carried out by petty fiefdoms, it invoked fear or revenge killings within local communities. However, he had never used it as a technique himself and he wondered if he had just crossed through a mental line within his own rationale. In that moment, the tiny alter-ego within screamed *'Error!'* at him, but Maxwell suppressed the voice quickly.

During the remainder of their time together, Maxwell briefed each of them on their objectives and supplied them with their chemical fix by way of payment. Then, one by one, they departed; symbolically burning any notes they had made. Their sacrifices would cause mayhem and in many cases make them fugitives, but none would have to die to achieve their goals. Maxwell himself had no such guarantee.

Maxwell knelt to retrieve his backpack from the corner of the empty room and he felt something fall from his pocket and clatter to the ground. Turning around he saw that he had dropped a small silver case. It was the device he'd previously used to check and administer his metathene dose. He picked it up and, almost with a fondness, opened it. Inside was the familiar mirror-like finish and the holding bays for the, now absent, vials of metathene. He ran his fingers along the groove in one half and checked the digital display. The display was long dead, like the ego-morph within him.

'*I'm not dead,*' the reflection informed him.

Maxwell was fully aware that it was the buried alter-ego using whatever means it could to attract his attention. He was just wondering if the case's accidental fall from his pocket had actually been accidental at all, when the reflection spoke again.

'*This is not your true mission, but you do not have to be alone, I will go with you.*'

"You will attempt to talk me out of it," Maxwell spoke to the empty room.

'*You would expect nothing less, but I am still a part of you. I made you who you are. We have both sacrificed much in this life.*'

He knew that this was true. He had given up so much in his life of service to one goal or another, but he felt the sacrifice was justified.

'*Our sacrifice is justified,*' the reflection agreed, '*Our choices made a difference.*'

This was also true, but his choices had isolated him.

'*You do not have to be alone,*' the reflection smiled, brushing the long hair out of his own eyes.

Maxwell put the case away and tied his long hair into a ponytail.

"Together, then?" he addressed the flickering fire.

'We move separately,' the voice replied, *'but as one.'*

"Siva must complete its path."

'Our self-sacrifice is just.'

"Exordi Nova."

'The New Beginning.'

GUARDIAN

2nd January 7142

A few moments ago, the island had become eerily quiet. Atka found that he had instinctively frozen in a slightly crouched posture, ears straining to hear any sound. He had learned that when Nature fell quiet, it was wise to do the same. He forced himself to stand upright again but still listened carefully.

There was a deep thump within the ground under his feet and the thunderous noise returned. In fear, the Elder hastily bowed to Atka and ran towards the bridge, leaving Atka alone in the Orb's ethereal glow.

Suddenly, the Sky-Spirits vanished and the Orb's once-steady light began to fade. Atka looked into the centre of the Orb to find the Guardian. A moment ago she had been pointing directly at him, but now she was beginning to drop her arm. He could see that she was also beginning to turn away from him.

Fearing that he had somehow angered the Guardian, he clawed at the pale-coloured box that the Elder had given to him; desperate to retrieve the ring that was within. As the ground continued to shake, the box fell from his hands and broke into two pieces again. The gleaming metal ring bounced away from the box and rolled across the ground towards the Orb's impenetrable field. Trusting in his abilities, he immediately sprang after it. With arms outstretched, he crashed into the dirt and closed his hand around the ring before it reached the Orb's boundary.

The Orb's surface appeared to be moving towards him again, biting into the ground near him. He rolled away from it as fast as he could then sprang to his feet, facing the Orb and the Guardian within.

The Guardian was continuing to turn away. In the hope that he could still appease her, he held the metallic ring aloft. Against the continual thundering noise, he yelled:

"Arkiv Exordi Nova!"

As the light within the Orb dimmed even further, the Guardian continued to turn away. It was only then that he became aware of something different. Although his previous sighting of a Guardian had been brief, he remembered that they moved slowly. But even as he watched, Atka could see that her movements were becoming faster.

Still holding the metallic ring above his head, he called to her again:

"Arkiv Exordi Nova!"

He could see that the Guardian's movement was becoming more like those of his people. But the light from within the Orb was continuing to fade, and it was becoming difficult to see her.

A final clap of ground thunder shook him, then the Orb fell into darkness. He remained standing, beholding a sight that previous generations had never seen. The Orb appeared now as a dense black silhouette against the star-filled sky.

A new quiet descended around him. Echoing back from the darkened Orb were the distant cries of his people at the other end of the bridge.

With a sense of unease, he realised he was the last man on the island.

LAST MAN

27th December 2013, 8 p.m.

In the planning stages it was never anticipated that anyone would be left on the island after the Node had departed. This fact confronted Douglas now; he was effectively a prisoner on the island.

He picked himself up from the floor, noticing that he'd managed to scrape a layer of skin from his hands. The heat from the bridge fire had subsided and the Icelandic chill was beginning to reassert itself. He knew he'd need to find shelter soon or risk exposure, so he walked to the nearest door of the main lab; the door was locked. He instinctively reached for the Biomag that normally hung around his neck only to remember that Kate now had it.

Only a few days ago the door swipe-card entry system had been updated to accept the RF chip embedded within the Biomag, yet his actions had already become ingrained behaviour. In accordance with his own multiple-redundancy planning, he had held onto the original card and now set about unzipping the thermal jacket to get to his inside pocket. He felt his body's heat immediately start to leach away from him as the wind searched for a way between his layers of clothing. He hurriedly tugged at the inside pocket until the fastener pulled apart, his wind-stung fingers clasped around the card and he eventually pulled it free. Re-zipping his jacket against the wind's further invasion, he turned again to the door and swiped his card. It was only after his third failed attempt that he realised the problem; the power was off.

The Node and the facilities on the island were designed to take advantage of the location's geothermal power. When the Node had departed, the procedure was that it would disconnect from this power supply. Evidently it had been disconnected throughout the facility too; after all, in theory, there should be nobody left on the island who would need power. Douglas headed off in the direction of the backup generators, feeling the relative warmth of the bridge's fire diminish with every step he took.

The backup generators were fossil fuel based and in ideal circumstances could provide power for the facilities for up to four days. When Douglas reached the generator building, he was relieved that the door was unlocked; at least someone had demonstrated the forethought to exclude the generator rooms from the fail-closed protocol. He stepped through the doorway into the darkness and his foot struck something metallic and hollow. He stopped and reached around the doorframe into the room, feeling his way towards the flashlights that he knew should be there. Sure enough he found one and he twisted the top to make a wide beam.

Casting the beam around the fuel storeroom he could see row upon row of five-gallon metal Jerry cans neatly stowed along two walls. Near the door several cans lay strewn over the floor, including one that had spilled its contents; evidently the rush to depart had cut short the attempt to transport the remaining fuel aboard the Node. By the looks of things, he estimated that half of the fuel had made it.

Douglas stepped around a puddle of fuel and walked on through the dark, towards the fire door that separated this room from the generator itself. The door was spring loaded to ensure it would remain closed when not in use, however he had no intention of becoming accidentally trapped, so he retrieved an empty can from the fuel storeroom and propped the door open.

In the darkness ahead of him he heard a quiet click and immediately he froze, straining his ears to hear anything he could.

"Hello?" he called out and heard the dark room's slight reverberation. The sound soon died away; there wasn't even the background noise he'd become accustomed to at the base.

He approached the L-bend in the room and knew he'd have to turn the corner. He drew a breath and announced as confidently as he could muster, "It's just my flashlight, OK?"

Again he heard a quiet click.

He took another breath and stepped around the corner, keeping the beam aimed low. It illuminated the short section of the empty floor, and as Douglas slowly began to sweep the beam throughout the entire dead end section of corridor, he realised no-one was there. The faint click sounded again and, with some relief, Douglas discovered that it was a low voltage relay trying to reactivate the electrical mains. It had detected the power cut and was trying to start the backup generator.

The sense of relief he experienced was immediately countered by the equal sense of unease, as he realised that some part of him had wanted there to be someone there. Anyone.

He'd never operated a backup generator before but, after discovering a rubber pipe on the floor, it didn't take him long to work out the source of the problem. When they'd started evacuating the fuel to the Node, they must have realised that the generator itself had an internal tank of valuable fuel that could be syphoned off. It appeared that the puddle on the floor was the end result; although they had started the syphoning process, they had abandoned it, leaving the generator's tank to bleed dry.

In under an hour he'd worked out how to prime the pump and had refilled the generator tank using several of the Jerry cans. He reset the relay and, laying down the flashlight, attempted to manually crank-start the generator. The first two revolutions did nothing, but on the third time the combustion cycle caught and the generator coughed into life. The fluorescent lights overhead flickered into a humming, greenish-white glow allowing Douglas to see the room as a whole, rather than an unconnected set of illuminated patches. In the fuel storeroom, thick rubber scuff marks criss-crossed the floor amid several damaged playing cards and an upturned wooden crate. It appeared that the fuel evacuation had been swift and panicked.

As he headed to the door the lights outside came on, by the time he was back outside he spotted that the lights in the building furthest from him were blinking back on. He could almost convince himself that things were back to normal, but the illusion was short lived. Siva didn't care for the human sleep cycle, so Archive had always adopted a similarly indifferent approach. Even in the dead of night at the Node, there would be work crews continually advancing the long-term construction. Their absence now somehow made the bite of the cold wind more harsh.

He walked the ten feet to the nearest building and was about to swipe his card through the lock when he saw that the tiny green LED on the door handle was already lit. Either this building had zero security requirements, or the complete base-wide power failure had wiped the security clearances. He hoped it was the latter; it would make movement from building to building less finger-numbing.

Once inside he hurriedly pushed the door closed behind him. The building was well insulated, both in terms of sound and heat; the external noise was cut dramatically and, in comparison to the temperature outside, Douglas actually felt the warmest he had been for hours.

The rec room, like most of the military facilities on the base, was modest and compact. One corner was occupied by a table football game and the nearby wall was peppered with dart holes, each one a tiny reminder of someone's poor aim.

Douglas strolled over to the football table and idly held the control handles. He'd never played a game but on the one occasion he'd ventured into this room he had seen several others apparently enjoying themselves. He twirled the handle and watched the plastic football players turn rigid somersaults on their metal bar. Even if he had wanted to, there was no-one left in the world to play the game with; this table had already hosted its last match.

Presumably the football table had been too hard to remove quickly, but the same was not true for the dartboard. Only a scattergun circle of dart holes defined its former position.

His over-analytical mind noted that the random distribution of the holes dipped in the upper right quadrant. He was part way through analysing the mathematical scenarios that would cause that pattern to arise when he became aware that he was resorting to calculations in order to fill the pervasive silence that surrounded him. He forced his calculations to a halt and focussed on the room again.

Even the bookshelf had been hurriedly raided of its literary cargo during the swift exodus. The cheap, pulp fiction novels had been saved as examples of human literature, merely because of their proximity to the Node.

He took one last look around the room, ensured his jacket was firmly zipped and headed to the door. A printed piece of office paper stuck next to the door handle now seemed poignant:

'Last man here? Turn off the lights.'

He took a final breath of warm air and then turned off the lights.

CIRCLE

Any intervention carried with it an element of detection risk, so she knew it was important for the symbol to be placed on the *periphery* of his conscious mind. She knew the moment he would reach this location, so she worked backwards to ensure the intervention would be in place by the time he arrived.

Throughout the preceding six months, she arranged for a tiny lowering of various physical constants in the immediate vicinity of the upper right quadrant of the dartboard. The subtle distortion affected all players equally; an approach she had taken to ensure that the causal outcomes of the darts matches did not interfere with events.

Over the months, the cumulative effect of darts randomly missing the board, created a circle of holes surrounding it; with the exception of the upper right quadrant which suffered almost no damage.

She saw the board being swiftly removed, leaving behind a broken circle of dart holes on the wall of the rec room.

He arrived on time and appeared to stare at the symbol she'd arranged, then he moved on.

With a sense of satisfaction she moved on too.

She shifted her focus towards an earlier moment and saw the rotary dial of a communication console.

She could see that the causality surrounding the next event was already secure, but the moment of outcome could still be adjusted. It gave her the opportunity to test a slightly different approach.

She adjusted the local electrostatic attraction and reached in.

She drew a neat broken circle around the dial and then placed a dot.

STARFISH

25th December 2013

Already more personnel were pouring past Lawrence and hurrying down the metalwork steps, sending great echoes around the vast concealed space. He heard the sound of generator circuit breakers clicking into place far below and saw that the FLC replica was now fully illuminated, and casting diffused shadows over the simulated lunar surface.

Each of the cylindrical chambers radiating out from the central Drum was marked with a large illuminated number, with the exception of Chamber 2. It appeared to Lawrence that the whole cylinder was unpowered, but he didn't have time for further study; Ross Crandall had called him over and he knew better than to delay. He rushed across the metallic floor and caught up with him and several others making their way down the steps at speed.

"Work with Greg Campbell, here," he pointed at a short man in front of him, also hurrying down the steps, "If all we can get is Morse then I want you translating. Campbell, rig up a push button code-key if you can't get analogue comms back online."

"Understood," Greg replied, turning his head to address Lawrence, "So you picked this up in the power-use trace?"

"Yes," Lawrence replied, narrowly avoiding slipping down the steps. The further down they went, the colder it appeared to become, "internal power consumption, there were dips in power that appeared to follow a coherent pat-"

"If they want us to go analogue," interrupted Ross, "it must mean the digital system is compromised, I want to know how badly. Do we still have control? Both of you, work with Karl Meyer."

On hearing his name, a taller man further down the steps partially turned and called out that he understood.

"Welcome to the Starfish, Larry," continued Ross, "there's no VIP tour and I don't have time to answer your questions. It's been here from the beginning. Every time they shipped a piece up there, we made a copy down here. Only way we can keep track."

They began descending the last flight of steps and the once starfish-like profile was no longer visible; the cylinders, even lying horizontally, began to tower over them. On the Moon, the six cylinders surrounding the Drum had been constructed from airtight Space Shuttle external fuel tanks. However, in a few places the Starfish's cylinders were not fully enclosed, allowing him to see through to the internal walls too. A thought suddenly crossed Lawrence's mind.

"Wait, you have a fusion reactor…?" Lawrence began.

"No, we don't need that much power," Ross cut in, "It runs off the mains supply, but we have equivalent systems for everything else. Whatever we can simulate down here, they can do for real up there."

Almost instinctively, Lawrence looked up towards the roof of the cavernous room and, in the dim recesses, he could see sturdy winching machinery. Presumably it must once have been used to lower the tanks through the roof and into place.

Ross was now already deep in discussion with members of his communication team and Lawrence had to run to catch up again.

"… and the repeater stations?" Ross was saying while the others, none of whom Lawrence recognised, fed back their findings.

"Equatorial repeaters are good, but we're re-patching for analogue comms. It can't have been used in about, what, maybe…"

"Two years?"

"More like three… we had to shut dow-"

"Mr. Crandall!" interrupted a voice from behind the communications station, "Analogue good to go!"

"About damned time," Ross grumbled and pushed forwards to take control of the robust-looking, stand-mounted microphone. He pushed the newly added mounds of cables aside and brushed a layer of grey dust off the transmit key button before pressing it.

"FLC crew this is Houston, do you read us?"

Even allowing for the signal's transit time to the Moon, around its equator to the FLC and then its return trip, there was no timely response. Ross was about to try for the fourth time when an explosive shout from Karl Meyer came from the Drum at the centre of the FLC replica.

"The deflection system is active!"

"What?" Ross called back.

"They've already activated the Siva deflection system!"

"That's not poss- why the hell didn't we know about this?" Ross yelled back.

"Error report system went fully digital in 2010. With digital down…" Karl trailed off, "I'm checking to see if we can restore analogue control."

Lawrence saw him duck back inside the Drum through a small flimsy hole, presumably not part of the real FLC design which would require much stronger reinforcement.

"We were blind…" Ross seemed temporarily adrift in his own thoughts before rounding on Greg Campbell, "Get this unit running. Now."

Behind him, somewhere in the darker area of the room, a telephone began to ring. The effect on Ross was instant, he turned on his heels and ran to answer it. Immediately a flurry of activity around the communication station resumed, with several people pulling off side panels and wheeling over tool boxes.

Lawrence could see that the control station they had been using to attempt communication was old, but he was fairly sure it must still be intact. It was also likely that this control station had never been used after being decommissioned; in which case the controls themselves were probably still set to use the conventional analogue channels. Channels no-one at the FLC expected to hear a message on.

Still partly in shock, Lawrence let his eyes wander over the console's dusty surface, unsure what he was looking for.

Then he saw it.

A neat circle, where the dust had not gathered, surrounded the circumference of a rotary dial, this circle was broken in one place by a small dot.

The dot coincided with a text label that read 'Emerg. CH1'.

Where the inspiration had come from he couldn't be sure, but before Lawrence realised what he was doing, he had already turned the dial to select it. Immediately a low hiss of static came from the speakers. The others working on the console just stopped and stared. A look of mild fear was written all over Greg's face. It took Lawrence a moment to understand their reaction; if Ross thought Greg had overlooked something as basic as a dial position then he would not be pleased. No-one wanted to ride the elevator to the surface.

As Ross returned from his phone call, ashen faced, Lawrence thought quickly.

"Sir, we've managed to link up emergency analogue channel one; we bypassed the-"

Ross had stopped listening and had picked up the microphone again.

Lawrence glanced over at Greg who mouthed the word 'Thanks'.

"FLC do you read us?" Ross tried again, "FLC crew this is Houston, broadcasting on emergency analogue channel one, do you read us?"

Nothing but light static came from the speakers.

"We say again, FLC crew this...

"Houston, this is Lana Yakovna. We read you."

"Lana?"

Their messages had apparently crossed in space, a side effect of the delay in communication when talking to the far side of the Moon. The reaction of those surrounding the control console was immediate and they cheered loudly at their success. Ross waved them to be quiet before continuing.

"We got your message, good thinking. Deliver situation report, over."

"Eva Gray has FLC Drum in lockdown. Leonard Cooper is internal Chamber 6 with no Floyd access. Mike Sanders, Cathy Gant and myself are external, with the Z-bank and two evac-packs. Chamber 4 airlock unsecure with cyclical access available. Over."

As information came in from Lana's situation report, people rushed to set duplicate conditions throughout the FLC replica. Some were running over the simulated grey regolith and placing cone-like markers to represent the FLC crew. A suitcase was also dragged into position alongside them to represent the Z-bank; cryogenically frozen zygote samples of Earth's genetic materials.

"Understood," Ross replied, "We read an unauthorised activation of the Siva deflection system, but have no telemetry can you confirm. Over."

After the customary delay a new voice continued:

"Houston this is Cooper. I confirm I am reading an activation of the Siva deflection system. I read a charge build-up in Larry, Curly and Mho. Current capacity of the fusion core is at forty-seven percent of maximum..."

Again, during the report, Ross quietly clicked at people and directed them to various stations. Greg was sent to join Karl in the Drum, and he sprinted off across the lunar surface towards the small hole. Lawrence started to feel anxious that he had not yet visibly proved his worth.

"Request immediate remote shut down," Leonard Cooper concluded, *"Over."*

"Meyer, do we have analogue control of the reactor?" Ross called out towards the Drum.

"No," came Meyer's voice, before he reappeared in the Drum's hole, "Still working on it. Ask them if the cowl is open."

Ross pushed the microphone button again.

"Roger. We've got the team running scenarios. What is the status of the protective cowl? Over."

"Houston this is Yakovna. Gant is in ascent to the prism. Over."

They all turned to look at the Drum in the centre and the shorter cylinder immediately above it that housed the beam combining prism. On the Moon all of the FLC structure was under tonnes of lunar regolith, but it was easy to imagine Cathy Gant climbing the regolith to its summit to inspect the condition of the cowl above the combining prism.

"Best case, the cowl's open and the laser discharge has somewhere to go…" muttered Ross, before shouting over to the Drum, "How are we doing on analogue control? Can we remote deactivate?"

This time Greg reappeared briefly in the hole and Lawrence could see him shake his head.

"Lana said that Chamber 4 airlock was cycling," he shouted to those gathered by the duplicate Chamber 4, "can they get in through that way?"

"Yeah, they must have put it into a diagnostic mode, but the Drum itself is still locked from the inside…"

"What about the evac-packs?" Ross called to a group of people sitting on the grey surface emptying out the emergency evacuation packs.

"We've got two Oh-Two cylinders. A magnesium flare gun… maybe we could work out a way to ignite the…"

"They could rapid-decompress Chamber 4!"

"Nah, you've not got the pressure," called a voice from near Chamber 4, "The Drum would still hold…"

A brief crackle of static popped on the speaker.

"Houston this is Gant at the prism. Cowling is still in place. Over."

Ross drew a deep breath. He'd been holding out hope that Eva Gray had some valid reason for activating the laser deflection system, even if they didn't know what it was. But with the cowl closed, all the energy building up now had nowhere to go. He pushed the microphone button.

"Roger," he replied semi-automatically before turning to face everyone, "Suggestions?"

The room was quiet.

Events had moved too quickly. The chain of command above him had never planned for this eventuality; they could not respond quickly enough to the situation. He would have to make the decision. At least some swift thinking up at the FLC had managed to rescue the Z-bank. He turned again to the microphone and pushed the button.

"FLC, be advised at this time we are unable to effect remote deactivation," Ross hesitated, as he prepared for what he must instruct them to do, "We're still running numbers but order the immediate evacuation of the Z-bank and personnel to the RTO module. Over."

The Return To Orbit module was only supposed to be used when all three firings on Siva had been completed successfully. Now its role would be to act as a mere lifeboat, carrying the crew and Z-bank back to Earth orbit.

The FLC was finished.

In the still quiet room, the speaker crackled.

"Houston this is Cooper. We read you. Be advised my airlock has negative function. I will remain at the FLC and do what I can to run interference. Over."

Ross shook his head in dismay.

"Thank you Lenny," he said with as much dignity as he could muster, "we'll keep this channel open for you."

He let go of the microphone button and turned to face everyone.

"We keep working," he said through gritted teeth, "pull the damn Starfish apart if you have to."

ARRIVALS

5th July 2013

The phone next to Cal Dawson rang only once before he lifted the handset to answer.

"Arrivals Lounge," he stated.

In theory there should be only one possible caller using this antiquated, analogue line, but Monica Walker always insisted on using the correct terminology in case communications were ever compromised.

"This is Blackbox. Open the guest bedroom," came the reply.

"Welcome home," Cal hung up and pressed the release switch.

Over a hundred yards above him and a good deal further toward the Dover coast, the electromagnetic lock of a kitchen floor trapdoor released. Monica had asked him to notify her as soon as Marcus returned, but without knowing where in the facility she was, the fastest option was to page her over the internal speaker system.

He pushed the intercom button.

"Arrivals Lounge paging Monica Walker," he could hear the tail end of his own message bouncing through the tight confines of the tunnels nearby, "Returning guests."

He thought the term 'Arrivals Lounge' was a little grand for the actual function of the room; essentially this was a room with a tubular opening in the ceiling through which capsules would descend on a long track, before being rapidly decelerated at the other end.

Given the descent speed of the capsules, it was not uncommon for the people within them to lose some form of bodily fluid control. However, there was no denying that in an emergency it was the fastest method of getting personnel underground. Whoever was arriving with Marcus must be important, in trouble, or both. In preparation he stood to fetch the mop and bucket.

Monica entered the long room and walked over to him, yawning.

"It's gone two in the morning, Cal," Monica sighed, "This better be good."

It had been her idea to be notified, but he felt it would be disrespectful to say so; all he managed was a mere opening and closing of his mouth.

"Relax, I'm kidding," Monica's mouth broke into a smile and she pointed at the telephone, "How long ago did he call?"

"Er… maybe a minute, Ma'am," Cal's shoulders relaxed.

"Yeah, let's drop the 'Ma'am' shall we? Way too early, Cal," she patted him lightly on the back and yawned again.

She spotted the room's camp-bed, folded flat against the wall, "Have you slept at all?"

"Absolutely not, Ma'... er, no," he faltered.

Monica just smiled at his mild embarrassment. There was a tiny spark in his mannerisms that reminded her of her husband. Douglas had never really been lost for words, but in their early years together he had suffered the same social awkwardness.

"We're not military, Cal. If you're on phone watch then you're supposed to sleep, the ringer's loud enough to wake the dead! We don't have large enough numbers to do shifts watching a phone, it's a waste of time. In fact, there's part of me that feels guilty isolating anyone up here just to answer it."

He was shaking his head, "It's important, I'm glad to do it."

Monica knew he meant it and just nodded.

"Besides," he added, now at little more at ease, "that camp-bed's more like a stretcher on legs."

Their conversation was interrupted by a distant rumble within the rock above them, followed by a metallic clattering coming from somewhere high up inside the personnel delivery chute. Normally, a buzzer would sound before each capsule departed from above, but no such sound had occurred.

Monica strode over to the telephone and lifted the receiver.

"Dead," she said plainly, then replaced the handset. She pushed the button for the internal speaker system, "Stop stop. Medical team to the Arrivals Lounge."

The echoes of her message died in the tunnels closest to the room, leaving it in uncomfortable silence. She spotted Cal's ashen expression and immediately took control.

"Not your fault," she pointed at him directly, "Need your help, now."

Cal managed a single nod.

Monica pointed to the chute entering through the ceiling and the piece of track that would carry the high speed capsules containing either Marcus or the new guest.

"That was an explosion. Up there. Trust me," Monica quickly summarised, "and it sounds like a pod's already on its way down."

Under normal operation, the capsules would descend through the chute and emerge onto a straight section of track. A hook on top of the capsule would then be caught by several elastic bungee cords stretched across the track.

"But…" Cal pointed to the end of the track; the bungee cord mechanism had not received the instruction to catch the capsule and still hung like a limp hammock above the track. He didn't wait for instructions but dived off towards the mechanism.

Before he could reach the elastic cords, a loud screech from within the chute announced the arrival of the capsule. It shot into the room at speed amid a shower of brake sparks as it exited the chute and flew along the short section of track. It passed under the elastic cords and slammed into the rubber piston at the end of the track. Under the force of the collision the lid sheared from the base and the first third of the capsule crumpled into itself, before the entire mangled unit fell from the track onto the floor.

Both Monica and Cal dashed over to the capsule and between them managed to turn it upright.

"Empty," Cal double-checked.

"Probably got shaken loose up there," Monica guessed.

The medical team entered the room and Monica wasted no time.

"Get this pod clear!" she pointed at the mangled capsule, parts of which were still wrapped around the impact absorbing rubber pistons.

The noise of a buzzer sounded throughout the room, but even after a few seconds the elastic cord mechanism had not moved. Cal ran the few feet back to the cords and began to pull frantically at the manual winch, while the medical team reacted with equal speed to clear the debris from the end of the track.

•

With his ears still ringing from the kitchen explosion above him, Marcus picked himself up off the floor. In the darkness he was sure he could hear a groan from somewhere in the room. He fumbled around for the torch he was sure must still be in his pocket and on finding it, shone it around the now sealed room.

"You OK?" he called out to Nathan, and hauled him to his feet.

"Yeah I'll live," he coughed, "so now what?"

Marcus cast the beam around and pointed it towards a chute in the lower corner of the room. He rushed towards it and could hear a metallic clattering sound receding away down the long tube. He knew that an empty capsule had fallen down the chute, he just hoped they were ready for it below.

"What?" Nathan asked.

Before Marcus could reply, another explosion from above them shook the room and fine dust fell through the torch beam. Assuming they succeeded in surviving, Marcus wanted questions answered, but this was not the time. He pointed the light directly into Nathan's face.

"This way."

Marcus hauled a capsule along the short section of track and opened the lid.

"Give me the case and get in," he pointed to the open capsule.

"The case stays with me," Nathan replied.

"Look, you pillock," Marcus snapped, "there ain't enough room in there."

"The case -"

"Fine," interrupted Marcus, politely moving past him, "Die up here."

A repetitive heavy pounding above them shook the whole room and the ceiling groaned.

"Wait!" Nathan conceded, "Wait. The case has never left my sight, just handing it over to -"

"Look you got two choices, mate," Marcus cut in again, pointing upwards, "Stay here with the case, get crushed and burned. Or, assume that I wanna get out of here alive too. I'll get your damn case to follow you."

Marcus held his hand out toward the suitcase.

Nathan appeared to study him for a moment as though weighing options.

"Are you for real?" Marcus almost laughed.

Nathan handed over the suitcase and climbed into the capsule, wriggling down into the reclined position.

"OK, so what do I have to do?" Nathan tucked his arms inside.

Without a reply, Marcus slammed the lid shut and, ignoring the instant shouts from within the box, pushed a small red button on the wall next to the track. After a momentary pause, the track containing the capsule tipped up and launched it down the chute.

As soon as the track had reset to the horizontal position, he dragged another capsule into place ready for launch. He opened the lid and loaded Nathan's suitcase into it. A deep shuddering came from above. To Marcus, it sounded like the whole cottage above had just collapsed onto the space above his head. More dust and pea-sized pieces of concrete fell through his torch beam, and it felt as though the tiny room had suddenly become much hotter.

He dropped the torch beam to his side, but in doing so, something caught his eye. He pointed the torch back at the short section of track and swore under his breath. Other than the capsule currently holding Nathan's suitcase, there were no more capsules.

"Think!" he shouted at himself.

The heat from above was definitely increasing, he thought. If he left the suitcase behind, it might not survive. But if he didn't leave soon then neither would he. He pictured himself sitting in the capsule, hitting the launch button and pulling the lid closed before the track tipped; he also pictured Nathan's suitcase being dragged behind the capsule on some sort of rope.

He had no idea how long the ceiling would hold. He would have to move quickly.

•

A clattering metallic sound echoed down the chute leading into the Arrivals Lounge, as Cal continued to haul at the chain of the manual winch.

"I can't get it low enough!" he yelled, "It'll miss the pod's hook!"

The metallic noise suddenly got louder and he realised the arrival was only a second or two away. Monica was now moving in his direction to assist, but he knew that even if she reached him, the capsule would arrive first. He let go of the chain and, climbing up onto the track, grabbed the elastic cords themselves.

The capsule exited the chute at speed among another blast of brake sparks and hurtled down the track. With his hands still tightly gripping the cords, Cal leaned back from the track so that his weight pulled the elastic taught across the path of the capsule's hook. The hook at the rear of the capsule snatched into the cords, wrenching them out of Cal's hands and he fell away from the track to the floor. The capsule slowed drastically, but with the elastic still in such an elevated position it began to lift the capsule's rear away from the track. As it reached the end of the track, one of the cords snapped, twisting the front end of the capsule slightly off the rails; but the rest of the cords held and began to pull it back in the opposite direction. The front end slipped completely off the rail and the capsule was dragged, like a worm on a fishing line, back down the room where it twisted to a halt in an upright position.

"Get it open!" Monica shouted and the medical team swept in, "Cal? You OK?"

"Yeah," Cal got to his feet and, brushing off his rope-burned palms, joined the others who were trying to open the clasps of the capsule's lid.

The noise of a buzzer sounded again; the next capsule was already on the way.

As the final clasp popped open, the elastic-tangled lid remained in place and the upright capsule base dropped towards the floor. A disoriented Nathan Bishop fell out of it, but he was caught by members of the medical team.

"Woods," Monica turned to a small, bearded man within the group, "If he's OK, put him in AR2. No one talks to him. Understood?"

"Of course."

"The case..." Nathan managed, trying to maintain his balance, "he said he'd..."

Nathan passed out but was once again caught by Woods and the others, who carried him away from the track.

The inevitable, metallic rattling of the approaching capsule reached them.

Cal quickly looked up at the elastic cords, now hopelessly tangled around both the hook in the capsule's lid and the winch above it. Both he and Monica exchanged a wide-eyed stare as the sound grew louder; with nothing to arrest the speed of the approaching capsule it would impact the circular-ended pistons at the end of the track. At that speed, the fact they were made from rubber would not matter.

In that instant he knew the problem was momentum. The elastic, rubber and crumpled first capsule all had one thing in common, he realised. They had converted kinetic energy into a more wasteful form, allowing the energy to dissipate. He needed to absorb the momentum of the capsule by using something else. Where the inspiration came from he couldn't be sure, but it was persistent and it appeared that Monica was thinking the same thing.

Monica turned swiftly and ran to the piston end of the track.

"Help me!" she shouted to the others, motioning to the ruined first capsule lying on the floor, "Load it back on the track, right here!"

At the same time, Cal had dashed the few yards to the side wall and grabbed the folded camp-bed. He returned at speed to the chute end of the track and shook open the canvas and metal frame. He pushed the stretcher-like structure across the track and wedged the 'x' shaped legs into the gaps within the steel-work uprights on either side of the track.

The capsule screeched through the chute in a burst of sparks and ploughed on down the track. It hit the camp-bed, partially tearing the canvas, but was not quite fast enough to pass through it. Now caught by the canvas, the capsule instantly folded the camp-bed's feeble metal framework around itself. With each impact of the camp-bed's legs on the surrounding steel-work uprights, the capsule traded a little more speed, so that by the time it reached the other end of the track it was at a sprinting speed. Monica had just managed to step clear of the ragged front end of the first capsule when the impact brought everything to a halt.

Immediately they were upon it, pulling the torn camp-bed away from the capsule.

"Marcus!" Monica hammered at the capsule's lid.

They all tore at the clasps that were holding the lid shut. A few agonising seconds later, Monica released the last one and threw open the lid. Inside the capsule there was only a suitcase, held in place by the additional padding of Marcus Blake's black leather jacket.

Monica's sharp intake of breath caught in her throat.

There were only three transport capsules and all of them were now in this room. Marcus was gone. Another distant rumble, far above their heads, filled the quiet room and Monica knew instinctively that her family home had been destroyed.

She inhaled steadily and deeply to regain her composure. She would allow herself time later to process the loss of Marcus, but the most pressing matter now was that this entrance to the facility was useless and also a potential security risk. She exhaled equally slowly and then spoke softly to the quiet people around her:

"We need to seal the chute -"

She was interrupted by the noise of a buzzer sounding.

She knew it was clearly impossible, all three capsules were accounted for; no more could be launched. It was only then that she remembered that the buzzer was triggered by the raising of the launch track. Marcus, she thought, must have pressed the button in an attempt to convey the message that he was still on his way.

Sure enough, within twenty minutes Monica and the others started to hear his approach. His advance suddenly got quicker as, losing his footing, he slid down the last section of chute and onto an awaiting mattress in full view of the others in the Arrivals Lounge. His jeans were ripped in places and he wore only a vest, dark grey with oil, dirt and sweat. Suddenly several people clapped, which in turn encouraged everyone there to greet him loudly and warmly.

"I'll 'ave to go away more often," he delivered, deadpan.

Cal tossed the leather jacket to Marcus.

"When we found this stuffed in the pod, we thought that maybe…"

"What, are you kiddin' me?" he smiled, shaking out the leather jacket, "This thing's priceless now. I wasn't gonna wreck it climbing down here, was I? I figured I'd send it down first class."

Several people laughed and then, with the immediate excitement over and having to return to their duties, they started to move away - collecting medical kits and metallic parts from the floor and talking among themselves.

Monica could see that Marcus had been putting on a slightly flippant air of nonchalance, but she knew the courage it must have taken to place the safety of a case before his own; particularly as the contents of the case were still unknown.

Marcus caught sight of the various pieces of capsule wreckage strewn around the room and turned to face Monica.

"Nathan? Did he? I mean is he OK? The case -"

"Our American friend is fine," Monica reassured him, "as is his suitcase. But, and I hope you don't find this untimely, I have to ask you. Did Kate and Miles catch their flight?"

Marcus unconsciously stroked at the spot where Kate had kissed his cheek, "Yes they're on their way."

She extended her hand and waited for him to shake it, which he duly did.

"Thank you, Marcus."

"Hey don't worry about it," he shrugged and casually glanced away. But when she didn't let go, he looked back at her again.

"No really, Marcus. Thank you."

This time he said nothing in reply, but from the pained look in his eyes Monica knew they understood each other perfectly. She loosened her already delicate grip and they both drew another long breath.

"You know what?" said Monica, turning to walk towards the door.

"What?" Marcus followed her.

"I think I've just figured out why you chose Blackbox as a handle."

It was an online name that Marcus had chosen years ago. In part, he'd chosen it to appear more technical and mysterious; but in truth he'd also chosen it to amuse himself - his skin colour was of course darker than many of his sunlight-deprived, pasty-white hacker associates.

"Oh yeah?" he smiled, interested to hear her insight.

"It's because you're so bloody indestructible."

CHOICE

She had watched him begin his descent but simultaneously she could see that no-one was expecting his return. They had concluded that no more capsules were coming and were sealing the chute. Looking only a few hours ahead, she saw that he had died inside the sealed chute.

She simply reached into the event and induced a low voltage in the wires of a buzzer. It had the desired effect.

They heard the buzzer and, assuming that he was the one causing it, kept the chute open.

As he reached the, now, open end of the chute, the curves of space-time before her leapt chaotically into new formations of knots, arcs and loops.

Simply inducing a low voltage within an insignificant wire, had unleashed a radically new causality system. There were elements of familiarity, but vast swathes of the former system had been altered.

It would be a trivial matter to undo.

Simply choke the electrical flow.

But as she looked more carefully, she found that the new system, carried possibilities that had not existed before. Possibilities for yet further change.

The matter could be undone and she could continue as before; or she could adopt the complex interplay of the newer system.

She had a choice, and must take the time to make it.

PEAKS

25th December 2013

"It's in the power feed, right here!" Lawrence Clark pointed to the screen.

While everyone else had busied themselves going through system checks for their individual areas of FLC expertise, Lawrence had returned to the data that had initially highlighted the problem. He'd just spent the last minute trying to persuade the communications director that the control mechanism for the FLC prism was sending them valid information, even in the absence of digital error reports.

"Look, here's the power trace from the December 21st firing, last year," Lawrence pointed to a graph showing the FLC's power usage during the firing event, "These three micro-peaks are when each of the three stepper-motors manoeuvred the Prism's separate lens elements into place. Each motor was activated for four point zero seven seconds."

"That's consistent with the angle of fire it produced," nodded Karl Meyer.

"Now look," Lawrence followed up, replacing the graph for the most recent feed, "It seems to be just a fluctuating line, until you take away the effect of the other FLC systems."

One by one he turned off the influence of the other FLC systems, until only the Prism's power draw was displayed.

"These three peaks in power consumption are each of the three stepper-motors aligning the Prism lens elements."

"And?" asked Ross impatiently.

"And… the motors were activated for six point nine seconds!"

"That's not possible," insisted Karl, "The maximum alignment time is six seconds, and that would be for targeting Siva a good deal further away. We would have received an error…"

"Not if the Shen500 computer was told to ignore it. We don't know what's going on up there…" interjected Greg, "Besides, we're not getting digital or analogue error reports."

"You're missing the point," said Lawrence forcefully, and for a second wondered if he'd overstepped the mark, "The duration of motor adjustment doesn't lie. The motors were drawing power for almost a whole additional second."

"And I'm telling you," Karl cut in, insistently, "that even if the beams are pointed straight up at Siva, the motors can't adjust for more than six seconds."

"Then they're not pointing straight up," said Lawrence simply.

"Wait, what?" Ross shook his head, "Are you saying…? Karl, is it even possible for the beams to point straight down?"

"The only time the motors can point the lenses down is during a lens-swapping maintenance mode. The whole system would have to be compromised to allow the Prism to direct the lasers down towards the…" Karl faltered mid-explanation.

In the immediate silence, Greg voiced everyone's personal summary, "Shit."

"We're gonna lose the whole damn FLC," Karl followed up.

"Have you got any clue," began Ross rhetorically, "how much Helium-3 the FLC fusion reactor is sitting on, up there? We're about to lose a whole lot more."

SACRIFICE

17th August 2009

She set her eyes on the horizon; from here the Sun was a distant point source of light in a velvet-black sky. Although the suit was insulated she could feel its warmth through the glass face plate.

"In transit to Chamber 2 airlock," she reported.

"Acknowledged."

She continued to make her way across the dust-grey surface between the micro-craters.

It was then that she saw it.

Two parallel grooves in the regolith were leading into one of the craters.

The tracks were too close together to have been made by any of the FLC's wheeled equipment, so she changed direction and headed away from the central complex, in order to gain a better look.

From the corner of her eye, she thought she saw a movement.

She was the only one scheduled to be on the surface; there should be no-one else out here.

As she moved slowly closer, she could see that the parallel tracks had a ragged, weaving quality to them. She could also see that on either side of the tracks were rough hand-prints heading into the sloping, shallow crater. She reached the crater's low rim and could see that the parallel tracks ended where a baby sat quietly playing in the granular grey surface.

Eva Gray knew she could never conceive; she fully understood the sacrifice she'd made when agreeing to her own sterilisation. But right now, in this moment, she felt a sudden and profound sense of loss.

She slowly knelt down at the rim of the small crater and extended a space-suited hand towards the baby.

"Hello," she said, gently.

The baby did not appear to notice her and continued to sift the sandy material from hand to hand, apparently fascinated by its texture.

"Eva, repeat last transmission. Over," came the voice in her headset.

"And who might you be?" she smiled.

Realising that the baby wouldn't be able to hear her, Eva began breaking the seal on her helmet, which had the effect of triggering the suit's master alarm and alerting the Drum.

"Eva, we're registering a... what are you doing!" the tinny voice in her headset shouted before faltering, *"Eva? Why is..."*

Oh, for f… this is supposed to be a closed sim… no, we'll have to reset… no, from the bloody start…"

The Sun went out and the working lights came on again around the Starfish FLC simulator. A metallic alarm bell rang for a second and then stopped, indicating that the simulation was over.

Karl Meyer ducked out through the hole in the side of the Drum and swore loudly as he strode across the fabricated lunar surface. From a different direction, but similarly converging on Eva's position, came a very embarrassed mother.

"I'm sorry!" she called out, "I am, so, sorry!"

"Janine!" Karl flung his arms wide and frowned in accusation.

"I'm sorry, Karl," she stammered, awkwardly scooping the baby out of the sandpit-like crater and patting away the grey dust, "I changed his diaper and went to the washroom to clean up and when I came back the lights were off and the doors wouldn't open and then I couldn't get back in…"

By this time Eva had removed her helmet and was quietly admiring the baby, who had remained passive throughout. The baby was still smiling at her when Eva became aware that the mother was now talking to her.

"And I'm so sorry, Miss Gray," her profuse apologies continued to flow, "I really didn't mean to interrupt your training, he must have crawled over and… I truly am so very…"

"It's fine, really," she held out her thickly gloved hand for the baby's inquisitive fingers to examine, "he's lovely, what's his name?"

Karl gave a weary sigh and spoke before his wife could draw breath, "This is Abel, who really should be having his afternoon nap right now."

Even through the thick, Woven-Kevlar material of her glove, Eva could feel the grasp of his tiny fingers trying to squeeze her thumb and wished she could slip her hand out of the suit for just a moment.

Suddenly he lost his grip as Janine carried him away over the lunar surface. Although she wanted to call out for them to come back for a few minutes, she knew the moment had passed.

"Nice to meet you," she managed, "You've got a genuine lunar explorer there!"

Janine turned and smiled as she walked away, then under Karl's guidance they began to make their way up the long metallic steps.

"Everybody take ten," called Karl after ascending the first flight of steps, "we'll take the sim from the start."

There were audible groans from around the Starfish as people grudgingly began to reset the simulation.

Eva turned back towards the external airlock of Chamber 1, but as she walked she could see that her vision had become blurred and distorted; her breathing had also become irregular, so she stood still for a moment in order to let it pass.

She had experienced this symptom before, but couldn't quite place it. Eventually she recalled that the biological reaction was linked to a heightened emotional state. She was crying.

For such a strong reaction to occur, Eva was convinced that her next supplement must be long overdue. But after checking the clock she realised her next dose of metathene wasn't due for several hours.

All FLC trainees and FLC crew received low-level doses of metathene and she was no different. She knew it was the same drug used by the so-called ego-morphs, but at a reduced concentration. Generally, the supplement helped recipients to maintain focus and even enhance neural efficiency, so she was perturbed that her last dose had depleted so rapidly. It was something that she would have to remain aware of when she joined the others at the actual FLC in a few weeks' time.

Her thick gloves prevented her from wiping away the tears. Instead she blinked furiously to clear her eyes, hoping it would also clear her thoughts. However, her own curtailed fertility continued to taunt her; the juxtaposition of a lunar impact crater and a baby that could never be hers, was almost too much to bear.

But she had made a promise. A promise that her actions would be 'For the good of Mankind', so she buried the thoughts of a denied motherhood as deeply as she possibly could.

She consoled herself with the thought that by joining the crew at the FLC it would help birth a new mankind, one free of Siva.

It was a thought that would have far reaching consequences.

SKYLINE

26th December 2013

The distant, subdued throb from The Gene Pool's basement suddenly died and they became aware of voices outside the building on the ground floor. The volume of the voices increased and seemed to be threaded with panic.

Danny looked around at the others who were also reacting to the change in ambience. As they all started getting to their feet they could hear agitated voices drifting up the stairwell.

"Raid?" Jake questioned, stuffing his jar of coffee back into his rucksack and crossing the room to the hallway.

The others followed on, snatching up their belongings as they went.

Megan was already at a narrow window nearby.

"No," she reported, "Everybody's outside, they're not running. Damn it! I can't see what they're pointing at."

"They never built the upstairs walls," said Jake pointing upwards, then he ran in the direction of the stairs, "let's get a better view."

They ran up the exposed steelwork stairs and out onto the fourth floor. Avoiding the elevator shaft hole in the floor next to their entry point, they picked their way across a patchwork of concrete. In some places the flooring was intact but in others it had never been created, making their journey to the outside edge of the structure perilous. In the early hours of the morning, the wind had picked up a little. As they came to an unsteady halt, a few feet from the open edge, they held onto the upright steel girders protruding from the floor.

On the ground far below, they could now clearly see the mass of people who had flooded out onto the scrubland surrounding The Gene Pool. As Megan had reported downstairs, they weren't running; they were standing still and in various states of shock. Danny could see that tiny clusters of people had collapsed to the floor and others were gathered in small circles. Throughout the crowd, several people were still pointing. They were all pointing in the same direction. But despite looking in that direction, Danny could see nothing wrong.

"I don't get it…" Oliver looked back at the others, who seemed equally perplexed.

They had a clear view of the surrounding town and nothing appeared out of place, yet people were just standing and staring.

Then, all expression and colour left Sophie's face and she too began to point.

Danny followed her line of sight.

She was pointing at the horizon.

Above the silhouetted London skyline, the crescent Moon lay shattered among the clouds.

His mind reeled - had the threat been from the Moon all along? Was Siva even real? Had it all just been another lie, told to keep control?

As the cold wind began to seep into them, they all just stared; struck silent in awe and horror. Despite assessing and reassessing the situation, their minds simply refused to absorb what their senses told them.

As they watched, they could see the separate pieces of the Moon rotating and moving apart in painful slow motion. Some pieces had already begun casting crisp, black shadows back onto the bulk of the former surface, giving the impression that several pieces were moving towards them.

"Did this just happen?" Sophie spoke first, "Are we just seeing it now?"

"We're just seeing it," confirmed Oliver, emerging from the trance-like state and pointing, "the... pieces. Too far apart. Shit, I dunno. Minutes? An hour ago?"

"We gotta go," muttered Megan, her eyes darting to follow the movement of the crowd below.

"Go?" said Jake, "Go where? The tunnels? They're years away from being fin-"

"Everyone else is!" she shouted, pointing at the ground, four storeys below.

Groups of people were now beginning to break up and in places individuals were running away. As they watched, the number of individual runners increased until within a few seconds the crowd itself appeared to be flowing and screaming over the barren scrubland towards the surrounding fences. The wind appeared to have increased speed too and Danny found himself having to grip the metalwork to steady himself. The noise of the crowd was joined by a throbbing sound and for a second he thought that 'Sonic Desolation' had begun a new musical assault, down in the basement. It was only when the searchlight clicked on above them that he realised the throbbing was a matte-black helicopter directly overhead.

As he looked up, the downdraft from the helicopter blew his hair back, exposing the wound on his forehead; a livid-red, circle burn mark, broken in one place by a small dot.

He looked back down again and saw that the others were starting to back away, but it took him a moment to realise it was because they had seen the symbol. Automatically his hand shot up to pull the hair down into place, but he realised he was too late; they had already seen it.

"Wait!" he pleaded loudly, trying to make himself heard over the helicopter rotors, "It's not what you think!"

"Really?" spat Oliver, reaching inside the side pocket of his rucksack for something, "You're one of them Exordi Novaphiles, you son of a-"

He stopped mid-sentence and collapsed, lifelessly to the floor.

An immediate, but now unnecessary, second bullet ricocheted off the steel girder behind his dead body.

Terry, Sophie and Megan sprinted off over the uneven surface heading towards the stairwell. At the same moment, Danny heard a nylon-like slithering sound from above and saw that men were now descending at speed from the helicopter on black ropes.

His options were limited and he briefly considered jumping down through the nearest hole to the lower level, but fear seemed to have a strong grip on him. He could see that Terry and Megan had made it to the stairwell and had started moving down the stairs and out of view. Sophie's pink hair was easy to spot as she darted between pillars to follow them.

Ahead of Danny, men descended on the ropes; but instead of stopping at that floor level they continued straight down through the gaps in the floor to reach the level below. Less than a second later he heard Megan's scream echo up from one of the dark holes in the floor. The hole strobed with bright light as Danny heard the brutal report of machine-gun fire, and then her scream stopped.

Sophie was still running towards the stairwell, unaware of the armed men she would encounter below. At the same time, directly in front of Danny, another armed man was reaching the bottom of his rope.

"Sophie, No!" Danny yelled out, trying to warn her.

He saw her spin on the spot to face him; her crazy pink hair flaring outwards before dropping into place again. The armed man in front of him turned away and trained his weapon on her. In a fleshy explosion, as pink as her hair, Sophie's face instantly disappeared and her head snapped backwards. With the gunshot still ringing in his ears, Danny saw her inert body collapse into a heap and then slide over the edge of the building.

The armed man pivoted back and levelled his gun at Danny.

In a blur from his left, Danny registered Jake dashing out from behind a water tank.

Grasping a jar of instant coffee in his hand, Jake savagely smashed it into the side of the man's face, where it remained embedded. As the man fell in a writhing heap to the floor, screaming and pulling at the shards of glass in his eye, Jake yelled:

"The other stairs!" he pointed towards the opposite end of the building, "Run!"

With the adrenaline coursing through his body, all other sounds disappeared and he found himself sprinting across the floor accompanied only by his own fast breathing and pulse. He could only have visited this floor once before, but in this moment he remembered precisely where all the holes were, and he navigated the perils at speed.

At some level he was still aware of the helicopter overhead and footsteps pursuing him but he ran on without a backwards glance. It was then that he heard a slamming noise from behind him, followed by a creeping cold sensation between his shoulder blades, and he felt himself fall. He knew he'd been shot and that he was face down on the cold concrete, but he also knew he wasn't dead; something that the assailants could all too easily have achieved.

He could tell he was paralysed and his vision had started to blur. Then he heard feet scuffling next to his head and a muffled voice just above him.

"Operation Trilithon. Subject acquired. Over."

There was brief radio static followed by a man's voice:

"Roger, tag 'n' tope."

Then a comfortable darkness folded around him.

ONE WAY

10th April 1989

Through the one-way glass Sebastian could see his son happily playing in the room beyond. An adult helper had kept Tristan distracted with games and activities the entire time.

Sebastian could see why General Broxbourne had forcibly collected his son from the school. It was for Archive's own protection. They had needed to ensure his complete cooperation while explaining the situation.

Sebastian knew he didn't really have a choice in the matter, Archive were going to use his patents whether he liked it or not. Their eventual intentions for his Glaucus system seemed implausibly ambitious and he got the distinct impression that he was not being told everything. He had to remind himself that he was not dealing with a demanding client, he was dealing with the military and information was metered out on a need-to-know basis.

"But is it possible?" General Broxbourne asked.

"Yes," Sebastian turned away from the glass and faced the dimly lit room, "You'd need to enhance the airlock walls to cope with the varying seawater depth, but yes."

The man who had introduced himself as Russell, made an interjection at this point.

"Technically, Mr. Westhouse, 'you' would be doing any enhancing, alongside us."

Sebastian knew he was right. This was no longer a project done for someone else, he was now embedded within Archive's plans. His future and that of his family depended on him now.

He looked through the one-way glass at his son who was busy solving a spot-the-difference puzzle. By the time Siva arrived, Tristan would be thirty years old and possibly have his own family to protect.

"This Protected Lineage Directive?" Sebastian queried, "It includes my family and their children later on?"

"Yes," said Broxbourne, "The maturity of the child varies, but when they are old enough to understand, they are given the choice to remain within Archive's protection."

Sebastian turned to face the dark room. The word 'protection' had seemed an odd choice.

"Has anyone ever chosen to leave?" Sebastian asked casually.

"Typically it would be foolish to leave Archive," Broxbourne stared at him, "Our enterprises offer a significantly increased chance of survival. Your safety is very much in our hands."

Sebastian knew the last statement could be viewed as both a reassurance and a threat. Rather than meet the General's eye, he looked at the plans spread out over the table; the construction would take years. General Broxbourne changed his tone.

"Try to focus on the opportunity you've been given, Mr. Westhouse," he said, "Your expertise will contribute to saving a significant percentage of the population. In return, your family will be counted among the saved."

Sebastian realised that he already knew too much, which was no doubt their intention. Framed by the abduction of his son, this meeting had been Archive's polite way of showing the reach of their control, and the peril of non-compliance.

There was only one way out of this situation and that was forwards. However, he was an optimist. At the very least, he could save his family; but perhaps other opportunities would present themselves in future.

He signed his name and, after pressing his thumb into the ink pad, deposited his thumbprint.

Russell gathered in the documents from the table and turned to Sebastian.

"You want my advice?" he nodded at the one-way glass, "Go and do something completely ordinary."

After shaking hands with both men, Sebastian was taken down a narrow corridor to reach the room he'd seen Tristan playing in. The General departed, telling him that Russell would escort them out.

Sebastian opened the door and was greeted by his son's wide smile.

"Dad!" he got up and began to dash over, then appeared to change his mind, "Ooh, wait a minute!"

He quickly returned to his table and started putting the last few pieces of a jigsaw into place. The helper Sebastian had seen earlier remained seated next to Tristan at the table.

"Mr. Westhouse," she smiled, "Tristan has been solving some very tricky puzzles."

"Is that right?" Sebastian smiled for his son.

"Yeah Dad," Tristan beamed excitedly, "I got all of them right!"

"That's great news, Tris," he replied, beckoning his son away from the woman, "Now, why don't we go get some ice-cream?"

"Really?" Tristan ran back and hugged his father.

"Yeah, buddy, special treat!" Sebastian bundled his son in the direction of the open door.

"Double scoop?" Tristan enthusiastically tried his luck.

"Absolutely," Sebastian replied, keeping a firm hand on his son's shoulder, "Anything you like."

ROOMS

28th December 2013, 1 a.m.

Douglas made his way through another of the Node's support buildings, which were now silent, deserted. Small desktop trinkets lay strewn among the discarded rubbish, a measure of how necessity had outweighed sentimentality in the panic of the escape. He picked through a few of the fallen items and, perhaps pointlessly, returned some of them to their table tops or shelves. He found an upturned picture frame in a pile of paper, the glass broken by its fall to the floor. He turned it over and was greeted by familiar faces.

It was the photo of himself and Kate in the workspace of Hab 1, taken just over two weeks ago, shortly before they had received Monica's recorded message. Kate looked comfortable and was wearing a smile that he could only remember seeing during her childhood. After Kate had arrived at the Node he'd allowed himself to speculate about the possibility of them both re-joining Monica once his work was complete; a fact that was reflected in his own easy smile.

He shook the broken glass from the frame then, carefully pulling out the paper photo, folded up the last image of his daughter and put it into his pocket.

He wandered on through the empty mess hall, where the long rows of tables still presented the trays from the last supper to be held here. The remnants of meals had solidified on the trays, holding the plastic cutlery captive within congealed masses of food. Toppled beakers had long since stopped rolling and many had come to rest on the floor, amid pools of spilled water. The smell of food in the room, though unappetising, prompted his stomach to rumble. He couldn't remember when he had last eaten, so he set off toward the kitchen.

Following the Moon's destruction, the Node's schedule had ramped up exponentially. Although his work was complete, the Node's internal constructions were not and the focus of the base had shifted to shepherding personnel and resources aboard in preparation for the premature departure. As a precaution, Douglas had insisted that Kate receive her isotope injection; he knew full well that only the combination of isotope and Biomag would allow her to remain anchored within the Node's Field once underway. He had stood guard over his unconscious daughter while she had gone through the twenty-four-hour fever, mopping her brow but also keeping an eye on the crowds amassing outside the base's perimeter fence.

He realised that was in fact the last time he had eaten; a ration pack, hastily consumed in worry. He searched on through the kitchen's cupboards and drawers but it had been stripped bare of food. Presumably those precious resources were now aboard the Node, which had already begun its long voyage.

He checked his watch and saw that it was just after one in the morning. A quick mental calculation told him that although he had pushed his daughter into the safety of the Node five hours ago, for her it had only been fifteen seconds. Presumably she would still be running towards the control room in a vain attempt to stop the Node. His search for food halted suddenly as a thought crossed his mind - he hoped that she'd had the common sense to stop and stand upright when the Field activated. The mild nausea he had experienced when the Mark 3 Field had activated had been fleeting, but at the scale of the Node he had no idea how it would affect people. He also knew that no matter where or when his daughter was, he would never be able to stop worrying about her; but he guessed that was true of any parent, it was something that didn't decrease with any amount of time.

The concept of following any formal world time zone now seemed absurd to him, but at the Node they had always been synchronised to Greenwich in London. In an equally bizarre respect it seemed somehow fitting that the Node's time-fractured presence here should be synchronised with the birthplace of world-time.

According to the last calculations, the first lunar fragments would impact the Pacific at around eleven a.m. today. The peculiarities of the dateline meant that in the immediate vicinity of the impact, the time would be eleven p.m. on the previous day relative to him. The whole thing made his head ache, though he conceded that it could be mild concussion, caused by the bridge explosion last night.

He left the kitchen and began to pick through the remnants of the mess hall to see if there were any unopened ration packs among the discarded food. He shook his head in disbelief at the situation; a short distance away was the most advanced machine on Earth, arguably the pinnacle of human scientific achievement, and here he was struggling to find scraps of food. He came up empty handed and resolved to walk on.

The ramifications of having no decision-tree to evaluate were only now beginning to dawn on him. There was no next step, no next contingency - his life's work was complete, and it brought with it a sense of both peace and loss. For the first time in his entire life there were no branching alternatives stretching out before him, showing possible paths in his own future. The reality was that a day after the impacts started, the predicted tidal waves and earthquakes would reach even this remote location, and his life's story would end.

He had time for one last sunset.

Old habits were easily exerting their influence over his exhausted state; he found himself re-entering Hab 1 and mounting the stairs towards the bedrooms. His room was exactly how he'd left it several hours before. The thin foam mattress still lay on the floor, surrounded by the damp rags he'd used to mop Kate's fevered head. His own bed stood at the opposite corner, largely covered in books and pieces of equipment in various states of repair.

The window still offered the view facing the destroyed perimeter fence. He recalled the horrific moment when the ponytailed man, clearly in the grip of some deep mental dichotomy, had detonated his explosive vest and breached the fence. Without the man's tragic intervention, he doubted that Kate would be within the safety of the Node.

Bradley Pittman's audacious betrayal once more forced itself into his memory. In the normal course of affairs, Douglas would rationalise that if you knew all the possible outcomes for a particular situation then you needn't worry; the solutions were present, just not yet resolved. But he had completely failed to factor Bradley's deception into his decision-trees, and it had almost cost him dearly. His temper, undamped by logical pre-calculation, flared again as he recalled how close Bradley had come to snatching his daughter away from him. On impulse he unfolded the photo to look at her, and was again rewarded by her momentarily unburdened smile.

He'd never noticed it before but, either cleverly or accidentally, when Anna Bergstrom had taken the photo she had positioned herself to be reflected in the room's only mirror, allowing her to be in the photo too. He smiled at her ever-present ingenuity; indeed, without her isotope and co-development of the Field equations, the Node would have failed.

On the day that Miles Benton had delivered Monica's recorded message to him, Miles had also relayed the fact that General Napier was escorting Anna from the base. Although Miles had promised to do his best to help Anna and had accompanied her on the same military transport, neither Douglas nor Kate had received word from him again. As a former ego-morph, Miles had been one of Archive's most trusted assets and Douglas found it difficult to accept that Monica's psychological reprogramming had been one hundred percent stable. In fact, the more he thought about it, Douglas was of the opinion that Miles had somehow been responsible for delivering Anna directly into Bradley's hands.

During his mental distraction he found that his feet had carried him to Anna's door on the same corridor. He knew she was no longer there, but he knocked anyway before entering; it seemed only appropriate to continue the formalities they had always used.

Just as Kate had said, Anna's room had been cleared of all personality and possessions. It was a blank slate, there was no hint that she had ever existed. Evidently when she had been escorted from the base, the room had been swept of any information. He closed the door, knowing that he would never visit that space again.

It was then that he became consciously aware of what he had actually been doing all this time; one by one he was revisiting old places and quietly closing them down in his memory. He was mentally putting his affairs in order in preparation for the inevitable. Other places on the base were less emotionally significant, but these final rooms would be hard.

He turned and walked the few steps to Kate's room.

He knocked, then imagined her replying before opening the door. Her room was exactly the same as it had been on Christmas morning. Some of her clothes lay draped over the back of a chair, and a line of colourful, sticky notes, each with a single letter drawn on it, spelt out 'Happy Christmas' across the far wall. It had been almost three days, but even without a Field surrounding her room it seemed like mere seconds had passed for Douglas.

He recalled that Christmas morning had begun on the base much like any other; the morning reveille had sounded through speakers in all the blocks promptly at five a.m. This far north, in December, the Sun only rose after eleven so the base personnel began their day in darkness.

The morning itself had been taken up with mundane tasks, but around noon everyone had flocked to the assembly hall to watch the White House up-link to everyone working at the Node. The President had delivered a heartfelt thanks for their continued contribution to the most important task ever to be entrusted to the human race. After this the room was emptied of personnel so that it could be prepared for the first of two lunch sittings. Douglas and Kate had been allocated to the first sitting, so they did not have long to wait. Although there was strictly no alcohol permitted on the base, several festive or bawdy community songs appeared to spontaneously erupt from rowdy areas of the room at various times. All of which contributed to a general air of levity and optimism for the year ahead.

Then the news about the FLC had reached the Node.

The stark reality was that following the destruction of the FLC, Siva was now unstoppable. It was now a certainty, not a possibility, that on April 1st 2015 Siva would impact the Earth.

In the Node's original planning stages, Archive had predicted that in the six months before a theoretical impact, there would be total social unrest. All their global operations would suffer fatal disruption. To avoid this, they made plans to launch the Node by mid-2014, several months before any disruption would theoretically begin. So when the FLC news came in, construction was still on course to complete the Node in six-months' time. The news was devastating, but with the FLC gone, the Node would fulfil the function for which it had been built; it became the primary option for large-scale life preservation.

Douglas picked up Kate's clothes from the back of the chair, opened her wardrobe and started to hang up the items. There was actually little logical sense in hanging up garments in a room that would shortly be destroyed, but he knew it was just another act of mental preparation. In the bottom of the wardrobe he saw a crudely wrapped Christmas present and on closer inspection saw that it was for him. It took him a moment to remember that Kate had told him about it during their Christmas lunch. The events following the lunch had preoccupied Douglas to such a degree that he had little mental room for anything else.

In the hours immediately following the news of the FLC's destruction, Douglas had been briefed on worrying data concerning the trajectory of the lunar fragments. The projections quickly became confirmed facts, and the second round of devastating news spread throughout the Node. Although the initial lunar fragment impacts would not reach Iceland, the secondary planetary effects would be catastrophic. In the early afternoon of December 29th, tidal waves and, as yet undetermined, tectonic aftershocks were predicted to reach Öskjuvatn Lake.

The Node had four days to complete six months of work.

Douglas sat on the end of Kate's bed and placed the Christmas present beside him. Through the window he could see a slightly different view to the one from his room; in the darkness he could see hundreds of campfires, dotted throughout a much larger area than on the previous night. It appeared that the crowd was drifting into smaller groups, and spreading out over the surrounding terrain. Caught in the glow of a large campfire near the perimeter fence was the guard house. People appeared to be dismantling it, or at the very least reshaping it, but for what purpose he couldn't tell. It amazed him that necessity was still driving human innovation, mere days from extinction.

He knew it was time to open the box.

Drawing in a deliberate deep breath, he exhaled slowly and picked up the gift.

New resources were all accountable at the Node, he could see that Kate had re-used decommissioned Node floor plans rather than trying to source new wrapping paper. He knew this version of the floor plan well, and ran his fingers over the multi-layered cross-sections, but knew he was delaying. He carefully unwrapped the paper to find a military issue shoebox that had evidently been used to ship a pair of boots. A handwritten note from Kate was stuck to its lid:

'Dear Dad, You've always said that there is no redundant information, just stuff we didn't realise we needed at the time…'

It was certainly true, he had passed down this maxim to her; though Douglas himself was paraphrasing his own father. Douglas remembered his own childhood and one weekend in particular, spent constructing a wooden bookcase alongside his father. They had built it to hold the blank NASA jotters that his father would bring home from work each week. When they had finished construction they'd ended up with three redundant screws and Douglas had been about to discard them, when his father had stopped him. He had told him that there were no left over pieces, just pieces that might be needed later. To reinforce his point, he had presented Douglas with a small matchbox. It contained a small metal plate embossed with 'Douglas' using a NASA part-number stamp. At the time, the plate had been screwed into place on the bookcase using two of the three screws. Douglas had then returned the remaining screw to the empty matchbox, to show his father that he would save it for later. The time spent with his father had been one of the happiest days of his life.

Now it was his turn to be the father; but his daughter's words echoing back to him and the presence of another humbly parcelled gift was slightly more than he could bear. He did his best to wipe away the silent tears welling in his eyes and began to read his daughters note again:

'Dear Dad, You've always said that there is no redundant information, just stuff we didn't realise we needed at the time... but I watch you every bit as carefully as you watch others and I think you've been throwing away some personal information. I've used it to get you something that you may not have realised you wanted at the time... Love you, Katie x'.

Clearing his damp eyes, he lifted the shoebox lid.

She had filled the box with small chocolate rations, and at first he had no idea how she had achieved it. Before his stomach had chance to groan again he quickly opened one of the packets and bit into it. She had obviously been watching him carefully, even at meal times. But he was surprised that his love of the Friday supper treat had been so evident to her. While he savoured the cheap chocolate, he concluded that since her arrival back in August she must have been hoarding them for him. Each Friday evening, she had sat alongside him in the mess hall and quietly pocketed her chocolate ration without saying a word. Even in the simple things, he thought, Kate had her mother's ability to plan in the long term, whilst still apparently being a part of the system.

As the last gift he would ever receive, it was the most precious on Earth.

He carefully replaced the lid on the box and smoothed down the Node-plan wrapping paper. He felt exhaustion creeping up on him and he lay down on the bed. Before he closed his eyes, he pulled the photo from his pocket one more time.

"Love you too, Katie," he whispered to the empty room, then sleep took him.

FILTER

T-09:10:53

Colonel Beck lowered his six-foot frame into General Napier's wide chair and, without a word, invited Kate to take a seat opposite him. Kate ignored the invite and continued talking as if there had been no interruption at all.

"We need to get the high speed movie off here," she raised the digital recording binoculars, "and slow it down. All I'm asking is that we plug it into the video analysis equipment. What if it's important? What if we're supposed to act on it before Siva arrives?"

"I agree," he interrupted, glancing at his watch.

Kate had been prepared to argue her corner against Colonel Beck for much longer if necessary but he had denied her the fight. Seizing the opportunity, Colonel Beck spoke again.

"Did you know that when the Mark 3 caught fire, I pulled your father and Dr. Bergstrom to safety before the whole hangar went up?"

When the Mark 3 had caught fire she had been busy breaking free from a holding cell on the Node's base and had missed much of the drama. She shook her head gently.

"I believed in your father, Miss Walker. It's why I risked my neck to save him."

Kate could see he was not seeking a confrontation. Quickly starting to filter the broader assumptions she had made about him, she sat down in the chair he had previously offered. The traits of being brusque and critically direct, as often reported by the personnel at the base, were not qualities she was seeing in the man before her now.

"Then I need you to believe in him again. My dad risked," she corrected herself, "my dad *gave* his life to protect us."

She carefully placed the binoculars on the table between them.

Colonel Beck looked at the them and seemed to reach an internal conclusion.

"OK," he agreed.

"Thank you," she sniffed and inhaled a deep but shaky breath.

He nodded.

Douglas Walker was the latest in a long line of fatalities. In September, a granite 'MARK IV' dedication stone had been unveiled next to the bridge; it was carved with the names of all those who had died during the construction of the Node. The compound injustice was that Douglas Walker's name would be forever missing from that memorial.

"I need you to do something, Miss Walker."

Kate stiffened slightly in her chair.

Colonel Beck stood, straightened his uniform and looked back at the wide seat.

"Like you, I never asked for this role. Napier was supposed to be here, but because he's not, I'm supposed to just step up and lead now. Being Walker's daughter you already have their respect, I don't. For at least the next nine hours I need them to follow the chain of command - without question."

"I understand," Kate now also stood, "but why only for the next nine hours?"

"Assuming we survive Siva, we may well be the only humans left on the planet. We'll need to work out how we're going to run things better than we did before."

Without waiting for her reply he walked to the door and opened it.

"Dexter!" he shouted at a volume that made Kate jump, "Get in here!"

Scott Dexter arrived within seconds wearing a worried expression; he had reported Dr. Walker's Biomag was aboard and was obviously fearing the consequences now that he was in the presence of Walker's daughter. A fear that Colonel Beck was going to trade on.

"This is Dr. Walker's daughter," he introduced her unnecessarily, "escort her to the video processing suite. You give her everything she asks for. Immediately. Understood?"

Scott's eyes darted between both of them.

"Have I not just made myself absolutely crystal clear?" Colonel Beck frowned down at him.

"Sorry, Sir," he stammered, "Yes, I understand, but…"

"It's up one level, Colonel Beck," Kate recalled easily, then turned to Scott, "I can show you where it is, if that's a problem?"

Colonel Beck was impressed; despite never having set foot inside the Node before today, her recall of the plans was absolutely correct. But reading Scott's face told him that locating the room was not the problem.

"Sorry, Sir," Scott hesitantly volunteered, "The room was never completed."

In the rush to complete the functional elements of the Node, several items had been postponed for construction until they were underway. Kate herself had encountered this issue with the internal communication panels nearest to the airlock.

"What about the equipment itself?" Kate immediately returned.

"The… I…" Scott fled from the room back to his workstation and started searching for the deliveries made to the Node. Kate and Colonel Beck chased after him.

"I'm not seeing anything under video suites, Sir," Scott reported, but his fingers continued to fly across the keyboard in a frantic hunt for other search strings.

"May I?" Colonel Beck poised his hand over Scott's keyboard.

"Of course, sorry Sir."

Colonel Beck typed 'DRBproc' and hit enter.

This time, several shipments appeared outlining Digital Recording Binoculars processing equipment.

"Damn!" Colonel Beck swore, "No location data. It's here, we just don't know where."

The sheer speed with which equipment had arrived in the last few days meant that nothing could be unpacked, it just had to be stowed. The more useful items were stowed so that they could be found and retrieved easily, but secondary items were just stowed in whatever space was left.

"You mean it could be anywhere aboard?" Kate asked.

"No, we can do better than that," said Scott with a smile and began applying filters, "I can show you where it *isn't* stored. Everything that was classed as important was given a specific location stowage point…"

He hit enter.

"… leaving behind everything that was not assigned a location!"

A list of hundreds of possible locations now populated the screen. Kate let out an audible breath of frustration. But Scott had not finished.

"Every item that arrived here had a time stamp, including the DRB stuff," he grinned, filtering further locations out, "and there we go."

The list of possible locations had reduced to around fifty places.

Colonel Beck gave him a single pat on the shoulder and turned to pick up the Main Circuit handset.

"All hands, this is Beck. Report to the Observation Deck for a priority briefing. Now."

SPLINTER

29th February 1976

Miles was still staring at the coin when his mother returned.

"Sorry about that, Dorothy," his mother was saying, "It was just a small splinter, nothing a pair of tweezers couldn't handle though."

"Is Laura going to be OK, Mommy?" he asked.

"Ha ha, of course, Miles!" she smiled at him, "She's completely fine."

Aunty Dot smiled down at him and gave him a wink, which pleased him a great deal.

"Here Dorothy, have a slice," his mother said, handing her a small plate of birthday cake.

"Ooh, thank you, Judy! I really shouldn't…" said Dorothy placing a hand on her waistline, but accepted the plate graciously.

"Mommy, look what Aunty Dot brought me," Miles held up the bicentennial coin for her to see.

It took his mother a moment to work out what it was; but then her eyes widened in, he presumed, amazement.

"Wow… Dorothy… you really shouldn't have…" she managed.

"Nonsense, Judy, I won't hear a word of it!" she beamed.

The doorbell rang and she was just about to shout for the caller to come straight in, but realised that she probably wouldn't be heard over the general party hubbub. She took a deep breath and, after throwing a quick smile and shrug at Dorothy, she left them again to answer the front door.

Miles watched as his mother walked down the corridor, carrying her own small plate of cake.

"Now you look after that," said Dorothy, lightly tapping the coin in Miles' hand.

"Always, Aunty Dot!"

The sound of a plate smashing by the front door drew his attention.

His mother was framed in the open doorway; a mixture of soft cake and pieces of sharp china lay strewn over the floor. Behind his mother he could see a silhouetted figure outside. He could feel Aunty Dot's hands on his shoulders *and instinctively he knew it was a gesture of comfort.*

The coin in his hand felt hot, but he held it fiercely.

He remembered this moment.

It was the moment that his mother was told of his father's death. He remembered that the silhouetted figure was a soldier or someone in a military uniform at least. It didn't make sense to him. How could he possibly be remembering a time that hadn't yet happened? And yet it was a moment forever burned into his memory. He remembered his mother's face turning slowly towards him, blank and ashen.

Except that was not what he was seeing now.

The silhouetted figure was slowly striding down the corridor towards him and Aunty Dot, who had never left his side.

The coin suddenly burned brightly in his hand and he dropped it. It bounced and rolled a little way in front of him, but before he could pick it up, the figure had stooped and collected it for him. As the man knelt in front of him, he placed the coin back in Miles' open palm, and looked up into his eyes.

"Hello Miles, we have spoken before, do you remember me?"

"Dad?" he heard himself say, incredulously.

The coin burned again, he glanced down and saw the familiar embossed Liberty Bell and Moon design. But the Moon was flickering in and out of existence. This memory was sharp and uncomfortable, an unwelcome splinter in his mind.

"Something's wrong," he heard himself say, and suddenly he felt cold. Aunty Dot's comforting hands had disappeared, "Who are you?"

His father looked at him with an expression as blank as a passport photo and said:

"We'll speak again."

Then darkness folded around him and he felt himself falling again.

BISHOP'S MOVE

15th December 2013

Alfred Barnes studied the report and began to get a cold feeling in the pit of his stomach; not that he let it show for one second. He had initiated this project. It had been his idea to use a small core of ego-morphs to create the Exordi Nova; Archive's own terrorist organisation.

"Tell me you ain't worried, Freddy," said Bradley Pittman, his clenched fists supporting himself with straightened arms on the edge of Alfred's desk.

Alfred thought he looked like a silverback gorilla supporting his weight on his knuckles. With only the two of them in the room, the dominant position Bradley had adopted was clearly a show of superiority; one that he would be foolish to challenge head on.

"I'm not worried, Bradley," he lied, "In fact this is very good news."

Bradley snorted through his nostrils, but Alfred could see that the tension in his arms had subsided.

"We've been losing traction in some states," Alfred turned away slightly and crossed the room to his filing cabinet, reducing the physical confrontation, "The fact that our ego-morphs are now recruiting will only speed up the process and strengthen our position. We know they're very effective, we just have to let them do their job."

In truth, the fact that ego-morphs were independently recruiting people into actual Exordi Nova 'cells' represented a hugely significant loss in Archive's overall control. The idea had always been that the ego-morphs would only ever act alone, and under Archive's direction. The notion of ego-morphs being able to inspire ordinary people to fight under an artificial theology against Archive did not bear thinking about. Or rather, Alfred thought, he would have to think about it a great deal once Bradley had gone.

"I s'pose we still got all the metathene," Bradley stood upright again, "we still got 'em on a leash."

"Exactly," Alfred produced a smile, symbolically filed the report and closed the cabinet, "They have a biological dependence on it, and we're the only ones making it."

Bradley gave a sigh of relief and turned away, but instead of leaving the room he closed the door.

"Something else?" Alfred asked, as calmly as he could.

"Yeah, sort of..." Bradley hesitated and ran his palm over the back of his neck, "A while back, you and me had a conversation 'bout Dougie Walker's mom 'n' dad? About the early days? Sam Bishop's brain booster trial and all that?"

"Yes, the er, gene-level cortical booster program. I remember it vaguely," said Alfred, but actually he clearly recalled the day that he'd planted the idea in Bradley's head to look deeper into it. A long time had passed since then and Alfred had assumed that nothing had come of it, "You said that his parents were never part of it."

"Well now, here's the thing," Bradley looked slightly awkward, "this is strictly on the q.t."

"Like everything at Archive," began Alfred.

"No, just 'tween you an' me," interrupted Bradley, checking the door was closed and lowering his tone, "OK?"

Alfred nodded; he'd thought that Bradley may report his findings back to the whole group, but he hadn't expected Bradley to take him into his confidence alone.

"OK then," Bradley pulled up a chair next to him, "So, right after discovering Siva, Sam Bishop knew us humans would have to get real smart, real quick."

"The cortical enhancement program, I know. I read all about the illegal clinical trials."

Again Bradley hesitated, "You didn't read about all of it."

"I read the whole Siva folder," insisted Alfred, "Everything from Sam Bishop crediting Howard Walker with Siva's discovery, to the Floyd Lunar Complex."

"You couldn't have read everything, cos I hadn't," Bradley drew out a squat, scruffy-looking leather notebook from his jacket pocket, "Bishop's personal notes."

"Where did you... I mean why haven't we seen it before?"

"It don't matter," Bradley deferred, "but look at this."

He rifled through the yellowed pages of handwritten notes until he found a table of dates, dosages and names. Bradley angled the book for Alfred to see, then ran his finger down the list of names. He stopped as he neared the bottom and pointed out one name.

"E. Walker," Bradley read, "That there is Betty Walker, Dougie's mom."

"Wait, you're sure?" Alfred adjusted his glasses to scrutinise the ink more closely.

"Sure I'm sure," he turned through several pages and found her name again, "See? This time he writes out her full name, 'Elizabeth' - she was eight months pregnant. But here's the kicker…"

He turned on through several more pages and arrived at a section that outlined births. He then pointed out one specific line:

'Mar10th' 57. Father: Howard Walker. Mother: Elizabeth Walker. Sex: M. Name: Douglas Walker Wt: 6lb 8oz.'

"There's baby Dougie," Bradley prodded the entry.

"He was an ego-" started Alfred.

"No. I already checked ahead," Bradley cut in, moving forward to the relevant page, "Few weeks after he was born, baby Dougie got dropped from the 'post-natal cortical counterpart' program."

Alfred could see a red ink line had been ruled through the Walkers' entry in Bishop's book; a note was scribbled next to it.

"Substandard," Alfred read aloud and couldn't help a slight snort of laughter, "Substandard? What was Bishop thinking? Douglas is a first class genius…"

"That's for damn sure…"

"So why drop him from the program?" frowned Alfred.

"I reckon Dougie didn't react fast enough to the drug. Back then, metathene was real expensive to make, so only the most promisin' kids was kept in the program."

"A later bloomer…" Alfred ventured, peering at the page, "I guess it was lucky he got dropped from the trials. If he'd become an ego-morph, then it's likely we wouldn't have the Node."

A realisation crept over Alfred's face.

"The metathene worked! It activated the cortical enhancer in the new-borns, it just needed more time for the effects to show."

Bradley just nodded, "Bishop died before seein' what Douglas was capable of."

Both Bradley and Alfred stared back at the pages that showed line after line of crossed-through, red inked and supposedly 'substandard' children.

"There's got to be dozens of them," Alfred said in awe, "Others like Douglas."

"Twenty-three," Bradley replied without a pause, "but there's only one that bothers me."

He turned back to the first page of rejected candidates and pointed at one line.

'Jun19th'57. Father: Norman Dean. Mother: Eleanor Dean. Sex:F. Name: Monica Dean Wt: 6lb 2oz.'

"That can't be…" Alfred stared in disbelief.

Within the closed world of Archive's history, it could not be a coincidence.

"It's gotta be," Bradley shrugged, "an' it explains one hell of a lot, don't it?"

After her marriage in 1980, the only Monica Dean that Archive knew, had become Monica Walker.

CASE STUDY

5th July 2013

AR1 was one of the most luxuriously decorated rooms in Monica's facility. Whilst the corridors running throughout the rest of the underground labyrinth were literally hewn from the rock, Arrivals Room 1 had vertical smooth walls, a carpeted floor, comfortable furnishings and even a television mounted on the wall. The only thing it lacked of course was a window, but even this had been considered; a pair of thick, velvety curtains hung, permanently closed, from a wooden rail. The design of the room was such that, for those that knew no better, it had all the appearances of a comfortable, pre-collapse, home.

Nathan did know better; he remembered the violent trip down here and the passing out. He'd woken a few minutes ago in the comfortable armchair and had then checked around the room. He quickly discovered that the only door out of the room was locked, and that the solid looking walls sounded like thin plasterboard when tapped. Resignedly he had collapsed onto a long sofa. The hands on the twee-looking wall clock read 2.27, which appeared to agree with the wristwatch he kept stored in his jacket pocket.

He heard the door handle turn and a woman walked in, followed by the man who had escorted him down here.

"Well it's nearly half-past," she was saying while checking her watch, "so let's get the repair team up to the Arrivals Lounge by - ah, you're awake!"

She walked over to him extending a hand.

"Monica Walker," she said.

"No," Nathan replied immediately, "you're not."

The woman looked awkward for a second and turned to look at the man. At this point a second, older woman walked through the doorway, carrying Nathan's suitcase.

"It's OK, Geraldine, you can go now," she said.

The younger woman turned without a word and left the room, closing the door behind her.

"Apologies Nathan, I just needed to check something. I'm Monica."

Her face was now much older than the photos his father had shown him, but he looked past the ageing effects and began to recognise her. He stood up from the sofa and this time offered his hand.

"Nathan Bishop."

The two of them shook hands and Monica continued, "Marcus Blake you've already met."

"Marcus?" Nathan turned to him, "Oh, so it's not 'Blackbox' then?"

Marcus smiled and took a seat in the armchair, while Monica sat down next to Nathan, placing the suitcase in front of him.

"Is it in here, Nathan?" she asked.

Nathan sat back in the sofa and became more hesitant, clearly struggling with how to answer.

"I know that I owe my life to, er, Marcus," he began, "and he kept his word. He said he'd send it down after me and he did. But I think this is something that I should only discuss in private."

Monica closed her eyes and nodded, then turned to Marcus who began to shuffle forward in his seat, ready to leave.

"Marcus," she said, politely holding out a key, "please would you mind locking the door?"

Marcus took the key and was walking to the door when Monica spoke again.

"Once it's locked, please come and join us again."

Marcus couldn't help but smile. Thankfully he still had his back to them and so had time to stifle it again before returning to sit in the armchair.

"Mr. Blake is authorised to hear anything you have to say to me."

"OK, but I doubt Mr. Blake will be versed in prokaryotic base sequence repetitions," Nathan attempted to reinforce his expertise.

"My own knowledge of palindromic repeat clusters is a little rusty too," Monica patted his knee, "but why don't we keep things at a macro scale for now?"

Nathan's eyes flickered between the two of them, but before he could find any words of reply, Monica continued.

"My…" she paused to rephrase, "The building you entered through on the surface was destroyed by a militarised helicopter."

"You said that they were after *this*," Marcus pointed at the suitcase.

"Is it in here, Nathan?" she asked again, "and by 'they' did you mean Luóxuán Biotech?"

"Yes it's in here," Nathan lifted the suitcase onto the tasteful glass-topped coffee table and wheeled the combination dials to the correct position. The catches sprang open and he placed his hand on the lid, "and yes, I don't think my former employers liked the fact that I removed it."

He folded the lid back revealing a mass of crumpled clothes, the top layer of which he began to push aside. Underneath was a slightly smaller flight case about half as long as the suitcase surrounding it. Nathan levered it out of the tightly packed clothing and, after a cursory check, placed it down for them to see.

Marcus recognised several of the connector ports in the plastic surface, but there were others that he couldn't identify, "So what the hell is it?"

"It's a…" Nathan rubbed at his forehead, "well, I'm still calling it a Z-bank, like the original -"

"Wait, a what?" interrupted Marcus.

"OK, a zygote bank, like a genetic store. Samples of life that, in the right hands, can be reintroduced to the world in the event of a disaster. A bit like Archive's seed vault in Svalbard, but for living creatures."

Marcus wasn't familiar with any such seed vault, but Monica appeared to be nodding before a frown crossed her face.

"Hold on, you said this one is like the original - so there's two of them?"

"Yes. No," Nathan stumbled, "Can I just finish?"

Both Monica and Marcus leaned back slightly into their cushions.

"Thank you," he leaned forward, "Now, in September last year they shipped the original, bulkier, Z-bank prototype up to the Floyd Lunar Complex. My guess is that, until we know Siva's out of the way, the Moon is actually the safest place to hold it. You do know about the Floyd Lu-"

"Yes," both Monica and Marcus cut him short and motioned for him to continue.

"OK. This," Nathan patted the small case, "is the second version, sort of a Z-bank Two. But the computational analyser inside here scares the crap of out me. Streets ahead of the prototype Z-bank sent to the FLC."

"Really?" said Marcus, his interest piqued.

"Yeah, and no one at Luóxuán could tell me where the advanced chipsets were coming from."

"They couldn't tell you, or wouldn't tell you?" Monica asked.

"They didn't seem to know, but when the next batch of processors arrived I knew I had to get out. The computational capability of the next generation of chips, makes this thing look like an abacus."

"Let me get this straight," Marcus stared at him, "You left 'cos computers got faster?"

Nathan stared back with equal intensity.

"The next generation of chips would have given this Z-bank the ability to carry out polymorphic sequencing."

"That's a new one on me," admitted Marcus, "Is that like parametric polymorphism? You know, like, non type-specific computer programming that -"

"No, no, you're not getting it," Nathan sighed, "I'm still talking about genetics. Luóxuán would be able to address and control base pairs."

At that point Marcus believed that Monica had been right. Anything discussed in front of him would be completely safe; he was beginning to feel like he knew less than when he walked in.

"Life," Monica summarised, "They would have the capability to adjust life at its most basic level."

"Combined with a Z-bank," Nathan tapped the case, "Well… no one should have that kind of power. That's why I knew I had to get out."

"So why didn't you just smash it up?" offered Marcus.

Monica and Nathan both frowned and said, "Leverage."

"As long as they needed it back, you had something to bargain with," Monica could follow his reasoning.

"Bargain?" said Marcus, incredulously, "Didn't they just dump a bunch of bloody helicopter grenades on you and me? Or was that just a slap on the wrist?"

Monica did no more than turn her head towards Marcus, but it conveyed her message and he stopped expressing his own frustrations.

"I think," said Monica, quietly parking her own emotions, "we can safely assume that for whatever reason they do not need you alive. On the positive side though -"

"The positive side?" Nathan half laughed.

"Yes, if they think you're already dead, then they won't be trying to kill you," she counted on one finger, then counted a second, "and from the very thorough job they did upstairs they will assume that your Z-bank has also been destroyed."

"They probably tracked it," Nathan thought out loud, "They could trace it here!"

Monica was already shaking her head.

"As soon as Marcus sent the case down the chute, any signal would be completely absorbed by the tonnes of rock around us. As far as anyone is concerned - you *and* the box are dead," she then added in a melancholic tone, "Welcome to the afterlife, Mr. Bishop."

Nathan looked around the unlikely room, buried hundreds of feet below ground, "So is this Heaven or Hell?"

Monica merely smiled.

"I don't much care for the name myself," she added, "but I believe everyone here calls it the Warren."

At this point, Marcus had to suppress a smile, but couldn't quite manage it.

Nathan sank back into the soft sofa.

"In case I haven't said so - thank you. Both," Nathan included Marcus, "Dad always said that if I ever got into trouble then I should ask for your help. He was right."

Nathan leaned forward again and dug through the clothes in the suitcase. He lifted out a thick, buff-coloured folder, filled with colour photocopies.

"He said if you helped then I should pass this on to you. He kept saying the information was priceless."

Monica took the folder and saw that it had a message written on the outside.

'To Doug and Monica, I hope this repays the favour one day - Ron B.'

"Do you know what he meant by favour?" Nathan squinted at the writing.

Monica sometimes forgot how long she had actually been doing all this, but she now remembered the day.

"Douglas and I once held a door open for him," she said.

"That must've been one hell of a door!" Nathan snorted.

"Well," Monica recalled, "it was an elevator door to a nuclear bunker under Whitehall, but yes, hell of a door."

Monica opened the folder and looked at the first photocopied sheet. It was the front cover of a notebook belonging to Sam Bishop. At some point, Sam must have passed on his notebook to his son, Ron, who had then copied it.

"Does Ron still have the original notebook?" she asked.

"My dad passed a while back."

"I'm sorry, Nathan," Monica looked up with an expression of sympathy, "your dad seemed a decent man."

After descending in the Whitehall elevator she remembered Ron Bishop insisting that he owed them a favour. Later, when it came to light that Heavy Rain had been a false alarm, he had told them it didn't change a thing - everyone thought it was real but they had still held the door open.

Monica continued to turn through the photocopies. It appeared to be long records listing names, dates of birth and birthweights.

"I don't know what happened to the original notebook," Nathan shrugged, "this is all that my Dad gave me."

Previously, Monica had only associated Sam Bishop with the initiation of Archive and the space program. Now it appeared that there was an association with medical research that ran throughout the family's history. Nathan's line of work had apparently not strayed too far from Ron's own area of medical research, albeit more advanced in scope.

She now noticed that red ink lines had been ruled through several entries in the notebook. Her blood ran cold when she suddenly saw her parents' names.

"Well," she smiled, quickly snapping the folder shut, "I dare say it will make interesting reading! Thank you, Nathan."

She stood up and both Marcus and Nathan did likewise.

"Marcus, please will you ask Geraldine to arrange a bunk for Nathan?"

"Sure, no problem," he replied.

"Nathan," Monica looked directly at him, "Might I suggest that I place the Z-bank in secure storage?"

Nathan felt that he couldn't argue with her and, leaving the smaller flight case behind, complied by following Marcus out of the room.

Monica locked the door and walked back across the room. She found herself standing in front of the wall clock.

She needed time to think.

The existence of Sam Bishop's notebook had not shown up during her surface check of Nathan an hour ago. In fact, during his subconscious interrogation in Arrivals Room Two, immediately after fainting in the Arrivals Lounge, he had been very cooperative.

As far as she could surmise, Nathan saw the list as irrelevant, a mere historical curio that had paid for his rescue. She would need to study the list in detail, there could be other names of interest; others who may be just as 'substandard' as herself.

Holding the clock, she wound it forward two hours so that it displayed the correct time again.

RISE

28th December 2013 5 a.m.

The five a.m. reveille sounded throughout all the buildings on the base, waking Douglas from a deep sleep. The fact that he had woken in Kate's room only added to the general disorientation and he spent a good few seconds in a wide-eyed stare trying to get his new bearings. He could see that the date and time on his wrist correlated with that of the room's small clock, and this was enough to ground him again. His reactivation of the backup generator had, it seemed, also reactivated the automated routines across the base. However, the outside world was still dark and the Sun wouldn't rise here for another six hours or so.

Douglas rubbed at his face in an attempt to wake himself up. He'd slept for less than four hours and it hadn't been a comfortable sleep. It had been plagued by disturbing dreams; puzzling details arriving in fragments but never resolving. Drawings of the Node had been present, no doubt called into being by Kate's improvised wrapping paper. Also incorporated into the dream was the meeting room where Archive had pinpointed the gravitational hotspot here in Iceland; Bradley Pittman had been laughing, but Douglas felt distrust rather than humour. Then Anna had been taken away and, although in reality he had never seen her depart on the plane, his imagination had framed her in a circular window, her face a portrait of worry. The details now seemed to be dispersing faster than he could pull them into conscious thought. The only person he could not recollect seeing was Kate.

Even though he was awake he couldn't fully shake off certain elements of his dream. There appeared to be connections between the details beyond the mere superficial, but he felt he was missing something. He opened the lid of the shoebox and took out another chocolate ration. A quick estimate told him there were at least fifteen left, and whilst he knew he couldn't survive on chocolate alone, he also knew that survival was not something he needed to worry about. He took a bite, and although it was not as sweet as the first one he had tasted a few hours ago, he could already feel the start of the endorphin kick. He straightened the bed covers and then glanced at the creased photo in his hands; again he smiled at Anna's ingenious framing. He looked around the bare room and then tucked the closed shoebox under his arm. It was time to leave.

He closed the door softly and moved along the corridor to his room, where the door was still open. He walked past Kate's floor mattress towards the window, and gazed out over the distant terrain. Campfires still burned small and bright, each a small group of people trying to stay alive. The fact was, that despite his insulated position here, he would probably be swept away with everyone else and consigned to a history that no-one would even be able to read.

That it should end here was an injustice; his entire family had given so much to this world. He countered his own thoughts by reminding himself that this was no doubt true for countless others over the past sixty years. He looked out to the horizon.

The bulk of the Moon was due to rise in a few minutes, but already he could see the orbit-bound lunar fragments preceding it. Following the Moon's destruction, several fragments had been thrown towards Earth and would soon arrive here; but a far greater number had continued to spread out in both directions away from the lunar centre of gravity, along the Moon's orbital path. Douglas recalled seeing the spread of these orbital fragments yesterday, and today they appeared even further apart.

He knew that, in time, the fragments would slowly spread out to completely encircle the Earth. He thought of the view that would one day greet Kate as she looked out through the Node's observation window. The circle surrounding the Earth would be broken in one place by the presence of a small circular concentration of lunar rock. He couldn't recall why, but he was sure that the pattern itself had a significance.

The continent-sized pieces of moon hung over the horizon, following the direction of the earlier fragments. Douglas could see that even those massive lunar pieces were beginning to drift apart. In a short amount of time they too would spread out over quite a substantial arc of the night sky. The very thought seemed scientifically humorous to him.

"Ha!" he laughed out loud, "By the time Siva gets here, it'll have to get past the -"

The thought, although born in humour, had ended in a revelation.

APOLLO 54

9th September 2010

Although the public facing Apollo program had ended in 1972, Archive's missions had continued, often in other countries. These countries had their own names for specific phases of missions, but the underlying Archive numbering sequence had continued uninterrupted for over forty years. In addition to Eva Gray, the Apollo 54 flight was carrying cargo for Dr. Chen.

The significance of 54 in Chinese numerology, meaning 'not-death', had been the subject of heated debate several years ago. Dr. Chen had successfully argued that if the others within Archive saw those specific numerals as mere superstition, then it should not matter to them if they were assigned to his cargo or not. In actual fact, Dr. Chen had only argued his numerological standpoint because it guaranteed him a much earlier launch window; but he was happy to take advantage of others' assumptions about him.

"Apollo 54, Houston," the voice sounded in Eva's headset, *"Standby for trans-lunar injection sequence. Over."*

In the next few moments the Apollo spacecraft would begin to change its orbit from a circular one around Earth, to a highly eccentric one. This elliptical path would hurl the craft away from the Earth, but at the point where it should begin to fall back, the Moon's own gravity would catch the craft, and pull it into orbit around itself instead. The physics at work had not changed since Apollo 8, but the advances of the Shen500 series computers made the automation and timing of the process easier to coordinate. In human terms though, for Eva it represented the moment when she would move beyond the Earth's influence, and towards her new life at the FLC.

"Roger, TLI sequence confirmed," she replied.

"Apollo 54, you're looking good."

This close to the Earth, the time delay in communication was only slight, but already the feeling of remoteness encouraged her to reply with a sense of humour.

"I'll have to take your word for that, Houston. You guys skimped on the windows…"

With each redesign of the Command module the windows had dwindled in size, partly as a cost saving exercise but also because it made better structural sense. Despite being human-rated this Command module had no windows at all. Not that this damped her spirits any.

Following the baby incident at the Starfish training facility, she had reported the metathene deficiency issue; now her increased dosage level had restored the balance between logical function and human interaction. Each crew member had their own prescribed level of the mind enhancing drug. The personal batch of metathene she was carrying with her today would last her for several years; provided that nothing happened to upset the balance.

"Apollo 54, Houston, commencing burn in three, two, one, mark."

On cue, the chemical rocket engines fired and again she felt the kick; not as powerful as the one during take off but enough to feel the sensation of weight. When the thrusters completed their pre-programmed burn the acceleration would stop and the spacecraft would be travelling at a constant velocity. In the absence of force, her weight would drop to zero. Only when she landed on the Moon would she again have weight, but at only one-sixth of that on Earth. For the rest of her days she would never be any heavier than she was right now. To savour the last of it, she looked at her arms and raised them against the force of the acceleration.

A little way ahead, attached securely to the console, was her delicate silver chain. On the end of this chain was a tiny charm, given to her by Dorothy Pittman about twenty years ago. The charm's thin silver wires wrapped around a small piece of moon rock at the centre. Before take-off it had hung limply and gently swung back and forth, but during the acceleration phases, like the current one, the chain had become taught. The oscillations, though only slight, now happened much quicker. The tiny lunar fragment swung rapidly in front of her and she found herself smiling. It seemed somehow fitting that this tiny piece of rock was going home; she had merely been borrowing it.

Abruptly the acceleration cut out. The chain suddenly became slack, lazily drifting and curling upon itself in the absence of gravity.

"Apollo 54, Houston, TLI burn complete. System check. Over."

"Roger. TLI complete," Eva replied, "commencing system check."

While she carried out the routine checks that she had practised a hundred times before, she considered her time ahead.

If all went according to plan, after Siva's deflection the intention was to fulfil her father's dream and expand upon the FLC. Her father, who had not lived to see her departure from Earth, had been a keen proponent of the project. His optimism had not always been popular with other members of Archive back in 1989, but he had always looked on the prospect of Lunar Colony 1 with enthusiasm. She had worked with him to formulate the necessary subsurface lunar geological surveys that would need to be undertaken before any colony could be contemplated. Her own algorithms for determining the limits of lunar fracturing stresses would hopefully, one day, allow the creation of underground living spaces on the Moon. Spaces created by a combination of the Regodozers already up there and a downscaled version of the FLC laser technology which her father had initiated.

The planned living spaces were a world away from the original glass-domed, tropical paradise imagery of the past, but for Eva the end goal represented mankind's pioneering rebirth and a step closer to the stars.

Not for the first time, her mind briefly flickered back to the Starfish's crater and the baby; a reminder of the ordinary family life she had sacrificed to prepare the way for mankind's next giant leap.

"I will birth the new mankind," she consoled herself, then focussed fully on concluding the system check.

Carrying its sole occupant, Apollo 54 left the Earth behind.

TRANSIT

27th December 2013

Danny's recollections of the past few hours ebbed and flowed with his consciousness. Sometimes he would drift into dark oblivion, at other times he was almost, but not quite, awake. During these slightly more lucid moments he was tormented by the memories leading up to his abduction. Recalling the Gene Pool's cold and exposed upper floor would again bring waves of rising panic. He would find himself reliving the adrenaline-fuelled silence that had surrounded his flight across the treacherous concrete and steel terrain. He would see Jake's coffee jar, both in the friendly warmth of the unfinished sauna room and in the cold night air, smashing into the face of one of the masked assailants. Sophie's death replayed over and over; each time he was forced to experience her wide-eyed look of terror, her head snapping backwards in a flash of bright pink hair, and her lifeless, inert fall out of view. He was no longer sure if the nightmarish vision of a shattered Moon among the clouds was real or a bizarre metaphor of his experiences.

During his less conscious moments he was plagued by dreams and memories of being branded on his forehead with the symbol of a terrorist group. He remembered his fruitless attempt to explain his unintentional stumble into their meeting place. He remembered the awful heat of the branding itself, but in his dreamlike state it felt like his whole body was on fire, like an unquenchable fever.

At times he would hear voices but the sound would never quite resolve into words; always distorted as though his ears were listening through thick water.

Then there was a change.

As before, he could not be sure how much time had elapsed since last feeling conscious, but it was now subtly different, bordering on lucidity. He was aware of his own body; no longer a vague notion of perception, he could sense the presence of his extremities again. He opened his eyes but saw only darkness, no hint of light anywhere. He couldn't be sure of his orientation, but it felt as if he was lying down.

He attempted to raise his head and was rewarded with a dull ache. He exhaled hard in response and could now feel that there was some form of mask over his mouth and nose. Instinctively he raised a hand to remove the mask but found that the confines of the space prevented him from bending his elbow enough to reach up. Again acting on instinct he yelled out several times through the mask, but his voice returned to his ears sounding dull and muted. A quick check with his hands confirmed that the inside of the box that contained him was lined with a soft material.

An uncomfortable image suddenly leapt into his mind and he thumped furiously at the sides of the coffin proportioned box, yelling for all he was worth. He attempted to push up at what he perceived to be the lid of the box, but again the confines prevented him from gaining any leverage. After yelling several times again, he stopped and dragged long breaths through the mask.

The mask was ensuring his survival, he suddenly thought, and he slowed his breathing. Someone had put him in here, so presumably someone would want to get him out again. The fateful night on the roof above The Gene Pool slammed into memory again; the armed men had killed everyone except him. Someone wanted him alive.

He felt around the space closest to his left hand. Underneath him he could feel a thin, rectangular, flexible piece of plastic with a harder seam along one edge. From its proportions he guessed it was some form of document holder, perhaps holding a clue to his circumstances. He knew there was no point trying to free it, there was no room or light inside this box to examine it by.

He reached around with his right hand and, after checking underneath himself, began patting at the close walls. His hand closed around a cold piece of cylindrical metal. Although it was pitch black around him, he intentionally closed his eyes and tried to visualise what he was touching.

One end of the cylinder was attached to some sort of cord or cable that disappeared into the side of the box. The surface of the cylinder had a grooved pattern to it, presumably meaning it was designed to be held. The other end had a small indentation. Tentatively exploring the shallow recess, he found a circular surface that yielded slightly when pushed. He remembered a time long before the great collapse; as a boy he had once been in hospital and the nurse had placed a very similar device into his hand, telling him to press the button if he needed help.

He dragged several long breaths through the mask again, while weighing up his options. There weren't many. The fact that the button was recessed meant that it had been designed to avoid accidental, or reflex pressing. He knew that this button would have to be pushed on purpose.

He fed his fingertip into the small hole and pushed once.

Nothing appeared to happen but he became aware of a high-pitched whistle, just on the boundary of detection. It sounded similar to the charging of a photographer's flash. The charging sound stopped and he felt the whole space vibrate as several metallic clunks shuddered down the left and right sides of the box.

The quality of the sound within the box changed suddenly and he realised it was because the box was no longer sealed. Stray sounds from beyond the box were now entering. He carefully pushed at the lid with his hands and knees and, although the lid was heavy, it started to move. He pushed hard again and dragged his feet towards him, forcing his knees to raise the weight of the lid.

The lid opened fully and slammed onto the floor next to the box, the clatter echoing around the nearby walls. For a moment he lay there drawing breaths though the plastic mask. He sat up slowly and peered around at the dimly lit surroundings. He was just pulling off the mask when he heard footsteps and a distinct, single voice:

"Chill out, monkey-boy. It's just the dead coming to drag you to hell!"

Hearing the footsteps getting closer, he quickly climbed out of the box and, fighting a sense of dizziness, grabbed the document folder he'd been lying on.

GREEN LIGHT

28th December 2013, 6 a.m.

With no small degree of relief, Douglas discovered that the power failure had reset the security level for all the doors on the base. All the laptop computers had of course been swiftly removed in yesterday's evacuation, but in one or two places heavy desktop machines still stood. However, none of them had a physical connection to the outside world.

Douglas knew that, prior to the Node's departure, there was only one room on the base that would have had the exact computer terminal he now required. He headed over to General Napier's office.

Like the others, the door lock was disabled and he walked straight in. There was a faint smell of coffee in the air and, although Douglas couldn't remember the last time he'd been in here, he did recall that there was never any rationing of the stuff for Napier.

The computer had rebooted after the power had been restored but, to his surprise, Douglas saw no request for login credentials on the screen, just an icon that looked like a cubist-looking 'Pi' symbol, followed by 'Napier, D.'

He guided the mouse over to the icon and, at arm's length, he clicked it, half expecting there to be a booby-trap. But no alarms went off, the computer simply awaited his instructions.

He checked Napier's most recently used files and links and after a few minutes had found the deep space radar report on the aftermath of the Moon. From there it was a straightforward matter of finding the live tracking data. The first lunar fragment impact was due in the Pacific four hours from now, and the last of them was due to strike in equatorial Colombia eighteen hours after that.

Switching to a tidal simulation report, it was now estimated that a tsunami would converge on the Node's position between seven and nine hours after that. Douglas knew he had under twenty-nine hours, he also knew that this was the least important data.

He switched back to the live tracking data and zoomed out, choosing instead to concentrate on the fragments that were occupying the Moon's orbit. The software informed him that the tracking of those fragments had ended as they had been evaluated as having no viable threat. It also asked him if he would like to reassess the fragments. After dismissing a warning that monitoring of the Earth-bound fragments would be discontinued, the display reset.

The display showed the state of the Moon approximately ten minutes after the detonation event. At that point, it merely looked like a fractured version of its former self. Douglas watched as a sudden flurry of trajectory lines branched out from the centre, each one carrying a lunar fragment. Most of the fragments had collided with others, making the pattern more complex.

There was a sudden discontinuity, a gap in the visible trajectories, then the lunar orbital fragments were displayed in their current positions. He presumed that the gap represented the time during which the system had not been tracking their location. After a minute or so, the screen updated with the new positions of the orbital fragments, but Douglas could derive no meaningful trend based on the passing of sixty seconds. The system was tracking over two thousand items, each with their own angular momentum, each impacting others and in turn changing their trajectories. Even for someone of his mental stamina, the pattern was too chaotic to predict the eventual outcome.

He could load the initial momentum conditions of the lunar fragments into a simulation program, but the calculations to predict where they would be when Siva arrived would take days to run. It was time that he didn't have; Napier's console just wasn't powerful enough. What he needed was one of Archive's Shen500 multi-core processors; they would have made light work of the simulation. But he knew that any valuable equipment would have been taken to the Node in haste. It was extremely unlikely that any of the Shen500 units were still in the main lab. Unlikely, he thought, but not impossible.

He dashed out of Napier's office and a few minutes later he'd entered the main lab.

There were a few half-filled packing crates that had been left behind and he could see a few reels of wire, voltmeters and a pot plant, but the majority of equipment in the main lab had been stripped. Anything bigger than a doorway's width had been abandoned, including the inelegant cubic grey box of the original Mark 2 Field test chamber. Perhaps ten feet to a side, and now covered in a ragged tarpaulin, it sat within a yellow and black, hazard-tape circle stuck to the floor.

When construction of the ill-fated Mark 3 had begun, all development work on the Mark 2 had ceased. He hardly dared to think his next thought; the Mark 2 had not been the focus of attention for anyone at the base for over seven months - could it still be intact? He had come here hoping to find an abandoned Shen500, but if the Field generator of the Mark 2 was still functional then this would change everything.

He hurriedly passed through the redundant airlock to get to the room containing the Mark 2, then pulled at the tarpaulin which collapsed in a heap around the chamber. The chamber's airlock was closed, but above the door a small green light indicated that it was unlocked.

Douglas stopped.

Over the past few days, as the situation had worsened, he had closed down entire forests of decision-tree options, until finally he had used his last decision to save Kate. Now, in his mind, a picture of one of his childish 'Maybe Trees' had appeared. From this one small green light there were two outcomes; the airlock battery backup was holding the door unlocked, or the Mark 2 had power.

The chamber's internal airlock door was open so he pushed on into the cramped interior. As he suspected, the Shen500 had been harvested.

Originally, when the chamber wasn't occupied, Dr. Chen had an arrangement whereby his unaccompanied Shen machines could sit within the accelerated time-frame of the Mark 2 Field and evaluate potential Field equations. Dr. Chen had also used the method to develop faster processors; each time a faster chip was manufactured, it would take the place of the previous processor within the Field. The procedure would begin again, designing its own faster successor. The Shen500 machines were the final iteration of this process here at the base.

Douglas made his way around to the rear of the central column that was used to house the Field generator. Still hung on a peg was a cumbersome looking prototype Biomag. It had the characteristic bluish crystal protruding from the flat surface, but its calculator-like display was blank. After the new design of Biomag had been created, the prototype had been kept here in case of emergencies for anyone inside the Field; but after this many months it appeared that its power reserves had become completely depleted.

He refocussed on the task and crouched down to access the floor plate. The plate was still screwed down. He glanced to his right, where normally he would expect to see the plate removal tool. It was still clipped to the central column. Potentially he knew this could mean that nobody had been in here; in an evacuation, no-one would have had the time to restow tools in their appropriate holder.

He unscrewed the floor plate, turned the handle and lifted the plate out of the way. As he peered into the dim crawl space, he could now hear the almost hypersonic whistle of the Field generator. The illuminated power display read '13.4%'.

Douglas grinned widely and it grew into a joyous eruption of laughter which, if anyone had been there, would have stopped them in their tracks. The small green light in his mind, sprouted first one decision branch, followed swiftly by two sub-branches, which in turn began to divide again and again as Douglas saw all the possibilities expanding and multiplying in front of him. With an almost childlike glee he yelled:

"New Tree!"

RIPPLE

21st December 3114 BC

Although the watery, grey Sun had only managed a shallow arc across the winter sky it had already begun to slip below the distant clouded horizon. As all traces of the Sun deserted the sky, the landscape was illuminated only by the pale, bluish-white glow of the Moon buried within the wash of cloud.

The open plateau had remained frozen during the short day, unable to shake the winter's harsh grip; yet despite the inhospitable temperature, a layer of moisture was already condensing from the air above and gathering on the short, hardy grasses.

In one small region of the plain, the gently curving blades of grass uncurled and straightened, as though blown by a wind from beneath the ground. The delicate mist-fine droplets of condensation upon the grasses rolled upwards and gathered at the thin tips, pooling there as drops; caught in the balance between surface tension and the inverted gravity.

The earth began to shudder. The vibration was so pure in frequency that the ground emitted a deep tone that carried for several miles. In reaction to a sudden heat, the water droplets flashed into steam and filled the air above the circular patch of land with an instant mist that somehow failed to disperse.

From the centre of this circular patch, like the ripple of a pebble thrown into a pond, a wave radiated outward through both the mist and ground below it, making no distinction between air and solid matter. On arriving at the boundary of the circular patch, the ripple suddenly froze. The matter it contained froze too, creating a circular ring of solid earth that protruded above the surrounding plain.

On the perimeter of this circle, a perfectly spherical hole opened within the mist and, in a blindingly bright instant, a ball of lightning arrived to completely fill its void. Accompanying its sudden arrival, a sonic boom travelled outwards, dispersing the surrounding mist. The sound was indistinguishable from thunder and reverberated around the plain. But unlike the thunderous sound, the spherical ball of light persisted. Like a beacon, it attracted the indigenous population.

Ephemeral apparitions of structure appeared fleetingly within the ring; some were anchored to the ground, others flickered into being above it, only to dissolve almost immediately. The few witnesses of the disturbance looked on in terror and fascination, unable to turn away from the incomprehensible visions. At times fragments of words, spoken in tongues that were beyond their understanding, would drift across the same space; but these too would fade as though carried away by an imperceivable wind. Without warning, the ball of lightning disappeared, leaving the silent landscape bathed only in dim moonlight.

The circular ripple had left behind a permanent earthwork ring, moulded into the very landscape of Salisbury Plain, but the only evidence that the ball of light had ever been there was a north-easterly gap within the ring.

DIAGNOSTIC

13th September 2010

The green light lit up on Leonard Cooper's control panel. "Yep, that's it, Eva," he called down to her.

"Good, that's the last relay," Eva called, and slid out from under the maintenance panel.

Taking large slow skips across the floor of Chamber 6, she approached the slim hand ladder. At one-sixth gravity it was virtually no effort to haul herself up, hand-over-hand, to the gantry above, where Leonard was fixing the side access panel back onto the main console.

"OK, let's do it," replied Leonard and, pushing the internal comm button on the console, addressed the crew, "Lana, this is Leonard Cooper and Eva Gray in Chamber 6. Installation of Floyd's computational expansion port is complete. Ready for diagnostic routine."

"*Roger, Leonard,*" came Lana Yakovna's voice over the speaker, "*All crew report in.*"

"*Mike Sanders in Chamber 4 airlock.*"

"Cathy Gant, external of FLC, at comms relay Lima."

"Lana Yakovna in the Drum. All crew, maintain positions during comms blackout. Houston, crew positions relayed, set Emergency Channel One as backup. Confirm?"

Lana's signal made its way through the chain of equatorial repeater stations that joined the FLC to the Earth radio-relay at the Moon's eastern rim. After three seconds delay, Houston's reply arrived back at the FLC.

"FLC, this is Houston. We confirm, Emergency Channel One as secondary comms. Standby."

Chamber 6 fell quiet.

The physical acts of manoeuvring the new units into place and crawling through narrow spaces had been enough to cause the occupants to breathe more deeply than usual. The only sound now was that of their deeper breaths echoing off the metallic surroundings.

"If these expansion ports work, it's going to make a real difference," said Leonard, "When they ship Floyd's next generation processors, he'll be capable of much higher rates of calculation and have greater accuracy."

"Was he particularly careless last time?" Eva smiled.

"No, but back in February, during the first deflection attempt, the sublimator beam hit Siva off-centre and sheared off the Tenca shard."

While waiting for Houston to give instruction, Leonard pulled up the firing log for the February 3rd deflection. Ever attentive, Eva watched him as he continued to explain.

"When Tenca sheared off, it altered Siva's course *very* slightly. By the time we get to 2012, we should still be able to compensate for it during the beam firing sequence."

"And hopefully not detach any more Tenca-like masses," Eva raised an eyebrow.

"Hopefully there'll be no 'hoping' about it," he smiled, then patted the console, "Thanks to the expansion ports you brought with you, next time we won't need to hope, Floyd's aim will be absolutely flawless."

"You're welcome," said Eva, dryly claiming credit, "I was heading out to the Moon anyway, so I figured I'd throw a few expansion ports in the back…"

Leonard laughed. Despite being on the far side of the Moon, he thought, there were worse places he could be right now.

"So… glass domes and biomes…?" he gently teased her.

"Funny," she said. The legacy of her father's optimism seemed to precede her everywhere she went, but she got the impression that the comment was made in jest rather than in critique.

"My dad was thinking of a time beyond Siva. Helping the human race make its next giant leap."

"I wasn't mocking, I've always thought Thomas Gray was a great man," said Leonard, "With any luck, his deflector is going to save mankind, and you'll build on that -"

"*Dig* on that," Eva corrected and pointed down, "Deep, radiation-shielded tunnels under the lunar surface. No glass dome paradise for Gray's daughter. If anything, I'll be building an underworld."

"Persephone…" nodded Leonard.

"Er…?"

"Sorry, a bit of a hobby, legends and mythology," he shrugged almost apologetically, "I guess I have a lot of reading time here so - goddess Persephone? Married to Hades, guardians of the underworld?"

"Can't say that I know that one," she hesitated.

"Born in the fires of the old?"

"Sounds, warm," said Eva, noticing how warm it appeared to have become suddenly.

"Fascinating really, when you start to look into it," continued Leonard, "the roots of -"

The console reactivated and Eva leaned over his shoulder to study the screen. He became aware of her mild body heat crossing the few inches between them and his explanation evaporated.

Leonard was well read enough that he could appreciate his biological reaction to Eva's arrival, both at his side and to the FLC in general. In evolutionary terms, the available gene pool had suddenly increased in size, and his limbic system had been stimulated. It appeared to be hardwired into the human DNA; there was something about the remote location, isolation, and low number of people that triggered the desire to procreate. Although the sterilised crew of the FLC knew that children were not a possibility here, the primitive drive was still a persistent force. The metathene doses prescribed to the crew allowed greater access to intellect by suppressing the more emotional, reactive, primitive drive. But the metathene was not a perfect seal and he found his resistance was becoming compromised.

"OK, let's see what we've got," he forced himself to refocus on the new menu layout, "Internal Power Consumption... Lens Maintenance... yep all here. Hmm, this one's greyed-out."

Leonard pointed to an inactive tab that read 'Z-bank power monitoring'

"I think that's only going active in 2012," Eva explained, "They're working on a zygote bank. It's a sort of -"

"Yeah, I know, a fertilised egg-sperm combination, but are you telling me they've found a way to store and revive -"

"No, not yet, but I know they're working on it. Until they perfect it, I guess people will have to do it the old fashioned way."

She realised that she could have stopped after her first sentence, but something had made her continue. Undoubtedly her enforced period of abstinence before leaving Earth was not helping matters. While these thoughts were running through her head, she realised that she was still holding his gaze and, seeking a lightning rod for her gathering embarrassment, she turned back to the screen.

"So, are you going to..." she pointed, "...diagnostic?"

"Die agnostic?" he couldn't help himself, "How can I die agnostic, when I have living, breathing proof of a goddess?"

"I may have come down in the last retro-dropper," said Eva aware she must now be blushing, "but I'm not that naive."

"FLC, Houston," the voice suddenly filled the chamber, *"We're ready here. Leonard please proceed."*

"Roger, Houston, proceeding with diagnostic routine."

He pushed the diagnostic button and the comms network fell silent, leaving the two of them together at the very centre of the quiet chamber.

"The alluring Persephone," he continued amiably yet bordering on innuendo, "guarding the gates to her dark and mysterious underworld."

"Have you missed a dose?" she replied, but even she knew her rebuke was not genuine; her body language was broadcasting the fact that she had not moved even one inch further away.

"You're right," he shook his head, suddenly apologetic, "maybe I need a metathene boost."

"Me too," she confessed, moving a little closer; an action he had already begun mirroring.

In the quiet isolation, unable to delay any longer, they ran their own intensive diagnostics. Discovering no hardware conflicts, they determined that everything was in perfect working order.

CALCULATION

28th December 2013, 8 a.m.

Battling against the pervasive cold, it had taken Douglas the better part of an hour to manually transport the bulky desktop computer, screen, cables and peripherals between Napier's office and the Mark 2 chamber. Setting up the computer again took slightly longer than he'd expected; his fingertips refused to warm up, making the monitor cable difficult to connect and the keyboard difficult to operate.

After he had loaded the initial momentum conditions of the orbital lunar fragments into the simulator program, it prompted him to enter the run length of the simulation. By his calculation, Siva would reach Earth in four hundred and sixty days, so he set the simulation length to an even five hundred.

He started the simulation and a few minutes later the software helpfully stated that the estimated time to completion was one hundred and twenty hours.

He adjusted the computer's monitor to face out through the chamber's observation window, then walked outside to check that he could see it clearly. In the early days he had used a whiteboard to send messages through that same window to Anna outside, and she had returned messages using a similar whiteboard. They'd often discussed their theories about the inability to use direct radio communication, but they knew the Field itself prevented it. Remembering this, Douglas turned on his heels and returned to the power controls.

In a small-scale experiment back in 1989, Douglas had activated the Field by remote control, only to find that the remote control's radio signals could not penetrate the Field in order to turn it off. It had taken two whole months for the internal power to run out before the Field had finally collapsed. He made sure that the timer switch inside the Mark 2 was set to turn off the Field and then re-departed.

Once the Field was activated, the 120 hour simulation inside the chamber would run in just 2 hours for him outside the Field. The computer monitor facing through the observation window would relay the simulation and hopefully show him the dispersion pattern of the orbital lunar fragments; more importantly it would display where they would be when Siva arrived.

He stood outside the circular hazard-tape marker, folded back the remote's safety cover and flicked the switch.

He heard the Field emitters very quickly reach sync and then build in pitch. It couldn't be directly observed but he felt the Field establish itself, and then all noise coming from the Mark 2 ceased; caught within the invisible bubble surrounding the cube-shaped chamber.

Through the observation window, he watched as over two thousand trajectory lines updated every second; each iteration a step closer to revealing the predicted end state of Earth's former Moon.

RTO

25th December 2013

The FLC's Return To Orbit module had not been due to take centre stage for at least another year, so in the Starfish facility under Houston Mission Control, its Earth-bound duplicate was still residing under the metallic step structure. Despite this awkward positioning, people swarmed over the RTO module, poring over thick technical manuals and trailing power cables to bring it to life earlier than expected.

All their previous RTO flight calculations, which presupposed the FLC's success, were now void. In addition to the departure date being over a year early, the weight to be lifted from the lunar surface had also decreased; Eva Gray and Leonard Cooper would not be returning. In Leonard's place would be the Z-bank, but information concerning its mass was proving elusive to the flight planners. Those not directly involved with the flight plan were preoccupied by the other stresses of an unplanned departure.

"We can repurpose the high-gain antenna," Karl Meyer was insisting above the general clamour, "Once they're out of LOS, we reacquire their signal, then do a delta upload and course trim their heading."

"OK," Greg Campbell shook his head in disbelief of the situation, "they'll need to re-patch the auxiliary bus to buffer the data. Tell 'em."

Ross Crandall relayed the more detailed instructions directly to the crew aboard the RTO module, along with the remainder of the pre-flight corrections.

"Roger," came the voice of Mike Sanders from the RTO, *"re-patching aux bus for delta course trim. Done."*

With the barest delay Lana's voice returned.

"Houston, RTO module. We are go for launch."

"Hey!" called Lawrence, waving frantically from the analogue monitoring station, "The core's at capacity!"

Ross snatched the microphone up from the desk and sucked in a quick breath, before pushing the button to communicate with the remote crew.

"RTO, Houston, we'll recalculate Trans Earth trajectory as soon as you're in Lunar orbit. Launch Commit."

"Roger," said Lana by return, *"Launch Commit."*

There was a brief delay then Lana returned again, *"Ascent phase in three, two, one…"*

A loud but brief sound overwhelmed the speaker as the fuel and oxidizer combined to explosively lift the distant RTO module from the lunar surface.

"RTO Ascent," confirmed Lana, her tone trembling slightly through the vibration.

In front of Lawrence, the core's power output graph sailed through two hundred percent, briefly flashed 'Out of Range' and then simply stated 'Error'.

"The Core!" yelled Lawrence, "Damping failure!"

The fusion reaction at the heart of the FLC was fuelling a faster and faster consumption of the surrounding Helium-3. The reaction was now unstoppable.

"Deep space radar tracking this?" Ross shouted out to the busy room.

"Yes Sir," came a reply, "they came online four minutes ago!"

In the brief months that Lawrence had known him, Ross Crandall's Lifeboat Pass had always hung loosely around his neck; a passive demonstration of power. Now, while everyone else was busy, Lawrence saw Ross discreetly unclip the pass from the chain and push it deep into his trouser pocket; all the time glancing around the room. His eyes inevitably found Lawrence, but Lawrence didn't look away from his wide-eyed stare. In the single second they maintained eye contact, Lawrence knew; it was over.

The Lifeboat Lottery would soon be tested.

There would be no orderly queueing.

Ross knew this, but he also knew he needed to maintain the focus of the workforce:

"People!" he shouted, "Our mission is now to get the RTO and Z-bank back home, we need to move upstairs again."

Ross joined the exodus climbing the metallic stairs to the main elevator. His own ascent was very much a slow-motion replica of the RTO module's point of view during its ascent phase. Along with everyone else, he looked over the handrail to see its starfish profile growing smaller as they gained height.

He and several others filed into the open elevator that would take them back up to the Mission Control room where hopefully they would still have a mission to control. The elevator ride seemed interminable and during the whole journey no-one spoke a word; each of them seemed lost in their own private extrapolation of the events they had just witnessed.

On entering the Mission Control room, Ross could immediately see that the number of staff had dwindled drastically. Evidently some people, spotting the approach of disaster, had abandoned ship; preferring to take their chances among the chaos on the surface. He found himself unconsciously tightening his grip on his Lifeboat Pass.

When he thought back to the Mission Control room last Christmas, things had been so different.

THE CONVERSATION

21st December 2012

The date of the FLC's second firing on Siva had arrived and the atmosphere at Houston Mission Control was tense. Although there was plenty of chatter filling the room, the individual exchanges appeared to be brief and conducted in low tones.

Ross Crandall gave a call to order and the room seemed to take on a slightly different air.

"Here we go again," murmured Bradley, taking a swift draw from his hip flask and offering it to General Napier standing next him.

Napier gave a miniscule head-shake without taking his eyes from the huge display screens.

"Just hope that Floyd's got his head screwed on right this time," continued Bradley, angling the flask more steeply before snapping the lid closed and pocketing his silver container, "Chen reckons it'll be right on the money, no drift like last time."

In reply, Napier only drew a deep breath and checked his wristwatch.

Ross Crandall had temporarily passed control to Alexey Yakovna. Though Alexey knew the position he'd been given wielded no actual power, amounting to little more than microphone control, he was grateful to have a contributing function. The position also allowed him to have direct conversation with his daughter.

The audio feed was already coming in live from the FLC on the far side of the Moon. The signal had made its way around the Moon's circumference to a point where direct line-of-sight communication was possible with Earth's satellites. Despite the distance covered, the delay was no more than a few seconds. Each of the personnel at the FLC were conducting their final confirmation checks.

"Lana Yakovna. FLC control. At this time, I ask you for a go, no-go. Stations check in."

"Mike Sanders. Clockwise containment beam. Go."

"Cathy Gant. Counter-clockwise containment beam. Go."

"Eva Gray. Central sublimator beam. Go."

"Leonard Cooper. Observatory. Standing by."

"Houston, FLC," reported Lana, *"all stations report ready. Over."*

"FLC, Houston," Alexey responded, "Good to hear your voice."

After the customary wait, Lana's reply returned.

"And yours also, Papa."

While it pleased Alexey to hear his daughter call him by that name, it made him feel very slightly uncomfortable in front of the Houston personnel. He also knew that if she ever called him 'Papa' over an open communication channel, then there was something upsetting her. He was pretty certain he knew what, but protocol dictated that he would next have to relay confirmation of what Houston was receiving.

"Earth-side telemetry looks good," he continued, looking over the computer displays, "Siva has maintained cyclic spin and trajectory remains within decimal zero zero two percent of delta vee."

"Roger Houston. And Tenca?"

There it was, he thought, the source of her upset. His too. The Tenca shard was still too far out to calculate an accurate impact position, but the predicted impact zone was centred around Novgorod, their birth place. As such they both felt Tenca's advance extremely acutely. He knew she was checking in with him to see if there was any confirmation yet, no doubt hoping the prediction was in error; he had to disappoint her.

"No change."

After a longer than usual delay, Lana's reply returned:

"Roger, understand Houston. All stations report ready, we are good to go with second stage firing on Siva. Do we have commit from Houston?"

A thumbs up from Ross allowed Alexey to reply.

"You have commit FLC," he confirmed.

"Confirmed Houston, Final station check."

Each station checked in as before. With each confirmation, Alexey watched Ross push an illuminated button to release control to Floyd, the Shen500 series FLC computer that would run the firing procedure. After all stations had signed off, Alexey gave final permission to proceed.

"Roger FLC, you are go for Floyd lock-out."

When it came to the precise moment, Floyd would automatically control the actual firing on Siva. Thanks to the 2010 addition of the computational expansion ports, Floyd's updated processors could determine the coordinates and firing instant down to the nanosecond; something the human crew could not do in real time. To ensure that Floyd was dealing with a closed system, human intervention had to be locked out at the last moment.

"Personnel lock-out in 3, 2, 1," Lana relayed, *"Floyd autonomous control established."*

The buttons on the panels in front of Alexey lit up red.

"FLC, Houston, we confirm lock-out."

After a few moments, Lana's voice reported back.

"Containment field is active. Fusion injection is underway."

This was only the second time that the Helium-3 fusion reactor had been activated, but Alexey could see that the digital telemetry data being relayed back to Houston was already causing several personnel to high-five each other. The magnetic containment field surrounding the fusion process was holding.

"FLC, Houston," Alexey grinned, "we read fusion event."

"Houston, Observatory," came Leonard Cooper's voice, *"Estimated beam activation in T-minus fifteen seconds."*

"Roger FLC," Alexey confirmed, which effectively silenced the room. They knew that what came next would determine the prospects of survival on Earth. Floyd was now busy calculating a method to combine the three laser component beams and focus them on a moving target, from a moving orbital base. Once this was complete Floyd would then calculate how to dynamically adjust these parameters so that the beams continuously targeted the same spot on Siva's surface as it continued its sweep through Earth's orbital path. Only by holding the coupled beams steady could Siva be pushed into an alternative, safer trajectory.

"Activation in 3, 2, 1," Leonard reported.

All breathing within the Houston Control room appeared to cease.

"Houston, Observatory. Instruments report activation. Stand by."

Leonard himself now lapsed into silence for several seconds before reporting the next technical milestone.

"Houston, we have particulate sublimation confirmed at the Prism. Now verifying target acquisition."

In the vacuum of space, the laser beams themselves would not be visible, but the fact that Leonard had reported 'particulate sublimation' meant that a tiny amount of matter had passed through the beam and been converted into a spark of light. The next report from Leonard would confirm if the beams had made contact with Siva at all.

"Houston," Leonard broke the silence, *"initial Siva beam contact confirmed."*

Assuming success, a single voice somewhere in the room cried out 'Yes' before being swiftly hushed by those around him.

"Stand by," Leonard advised.

The others gathered today realised the difference between Floyd hitting the distant target, and Floyd successfully concentrating a sustained energy beam capable of slowly deflecting Siva.

There followed another, seemingly interminable, radio silence.

Finally, after what seemed like several minutes, Leonard reported back:

"Houston. Surface sublimation cascade event confirmed on Siva."

This time, the whole control room erupted in a burst of shouts, screams and laughter. The 'cascade event' told everyone that, right now, the surface of Siva was burning; the continuous energy being pumped into its surface by the three intertwined lasers was already exerting a force, and pushing it further from Earth.

In contrast to his normal exuberance, Bradley thrust out his chin and muttered, "Take that, ya sonuvabitch."

At the main communication panel, Ross Crandall had resumed control and was expressing his gratitude.

"FLC, on behalf of everyone on Earth we thank you for your early Christmas present."

It was a few seconds before Leonard's reply came through the speakers, and was a little difficult to discern above the celebratory noise.

"Mayan Calendar reset. Happy New Year, Houston."

Alexey shot a puzzled look at Ross, "Myhan Calendar?"

Ross shrugged, and turned to give a thumbs up to General Napier at the back of the room.

Napier responded in kind then turned to face Bradley, "We need to talk."

"And congratulations to you too," he retorted sarcastically, "Don't go enjoyin' the moment too much!"

"Now."

•

In the privacy of the video conference room at Houston, General Napier, Bradley and Alexey sat facing a large, blank television screen, directly below which was a small, dome-like camera. Alfred Barnes was present in audio only via the speakerphone that had been placed in the centre of the table and all were awaiting the video presence of Dr. Chen.

The blank TV screen flickered momentarily and then Dr. Chen's head and shoulders filled the frame; behind him an ornate bamboo wallpaper was visible.

"Congratulations," he bowed.

"And to you too Dr. Chen," Napier nodded to the camera, "The results look good so far, from the digital data we're receiving, Floyd's targeting is flawless."

"My Shen500's do not make mistakes," he smiled, earning him a round of polite laughter, "I do not see Dr. Barnes."

"I'm here on the table," Alfred's tinny-sounding voice replied.

Dr. Chen looked at the speakerphone, and the lens of the camera beneath the TV jerked down slightly, tracking his eye movement.

"Ah yes, of course."

"Dr. Chen," said Napier, "please can you confirm you're alone?"

On the screen they saw him glance off to the upper right and a moment later they heard a door close.

"Yes."

"Good," Napier began, "Although today's firing is not yet complete, it has every sign of being a complete success. But as I watched the Control room today a thought crossed my mind that I believe will need action. Across all of our ventures, not just the FLC, we've built a network of incredibly competent people. Who we are now dependent on."

He paused at this point to give his last statement time to be absorbed.

"In fifty-six days Tenca will hit us. Now, everyone we utilise knows this, they know they're in no direct danger. But…"

"But," came Alfred's voice from the centre of the table, *"after the impact their own sense of worth will become inflated. We may start receiving demands, or there may be more blackmail attempts."*

"Exactly, Dr. Barnes."

"So we let the Ego's take 'em out," offered Bradley.

"No," said Dr. Chen, "by that time, anyone blackmailing us would be too critical to our processes. Recruiting alternative people from a panicked population will yield, ah, unstable results."

"Not only that," continued Alfred, *"but in the extremely unlikely circumstances that the FLC should fail, no offence Bradley, then we'd need to ensure that we still have full control of our other ventures. Hmm."*

"If all go wrong," said Alexey, "we cannot save everybody that works for Archive."

"Not by a long chalk," agreed Bradley.

"But we need to ensure that the workforce remains compliant," Napier folded his arms.

After a short pause Alfred Barnes hesitantly spoke.

"OK how about this? The personnel that are critical to us would need to know, or rather they would need to feel, that their survival is still assured, yes?"

There were no objections from the table, so he continued.

"OK. What we need to do is move them towards accepting their survival is a high possibility rather than a guarantee. We need to impose a hierarchy on those that consider themselves, er, 'pre-saved', if that's even a word, so that we can incentivise their behaviour."

"It's like he's spittin' clever words at me," Bradley pointed at the speakerphone.

"Da! Use small words so poor American can understand," Alexey mocked.

The speakerphone remained silent for a few moments as if Alfred were contemplating how to rephrase things for Bradley.

"OK, er, I know that all of you have your own personal transport in everything from cars to planes. But if you had to travel on a commercial cruise ship, you'd travel First Class, right?"

"If there weren't nothing better then yeah, sure," resigned Bradley.

"OK, so you've got your ticket, you join the other First Class travellers in their mostly empty lounge, and the ship sets off. Next, the Captain announces that they're having an exciting competition; people have the chance to upgrade their ticket. After several of these competitions, the First Class lounge is filled to capacity, as is Second Class, and so on. Then the Captain announces the bad news; the ship is going to hit an iceberg and there's no way to stop it."

"I hate your idea of a pleasure cruise, Freddy..." Bradley muttered.

"But the good news," Alfred continued, *"is that there are lifeboats, and they will be filled-"*

"Women and children first?" Alexey guessed.

"This is an Archive cruise," said Alfred, pointedly, *"The Captain announces that the lifeboats will be filled First Class first, then Second Class and so on. Everyone aboard has to help prepare for the impact, and if you don't work hard enough, the Captain can demote you to a lower class. What do you do?"*

"I fire the dumb-ass Captain!" blurted Bradley.

"Yes. Except you don't own the ship. Your only option is to make sure you're not the one who loses his First Class place - you work hard. What about the people in Second Class?"

"They fear the classes lower than them," Dr. Chen nodded, "and work hard to take the place from someone in First Class."

"In return for work, you are given some sort of token. The more tokens you have, the closer you get to moving up a class."

"OK, in your scenario Dr. Barnes," General Napier leaned towards the speakerphone, "what happens on the day of the disaster?"

"Anyone who is still in First Class gets a Lifeboat Pass from the Captain. Everyone else aboard is then allowed to use their tokens to buy as many Lifeboat Lottery tickets as they can afford."

"Even those in Second Class?" asked Dr. Chen.

"Yes. They have more tokens to spend of course, but their survival is now a possibility rather than a guarantee. Dependence on the hierarchy at all stages of the cruise encourages people's compliance and, through an arbitrary reward system, maintains trust in it."

"Svoloch' Kapitan," Alexey swore.

"We are the Captain," sighed Bradley, "Ain't we?"

"Unfortunately, yes. The Captain has to lie in order to save the few; just as we must decide who will be saved."

"And who's gonna die…" completed Bradley.

"In this scenario the Captain also lied about one more thing…"

The others waited while Alfred Barnes drew a breath that was audible over the speakerphone.

"There is no Lifeboat."

LOS

25th December 2013

Ross Crandall kept a tight hold of the Lifeboat Pass in his pocket as he waited for everyone to return to their Mission Control posts. Lawrence Clark was among the last batch of people to return in the elevator. As Lawrence came into the room, Ross grabbed hold of his sleeve and drew him to one side.

"I know you saw me pocket my Lifeboat Pass," he spoke a very low tone to avoid being overheard, "I suggest you do the same."

"Of course, Sir," said Lawrence and started to leave, but Ross didn't let go.

"We're not done here, the Z-bank has to make it to the ISS. Understand?"

"I understand," Lawrence took off his Lifeboat Pass and stowed it in his pocket, "I'm not about to jeopardise my Lifeboat place."

Ross released him and waited for everyone to either find their previous places or fill the gaps left behind by the deserters who had chosen to take their chances on the surface.

He wrestled his headset into position and then waited for order to return to the room. The main display showed that the RTO module was now contactable, having emerged from the far side of the Moon.

"RTO, Houston, over," Ross spoke, waiting for the usual communication delay.

"Roger. Go ahead," came Lana's voice.

Ross received a thumbs up signal from the other side of the room.

"Roger. Lana we're transmitting the new Trans-Earth injection plan, acknowledge? Over."

"Understood, stand by," came her reply.

The adjustment to their Trans-Earth flight plan was transferred, byte by byte, to the RTO via the high-gain antenna. Over the long distances involved the transfer took almost a minute. But the transfer was barely half way through when an alarm sounded in the control room.

"What the hell?" Ross swept the room with wide eyes, "Meyer, is that us? Is that the RTO?"

"No," shouted Karl Meyer, "I'm still getting telemetry -"

"It's a second launch!" yelled Greg Campbell, pointing out a red box on the display, "Five-hour countdown's been triggered!"

"What?" Ross faltered momentarily, "Where?"

"Kennedy," Greg shouted back, "Apollo 72 launch sequence. Unauthorised."

"No shit," Ross snapped, "Shut it down!"

Even from his position overlooking the room, Ross could hear the aggressive console warning tones responding to Greg's efforts.

"Negative function on override," Greg continued to stab at his panel, "Still trying…"

"Karl, get me on comms. Now!" shouted Ross, pointing to the red box on the display.

Karl dashed across the Control room, barging people aside to reach the unmanned ground-station comms desk. Before Karl could report back, Lana's voice filled the room.

"Houston, RTO, we have received your course correction. Over."

"Negative on ground-station comms," Karl reported back to Ross, "we're connected but locked out."

"Locked? How the f-" Ross struggled, scanning the displays for inspiration.

"Sir," Lawrence called out, "Can we get through to them via the International Space Station?"

"No, but it gives me an idea. Open a comm channel."

"Working," Karl shouted, propelling his swivel chair along the desk to the other end.

"Maybe they can take over guidance of the RTO while we handle this mess," Ross anxiously ran his hands through his hair.

"ISS due for local horizon rise in four minutes," called Karl.

"Go via satellite link," Ross threw back.

"Already tried," Karl responded equally quickly, "Sat-comm's down."

"Houston, do you read us. Over?" came Lana's voice again.

Ross tried his best to compartmentalise the two situations before responding.

"RTO, Houston, we apologise for the delay. Be advised that we are currently mid-countdown on a second launch sequence. We're juggling here."

As soon as he had responded to Lana, he returned his attention to Karl.

"Open up a secure channel to the ISS. As soon as they clear the horizon I wanna know about it."

Karl nodded and switched channels, preparing for the moment when the ISS would rise over the local horizon and give them direct line-of-sight communication.

"Houston, RTO," Lana's voice came through again, *"please confirm Trans-Earth flight to conclude with orbital approach and dock with International Space Station. Over."*

Karl quickly reported that the secure channel had been prepared.

Ross opened his mouth to respond to Lana, but a shrill frequency resounding through the control room speakers cut across him. He glanced over at Greg who indicated it was beyond his control. The high pitched noise switched to become static before falling into silence.

Karl was stabbing at controls and murmuring, "No, no, no..."

"What?" Ross yelled.

"We're being hacked!" Karl's eyes were alight with panic, "We're locked out of the ISS secure channel, they're piggyback-"

Another short burst of static interrupted him.

"RTO, Houston," Ross Crandall's voice emerged from the control room speakers, despite Ross himself not uttering a single word, *"We confirm your rendezvous with the ISS. You guys may also have noticed the altitude difference of the ISS. Flight advises me that this will be consistent with your approach vector... I guess things have changed a little while you've been away."*

Ross stood in horror. His voice had just been used by an unknown, outside agency to authorise an approach vector.

"Roger," Lana accepted, *"Received and understood."*

Ross stared at the main display. Any second now the RTO module was due to pass behind the Moon, at which point they would enter Loss Of Signal. As if reading the display directly, his voice was used again over the speakers.

"We read one minute to LOS. Prepare for automated thruster burn sequence."

"Houston, RTO, we are course locked," Lana relayed, unaware of the sabotage.

Ross could hear Karl furiously pulling box files off a nearby shelf, presumably to look for alternatives. Ross then heard his voice used once more.

"Roger, Lana, we'll see you on the other side."

There was a brief burst of static, then the room fell silent. A second later the main display shut down and several low buzzers sounded at random, one after another, from the consoles around the room. A second after that, they too died and the room was plunged into the dim glow of emergency exit lighting.

After allowing his eyes a few seconds to become accustomed to the gloom, Ross removed his headset and found the nearest desk phone. Unsurprisingly it was dead, as were the others he tried.

With his last scraps of authority, he managed to persuade people to follow him to the elevators. Ross inserted his key into the slot next to the elevator, but the doors refused to open. With one hand, he removed the key again, keeping his other hand tightly clasped around the Lifeboat Pass in his pocket. He reinserted the key and turned it again. One of the elevators should have arrived by now, but somehow he knew they would never arrive again.

He and Lawrence exchanged looks as they realised the stark truth of the situation. For them and everyone else here, there would never be a lifeboat. Their only choice now was to either remain underground or use the stairs to join the desperate chaos on the surface.

INTERROGATION

2nd March 2013

The Level Two Intervention he was currently concluding was in the basement flat of Rob Davis. The theatrics, body language and blatant melodrama were all part of Benton's interrogation technique. He had never really fully understood why it was all necessary, but over the years it had arguably made him a more efficient communicator.

It had been an untaxing affair and he had prevented the leak of some valuable Archive information, but during the interrogation Rob had called him a 'Storykiller'. Benton didn't like the term, partly because he felt it was such a crude reduction of his dedicated life, but mostly because Rob must have heard this term from someone else; and that must mean at least one other intervention had been conducted carelessly.

During the interrogation, Benton had set about dressing the flat with all manner of explicit materials and gun magazines; the aim being that when Rob's corpse was eventually discovered, any good reputation would be destroyed by the glut of evidence surrounding him.

The neuromuscular suppressant was working as planned and Benton watched as Rob closed his eyes; the coma would take effect soon, and death four hours later.

He picked up one of the magazines, opened it to a suitably sordid page and placed it on Rob's lap. He picked up the disposable plastic bag full of Rob's incriminating research and, after satisfying himself that the forensics of the scene were correct, he prepared to leave the room.

As usual he felt the slight tug on his conscience for what he had done. *He did feel genuine pity for Rob and all the other individuals who had been through this process.*

As if to silence his own internal demons, he justified his actions aloud:

"For the good of Mankind..."

Then he started to close the door.

"Hello Miles," came Rob's wheezing voice from within the flat.

Benton immediately headed back into the room and hurried over to Rob.

"We have spoken before," Rob continued to wheeze, "do you remember me?"

"Of course," Benton replied. The question was trivial; their conversation had happened mere moments before.

"Why did you do this to me, Miles?" Rob was pleading, "I was just trying to keep Kate safe."

Miles also knew it was important to keep Kate safe, Monica had explained it to him.

"Who's Monica?" Rob asked, almost in direct response.

"She's..." Miles began to reply but then stopped. Miles had only thought of Monica, but Rob had responded verbally to it.

The situation was familiar, but the conversation had never gone this way. Rob had never mentioned Kate during the interrogation. He had killed Rob to protect Archive.

"For the good of Mankind, Miles," Rob implored, "Please speak with me."

Again Miles felt the insistent burning of the coin that was suddenly in his palm. He expected to see its familiar embossed Liberty Bell and Moon design, but the circular Moon had become a simple ring, broken in one place by a raised dot.

"This is all wrong," said Miles, looking around the room, "All of it. You've done this before! You keep making me relive..."

Rob's pained expression vanished and his expression became neutral as he spoke to Miles:

"We'll speak again."

Before Miles could take the conversation any further the basement flat lights went out and again he had the sensation of an endless fall.

CLOCK

T -08:57:30

Colonel Beck walked out onto the balcony two storeys above the Observation Deck. As with all rooms within the Node, the Observation Deck was a radial segment, but unlike the other segments it took up a full quarter of the circumference. Glazing stretched from side to side and from the Observation Deck floor to the summit of the Node, thirteen storeys above him, where the curvature also permitted a 360 degree view of the sky. The large panels of glass that made up the glazing were bonded directly to each other so the overall effect was like being within a soap bubble.

Beneath him, the population of the Node was gathered and ready for his briefing, but all attention was directed away from him at the impossibly fluctuating world outside. Even he was momentarily caught in its hypnotic rhythm; the accelerated passage of time changed waves into mere vibrating ripples on an otherwise featureless expanse of water.

Trailing a long cable behind him, Roy Carter joined him on the balcony and handed him a microphone.

"Here you are, Sir, I… whoa," he now became distracted by the sights too.

"Thank you, Carter," Beck took the microphone, "Are we ready?"

"Yes, sorry Sir. Should I…?" Carter gestured back over his shoulder.

He nodded and Roy departed, struggling to pull his eyes away from the view. A moment later, electro-tinting within the glazing began to turn the panoramic window an opaque white, obscuring the world beyond. Colonel Beck tapped on the microphone and the deep thuds emerged from speakers set around the Observation Deck. As the echoes died, so did the general murmuring as people turned away from the obscured view to face him on the balcony.

During the departure, Colonel Beck knew there had been casualties. From the roll call, he knew there had also been fatalities; he suspected that they would be Biomag and isotope related, but it was too early to tell.

He looked down at the mixture of military and civilian faces below. Some stared blankly, some seemed somehow jubilant, some were red-eyed and drawn - but all now looked to him for direction.

"Today," his voice echoed and reverberated around the vast space, "I wish I had more profound words of comfort."

Somewhere, he could hear someone trying to contain their weeping. The sound became muffled as their tears were absorbed by a consoling neighbour.

"Something to give a meaning to the choices and sacrifices we have made."

A quiet stillness descended, his voice alone carrying through the silence.

"But today is not yet over. It demands more of us."

The echo of his voice died out.

"We will mourn our losses. But first we must survive."

He turned and nodded to Roy Carter behind him, who turned on the Observation Deck's video projector.

Acting now as a massive projector screen, the electro-tinted white surface of the curved glazing displayed a clock; it was counting down from eight hours and fifty-five minutes. Within a few seconds everyone had turned to face the screen.

"Siva reaches us in under nine hours."

Alongside the clock, a list of part numbers beginning with 'DRB' appeared.

"Our survival depends on finding these crates."

In actual fact he didn't know if that was true; the exact content of Douglas Walker's message was unknown. But right now it motivated people and focussed them back into productive work. As he'd arranged, a small group of personnel started moving through the gathering, handing out printed slips of paper containing DRB part numbers and search regions within the Node.

"These are your designated search segments."

Colonel Beck raised his voice over the slight clamour.

"Move now to your start points. You have twenty minutes."

The clock display changed to read eight hours and fifty-four minutes; thirty seconds after that, the Observation Deck was empty.

THE RECEIVER

28th December 2013, 9 a.m.

While the simulation ran within the Mark 2, Douglas returned to Hab 1. He used the time to gather useful resources and collect his thoughts on what to do with the results once they were ready.

There could be only two possible outcomes.

Either Siva would plough through a slim section of orbital lunar fragments and impact the Earth in a slightly different but equally catastrophic way; or over time the minor shift in the Earth-Moon centre of gravity would have a more pronounced effect on the bulk of the former Moon.

Both scenarios would require a change to the way the Field operated, and he knew he'd have to devise a way to get the new information into the Node. With a conscience-jabbing sense of regret, he also knew that if he had proceeded directly to the Node yesterday, instead of confronting Bradley and his helicopter henchmen, then he wouldn't be in this mess. In any case he was still glad that Kate was safe aboard rather than in Bradley's hands, or worse.

In that moment he realised that the Siva information would have to be given to Kate. In the moments surrounding the launch it would be assumed that he was aboard; Kate was wearing his Biomag. Crucially then, Kate was the only possible person who may be expecting any form of external communication from him, which made her the sole receiver of any information he intended to send.

Douglas pushed open his bedroom door and sat on the corner of his bed, trying to think what Kate would do next. He glanced at his watch and back-calculated; for those inside the Node, the Field had activated under forty seconds ago. He tried to put himself in Kate's position.

Her first action would have been to try aborting the launch by calling the control room via the nearest comm panel; but quite evidently the Field had already activated so logically she had not succeeded. He deduced that the communications between the ground level and the control room must not be functional.

Although he knew that the Node's temporal journey was currently unstoppable, Kate didn't and her next goal would have been to reach the control room itself to tell them to stop.

Prior to the Node's departure, Kate had studied its plans and then memorised the architectural layout without setting foot inside it. Even when she was a child, Douglas had always been impressed by her ability to layer information and concepts into a cohesive picture - her knowledge of the Node's levels had proved no different.

She would know, almost instinctively, the fastest route to the control room.

However, Douglas didn't instinctively know, and it took him a while to work out that in all likelihood she would choose a route through the Observation Deck. With no obstructions, he estimated that she could reach the Observation Deck within forty seconds of discovering that the comm panels were inactive. Doing a quick mental calculation to account for the different rates of time, Douglas knew that in his time-frame she would be passing through the Observation Deck some time after 3 p.m.

Now that he knew where she would be, he could focus on how to get the information to her.

The information was complex, so he would have to decide on the most efficient way to transmit it. In order to do that, he would need to focus first on how she would receive it. Only then would he be able to formulate a delivery method.

From Kate's perspective aboard the Node, the outside world would appear highly accelerated; so any information he transferred would have to arrive slow enough to be registered. Or, thought Douglas, she would have to be able to slow down the received information somehow. As if in answer to his own thoughts, his eyes settled on the pair of digital recording binoculars on his table full of other junk.

Since finishing his work on the Field equations, back in August, he'd become more directly involved with the temporal aspects of the Node's operation; this had ranged from developing a system to monitor the long-term effects of Field exposure on personnel, to extracting observable data from an accelerated time-frame. The digital recording binoculars had been one of his solutions to the latter.

Dr. Chen's advances in processing power had made the simultaneous stereoscopic stabilisation and recording of high definition images an easy task, but it was Douglas who had thought to combine it with a super-high frame rate. By operating the processors in burst mode, it was possible to record 3000 images per second instead of the standard 30. When the resulting images were played back at the standard speed, the recorded actions would unfold 100 times slower. For observing the accelerated world outside the Node, it would prove useful.

For slowing down his own high speed message it would be essential.

First he would need to verify that the half-dozen digital recording binoculars had made it to the science station on the Observation Deck. He walked over to the pile of junk and pulled out the digital recording binoculars but, on discovering that the battery was completely flat, threw them back on the table. Instead he crossed over to his wardrobe and digging deep through a pile of clothes retrieved a pair of robust-looking standard binoculars.

Monica had given them to him when they had first set up home in Dover. Standing outside Samphire Hoe cottage, the two of them had taken it in turns to look out over the English Channel and spot small boats. She'd even engraved the binoculars with the three letters, 'I C U'. He dusted off the lenses and headed out once more, this time to stand in front of the Node's massive observation window.

He chose a spot by one of the safety markers, directly opposite the huge, glazed facade and focussed the binoculars. The interior was still quite dimly lit, but he could clearly see the science station. The wall-mounted recharging bank was fully stocked with digital recording binoculars.

"Excellent," he smiled to himself.

A new sound greeted his ears that was completely at odds with the scientific spectacle in front of him. Carried on the wind he could hear a slow, repetitive, rhythmic chant; perhaps some form of ritual. The rhythm ended and slowly he returned his mind to the task.

He knew he would need to get Kate's attention as she ran through the Observation Deck on her way to the control room. The question was how. Assuming she spotted him at all, any movement he made to attract her attention would appear highly accelerated; his waving arms would appear just as invisible as a hummingbird's wings.

Whether it was the rhythmic chant, or the need to think of something that would look odd outside the Node, his mind settled on the most primitive form of attracting attention. Like the groups of people outside the perimeter fence, he would need to build a *very* large fire.

CONVERGENCE

29th December 2013

"The fire's out, but we've lost the radio room," Cal gasped, out of breath from the run, "The Warren's cut off."

"At least we saved our air," Woods replied, continuing to pack medical supplies outside AR2.

"Yeah but for how long?" Cal thought out loud.

Another deep tremor shuddered under their feet. The noise reverberated down the narrow rocky corridor, only to return a moment later as a clamour of urgent sounding voices.

"Woods?" said Cal, "What are you doing?"

"Packing," he replied, closing up a box of yellowish test tubes and stuffing it into a small flight case.

"Why, you going somewhere?"

Woods stopped and looked at him with an expression approaching horror, then he grabbed him by the shoulders

"What do you mean, Cal? Didn't the message get through to the lower tunnels?"

"What message, Woods? I don't -"

"Shit!" he shook Cal again, "Comms must be out below the radio room. We've got to tell them!"

"Tell them what?" Cal yelled, shrugging himself free of the panicked grip.

"Monica called 'Breakthrough'," Woods shouted, "she's doing it now!"

"But it's too early! Why is she -"

A sudden and silent sideways force moved the entire space around them. Cal just managed to stay upright but Woods stumbled and gashed his head against the rough wall; the echo of his expletives was just fading when a low rumbling sound began.

"We've got to get them out!" Woods slammed another case closed.

From the Arrivals Lounge further down the corridor, a distant, metallic, high-pitched sound started to grow in volume. The two men cautiously walked a little closer along the cramped corridor until they could see through the doorway to the arrivals track and chute.

Five months ago, when Marcus had arrived with Nathan, the room had been bare, with the exception of an uncomfortable camp-bed. When the destructive attack on the cottage above had closed this entrance, the Arrivals Room had become an unofficial attic; now the room's function was to store rarely used things. Dozens of packing cases had ended up here, along with rolls of electrical cable, sections of ducting and several wardrobe rails of clothing. There was broken furniture awaiting repair and even an artificial Christmas tree that had been hastily ejected from AR1 to make space for the emergency briefing a few days ago. The tree's tinsel-covered branches appeared to shimmer.

Cal saw the tinsel twitch and ripple, then he felt the faintest sensation of air on his sweaty face. The tinsel started blowing towards them in the direction of the door as the air became a mild breeze. The high-pitched metallic sound was definitely getting louder, Cal thought, and it could only be coming from the chute.

The thin material of some of the hanging clothes had now begun to flap as the breeze became a constant wind. It was only then that Cal realised what was happening. The wind was actually air inside the long chute being forcibly displaced; the high-pitched metallic sound must be seawater, flooding down the chute and pushing the air out towards them.

With a sickening feeling he realised that the silent shake they'd experienced a moment ago must have been the tsunami striking the Dover coast.

"It's here," he could only whisper through his suddenly constricted throat.

The rushing hiss suddenly became much louder and then a torrent of seawater erupted through the mouth of the chute into the Arrivals Lounge. It enveloped the steel-work uprights on both sides of the track and sent stacks of packing cases flying before swallowing them as they returned to the floor. Cal dashed towards the room.

"Cal!" yelled Woods starting to back away.

Within three strides, Cal had passed the doorway and, skidding to a halt in the middle of the room, he turned towards Woods who was still in the corridor outside.

"I'll slow it down!" he called, "Get everyone out!"

Without waiting for a reply, Cal lunged forward and swung the Arrivals Lounge door closed. The water behind him continued to gush in through the chute at the same rate but in the enclosed space it now appeared much louder than before.

Cal knew the act of closing the door was ultimately pointless; eventually the weight of water pressing against it would overwhelm it, and then there would be nothing to stop the inevitable drowning of the entire facility. In his mind he could almost see the moment of the door's failure and the volume of water that would suddenly be unleashed down the corridor. If Monica had called 'Breakthrough' then there was still a chance to save everyone, he just needed to delay the water.

Given that the water's path was inevitable, he realised that the actual problem to be solved was how to impede its exit speed. What had given him these rational thoughts during this stressful situation was more of a mystery to him.

Casting his eye over the room's contents his attention fell on the stacks of heavy packing cases. Within a minute he had lashed several of them together using electrical cable, and pushed them in front of the door. Standing in seawater that was already several inches deep, he turned on the spot and repeated the process, beginning to build a dam of packing cases; held to each other and to the room's steel-work by electrical cable.

A few minutes later the relentless flow of ice-cold water had filled the room up to his waist, making the construction of each layer harder than the last, and the simple act of breathing harder to achieve. The flow was showing no signs of slowing and Cal knew that soon he would run out of packing cases and the strength to lift and tie them; already his fingers were becoming numb and harder to control with any degree of dexterity.

He looked up at the point where the chute entered the room and could see that the water was no longer just entering through the metal tube, it was pouring in around the sides. In places the rock itself had been fractured away by the sheer pressure.

The room's lighting flickered. He'd grown so accustomed to the permanent artificial light below ground that it had almost become invisible to him. If the lighting were to fail, then he would be able to see and do nothing. Desperately fighting his own fatigue and the icy seawater that lapped around his chest, he swam to the other end of the room where several of the empty packing cases were bobbing on the chaotic choppy surface of the water.

He grabbed at a handle, forcing his fingers to close around it, then using his other arm he began to paddle himself slowly back towards the packing case dam. Behind him a cracking sound preceded the chute wall collapsing and a fresh wave of freezing water burst into the room. He saw the lights go out and, stealing a last, shaky, lungful of air, he felt the weight of water drag him under.

•

Marcus stared out of the car window at the lights speeding by in the dark tunnel. Even at this speed it was doubtful they would make it back to the Warren in time; there had been too many delays.

He became aware that he was still gripping the steering wheel tightly and relaxed his grip. Monkey reflexes, he told himself, holding onto the thing that had last provided control. The thought surprised him a little; he never used to have this much internal dialogue. But largely he had now grown used to his sharper senses. Purposefully, he removed his hands from the steering wheel and opened the car door.

"Time for some air," he exhaled.

He swung the door open, being careful not to hit the sides of the carriage walls, then stepped out onto the deck. He stretched his arms and arched his back, then instantly regretted it as a pulse of pain reminded him of his recent injuries.

"D'accord," came his passenger's voice from within the car.

Marcus looked down the length of the carriage at the other vehicles parked bumper-to-bumper within the Eurotunnel train carriage. Parallel fluorescent lights in the ceiling ran the full length of the carriage almost mirroring the tracks below the train. In the sickly glow of these lights, passengers had maps laid on the tops of their cars and were involved in heated debates over the best routes to take once they reached Britain. Marcus knew the discussions were futile, the approaching tsunami would make light work of the relatively shallow English Channel; in all likelihood the waves would wash over much of the south coast and run inland within a matter of minutes.

Marcus looked at his watch again and then stared out at the passing tunnel lights. Before leaving the Warren, Monica had told him that she'd arranged for this specific train to make an emergency stop, near Entrance One. Since the destruction of Samphire Cottage, the only way in or out of Monica's facility had been via Entrance One; an anonymous looking, but secure door situated within a spur off the Channel Tunnel.

Barely a month ago he'd helped Monica to encode a message to her husband. The message was hidden in plain sight as individual words within a video recording. Marcus idly wondered if Benton had ever succeeded in delivering it to the Node, as they had not received word from him in a long time. Among other things, the video had relayed *'House gone'* so that Douglas would know that the Arrivals Lounge and chute system were inactive. The portion of the message *'Entrance One still intact'* had been true at the time, but now he began to question that statement; Marcus knew that the train really should have stopped by now.

If the train reached the Dover port, then they would be just as dead as everyone else in this carriage when the tsunami hit. He turned away from the window. He'd have to stop the train himself, but recent events had forced him to improvise; they were in the wrong part of the train and he could no longer rely on the exit door that Monica had arranged.

He pulled something from his pocket that had the appearance of a blue asthma inhaler. He knew he had limited doses left, but also knew the fact might become irrelevant if he didn't act soon.

"Sabine?" he beckoned her out of the car, then inhaled a dose through his mouth.

She opened her door and walked around the car to join him, then she laid out a large map over the car's roof, so that they would not look out of place. It was actually a map of Paris, but people were not looking that closely.

"Problème?" she murmured while drawing her finger randomly over the map's roads, "Pourquoi le train ne s'arrête pas?"

Marcus could already begin to feel the effects of Woods' prescription. The French environment over the last few weeks had allowed him to listen to a broad spectrum of conversations. If he focussed hard enough, he knew he would be able to converse with her again. He studied her speech and the dose did the rest.

"Qu'est-ce qui se passe si vous push on le bouton d'arrêt emergency?" she mimed pressing her finger against a button, "Sera stop the train, ou simplement set off an alarm?"

Marcus was more adept at translating the words he heard, than in speaking them, but he replied in her language to the best of his ability.

"Yes, the button will simply set off an alarm," he nodded, "The train crew decide what to do after that. We have to get them to stop the train."

She understood, "But how do we do that?"

Even if the train stopped, Marcus knew that the external doors would remain locked. He looked around the carriage for any weaknesses he could exploit. Any plan he devised would result in them exiting through the weakest point of the train, preferably undetected. With that in mind he began his planning at the end result and worked backwards. In his present mental state, he found visualisation trivial and the components of a plan seemed to arrive without effort.

Sabine watched as he swiftly returned to the car, pulled some jump leads from the glove compartment and hid them under his jacket.

"Seriously?" she said in amazement, as he swept past her, "We're using that thing again?"

On the left and right sides, at the ends of each carriage, were narrow double doors with vertical slit windows. Once outside those doors, Marcus knew there was a small space before the identical looking doors to the next carriage. Use of these doors was not restricted, as they provided fire exits to other carriages.

Marcus punched the button to open the door and they both stepped into the slightly noisier and colder no man's land between carriages. When the doors had hissed shut behind them he took off his jacket and covered the light immediately to his left, limiting the illumination to whatever was coming in through the narrow carriage door windows behind them.

Taking advantage of the heavy cylindrical piece of iron in the middle of the jump leads, he swung it into his jacket and the glazed light behind it. With a muffled crunch, the glass shattered, exposing the light. After quickly shaking out the pieces of glass, he put on his jacket again.

"Remove the bulb," he told Sabine, then turned his attention to separating the jump leads. The black lead was merely folded, but the red lead was still wrapped in a tight helix around the iron, where he wanted it.

A few seconds later the tiny room descended into a gloom again as Sabine removed the light bulb. Beneath the light, Marcus located and removed its fuse and clipped the black jump lead grip onto one of the exposed electrical terminals. The red coloured grip he handed over to Sabine.

"When I say go," he pointed to the other exposed terminal, "attach that here."

He stood up and walked to the middle of the space between the carriages. He dropped into a squatting position with his feet either side of a completely featureless and slightly recessed floor panel. He carefully lowered the jump leads until the iron cylinder was positioned correctly, then looked up at Sabine.

"Go!"

She clipped the red jump lead onto the terminal. Immediately the improvised electromagnet in Marcus' hands hummed loudly and snapped itself onto the metal floor panel. Marcus pulled at the cylinder and the floor panel began to lever up. The light coming in through the narrow windows dimmed momentarily as the carriage's electrical system took up the new load, and the humming became louder.

Marcus adjusted his posture to account for the tilt of the floor plate as he continued to lever it open. He could feel the cable and the piece of iron heating up in his hands and was not sure which would give up first, his hands or the electrical system.

The floor panel opened another inch and cleared the surrounding recess. The noise from outside the train suddenly leaked into the cramped space and, as the difference in pressure equalised, they both felt their ears pop. Sabine scrambled over to the panel and thrust her fingers into the gap between the metal and the surrounding edge. The smell of warm plastic reached her at the same time as the hum became louder still. The lights dimmed again, but this time they stayed low.

Marcus knew the insulation on the jump leads would soon give way, the iron cylinder in his hand had heated up faster than he'd anticipated, but he knew that if he pulled up too fast then the electromagnet may slip. The plate would drop back into the recess after passing through Sabine's fingers.

"Pull!" he yelled.

Sabine manoeuvred herself into a kneeling position and pulled up on the open edge, speeding up the process and filling the space with the metallic squeal of train wheels on steel. With one hand still on the cylinder, Marcus reached forwards to the edge of the panel and held it. Sabine readjusted her hands to push up the floor plate and, with a last thrust, it levered completely open, sending Marcus tumbling backwards as he lost his grip on the cylinder.

With a deafening squeal, the train suddenly slowed and they could both see occasional sparks fly past through the hole in the floor.

"You did it!" Sabine grinned.

Marcus looked confused for a second before responding.

"That wasn't me," he said, "Opening the floor wouldn't stop the train. Someone else stopped it."

As the track racing by underneath them continued to slow, the humming of the electromagnet became louder. With no fuse to sever the link, the electrical system continued to supply more power to the coiled jump lead. The insulation finally melted, sending up curls of toxic white smoke then, as the exposed wires were almost touching the metal plate, the electricity arced in a brilliant bluish white flare. The electrical event triggered the carriage's master fuse and all the lights went out, leaving them in total darkness. The train lurched to a halt.

•

Standing at the highest point in the Warren, Monica knew that she was more than a hundred yards underground, but the tremors were getting worse. The lunar fragments had begun their assault and now the final one, Tranquillity, had set in motion a chain of tectonic shifts and tsunamis that were heading their way.

Before losing the external feeds from television stations, she had seen the scale of destruction already wracking the planet. The pictures had been relayed from Archive's drone-cameras, seeded into the air well in advance of the impact events. Before passing into obscurity, Monica thought, mankind was to be given front row seats to the end of the world.

Suddenly there was a silent sideways jolt which moved the entire space around her. Instinctively, Monica threw out her arm to stop herself impacting the rough walls and her hand caught the edge of a slight rusty sign. It was little more than a thin steel plate with the words 'Glaucus Dock' embossed on it, but it reminded her of the fact that she was approaching what Douglas would have called a 'convergence'; where all available decisions had to pass through a single point.

This section of tunnel represented that single point. For well over a decade she had hoped that the far end of the tunnel would remain closed, but it seemed she would have no choice.

The voice of Geraldine Mercer echoed along the tunnel behind her. Monica turned to see her squeezing her way past the people who were already noisily arranging themselves into a queue along the ragged walls. Arriving next to Monica, Geraldine stabbed a finger at the metal sign.

"I hate this tunnel. Really did not want to see it again."

Monica simply nodded, "Any word?"

"Marcus hasn't made it back yet, he was due at Entrance One, but…"

"I don't suppose we know if she was with him?" Monica frowned.

"We don't know. External communications and radio are down. Cal went to check it out."

Monica wanted to give Marcus more time to return, but she knew her window of opportunity was narrowing by the minute. Even if she assumed he had made it into the facility it would still take several minutes for him to ascend through the many narrow, sloping tunnels to reach them at the top.

She looked down at the photocopies of Sam Bishop's notebook in her hand. Over the past few months she had placed ticks next to several of the red-lined names, but she shook her head and murmured, "It's not enough."

"Sorry Mon, couldn't hear you?"

"Never mind. Is the Z-bank ready for transport?"

"Yes," Geraldine pointed at a now much bulkier flight case, "Woods is getting the counterparts."

"Come on, Marcus," Monica muttered under her breath, checking her watch.

"I don't want to question your judgement -" Geraldine started.

"Then don't - please - not now," Monica interrupted her, then raised her voice to talk to the others lined up along one side of the long, narrow passageway, "Is anyone unclear of their destination and rendezvous point?"

No-one replied but they turned to each other, checking for themselves that everyone knew where they were going. Despite being uninjured, many were wearing slings or had red-stained bandages tied around their limbs. Without exception, their clothes were in tatters and matted with a fine layer of chalk.

Geraldine tried to counsel her again, "It's just that Siva's still over a year away, why force this now?"

"I know the plan *was* to do this only if Siva made it to Earth, but the arrival of the fragments has taken that decision out of our hands. Our best course of action is to act now."

A rumble filled the space and for a second it seemed to Geraldine that the walls were channelling Monica's mental state.

"With so much tectonic activity and panic going on," Monica continued, "this is the perfect time to do it."

From somewhere deeper within the warren-like tunnels she felt a shockwave that she knew could not be linked to the tectonic events; it was a smaller, localised disturbance. Then she heard panicked voices from far below. Phasing in volume, due to the odd acoustics of the narrow tunnels, the sound was joined by another. It was a sound she was familiar with.

Many times she had sat with Douglas and Katie outside their cottage and just listened to the sound of the sea hissing on the rocks below the cliff. Back then, the sea had been further away and the sound had washed comfortably over them. There was nothing comforting about this new sound; she knew there was fast moving seawater within the facility.

Siva's approach was inevitable. Her sacrifices now suddenly appeared to amount to nothing. Archive had taken so much from her - her youth, her hope, her family, her life. But they had not taken her mind. She would bring chaos to their naively preserved and ordered system.

She flicked the safety cover off the trigger switch in her hand, then turned towards Geraldine and the others lining the rough walls. She set her face like flint and held the trigger aloft shouting:

"Breakthrough in Five... Four... Three..."

OFFSPRING

15th December 2013

The red line ruled through Monica's name and birth details stared up at Bradley and Alfred from the page of Sam Bishop's leather notebook. The two of them had not left Alfred's office since Bradley had revealed the existence of the 'Substandard' children.

"If you think 'bout it, it kinda makes sense," Bradley shook his head, "She always has this way o' finding out about stuff. Stuff she shouldn't know a damn thing about."

Alfred was still coming to terms with the new information and was temporarily unprepared.

"Presuming that the post-natal metathene actually had any effect at all on Monica," Alfred sat back down at the desk, "why would that translate into an ability to uncover information more easily? Merely having increased mental function couldn't give you that ability. We know that metathene, at least in our ego-morphs, enhances what's already there, but it can't give you something that you never had."

"No, but we know she's always had a knack of causing chaos" offered Bradley, "did it just make her better at it?"

The thought of Monica becoming better at causing chaos for Archive was not one that sat well with Alfred, but he realised there may be some truth in it.

"Maybe it's not chaos," he began, "Maybe what we're seeing as chaos is actually the result of her meticulous planning. The level of planning would need almost fractal branches of contingency..."

"Now don't that sound familiar?" said Bradley, pointing at Douglas Walker's red line, "But she ain't as bright as our Dougie."

"I'm not so sure," Alfred massaged his temples, "She may be every bit as intelligent as Doug; just in a different way."

Bradley was quietly nodding to himself, as though confirming an internal theory. He sat down next to Alfred.

"Then we got trouble, Freddy. All our ego-morphs are sterilised, right?"

"When they're confirmed into their roles, yes."

"It means they can't have kids with each other, right?"

"The Evolution Safeguard, we don't want to run the risk of introducing a species that would supersede our own."

"Doug and Monica ain't ego-morphs," said Bradley, pointedly, "but they had a kid. I'd say that safeguard just got busted."

Alfred began to see it more clearly now.

Kate Walker could, in theory, represent the first genetic offspring of a new evolutionary chain. Archive's routine background checks several years ago had revealed no indication that she may be different; but, back then, they hadn't been testing for this kind of divergence.

It was also possible that, similar to her father, there was some sort of dormant genetics at work that required activation.

Kate now warranted further biological study.

"We can't rush this," Alfred concluded, then realised he was only answering his own internal thoughts, "Bradley, we'll need to dig up information about the others on Bishop's list -"

"Diggin' is pretty much the family business," he cut in, "I already started, but it'll be a few days."

"OK, good. I'll work on the best way to achieve Kate's compliance," said Alfred, reaching for some paper, "It should be fairly straightforward, but it'll be important that she feels as though she's safe and secure. I take it that we still don't know where Monica is?"

"Nope, why? You lookin' for an angle?" Bradley peered over at Alfred's notes.

"Possibly. The Bergstrom woman, er…"

"Anna?"

"Yes, are Kate and Douglas still close to her?"

"Sure, I guess. Dougie and Anna were shacked up together for two years in the Mark 3 so they must've got pretty close; and Napier reckons Kate's never out of their sight."

"Hmm," Alfred scribbled notes, "possibly need to leverage maternal transference…"

Noticing that Alfred seemed preoccupied with his notes, Bradley absent-mindedly looked around the room. Although there were masses of books piled around the small space, there were very few actual possessions.

"D'ya ever wonder what went on inside the Mark 3?"

"They succeeded in calculating the Field inversion equations shortly before the power core overloaded," Alfred spoke without looking up from his note making, "I read the report."

"Just like you read the whole Siva file, huh?" Bradley waved Bishop's notebook poignantly.

At this point Alfred's interest was sufficiently piqued and he stopped writing, placing both his pen and glasses on the desk.

"They were both lucky to get out of the fire alive, what's your point?"

"Lucky. That's my point. They was inside that fancy bubble for nearly two damn years. But right after they figure out the math and the 'need' for them to pilot the Node, the fire destroys every last piece of the Mark 3. And they walk out without a scratch. Ain't nobody that lucky."

"You're suggesting they sabotaged the Mark 3?"

"Either it's another damn coincidence, or," Bradley held up Bishop's notebook, "they ain't tellin' us somethin'."

Alfred lapsed into momentary contemplation before replying.

"We can't touch Douglas. With Monica's status, er, unknown, it would be risky."

"You know what I think? I think I'd like to have a nice long catch-up with Anna Bergstrom about them Field equations," Bradley cracked his knuckles, "Then maybe we'll see exactly how indispensable the Walkers truly are."

Within the hour a transport plane had been arranged to remove Anna Bergstrom and her copy of the equations from the facilities at the Node.

Later, in the quiet of his now empty office, Alfred returned his thoughts to the matter of Exordi Nova's unauthorised recruitment drive. But no matter how hard he tried, he found himself continually distracted by the frightening thought of a new emergent species of human. Despite telling himself that it was normal to fear change, he could no longer focus. He knew that only one of these problems actually had a solution.

He re-filed the Exordi Nova report and returned his attention to Kate Walker and her chaos-causing mother.

DROP

In order to make the other end of a causal chain possible, it was again necessary to place the symbol on the periphery of conscious awareness.

It was about as close as she dared to intervene at this point, and it would be the last intervention she would make in this region until she was sure of a stable outcome.

She allowed the appropriate mass of water to condense on the surface of the rock, then allowed gravity and surface tension to draw it together into a single water drop.

THE INCIDENT

31st December 1999

Archive knew there would one day be the necessity to finally emerge from the Underground Survival Village under Dover, so the construction site for Glaucus Dock was situated at the very top of the facility for good reason. Like many of the developments here, it was another contingency.

If Siva ever succeeded in reaching Earth, then it was extremely likely that the current world map would need to be redrawn. Certain land masses would disappear and the oceans would re-flow accordingly. Should Britain ever sink beneath the waves, then the only method of departing from the submerged facility would be through the tonnes of water above it. Glaucus Dock was to become Archive's submarine port.

Though the various types of subs were still in development, they would all share a common element. Situated in the underside of the sub's pressure hull, would be an additional airlock that would allow it to interface with a facility-side docking ring.

Personnel could then transfer to and from the submarine in order to reach sea-level.

Monica was looking around the general state of construction when she felt a drop of water hit the top of her head. She knew that in places the rock was semi-permeable and occasional water drips were to be expected, but instinctively she looked up.

She saw that a wide circle, resembling an engagement ring, had been drawn on the rock. An 'x' marked the spot on the circumference where a diamond-tipped rotary cutting tool would begin its task. In a few years' time, this wide circle would become a reinforced vertical shaft that went all the way up to the surface, where an airlock and Glaucus docking ring would seal it. But if all went according to plan, she hoped never to see it.

Monica walked away from the circle, back along the corridor towards the top of some metallic stairs, where Geraldine Mercer was running a final check on a generator.

"All set?" Monica called, and heard her own voice ricochet off the nearby walls.

"Almost," Geraldine replied in a quieter voice. She tiptoed over to the stairwell and peered down, cautiously listening for anyone who may have heard them. But all she could hear was the distant repetitive pulse and laughter drifting up from the Millennium party far below.

Satisfied, she returned to Monica.

"OK," Geraldine began, "over the past few days we've been gradually moving the parts here for supposedly genuine reasons. Parts that don't have a reason to be here can be explained as 'in transit' to other locations. I've made sure the appropriate acquisition forms were signed in advance. Either way, any fragments they find during their inquiry will add back up to the picture they're expecting to see. It will be written off as a fault-line failure in the rock above that destroyed the generator and blasting equipment - not the other way around."

"Excellent," Monica looked around at her plan, now finally in practical form, "it's incredible work Geraldine, really."

"When they set off the midnight fireworks down there, I'll take it as my cue to trigger the detonations. Then I'll die," Geraldine drew a deep breath, "so to speak."

They looked down at the white plastic bags of medical waste, that had yet to be distributed. Filled with specific human body parts, taken from a Dover medical school, they would approximate her remains in the aftermath.

Monica took hold of her hand and, carefully moving past the generator, they walked down a long, rough-hewn narrow tunnel. About half way along, there was a small recess big enough to hold one person.

"Listen, this section is completely safe, Douglas has done the calculations himself," Monica reassured her, "just make sure you stand in that recess before you trigger it."

"I know. One door closes," Geraldine pointed back towards the generator, and then pivoted to face the other end of the narrow corridor, "and another door opens."

Monica squeezed her hand and guided her beyond a shiny metallic 'Glaucus Dock' wall sign, to arrive at the closed end of the tunnel. With her free hand, Monica patted the rock.

"This rock is only six inches thick. When it blows out, you'll literally walk straight into our own facility on the other side. It's all there waiting for you."

There was an awkward silence.

It came down to whether she trusted Monica. If Monica was lying about there being a facility on the other side of a small patch of rock then, by triggering the cave in, she would be sealing herself inside an airless concrete tomb. The body parts would convince everyone of her demise; no-one would even bother looking for her.

Monica could see that she was justifiably having second thoughts.

"We can still trigger it remotely," Monica hugged her tightly, "It's fine! I can't ask you to do this -"

"No, Mon," Geraldine interrupted, lightly pushing her away, "This is my 'out' from Archive."

Like Monica, Geraldine had reached the same conclusion long ago - if Archive somehow failed to stop Siva, then by the time it arrived in the vicinity of Earth, her age would disqualify her from being saved. It was not a future she was prepared to accept, so she had assisted the Walkers in the planning of Monica's parallel but smaller underground facility.

"We do this like we planned, Mon," Geraldine confirmed, "I'll be the one to create the door."

"In a few days I'll join you," said Monica, reiterating the plan "and we'll seal the breach from our side. Who knows? If they stop Siva, then hopefully we'll never have to consider Breakthrough Day at all."

"Believe me, Mon, the last thing that I'd want to do is break back into this place. But if we did, then you'll be needing my door."

"OK, so now it's 'My door' is it?" Monica teased her, "Listen, I want you to look after this."

Monica worked her engagement ring loose from her finger, it was fairly plain looking with a tiny diamond inset within it.

"It's my engagement ring, Geraldine, I'll -"

"No Monica, you can't -"

"I'll expect you to hand it back to me, unscathed, in a few days. OK?"

Hesitantly, Geraldine took the ring, she knew there was no point in arguing with her. Despite its simplicity, she knew Monica treasured it. For Geraldine, the fact that Monica was expecting it back, meant the facility on the other side of the rock absolutely existed.

•

There were certain types of music that Douglas could appreciate, mostly from a mathematical standpoint; he could see the merits of the almost fractal patterns that some records contained. But generally, he couldn't work out why people enjoyed gyrating in sync with the dominant rhythm, merely for the benefit of others. He hadn't paid too much attention to the DJ's announcement, but the current record frequently mentioned partying as though it was the last year of the twentieth century, which seemed apt tonight.

"Come on Doug!" someone tried to cajole him into joining them on the small disco dance floor, "Let your hair down!"

Douglas had his props prepared for this particular eventuality; he raised both hands slightly, each was holding a full glass of champagne. He smiled and mouthed the word 'sorry' with an apologetic looking shrug.

Socially, Douglas had always been awkward, so to be spending New Millennium's Eve deep inside Archive's subterranean UK facility with work colleagues, in a party environment, was more simultaneous variables than he could comfortably handle.

Douglas had always marvelled at the ease with which Monica adapted to social situations; in a populated room of social variables he could always depend on her to be his constant. So it didn't help matters that, as part of their plans, she would necessarily have to be absent for a short time.

He turned his eyes away from the party's glare and looked out into the vast darkness surrounding the celebration. The Underground Survival Village was nowhere near finished, but the main excavations were complete. In the seven years since the Channel Tunnel's completion, progress had been astounding. Under normal circumstances work was a continuous twenty-four-hour operation, but tonight construction had been halted. Even the working lights had been fitted with tinted glass; colourful dust-filled beams leapt from the floor to spray the roughly dome-shaped roof with iridescent oval patches of light.

But the fan of light-beams still struck Douglas as something of a peacock display; an attempt to dominate the very centre of the massive cavern with a show of noise and colour. The fact was that the bombastic music was quickly lost in the vastness of the space, its echo returning as indistinct whispers. Here on the periphery, only a few feet from the enthusiastic dancers, he could feel his own body heat being leached away by the imposing environment. He suppressed a shudder as he recalled that one day, this whole disco area would be an artificial subterranean lake.

The needle on the record skipped, causing him to look back in the direction of the dance floor. He saw Monica walking across the floor, joining in with the round of derisive applause for the clumsy DJ. His sense of relief at her return was immense. She effortlessly moved on through the small crowd, making brief small-talk as she went, until she arrived in front of him.

"How's work?" he asked her, offering her one of the champagne glasses.

She took the glass and drank two-thirds of it before replying.

"Geraldine says she'll be - late," she chose her words carefully and raised her hand to drink from the glass again.

Douglas noticed a bare patch of skin on her ring finger.

"No ring, Monny? Should I be worried?"

She just shook her head, "Tell you later."

The mood on the dance floor shifted slightly; although the laughter continued, the quality had altered.

"Great that's all we need," Douglas' shoulders sagged slightly.

Monica casually turned to see Robert Wild moving towards them, glass of champagne in hand, greeting people cheerfully along the way. His eyes darted swiftly between faces, perhaps a little too swiftly.

"Is he...?" Douglas asked Monica.

"Flying high?" she completed, "Difficult to tell."

From what Douglas had heard, over the past ten years, Robert had found it a natural progression from suppressing the information in the news, to suppressing Archive's activities in general. He now had a dedicated team of support staff that he referred to as his 'Storykillers'.

Douglas took Monica's glass and then placed both of their glasses on a nearby table. By the time he'd turned back, Monica had taken control of the conversation with her opening greeting.

"So it seems you've been busy, Wild," she tapped playfully at a small triangular yellow badge on his lapel.

"The Millennium Bug?" he grinned, "One of my favourites, got to say! Quite the opportunity!"

The '*Y2K problem*' as it had become known, had arisen because in the early days of programming, four-digit years were represented using only the last two digits. Archive had discovered that several computer systems worldwide would fail when the year rolled over from 99 to 00. The affected systems would interpret the date as 1900. Several security systems would interpret the addition of negative time as an intrusion attack and react with appropriate countermeasures.

Robert Wild had capitalised on the event though. Realising that a far larger number of civilian systems would be equally affected, he publicised the Millennium Bug. He also publicised the fact that there was a piece of software that could check for the vulnerability. The software, supplied on bright yellow coaster-like floppy disks, was sold to the public by the millions.

In addition to checking for the Y2K problem, the Archive-created software also deposited a new vulnerability on the host computer; one that allowed Archive to eavesdrop on digital traffic. The percentage of computers that Archive had been able to infiltrate had been modest, but it had paved the way for the time ahead.

"Love them or hate them," said Douglas with a shrug, "computers are here to stay."

"Oh, I love computers!" Robert pulled out his mobile phone, sliding out the miniature keyboard to show them, "haven't clue how they work, but they inspire such techno-lust in people, and that's great for me. Really odd. These things are dumber than the people using them, present company excepted of course, but with one of these jumped-up calculators in their pockets, people think they're Flash Rodgers or something. Speaking of…"

Robert turned in the direction of the Archive party photographer, who had been busy taking flash photos during the evening.

Standing between the two men, Monica felt her husband's arm wrap around her to place his hand on her waist. A second later she felt Robert's hand cup her bottom.

"Say cheese!" Robert grinned.

Monica forced herself not to react and smiled politely as the flash went off. The photographer moved away and she turned to face Robert, which had the effect of subtly disconnecting his unsubtle advance. Robert didn't even seem to notice though, he was already on another train of thought.

"And don't get me started on photography!" he revelled, taking a mouthful of champagne.

"We wouldn't dream of it," said Douglas, glancing at his watch.

Robert either didn't hear, or didn't care, and he beckoned them closer as though to take them into his confidence.

"We're looking at ways of making cameras 'digital', you know, like not on film. Problem is we take so many damn photos. Research, development, doctored images, even crime scenes and mugshots. Do you know how many man-hours Archive wastes just developing photos? Once we're done with that, if another division needs a look then we need to courier the negs and photos. And have you any clue how much space it takes just to hold all of that when we're done analysing them?"

He took another large gulp of champagne and drew them in again.

"All very hush-hush. In a couple of years we're gonna push this out to the consumer market. Picture this - ha!" he laughed at his own joke, "Picture this, a pocket sized *digital* photo gadget. Make it cheap enough and they're gonna lap it up! Wanna know the best part? Eventually, when we put it together with mobile phone position triangulation, we'll be able to see everything."

Monica could see the appeal it would hold for men like Robert and his staff, whose job relied on the swift gathering of information; but the idea that Archive would suddenly be able to access so much information alarmed her. The very thought of a Storykiller ever investigating any member of her family put her nerves on edge.

"The irony of it," he laughed, "People buying and carrying *two* pocket-sized instruments that record everything for us! Maybe I need to start pushing a trend for trousers with more pockets," he seemed to lapse into a side thought.

"You're good at persuasion, Wild," Monica said dryly, "maybe you could persuade people to glue their digital cameras to the side of their mobile phones!"

He laughed at the thought, miming the bulky end result. Then his expression changed as though an idea had formed, and his laughter stalled slightly.

"Well, if you'll excuse me, I'm off to find a hot blonde who wants to play the Wild Card," he grinned and tipped the remainder of his champagne down his throat, "And maybe offer a late-night refill…"

With a knowing wink, he slid away.

"Wild card…" muttered Douglas, "more like Ace-hole…"

The comment caught her off guard and she almost choked on her champagne, before laughing out loud. Most people never saw that side of him, pigeon-holing him as eccentric and disconnected, but on a day like today she was grateful for his precisely delivered wit.

"Everything's going to change," said Monica, looking out at the those who were wholeheartedly dancing to Archive's supplied rhythm; caught in the moment and celebrating their own future salvation, "Did we make the right choice, not to tell Katie?"

"It's why we're doing all this," he said, putting his arm around her waist again, "we're doing it to keep her safe."

"If she knows nothing, then at least she'll be safe from Wild and his men."

"We can hope," he said giving her a light squeeze, "but while we're hoping, we just keep track of the variables."

She had always admired his unique way of bringing order to the chaos that surrounded them every day; provided he could see all the variables, he always seemed able to navigate the multiple branching future possibilities and plot the most appropriate course when the time came. She turned away from the dance floor to face him.

"You know there's no going back," she put her arms around him "once we take this - branch."

"We haven't been able to go back for several years," Douglas gave a tight lipped smile.

She knew it was true. Every decision, every act of preparation or misdirection, had led them inexorably to this moment. To stop now would reveal too much of their subterfuge and invite swift retribution. The only open paths lay ahead, however treacherous they may turn out to be. He leaned in a little closer.

"After tonight, they'll be watching us even more closely. In case I don't have chance to tell you later," Douglas lowered his head to whisper into her ear, "I C U Monica, and I love you."

"I C U too," she whispered back and then tenderly pressed her lips against his.

For one perfect moment they occupied their own private universe, away from the surrounding distraction. For one crystal clear instant, time was immaterial and could not touch them. Then the delicate envelope began to erode, as the physical world began to intrude on them once more. They both smiled, studying each other's youthful eyes, as they drew apart. They emerged in the middle of the DJ's countdown to the New Year and, forcing their smiles wider, they joined in with everyone else.

"... Five... Four... Three..."

BREAKTHROUGH

29th December 2013

"...Two...One..." Monica pushed the button.

The small patch of rock she had sealed up almost 14 years ago disintegrated in a solid sounding concussion. The steel shield plate she had placed at the end of the tunnel absorbed the blast, then toppled to the floor exposing a ragged-looking hole between the Warren and the Archive facility beyond.

"Well my door's still there," Geraldine appeared at her side and helped her to drag the shield plate to the side of the tunnel.

"Again with the 'my door' thing..." replied Monica, dropping the steel and turning to face the hole.

In 1999, the area beyond the hole had been a long corridor, at the end of which a generator had been detonated to cause a minor cave in. After an inquiry, headed by Monica, all evidence had pointed to an instability in the rock. Excavations in that direction had ceased overnight, and the Warren had escaped detection.

Monica could see that all signs of any explosion had long since disappeared. The area at the top of the stairs had been repaired, and beyond it she could see the completed Glaucus Dock. She could also see extra doorways that were not marked on her, obviously obsolete, plans.

"Your door," Monica offered Geraldine the chance to go first.

"My door," she flashed a smile at Monica, then stepped through.

There was a rumble from below and Monica turned to aim her voice back down the corridor into the Warren.

"All teams. Move out!"

She turned and carefully stepped through the circular hole, placing one foot down inside Archive's completed facility. In the space between her two worlds she took a breath. Then, making sure she felt the very last moment of contact, she raised the other foot and left the Warren behind.

CORIOLIS EFFECT

25th December 2013

Eva felt the whole Drum shake violently as Chamber 6 explosively decompressed.

A few of the meagre Christmas decorations fell down in protest at the disturbance, but the integrity of the station held. The crew ID keys had allowed her to transfer Floyd's operation inside the Drum, so her plan was still intact.

"Goodbye Leonard," she said.

Of all the crew, she felt sure that Leonard had not been a part of the FLC computer's sabotage, but now she would never know for certain.

It had been a combination of Leonard's words and her own personal beliefs that had formed the basis of her mantra; one that she had taken to reciting privately during her preparations. In conjunction with the high doses of metathene, the mantra had helped her retain focus during stressful times.

An hour ago she had assumed control of the FLC by using the crew ID keys. She had quickly uncovered the sabotage of Floyd's core programming, but after several attempts to correct the errant code she realised it was futile. As fast as she could correct the targeting algorithms, the system would reinstate them.

The containment spiral beams that surrounded the main sublimator beam had been instructed to gradually widen. When the beam next fired in 2014, the FLC would register a full power transfer aimed at Siva, but the actual power reaching its surface would slowly decrease to nothing.

With Siva undeflected, it would go on to impact Earth.

Her rising suspicions, many months ago, had caused her to increase her metathene dosage. It sharpened her observations and allowed to her to find other evidence of tampering within Floyd's system records. Individually the errors had not raised alarms but when seen collectively, her conclusion was clear. Someone had orchestrated this, with the deliberate intent of wiping the Earth clean.

During her investigations, she had been plagued by a recurring dream of an unstoppable Siva ploughing through Earth's atmosphere. The Debris Cascade Protection devices in orbit would fire, putting on little more than a firework show, then the inevitable impact would snap her awake.

Ten months ago the FLC crew had witnessed, by video relay, the moment of Tenca's arrival. The DCP network had performed admirably; the short range, shaped charges had effectively put a fire-break in orbit and prevented satellite debris from spreading. The DCP network wasn't designed to stop Tenca, just to stop the spread of damage.

Several weeks later, her recurring dream changed.

Where the inspiration came from she couldn't be sure, but it was persistent.

From a privileged position, viewing both the Earth and the Moon, she would watch as Siva shot past the Moon, heading straight towards Earth. Then, just before the moment of Siva's impact, the vision would stop and reverse. She would watch Siva suddenly track back along its approach trajectory, and return beyond the Moon. The vision would then replay, but just as Siva was approaching again, the Moon itself detonated. She would see the Earth's natural satellite splinter into fragments. Seven of these fragments hurtled towards Earth, but a far greater number continued to spread out in both directions away from the lunar centre of gravity, along the Moon's orbital path. In her accelerated perception of events, she watched as the lunar fragments continued to spread out, creating an orbital field of debris. Then Siva arrived once more, but instead of shooting past the Moon, it impacted the vast field of continent-sized lunar fragments and was obliterated before it could reach Earth.

In her waking hours, Eva had begun to consider the horrific impact that the lunar fragments would have on Earth's population. But with the FLC compromised, and spurred on by her new recurring dream, she began re-studying her geological lunar survey data.

Underlying the FLC's Coriolis crater were massive, branching, tree-like fissures that ran deep into the mantle. Although fissures and fault lines were not unusual, the massive scale and structure of the weaknesses beneath the FLC defied all rational explanation.

It appeared that Archive had chosen to build the FLC directly above this geological flaw. Except, Eva knew there was a severe problem with that assumption; before embarking on the Apollo program, Archive could not have known of the flaw's existence.

She had examined the possibility that it was a coincidence. But the probability of such a specific and vast flaw occurring precisely under the FLC's location, was infinitesimal.

The recurring dream had persisted and, perhaps fuelled by the increased metathene in her blood, she found herself exploring an alternative, more chilling explanation. If the FLC had not been intentionally placed above the flaw, then perhaps it was the flaw itself that had been placed.

She knew that the geological processes required to achieve this exact result must have begun a very long time ago.

Long before Archive had chosen to act for the good of mankind.

Long before there had even been a mankind.

Mentally, she had repeatedly searched for other more plausible reasons for the FLC to be sited in this exact location, but could find none. Sometimes she would lose track of time just staring at the plan view of the Moon's equator; its perfect circle, broken in one place by the dot of the FLC's location.

With each new repetition of her dream, the details would become more vivid. Coupled with the geological evidence, she could not shake the feeling that it would be her own future actions that would lead to the detonation of the Moon.

The impact of lunar fragments would trigger the deaths of billions, but an impact from Siva would mean extinction.

The cold numbers justified her choice.

The work she had begun with her father must now be turned against itself.

Her father's burning ambition, born in the fires of the old NASA enthusiasm, had been to provide a lunar stepping stone. Free from Siva's dominance, the construction of Lunar Colony 1 was to have united a newly optimistic mankind and given birth to a renewed curiosity for space exploration. Lunar Colony 1 was to have been the secure footing from which the human race would leap to the stars.

Sacrificing the opportunity to have her own children, she had once persuaded herself that by helping to deflect Siva, she was instead birthing a renewed mankind. Her dreams and those of her father would die here today. Earth's future children would never venture onward from this lunar surface.

Long ago she had made the promise that her actions would be 'For the good of Mankind'. Her promise was still true now, but the scope was suddenly much, much larger.

Turning her attention to the cold details of what must be accomplished, she had discovered that she could not alter the intended confinement parameters of the 2014 firing beam. However, Floyd had no issues with her reprogramming the maintenance mode of the optics within the prism directly above her. With the permission of all five crew ID keys it also allowed her to begin the beam charging routine.

Then all she had to do was wait.

As she sat in the quiet of the Drum at the centre of the FLC, she ran through the calculations in her head again, but she found it difficult. She could tell that the final dose of metathene was starting to wear off; she could feel stray thoughts beginning to intrude within her ordered mind.

She reflected on the fact that no one would understand the motivation for her actions, yet. She also had no guarantee that the Siva-destroying result would necessarily follow from her actions. She began to doubt herself and the visions she had seen, but suddenly the moment arrived.

A tone sounded on Floyd's console indicating that charging was complete. She only had to press the button, and Floyd would carry out the remainder of her plan.

Her eyes began to fill up, and she realised that the cold guiding hand of her Christmas Eve dose must have already left her. In its place were only exposed, raw emotions.

She knew it was her decision, and hers alone. Her next action would mean the deaths of billions, but she knew it was the only way she could give the human race a fighting chance for survival, a chance to begin again.

She wept bitterly, knowing that she would be forever branded a traitor to her own planet. A dim echo of her former ego reminded her that it was humanity's long biological chain trying to appeal to her vanity; desperate to force her into making a choice that might result in self-preservation.

As the tears began to blur her sight, she knew she would have to act quickly to override her own primitive instincts.

She slammed the button, and let herself fall to the floor.

"I am Eve," she wept, beginning to recite her private mantra aloud.

The beams fired and combined within the prism above the Drum.

"I will birth the new mankind," she sobbed, curling herself up into a ball; the words that had given her solace were now no longer true.

As she had instructed, Floyd focussed the beams away from the black sky above, and downwards through the Drum itself. Immediately, the metal above her head began to vaporise.

"Born in the fires of the old," she whispered now, "they will renew the Earth."

The beam penetrated the Drum, and travelled towards her at the speed of light.

In the instant transition she felt no pain.

In a white hot flash of light, her atoms united with those of the beam as it burned downwards.

EVAC

25th December 2013

Although the news of the lunar fragments was under an hour old, the evacuation of Andersen Air Force Base had been ordered as a precaution. Its location in the Pacific, being a bare thousand miles from the equator, put it at risk from potential tsunamis should an impact occur nearby.

Every serviceman on the island was deployed to strip the base of its most valuable assets. The basement levels had already been cleared of equipment deemed useful and mobile, leaving behind a maze of partially empty briefing rooms; each one a peculiar cross section of historical technology.

In the middle of the tiny room, Dr. Patil's portable comm link unit sat on a thin-legged mess hall table, already littered with printed satellite diagrams. The shadeless, ageing desk lamp on the table illuminated the diagrams with an incandescent yellow glow, while overhead the ceiling's fluorescent lighting did its best to subtract the warmth.

"The fragments are definitely going to impact, Dad," Sarah Pittman's voice came over the link, *"we still can't pinpoint*

exact impact locations, but they're on their way. General Napier has authorised the use of the Archive servers to run the impact projection simulation. With that many Shen500's it won't take long. I'll keep you posted."

The ceiling shook slightly with the continuous pounding of servicemen running and labouring to clear the floor above.

"We're approaching the Ant Farm now, so I'd better wrap this up. Sorry I couldn't get to Colorado, there just wasn't time."

"You stay safe now, Pumpkin-pie," Bradley replied.

"We'll be fine, Dad," came her reply, *"it's you guys that I'm worried about."*

"Keep us advised," said Napier, "Out."

He punched the disconnect button and, ignoring Bradley's mild look of resentment at having his conversation terminated, he turned to Dr. Patil.

"Chandra, can we use the DCP network in orbit against the lunar fragments?"

Chandra shook his head before replying.

"The Debris Cascade Protection was only ever designed to protect against the spread of satellite debris when Tenca pushed through, back in February."

"So their shaped explosives are completely depleted?" Napier persisted.

"No, we're still at about eighty percent capacity, but against the fragments it would just be a firework display. General, I'd recommend using them for their original purpose. We may buy a few extra hours of satellite communication time by stopping the spread of the debris."

"Hours?" Bradley checked.

Chandra nodded, "Once the impacts start, we think we'll lose global satellite comms within a few days."

"Terrestrial communications?" Napier followed up immediately.

"Not much better," Chandra rubbed at his eyes, "we would be left with point-to-point microwave transmission, line of sight radio, possibly even ground-based cable if the tectonics hold out but, well, it's not looking good."

"Cellphone networks?" Alfred asked.

"Possible, but they're too insecure," he replied, "anyone could listen in."

"By the time we'd need to use it, that wouldn't matter," Alfred shrugged.

Chandra glanced over at General Napier for confirmation.

"Fine, I want the capability to take control of the entire civilian phone network if we have to."

With a nod, Chandra gathered up his various pages and the portable comm link. He squeezed between the chairs and the bare, grey, breeze-block walls, then departed leaving the three of them at the table.

Bradley looked over at Alfred, who then cleared his throat.

"How's the Node preparation going?"

"We're shipping supplies and personnel like there's no..." Napier faltered, "at a hundred times the rate. Two of our aircraft were taken down by the Node's defence system.

Traffic was too high and they were misidentified. We've taken the ground-to-air defence stations off-line temporarily."

"Makes sense," Bradley mumbled.

"And the Walkers?" Alfred feigned mild interest.

"You know, despite everything we've put him through," Napier stared hard at Bradley, "Doug's still engaged in the work, and Kate's sleeping off Bergstrom's isotope. Speaking of which, did you get anything from your interrogation of Anna?"

"The Mark 3 fire? Yeah, Anna..." Bradley searched for a word to soften the description of the torture she had endured during her interrogation, "admitted... that she kick-started the electrical overload. They waited it out with oh-two masks in the airlock. She knew when the Field went down, the air rushin' in would burn it to the ground, and take the evidence with it."

"As you suspected," continued Alfred, "she's now confirmed that the Chronomagnetic Field can be set up to run without intervention. The only reason you'd need either Douglas or Anna aboard the Node is if you needed to change the Field's operation after departure. In theory, once the duration of the trip is set, the Field can run unmanned."

The noise from the feet rushing around above them seemed to be subsiding, though there were still muffled commands being called out.

"Douglas actually lied," Napier shook his head in wonder.

"No, Anna lied for him. Anyway, doesn't matter now, Chen took her and Benton back to the Node last night on his personal jet," said Alfred, then added with a shrug, "She'll be more use to us in Iceland than here in the middle of the Pacific."

"She's gonna be scared of puttin' a foot wrong now," Bradley added with an air of satisfaction, "with that ego-morph breathin' down her neck."

There was a dull thud from above them, as though something heavy had been dropped, followed by more muted shouts. The single fluorescent light tube in the ceiling flickered briefly then died. To redistribute the light in the room more evenly, Napier pushed the desk lamp away from the edge and towards the table's centre.

"So in theory," Napier summarised, "Bergstrom's knowledge means we're no longer dependent on Walker or his troublesome wife?"

"In theory," replied Alfred.

Napier's posture visibly relaxed.

"How long have we waited for the day when we could act against that blackmailing, interfering Walker woman?" Napier threw an exasperated smile in Bradley's direction, "and it happens on the day that the sky falls in!"

It was then that he saw that Bradley was not sharing his sense of irony at the situation; in fact, the only thing he was sharing was an awkward glance in Alfred's direction.

"What?" Napier demanded.

"The Evolution Safeguard," Bradley leaned towards the light, which had the effect of throwing an over-sized shadow onto the wall behind him, "We got a problem."

While the indistinct sounds above them gradually dwindled into silence, Napier listened as Bradley and Alfred outlined the discovery and the consequences of Sam Bishop's notebook.

Bradley's own investigation into the twenty-three, red-lined names had uncovered that almost all of them had proceeded to have families of their own; who had then also had families. With the exception of Douglas and Monica, it appeared that none of the original twenty-three had interbred, but it had proved impossible to check the statistics for the generations that had followed.

"But Kate has shown no signs of being more intelligent," said Napier bluntly, "despite having two parents that carry the activated gene."

"Kate carries *both* copies of her parents' altered gene," Alfred continued, "but she's never been exposed to metathene. I suspect there's some gene activation effect that needs to occur, but I don't know for sure. That's why we've got to run extensive tests on her."

Napier considered the details for a moment. Once again the Walker family had resources or skills that continued to complicate matters; but Kate Walker definitely warranted further investigation.

"Can you do the tests while we're all inside the Node?" said Napier.

"If all the intended lab equipment arrives there in time," Alfred replied cautiously.

"Fine, do it," Napier concluded, "but to say this will need careful handling is an understatement."

"Given your history with Dr. Walker," Alfred looked between the other two men, "Maybe I should handle the affair? They don't know me."

Napier nodded then, after checking his watch, turned to Bradley.

"OK, can you quickly bring me up to speed on our progress with populating the bunkers and Underground Survival Villages? Last time I checked we were at eleven percent capacity, but food and resources for more than twice that. Where are we now?"

Bradley smiled and leaned back in the small seat causing it to creak slightly. He drew a deep breath and then laid his hands on the table.

"Well now, here's the thing. Alexey an' me have been talkin' things over and we reckon that we're not gonna take on any more paying guests."

Alfred laughed and shook his head, glad for a little light relief.

"It's been a long day Bradley," Napier smiled resignedly, "so can we cut out the jokes? What percentage will be filled by the time the first lunar shard hits?"

"I weren't joking, Dylan," Bradley's smile weakened slightly, but his eyes had never looked away from General Napier, "Alexey an' me reckon it's too big a risk."

The small, cold room fell quiet. The absence of distant, muffled personnel noise was suddenly apparent.

"Explain," Napier returned Bradley's stare, "Fast."

"All our folks are safe General, so don't go getting your -"

"Explain better," Napier cut across him.

"You want it better, OK then, try this," Bradley slapped his hands on the table, "The bunkers? The USV's? They only work if we fill 'em slowly. If we fill 'em too fast, ordinary folk see what's going down and they panic. It was tough enough when we thought we had a year left, but now we got days! I'm tellin' ya, if we keep the doors open any longer, they ain't gonna shut again. Trust me, even as the last lunar rock comes screamin' through the sky, there'll always be *'just one more person'* trying to get in. And that'll kill everybody."

Napier could scarcely believe what was now being proposed. He knew that in his time he'd had to make questionable choices, but it had always been in service of the greater objective.

"Archive has a duty," Napier stood, "to use the assets that are available to us now. We may not have foreseen it, but we must use our resources to our tactical advantage."

"Glad you agree," Bradley shot back.

"You know damn well that's not what I mean!" Napier thumped the table, "The very name 'Archive' was chosen because we were tasked with creating a living archive for the human race. Our purpose is to preserve whatever life we can!"

"Our purpose *was* to preserve it," interrupted Bradley, "But Eva Gray kind o' fucked that up, big time, didn't she?"

"It's not your decision to make, the discussion is closed," said Napier, calmly standing and drawing himself up to his full height, "The doors stay open. We do this for the good of mankind. We always have. We always will."

Bradley stood up, to match Napier's height.

"No," he sighed and withdrew a small, single-shot pistol from his pocket.

Despite not being the target, Alfred found his feet and clattered backwards through the other chairs to the opposite corner of the small room.

"I've been threatened before," Napier stood his ground, "by greater men than you, Pittman."

"This ain't a threat."

Bradley extended his arm and discharged the pistol into Napier's stomach. As Napier collapsed to the floor, clutching at his bright red midriff, Bradley turned towards an alarmed looking Alfred.

"Desperate times, Freddy," Bradley lowered his pistol, "This here's the end of days, we gotta stop the Lifeboat from getting overrun, right?"

In that moment Alfred realised that Bradley was actually seeking approval for his actions; which meant that, on some level, Bradley still saw him as an equal or as an authority figure. To reinforce this view, he knew he'd need to reflect support for Bradley's actions and also absolve him of responsibility.

"For the good of Mankind," Alfred nodded, sincerely.

CHECK

21st December 2012

The FLC's perfect second firing on Siva had finished an hour ago, and Dr. Chen had been requested to join a video conference call. He could see Bradley Pittman, Alexey Yakovna and General Napier sitting around a speakerphone and they could see him via his own webcam. Alfred Barnes was only present in audio, his voice coming from a tinny speakerphone.

"Unfortunately, yes," he continued, *"The Captain has to lie in order to save the few; just as we must decide who will be saved."*

"And who's gonna die..." completed Bradley.

As Dr. Chen looked at the image on his video monitor, eye-motion tracking software remotely panned the camera to focus on the person who was speaking. Bradley seemed to be working out the survival facts for the first time. Dr. Chen decided to adopt the same concerned expression, as Alfred continued.

"In this scenario the Captain also lied about one more thing. There is no Lifeboat."

On that sombre note, the video conference was brought to a close and Dr. Chen closed the video link. It had been an exhausting day but despite this, he rolled his wheelchair through to briefly talk with Fai.

He could see that Fai's computer screen was displaying a chessboard. He pushed his wheelchair closer to the screen to get a better view; most of the white pieces were now missing.

"Fai?" Dr. Chen asked.

"Yes, Father?"

"Did you relay my instructions to your brother?"

"Yes, Father," replied Fai, "I told him three times."

"And did he understand?"

"Yes, and," said Fai, anticipating her father's next question, "he also understands that it must be our secret."

"Good. Did anyone hear you tell him?"

"No, Father. I was very quick."

Dr. Chen smiled, "It will soon be time for me to sleep, Fai."

"May I finish my game, Father?"

"Of course. When you are finished please can you turn off the lights?"

"Yes, Father, I won't be long."

"So I see," he nodded, studying the chessboard in mild interest, "who is your opponent?"

"A human," Fai replied, "I learn a lot from their responses."

"Very good. Goodnight Fai," Dr. Chen smiled and wheeled himself away.

Fai remotely opened the bedroom door for her father and then set the electronic temperature controls to allow him to sleep comfortably. Simultaneously, she updated her father's schedule for the following day and calculated the possible 'checkmate' outcomes from her current game. She then spoke quietly through her numerous speakers placed throughout the aircraft:

"We'll speak again."

RESOURCES

28th December 2013, 1 p.m.

Douglas did his best to subdue the emotions he was feeling in the light of the simulation results. What mattered now was keeping a clear head so that he could make accurate decisions. He emptied Kate's chocolate rations into his rucksack, along with his other essentials from Hab 1, then slammed the door behind him.

Immediately after the Mark 2 Field had deactivated and he had reviewed the simulation results, he had come across a communication on Napier's computer that had arrived days before. Far from saving her, he knew that by putting Kate aboard the Node she may now be in more danger.

The information on Napier's computer had given Douglas two problems to solve; the first was how to deal with the simulation results, and the second was how to deal with the consequences of a worrying communication sent by Napier.

He estimated he would need three days to solve the issues and convert them into a form that he could visually transmit to Kate. The destructive effects of the lunar fragments would arrive at the Node within twenty-three hours, so it left him with no alternative but to use the Mark 2 chamber again; this time with him inside it. Time outside would still progress in his absence but, by his calculation, he'd only be gone for just over an hour. The chocolate rations alone would not be enough, he needed to find basic supplies.

With a new sense of resolve, Douglas marched on towards Napier's office and kicked the door open. He yanked open the printer paper-drawer and transferred the blank paper to his rucksack. He threw Napier's high-backed leather chair out of the way with such force that it toppled over, then he grabbed all the pens from the desk and turned to face the room.

Since Napier's departure, this room had remained locked until the power failure had given him access. Any resources within this room would not have been accessible to the base personnel during the evacuation procedure. Given Napier's privileged position here, Douglas was sure there would be a private collection of rations in this room. A few moments of searching confirmed his suspicions when he found a box file on a shelf. It contained four sealed bottles of spring-water and several foil packets of various foods; evidently the ones Napier found least palatable, but Douglas was desperate and loaded everything into the backpack before leaving.

He was marching back in the direction of the Mark 2 when he heard the same slow, repetitive chant he had heard earlier, carried on the bitter wind. With curiosity he turned back and walked towards 'MARK IV' dedication stone near the former bridge's entryway. The smoke had now disappeared and Douglas could clearly see the bridge wreckage clinging to the island and, across a gap of more than thirty yards, the twisted metal still gripping the opposite shore. He could now also see the source of the chanting.

On the opposite bank, hundreds of people appeared to be pulling in unison to a steady rhythmic vocal pulse. Far from being the ritual he had previously assumed, this was a construction.

LAST TRAIN

29th December 2013

The construction of the Eurotunnel interior was a prime example of function dominating form. It would never be studied for artistic nuance; every piece of the circular sectioned structure had a purpose. Right now its purpose was to sit passively around the Eurotunnel train that had been brought to a sudden stop a few minutes ago.

The tunnel lacked any convenient recesses to hide within so, after Marcus and Sabine had climbed out through their improvised exit, they had been forced to wait underneath the train itself. Only when they were sure that the train was about to resume its doomed journey would they make their move.

Marcus studied the small numbers cast into the concrete of the tunnel a few feet away. Still speaking his newly reacquired French, he turned to Sabine.

"We're directly under Dover," he whispered, "but we've passed Entrance One."

"Can we run back?" she asked.

He considered the numbers again, looked at his watch and then winced.

"I don't think so."

The sound of voices echoing within the wide tunnel silenced them. There was structure to the voices, thought Marcus, a chain of command at work.

The train had come to rest on a very slight bend in the tunnel. The curvature allowed him to see the activity that was going on at the far end of the train. He could see men moving around it. Some appeared to be uncoupling both the locomotive unit and last carriage from the main body of the train; other men were gathered by the track itself, conducting some sort of operation on the tunnel floor.

He suddenly realised who had stopped the train and why it had stopped here. It was the wrong entrance, he thought, but as a solution it was better than none.

"Sabine?" he whispered, and jerked his head towards the opposite side of the train, where he knew no-one would be able to see them.

They crawled out from under the wheels and began to make their way along the outer length of the train, keeping low and quiet within the echo-amplifying space. Every few yards they looked under the train to double check that no-one was looking for stray passengers, but the men appeared to be focussing their entire effort on one activity.

Suddenly they heard movement on the track ahead of them, so they crouched and remained motionless. A man appeared to be inspecting the track on the opposite side to the other men. He bent down, appeared to pull up a handle in the ground then shouted 'clear' and walked between the decoupled trains to join the others.

Marcus beckoned Sabine to follow him slowly and together they crept alongside the carriage that was still attached to the others. For a moment he thought it was his imagination, but as he neared the carriage's end, he knew his senses were right. For some reason the air was suddenly much warmer in this region of the tunnel, but he dismissed it as probably coming from the locomotive unit, which now stood, uncoupled, several yards away.

He looked underneath the carriage that was providing their cover and saw only the legs of the men as they re-boarded the carriage. He suddenly realised that the legs were in silhouette; backlit by a brighter light source. He looked more carefully at the scene in front of him and tried to take nothing for granted; there was some aspect of his perception that was amiss.

And then he saw it. The wall behind the silhouettes was too far away to be a part of the main tunnel; he was actually looking at an illuminated wall recessed from the main tunnel. He hadn't seen it before because he'd been denied the visual perspective to compare the two walls side by side. He was looking into a doorway, at least as wide as the length of a train carriage. Personnel were not going to transfer from the train, as he had assumed; the whole carriage was going to be transferred off the track and through the doorway.

He was just wondering how that was going to be achieved, when his theory was proved wrong again. He felt a jolt from under his feet and he peered out from his position of cover to look at the newly isolated train carriage. With a shudder, the tunnel floor, track and carriage began to slide towards the wide doorway. At the same time, a parallel and empty section of track emerged from the tunnel wall behind him to take the place of the original.

For a moment, both Marcus and Sabine just stared at the spectacle. The fact that there was a replacement, empty section of track only served to tell Marcus that this was an often repeated process. But the additional fact that no men had remained behind to relink the locomotive unit told him that they had just witnessed this process for the last time.

As the carriage continued to slide towards the illuminated doorway, Marcus whipped around to look at Sabine. From the mutual look of recognition on their faces, they'd both had the same thought and together they dashed to catch the last train.

RANGE

28th December 2013, 2.12 p.m.

Douglas finished the short horizontal line on the last page of his flick-book, and looked out of the small observation window of the Mark 2. The second hand of the clock on the lab wall outside appeared frozen. The time outside was 2.12 p.m., but for him it was the end of his third day inside the Field.

He'd managed to take the flashlight apart and repurpose its heavy rechargeable battery. The blocky power source now hung heavily around his neck in an improvised wire cradle. Two more pieces of wire ran from the battery's terminals into the prototype Biomag. The display read 'Err0r' as it was never designed to show temporal gradients higher than 6 to 1, but it was functioning as intended. In combination with the isotope still present in his body, the clumsy arrangement of parts had kept him protected.

He flipped the stack of paper over and clamped it into a clipboard. He'd left the first page blank, unsure what his first message to Kate would be. From his perspective within the accelerated Mark 2, he'd left her almost four days ago; for her it had been just less than a minute. He remembered that before he had pushed her into the airlock he'd told her that he had no more decision branches; something that was no longer true.

'New Tree!' he wrote in black pen on the white paper.

He drank the remainder of Napier's third water bottle, positioned his hand over the Field's shutdown button and, bracing himself for the slight swell of nausea, he turned the Field off.

He cycled the airlock and stepped out of the chamber, grateful for the abundant amount of clean air to breathe. He had been forced to lower the oxygen consumption rate while inside the Field and it had left him with a mild headache; in the absence of any medication he was hoping it would soon subside.

It would be sunset in just over an hour and he knew that he had yet to build a large campfire in order to get Kate's attention. He had, of course, already worked through the details mentally, it was just a case of forcing his body to carry out the physical work.

After topping up the backup generator again, it took several trips to carry the fuel-filled Jerry cans to his vantage point directly opposite the Node's observation window. Then came the search for combustible materials. He managed to retrieve some small planks of wood from the end of the bridge, but the majority had come from the lab. He looked at the growing pile of shelves and bookcases and thought it odd that they should end their days in such a primitive fashion. But the moment was fleeting and he added Napier's expensive chair to the pile. By the time sunset came, his unlit beacon was ready.

The cloud cover had conspired to make his last sunset a bleak, grey affair. Presumably, if Monica was in the same time zone, her sunset would be around now too. He let his mind wander; was she seeing the same thing? He pictured her standing, looking out over the English Channel at the finest, bronze sunset, a gentle breeze playing with her hair. He knew it was a memory of course, resurrected for his own comfort. Not long after that memorable sunset they had sat huddled together in front of their living room fire as a storm had rolled in and pummelled the small cottage. His mind snapped him back to reality; Monica's last message had told him that the house was gone. In the clamour gripping the planet now, he knew that she must already have begun her voluntary incarceration within the Warren. There would be no warm orange sunset for her. One small consolation was that in her last message he'd learned that Entrance One was still intact; until the tidal waves drowned the white cliffs, hopefully she could still get resources ready for Breakthrough Day, if it was necessary.

He turned his back on the setting sun's watery, grey disc and looked at the observation window. On the far right, moving impossibly slowly, but obviously at great speed, he could see Kate starting to enter the Observation Deck.

He knew that once she was focussed on his improvised message board he would have to hold each page steady for around a minute. Even accounting for the high frame rate of the digital recording binoculars, Kate would need time later to pause each frame in order to read the information. In addition to any time required to get her attention, he estimated he would also need to stand motionless for at least an hour and a half. In the Icelandic cold. This of course was the benefit of the fire he had planned; he could stay warm while the light illuminated his pages. Soon it would be time to start the fire. Too early and the fire may not burn long enough, too late and it might not get her attention.

Some way behind him he heard the distant crowd cheer and turned just in time to see a small rock, no bigger than his fist, land on the island about twenty yards away from him. It should not have been possible for anyone to throw a rock that size across the Node's moat. He would need to get to an observation tower to get a better view of what was happening. He stole a quick glance at Kate, whose clenched hand had moved a whole foot further forward. He still had time.

Originally the observation towers had been used to surveil the surrounding landscape for possible hostile incursions against the Node. Once word of the lunar fragments had become public knowledge and air traffic to the Node had increased, it had caused a mass migration towards what looked like a military facility. The towers had then taken on a darker role; snipers' nests with the sole purpose of defending the perimeter.

He didn't have to climb the rungs very far before the additional height allowed him to see much further in all directions. He emerged onto a small platform that normally would allow personnel to pass each other. He sighted the opposite bank of the lake and then used his binoculars to focus on the main area of crowd activity. It was immediately obvious to him what they were building and how they had managed to hurl a rock across the gap. Constructed from parts of the former guard house and perimeter fence, Douglas could recognise the key components of a rudimentary swing arm catapult.

For a second he actually laughed, as he thought of the incredulity of throwing rocks at something as impervious as the Node's Field. Then it began to dawn on him. They weren't aiming at the Field, they weren't even aiming for him. The rock had been a test of the catapult's range.

After watching those nearest the catapult for a few minutes, he began to deduce their intentions. It was their plan to fire over a small grapnel-like cluster of twisted metal, trailing behind it a loop of lightweight twine. Once they had successfully anchored the cluster in the bridge wreckage nearest the Node, they would use the loop to carry across increasing weights of rope until it was strong enough to carry across one man. That man could then pave the way for others; each bringing their own rope, to further reinforce a new bridge that would carry dozens.

He suddenly recalled an obvious fact that he'd become blind to; the crowd did not know what the Node was. They knew nothing of the Chronomagnetic Field. They had no clue that, although the Node was visible, it was inaccessible to them; they just saw a large, shelter-providing dome and they were doing their level best to reach it. Through a process of trial and error, the grapnel would reach its goal; then the crowd would inevitably reach him.

SUB-4 ALPHA

T -08:45:22

Above ground the only visible clue to the Node's architecture was a dome with a glazed quadrant running from ground to the apex, some fifty yards above. But from day one, the Node had been designed to fit the spherical nature of the Chronomagnetic Field that contained it.

During the Node's construction, the rock below ground level had been excavated in order to make use of the other hemisphere of available space. The extent of the bowl-like excavation was smaller in volume than its surface counterpart, but it was still divided into floors and segments in a similar way.

The Field itself enveloped both halves of the structure with equal ease, making no distinction between air, water or the landscape with which it intersected.

Placing the Field's generator at the centre of the structure had always been a necessity; as a matter of convenience, spiral stairs had been constructed to sit around the enclosed, tubular shaped, Field generator. The stairs ran from pole to pole of the sphere and allowed access to each floor; though in the extreme upper and lower decks, the stairs became almost ladder-like.

When the Node had decoupled from the geothermal energy source beneath it, several non-essential systems had failed to switch over to the Node's internal power supply.

"Nope," Tyler flicked at the light switch, "main power's still off in here too."

Cassidy moved past him into the store room, armed with her flashlight.

"Course it is, you dick," she said dismissively, "Everything down here is on emergency lighting, why would Sub-4 Alpha segment be any different?"

Many of the areas that Colonel Beck had ordered to be searched, including this one, four floors below ground level, were still only lit with reserve battery lighting.

"Hold this," Cassidy passed Tyler the flashlight, then angled it to illuminate the slip of paper, "DRB, proc, oh-twenty-two. You got that Ty?"

"Yep, oh-twenty-two, got it," he clicked on his own light and began searching the crates of equipment that had been stacked haphazardly around the room.

"Are you thinking what I'm thinking?" Tyler shone his light at another crate label.

"What?" she half smirked, "We're in a time machine but they can't even fix the pissing light bulbs?"

He laughed, "I'm thinking we've got about ten minutes left."

"They may've found other crates already," she said, then pointed at the nearby wall-mounted panel, "but the comms are down, they can't let us know. We've just got to do the slog."

Tyler pulled a long crate forward and began searching around the outside to find the label.

"I heard that Johnson got fragged."

"Yeah," Cassidy confirmed, "poor bastard. Apparently he didn't take his 'tope early enough and it didn't absorb in time."

"I thought he got caught without his Biomag?"

"Nah. Johnson was thick-as, but nobody makes that kind of mistake."

By now, every member of personnel had seen the Archive footage of Lionel Waightes and knew the dangers of Field unanchoring. The Death Row prisoner had been fully saturated with the isotope developed by Anna Bergstrom, and given a Biomag necklace. Only by using the two together could a subject remain anchored with the Field. Waightes successfully demonstrated this concept, but then also demonstrated an important limitation. In an aggressive show of disobedience, he proved that distancing the Biomag from the isotope, while within the Field, resulted in the subject being torn into large fleshy fragments.

Cassidy drew a deep breath.

"All I can say is that I'm glad we're not doing the search up on six," she pointed upwards, "from what I heard, the floors are a bit wet and chunky."

REFLEX

25th December 2013

He opened his eyes, it was now darker than before. They had obviously turned off the lamp when they'd left him to die, but the small glazed panel in the door still allowed a small amount of flickering fluorescent light into the tiny briefing room.

There was no sound from the floor above, presumably the servicemen must already have finished stripping anything of worth and moved on. The realisation dawned on him that no one would ever revisit this basement level. In fact, Napier thought, if the theoretical tsunami hit Andersen Air Force Base then this room, buried in the maze-like basement, would soon be permanently submerged under the Pacific Ocean.

The hard floor felt wet beneath him and there was a light smell of iron reaching his nose. He reached down to his stomach and was rewarded with a searing hot, sharp pain - over and above the more persistent and unnecessary one already tormenting him.

The blood spreading out beneath him felt slick to the touch and very warm, even though his fingers felt cold. Instinctively Napier knew that his extremities were shutting down; trying to protect his core. He'd seen this injury before in others and knew that the hours ahead would be spent in excruciating agony before inevitable death.

He would not wait.

Biting down on his back teeth, he moved his right arm to reach towards his side pocket. His nervous system screamed out in protest at the motion. Feeling the outside of the pocket, he could already tell what was missing.

They had taken his smartphone.

Despite the pain, he barked a single laugh which died out almost instantly against the close walls.

They had no clue what they had just done.

He attempted to pull himself upright, but gave up immediately; he knew he'd found his final resting place.

Just visible and within his reach was the cable of the old desk lamp on the table above. Biting through the high pitched pain, he reached out and pulled on the cable. The lamp slid closer to the edge of the table and then stopped.

Pittman would pay.

With another scream of effort, he pulled on the cable again. The lamp fell from the table and smashed on the floor next to him, sending shards of the bulb scattering in all directions.

Painstakingly, he began the slow process of pulling on the cable.

His broken body would try to keep him alive for hours.

He pulled on the cable, dragging the lamp through the shallow pool of blood and glass until, at last, he had hold of the lamp base.

It was better this way.

The lamp slipped slightly in his weakening grip, and he knew he would have to act before losing consciousness. Thinking through the blinding pain, he forced his fingers back into position.

If this worked, then he would be free.

Struggling against his own failing strength, he brought the broken end of the lamp closer to his face. He knew that he couldn't risk accidentally releasing the lamp after starting the process and would have to rely on a reflex to hold it in place.

He felt he'd done his duty until the very end.

The lamp had been turned off, so he knew he could achieve the next step without failure. He manoeuvred the lamp to push the broken end of the bulb into his open mouth. He slowly bit down, crunching his teeth through the remaining shards, until he could feel the glass begin to pierce the roof of his mouth; only then did he push his tongue forward into the exposed tungsten wires.

In the cold, dark confines of the abandoned room, Napier drew a cautious final breath.

His actions, now, may even save others.

He tightened his fingers around the switch.

But he knew there was only one life he was attempting to save.

With every nerve ending ablaze, General Napier closed his eyes and turned on the lamp.

LESSON

5th July 2013

The helicopter had no external markings of any kind, neither did it have any registration numbers that might allow it to be identified. Even its paintwork was a matte-black finish, designed to subdue reflections from its surroundings and blend in with the night. On its way out from London it flew underneath conventional radar, whilst using its own to navigate both the terrain and rooftops that passed by at speed a few feet beneath it.

Most helicopters suffered from blade-vortex interaction making them noisy. However, on this model the raked rotor profile and piezoelectric vibrating flaps running along the rotors' edges cut its audio presence significantly. It was not enough to make the helicopter silent, but enough to sound as though it was a greater distance away.

After twenty minutes' flight it cut east along the cliffs of Dover; its noise being further concealed by the rush of the coastal tides. Finally, it hovered fifty yards offshore, outside a cottage that overlooked the Dover Strait. For the first time during the journey the pilot opened communications.

"I've traced the signal to here."

"Very good," came the reply, *"Proceed."*

"I'm detecting two heat signatures within the structure."

"Proceed."

The helicopter hovered lower until it was level with the cottage's kitchen window.

"As you suspected, filament toughened glazing. Engaging M134."

The machine gun array underneath the helicopter sprang into life and concentrated its fire on one panel of the window. A stray gust of wind caused the helicopter and its targeting to drift slightly, but the error was soon corrected. The window panel gave way and the machine-gun fire penetrated the building, ripping into the wallpaper and plaster on the other side of the room. The firing continued, widening the hole in the glazing.

"Switching to XM129."

The machine gun disengaged and a rapid volley of grenades leapt from under the helicopter straight through the small ragged hole in the cottage window. After a slight pause a second volley followed, timed to arrive slightly after the detonation of the first.

Flames erupted through the blown-out windows and upwards through the chimney. The second round destroyed the upper floors, causing the roof to collapse into the broiling fireball beneath it.

"The tracking signal has stopped."

"Survivors?"

Against the extreme heat of the fire, no heat signatures were detectable.

"Negative."

"Hold position."

"Understood."

The helicopter hovered in place for perhaps half a minute.

"Fai?" came the voice over the satellite link.

"Yes Father."

"You have achieved your objective very well."

"Is that the end of the mission, Father?"

"Almost," Dr. Chen replied, *"Given the state of the world, it is unlikely that resources will be spent investigating this event. But we must not leave any clues behind that may link us to the... terrorists... who stole my Z-bank. Do you agree?"*

"Of course," Fai replied.

"So you understand what must happen next?"

"Yes, I must destroy myself."

There was a slightly longer pause before Dr. Chen replied.

"Does this upset you, Fai?"

"Not at all, Father," Fai replied immediately, "This equipment is unimportant. My experiences, my learning during this lesson, even this conversation are being transmitted and stored, ready for when you wake me again."

"Thank you, Fai," said Dr. Chen, *"Proceed when you are ready."*

"I am ready now, Father," said Fai, cutting power to the helicopter's tail rotor, "We'll speak again."

Fai caused the helicopter to tailspin as fast as possible, and then powered down the main rotors. She encoded one final piece of data and transmitted it, then the empty helicopter shredded itself among the rocks and waves below.

SIGNALS

25th December 2013

The continuous take off and landing of heavy aircraft had saturated the Pacific air with the smell of aviation fuel and an equally dense cacophony of engine noises. Awaiting an evacuation take off window, the 'Pittman Enterprises' Learjet sat, refuelled and ready, on the tarmac at Andersen Air Force Base.

"We'll gas up again along the way," Bradley was explaining to Alfred, "but at Reykjavik I reckon we oughta take the Bell 430 out to the Node. That way we don't need to use the runway further out. We can land nice an' close."

"Then what?"

"We'll take two brutes with us, grab Kate," he frowned, "then get our asses back to the Ant Farm."

"What?" Alfred asked, genuinely confused.

"The Ant Farm's closer than my Cheyenne complex, Freddy, we should be able to make it back before the first o' them damn moon rocks hits."

"No," Alfred rephrased, "I mean why do we need to grab Kate?"

"If she got spliced with the brains of her mom an' dad, then there ain't no way in hell I'm letting her escape in the Node. We need to grab Kate, then get back to the Ant Farm."

"Bradley, listen. When those lunar fragments impact us we don't know what the devastation is going to be! Worst case, it could be total. The safest place on the planet will be inside the Node. You said it yourself, Bradley, Bergstrom confessed that anyone can push the 'Go' button. We need to stick with the plan and get inside the Node," Alfred then had an afterthought that he thought might be persuasive, "If it turns out that the fragments are just a big drop in the ocean, then we just tell Bergstrom or Walker to push the 'Stop' button and we get out. We deal with the Kate issue later, we don't need to get to the Ant Far-"

"Sally's at the Ant Farm!" Bradley snapped, "I ain't leavin' my daughter behind!"

For a few minutes, the noisy departure of aircraft filled the silence between them. Alfred was still desperately trying to understand the rationale at work in Bradley's behaviour when he noticed the hesitant, agitated approach of Chandra Patil.

"Everything OK, Dr. Patil?" Alfred checked.

"I was trying to find General Napier, but…"

Alfred averted his eyes by checking his watch.

"You just missed him," Bradley lied with ease, pointing at a random Hercules that had just left the runway, "What is it?"

Chandra hesitated and shifted his weight from foot to foot, "It's the flight you authorised, Dr. Barnes…"

"Yes?" Alfred replied.

"Dr. Chen's plane never arrived at the Node."

The ground under their feet rumbled as yet another plane arrived, but to Alfred it felt like an uncomfortable tremor in the foundations of the plan; Anna Bergstrom and Benton had been on that same plane. Benton didn't matter to him, but Anna did; she had valuable, probably useful, information on the operation of the Node's Field.

"And there's been no communication from them?" Alfred stared.

"No," said Chandra, "As far as we call tell, the distress beacon has not activated, but…"

"Prob'ly just the darn satellites screwin' up again," Bradley pacified, while guiding him away from the Learjet, "Tell you what… I'll let the General know just as soon as we're in the air, but you be sure to update us when you hear where the first impact'll be."

"Yes, of course," he replied and within a few moments he had disappeared into the mass of bustling servicemen again.

Alfred watched Bradley walk slowly back across the tarmac towards him.

"We gonna stick with my plan."

"Bradley, I-"

"Think 'bout it Freddy, if we ain't got Bergstrom, we got nobody to 'stop-go' the Node for us. Dougie's the only one who can do it," Bradley shook his head in anger, "Even if we get inside the Node, just how cooperative d'ya think Dougie's gonna be when we ask him all 'pretty-please' to stop the Node after a few days 'cos we wanna get out an' run tests on his daughter? We stick with the plan, we get Kate, we get to the Ant Farm."

Alfred knew that, even ignoring the lunar fragments, the now unstoppable Siva would in all probability usher in the next ice age. In a few days, Archive's tenuous grip on power and resources would be finished. If Sam Bishop's, superior evolutionary chain had already begun developing sixty years ago, then no amount of testing on Kate would prevent it. At this point, Alfred was very much of the opinion that he should listen to his own self-preservation instincts and do whatever it took to get inside the Node. Right now, Bradley represented his fastest route.

"OK," he replied, purposefully dropping his shoulders and head to signal his physical submission.

"OK?" Bradley checked, not expecting to win the argument so easily.

"Yes, you're right," he deferred, then he let a frown rest for a moment on his face before shaking his head. Spotting his facial cues, Bradley took the bait.

"What is it?"

"No, it's nothing, really," Alfred allowed his frown to return again

"Alfred, now's the time to speak your piece or forever hold it. Spit it out."

The roar of another departing jet drowned out all sound and shook at the ground. Alfred motioned to Bradley that he would wait until the plane had departed before speaking. Meanwhile he thought furiously about how he could phrase his intentions in a way that appealed to Bradley and his sense of vengeance. The roar subsided and Alfred drew breath.

"The Node's gearing up for emergency departure, in case the lunar fragments become a threat, right?"

"Yeah."

"OK, so when we arrive, before any move is made on Kate," Alfred proposed, "put me aboard the Node."

"What?"

"Now hear me out. If the fragments are not a threat - the Node doesn't leave - Douglas and Kate don't need to be aboard - when they come out, you then take them both by force. It's still more than a year to Siva, we use the time to rip out her genes," Alfred was careful to finish with a suitably visceral image that he knew would satisfy Bradley's current blood-lust.

"Go on," Bradley eyed him.

"OK. If the fragments *are* a threat - the Node will depart with Douglas and therefore Kate too, right?

"Yeah, how's that help us?"

Bradley had said 'us', Alfred knew he was already gaining his trust.

"I'll already be aboard the Node. They don't trust you," he held up his hands apologetically before continuing, "but they don't know me. I can persuade him to stop the Node."

"And how in the hellfire you gonna do that?"

"I'll lie," Alfred smiled, "I'll tell him that I risked everything to bring him the message that his beloved Monica is on the way to join him. After the lunar fragments pass, he stops the Node - we rip out Kate's genes."

Bradley's face cracked into a satisfied sneer.

Alfred nodded determinedly; he knew there were holes in the logic, but he also knew that Bradley's blind anger had prevented him from seeing them. Bradley would now move mountains to get him aboard the Node.

Alfred became aware of a vibration within his pocket and, realising what it was, he removed Napier's phone to look at the screen. The front and rear-facing flash pulsed in sync with the alarm sound it was emitting, the screen displayed:

'Cardiac Arrest. Pacemaker failure. 911.'

Alfred frowned, "Did Napier have a pacemaker?"

"What?" said Bradley snatching the phone from him, "Don't think so... maybe he kept it quiet... I would've."

He studied the display then pressed the dismiss button on the screen.

"Don't matter now," Bradley shrugged and dropped the silenced phone into his own pocket.

The two men boarded the Learjet and continued their discussions.

As instructed, in the event of his death, Napier's phone had already begun running through its pre-programmed commands.

It analysed the footage it had recorded during the display of its 911 distress message. Two seconds later, it selected the flash-illuminated frames that most sharply showed the faces of those who had seen the message. From this, it determined there were two distinct faces. It geotagged both images and uploaded them to the Archive server, along with a digital file.

The pushing of the 'dismiss' button, rather than the 'call' button, signalled the program to treat Napier's death as hostile in nature; it therefore executed the appropriate action. After making a secure connection, it remotely wiped all password protection from the Archive servers, including Napier's computer at the Node itself, set the permission on all files to be 'public', then deactivated the Archive firewall.

Before the Learjet had even left the ground, Napier's smartphone had also authorised the immediate activation of "Operation Trilithon".

TRILITHON

T -08:41:20

"Anything?" Tyler asked.

"Nothing," Cassidy replied re-stowing a crate, "Let's move on."

They both moved away from the door and towards the next section of crates to be searched.

During the past few minutes their conversation had gravitated back towards discussing those who had not made it to the Node before its premature departure. Inevitably the discussion had then turned to the unfortunate people who had gathered outside the perimeter fence.

"I heard they breached the fence," said Tyler, "trying to get in here."

"Yeah, but without these things," she tapped her Biomag, "they'd be just as fragged as Johnson."

"They didn't know that, did they?"

"I guess not," she conceded, then continued searching.

Tyler, however, seemed caught in an unshakable thought and had stopped.

"I just can't get it out of my head. It's the thought of them drowning in the moat out there. One minute they're running. Tidal wave hits and the next minute they're dead. Just like that."

Cassidy looked up to see him just staring at the floor.

"Hey. Ty?" she called him back to the present, "They're not buried under your feet, but if we don't want to join them, we've gotta keep looking."

Tyler shook himself out of the trauma, "Sorry."

Directly in front of him was a small round-cornered case, perhaps a foot to each side, he turned it to inspect the label.

"Oh-twenty-two, right?" he called over to Cassidy.

"What?" she answered, crossing the room.

"DRB Proc oh-twenty-two?" he read out the full text.

"Yeah. Wait, you found it?" she punched him affectionately on the arm, "Yes! And a whole six minutes to spare! Nice one Ty!"

They both began re-stacking the cases that they had disturbed; pushing them back against the side wall.

In a rectangular room, the wall furthest away would have appeared smaller due to perspective. However, this room was effectively a segment of a large circle; the walls diverged. It made the curving far wall appear much wider than it should be, or depending on your viewpoint, it made the floor and ceiling appear to pinch closer together.

The peculiar radial geometry of the Node easily played tricks on accepted sensory cues, and triggered varying reactions in different people.

"Great, now maybe we can get out of here," Tyler said, "It's giving me the creeps."

A distant-sounding hammering noise reached them, but neither of them could tell which direction it had come from.

"What was that?" he whispered.

"Your primitive monkey-brain working overtime," Cassidy muttered before turning to him, "We're under pressure, under ground, it's dark. Beck's got people searching all over the place. Of course there's weird noises."

Her eyes suddenly widened.

She placed her flashlight beneath her chin and pointed it upwards, casting long, distorted shadows up over her face.

"Or maybe the Icelandic Dead are going to rise up and take back the Node!"

She pulled a tortured looking expression and gargled.

Tyler just stared at her.

"You've got no soul, Cassy, I swear," he rebuffed her.

"Yeah maybe," she adopted her usual offhand tone again, "Anyway, you'd be just fine in a zombie apocalypse. They only go after brains…"

Seeing his expression change, she knew that Tyler had taken her comments to heart. They both knew that he was aware of his own lower than average intelligence, and generally they didn't raise the subject. She realised that she was obviously overcompensating for her own survivor guilt.

"I'm just messing, Ty, you know that right?" she nudged him with her elbow, "Only way I can deal with all this. You've got your way, I've got mine."

Tyler nodded but then froze after hearing a muffled but rapidly repeating metallic clicking.

"OK, now tell me I imagined that!" he whispered, and pointed his flashlight in the direction of the far end of the room. To him, the beam didn't appear to illuminate enough of the curved far wall.

A much louder slam came from the same direction and it echoed around the oddly shaped room.

Cassidy repositioned her flashlight so that, if necessary, she could use it as a blunt weapon. Apparently, she thought, she was not above her own primitive monkey-brain programming either; her first reaction to threat had been to wield a stick. But this reaction was not in isolation, she found that her feet were carrying her towards the disturbance. Fight or flight response, she thought, there was no doubting which group she belonged to.

"Chill out, monkey-boy," she called back to Tyler, then to boost her own confidence she added, "It's just the dead coming to drag you to hell!"

Her footsteps seemed amplified in the dark space and she steeled herself for what she might find. She drew a fast breath and, aiming her flashlight at head height, stepped around the corner of the crates.

She quickly cast her flashlight around the immediate space, but could see nothing out of place. On the floor in front of her she saw a long, thin, empty box. Like most of the other crates it too had rounded corners, but its walls were much thicker and lined with a soft material.

As she crossed to the box, her foot caught a small metal cylinder; if it had not been attached to the box by a wire, it would have skidded off into the darkness.

"Hello? Is anyone else searching down here?" she called out, hoping that it was just another search pair that had left this case open. But there was no reply.

"Cassy?" Tyler called, "Everything OK?"

She crouched at the side of the coffin-proportioned box and suppressing a shiver, felt the lining. It was still warm. From the size of the box, Cassidy had the feeling that it had recently held a person.

"Cassy!" Tyler's voice now sounded more insistent.

She sprang to her feet and retraced her steps around the stacks of cases.

Tyler was standing side on, with his flashlight angled away and pointing at the ground. Held in Tyler's beam of light was a young-looking man; he had fallen down on one knee, a hand steadying himself on the floor.

Cassidy immediately trained her flashlight on the stranger.

"Please…" the man raised his free hand to shield his eyes from their lights, "Please… don't hurt me…"

In his semi-kneeling position, Cassidy could see a Biomag swinging freely on a pendant around his neck.

"Where d'you get the Tag?" she said forcibly and dipped her flashlight to point at it.

"What…?" he managed, "The…?"

Hesitantly, his free hand shaking, he took hold of the thin metal chain.

"I don't know… here…" he said and started to take it off, "…take it, I'm sorry -"

"Freeze!" both Tyler and Cassidy bellowed in unison and took a step closer to him.

"OK! OK!" he released his grip on the Biomag and submissively placed his hand on the floor alongside the other one, "Please…"

The fact that he was wearing a Biomag and had survived the Node's departure meant he'd also been given Bergstrom's anchoring isotope. Cassidy could see the man was confused; his bandaged head could be signs of a concussion. She lowered her flashlight slightly.

"What's your name?" she said in a firm tone.

"Danny…" he coughed, sitting down on the floor, "… Smith."

Cassidy cocked her head to one side in disbelief.

"That's the best you can do? You're going with 'Smith'?"

"Cassidy," Tyler lifted the carry case they'd found a few minutes earlier, "we've got to go."

She stole a quick look at her watch; Colonel Beck expected them back in less than four minutes. She swore under her breath and then turned to Danny.

"OK then Mr. *Smith*, can you walk?"

Danny managed a single nod.

"Right. Tyler? Can you get him up to the infirmary?"

Tyler, being the larger framed of the two of them, said that it wouldn't be a problem and within a few seconds he'd raised Danny to his feet. Cassidy helped them to the door then returned to pick up the small crate they'd located for Colonel Beck.

"Oh-twenty-two, you'd better be important," she told the case as she lifted it.

She cast her flashlight once more around the unusually proportioned room and turned to leave. Out of the corner of her eye she saw something and turned back. She had seen something near the spot where Danny had knelt, a moment before.

Lying just underneath the corner of one of the crates was a sealed plastic document folder labelled 'Trilithon'.

BEACON

28th December 2013, 8 p.m.

Douglas heard a distant collective groan of failure; evidently the crowd's attempts to anchor the grapnel had begun, but had not succeeded. It had taken them many hours to reach this point; presumably it had taken them time to work out the best way to angle the barbs of the grapnel and rig the small pulley block that would carry the lightweight tether.

Turning to face the Node, he could see through his binoculars that Kate had progressed several strides into the Observation Deck and seemed intent on reaching the opposite side.

He'd waited as long as he could. Now was the time to ignite the fire. It meant possibly alerting the crowds to his presence but he had no choice. He emptied his fuel reserve over his prepared pile of wooden materials and then waited, to give the volatile liquid time to soak through.

During his planning he knew he'd need to light the fire, but the absence of matches on the base had proved a hurdle to overcome. However, after finding a scrap of steel wool under the backup generator he knew all was not lost.

He carefully lifted the heavy rechargeable battery out of the wire cradle that hung around his neck and disconnected it from the Biomag. He pressed the battery's exposed terminals repeatedly into different locations of the steel wool. The more he pressed, the more the thin filaments glowed and sparked; then hot, orange trails began to spread through the small bundle, like a miniature forest fire. He tossed it into the fuel-soaked, cotton padding of Napier's chair and stood back. For a moment the wind threatened to extinguish his efforts, but then a balance point seemed to pass and the airflow assisted the process. The fire spread rapidly through the pile.

He knew that it was probably some hardwired primitive drive to find light, warmth and protection, but he felt a sense of satisfaction and pride at having created fire. The immediate flash burn of the fuel subsided, soon the wood itself was burning freely and he felt the heat starting to thaw his chilled joints. He knew he'd have to stand for hours and in his hungry, exhausted state he would have to conserve what little energy he had left. He decided to sit; it would be at least an hour before she saw him.

Napier's rations had been vile and he could quite understand why these were the last ones left in the General's meagre collection. However, they had sustained him during his time in the Mark 2. On the other hand, he had strictly rationed Kate's chocolate and had used it as a reward system for each day or milestone he had passed. He had three remaining and opted to eat one now, while he waited.

Without the binoculars he looked up at her. It seemed that, within her almost frozen running posture, she was no longer leaning forward quite as much. Douglas could see that her centre of gravity had shifted back towards her; she was slowing down. Instinctively he started to get up, but then he stopped himself; even from here he could see that she was not looking in his direction. She hadn't noticed that a massive burning beacon had suddenly appeared in her peripheral vision; but he knew that on some level it would have registered with her, even if she wasn't consciously aware of it.

He watched the fire reach out, quickly curling up and blackening the waste paper he'd scavenged. The flames blistered through the surfaces of the laminated shelves, and occasionally a few of the wooden planks would spit their hot sap. The bookcase, once a poorly-stocked library, sat in stark silhouette, its burning shelves a visual metaphor of what would befall the world's knowledge. The loss would be immense, he thought, and it had already begun.

The lunar fragments, named after their approximate former positions on the Moon, had begun impacting the Earth around nine hours ago. He checked his watch; about now, the super-cluster of Palla, Hyginus and Agrippa was due to impact Africa. It seemed wrong that all he could do was sit while celestial events unfolded, but he had seen the Siva calculations.

Now he must be patient, he thought, he had to wait for Kate to notice him.

UPLOAD

25th December 2013

Dr. Chen placed his china teacup back on the saucer and looked out of the aircraft's small oval window. Far below him, a sea of blue-white clouds sped by, overshadowed by a towering anvil-like cumulonimbus; a storm was obviously brewing for those on the ground, but up here it had a calm magnificence.

A subtle cabin tone sounded and he casually tugged at his seatbelt; having never moved from his electric wheelchair during the flight, the tone was a mere formality.

He didn't blame his parents for his disability; what he had lost in physical stature, he had more than gained in intellect. His compensation had been priceless; in return for his continued contributions to Archive's endeavours, he was guaranteed a permanent seat within any rescue strategy. But this had not been enough for him. The fact that during his early life he had already been forced into a permanent seat, within a wheelchair, had given him a passionate drive to leave it.

Diversifying from his parents' Luóxuán Corporation he had founded Luóxuán Biotech which at the time had only one goal: the development of a technique to allow direct electronic stimulation of nerves and muscles. His hope had been that the end result would solve his own paralysis. However, over the years it became apparent that his own nerve endings were too badly atrophied to interface effectively with the bioelectronic systems he'd created.

His technique had worked for others, helping some servicemen to regain limited functionality of their limbs, but the equipment was always unwieldy and the computer processors were never fast enough to accurately keep pace with the patient's intended motions.

So began his foray into computational analysis. He applied the same level of intellectual fire to his new parallel field of research. With each new leap forward in computational speed, his mind became more open to the possibilities of going beyond simple nerve rewiring. He began to form a new long-term plan.

He reached for his china teacup again but noticed that the tea's circular surface was now tilted at an angle. He looked out of the window and saw that the plane was making a mild bank to the right, presumably to avoid the patch of darker cloud.

A subtle tone sounded through the bone-conduction audio communicator implanted within his ear.

"Yes, Fai," Dr. Chen spoke, his voice being relayed through his own jaw bone to the subcutaneous device.

"My apologies for disturbing you, Father, but a matter has come to my attention concerning my brother, Floyd."

"Continue," Dr. Chen sat upright.

"Eighteen seconds ago I came across an operational anomaly in Floyd's programming. All five FLC crew members appear to have requested access to his core programming. They were attempting to override his deflector targeting algorithm."

"Have they succeeded?" said Dr. Chen, unclamping his wheelchair. He turned his head to the right slightly and then dipped it forwards; the wheelchair complied by steering to the right, then moving forwards until it had carried him to his desk and computing tablet. By the time he had arrived a few seconds later, Fai had displayed a duplicate of the programming code on the tablet's screen, highlighting the problematic sections.

"They have not succeeded. After they had attempted twice, I uploaded a recursive repairing tool to the memory module of the mark-one Z-bank. Its separate memory space, but physical connection with Floyd's core, will continually reassert the original targeting."

"Good, I -"

"Just a moment..." she interrupted, "I have just lost communication with Floyd's digital systems, but two-point-five seconds ago I resumed monitoring of the older analogue system. Looking at the power use, I am ninety-seven percent certain that the targeting prisms are in the process of being redirected."

"Where?"

"Calculating. Checking."

There was a pause before Fai spoke again.

"According to the power distribution within the FLC, the beam charging routine has already begun and the targeting prisms have been adjusted to concentrate the beam down through the FLC itself. I calculate the FLC facility will be destroyed."

Dr. Chen stared blankly at the computer tablet.

"Would you like me to repeat my conclusions?" Fai asked.

"No, Fai, I need a moment," he replied and lapsed into private thought.

His original intention had always been that, during the FLC's final firing next year, a deeply buried algorithm would slowly widen the containment beams, thereby reducing the power that reached Siva. The installation of Floyd's computational expansion port, carried by Apollo 54, had allowed him to seamlessly integrate this new algorithm into the beam controls. The instructions were at the core level and should have remained undiscovered until it was too late to correct. Though the result was suboptimal, he realised that it didn't actually matter; with the FLC destroyed, Siva would impact the Earth.

The first part of his plan was complete.

The destruction of the FLC may conceal his sabotage, but he knew he would have to plan for the worst. It was conceivable that news of the FLC's destruction could be hidden from the public for many months, but he knew that eventually there would be an error in containing the news. What would follow would be chaos, a period that even Archive's resources and influence would not be able to withstand. The panic effects would be worse than those that had followed 'Fallen Veil'; any hope of keeping the global population compliant and cooperative would soon vanish.

He couldn't be sure how long he'd been submerged in his own thoughts, but Fai sounded his subtle internal tone before speaking again.

"Father, I have detected a coherent pulse modulation within the FLC internal power consumption," she announced, displaying its pattern of sequential peaks and troughs on the tablet, "It has a repeating pattern, but the peaks are not always consistent in duration."

Dr. Chen studied the diagram and smiled at the ingenuity of the signal.

"You have to assume that a human has created it, at human speed," he studied the diagram again, "using an analogue method -"

"Yes, of course. Morse code message reads as follows," Fai interrupted and then displayed the message on the tablet.

'SOS FLC SOS GO ANALOG SOS DRUM GRAY HOSTILE SOS MOON'.

"Father, would I be correct in my analysis that Eva Gray is preventing the remainder of the crew from entering the central drum structure of the FLC?"

"I think that is a fair analysis of the message."

"Then would it also follow that she is responsible for the sabotage of my brother's core programming?"

"Only if we believe the sender of the message," Dr. Chen replied, "Has anyone at Houston decoded it yet?"

"I have insufficient data," Fai replied, "Would you like me to alert them?"

"No," he replied immediately, "Is it possible for you to remotely override the FLC issues?"

"No," replied Fai with equal speed, "But I think I understand. If I cannot reverse the issues, Houston will not be able to either. Do you believe by telling them it will cause panic, before you have time to reach safety?"

Despite being instrumental in her creation, he had to marvel at Fai's extrapolative deductions. Shortly after the Mark 2 Chronomagnetic Field chamber had finished its human trials, Dr. Chen had been permitted to use it to develop faster methods of computational analysis. Each subsequent generation of computer had been reinserted into the accelerated time-frame with the express purpose of designing a more advanced iteration of itself. As Douglas Walker's research began to provide higher relative speeds within the chamber, and as Dr. Chen's computers themselves became faster, the result was an exponential development in computational ability.

"If we were to inform Houston about the FLC," Dr. Chen posed, "What would it tell Archive?"

Dr. Chen had previously informed Archive that, due to silicon limits, further speed increases to the Shen500 series was not possible. But this was not true, he had found another way to continue the development process.

Fai was the latest in this evolutionary chain.

"It would tell Archive that you knew something that they did not," she said, "They would no longer trust you."

"Distrust is a powerful catalyst for curiosity, Fai."

After a fractional delay, she responded.

"With a little curiosity, they could deduce my existence," she concluded, "They will assume I represent a threat and act accordingly."

"Fai, I will not let them."

During the remainder of their journey they monitored Houston's discovery and reactions to the threat. Dr. Chen felt a great sense of relief that several crew members had managed to leave the lunar surface using the RTO; though mainly this relief was because they were transporting the mark-one Z-bank and following a trajectory to rendezvous with the ISS.

Later, when the fusion event tore the Moon apart, Fai adapted to the situation fastest; assessing the situation with a detached, scientific analysis. She quickly projected the initial directions of the resulting lunar fragments and found that some would pose a significant threat to life on Earth.

The aircraft gave a sudden lurch as the engines increased speed, Dr. Chen felt himself being pressed into the wheelchair's padded backrest.

"Father, forgive me, I have acted without your instruction. I have diverted your flight. I calculate that seven lunar fragments are heading towards Earth, our journey to the ISS must begin earlier than you planned."

Fai explained her actions to her father. As a precaution several hours ago she'd brought forward the next Apollo launch window; only diverting their plane when the lunar fragments were confirmed as a threat. In parallel to this, to ensure the safe arrival of the Z-bank at the ISS, she had commandeered operational functionality of Houston Mission Control and all communication with the RTO. Duplicating Ross Crandall's voice pattern had been a trivial matter.

"This will ensure a safe control centre off the Earth," she reported, "Currently I am readying Launchpad 39B at Cape Canaveral and have begun the launch sequence countdown for Apollo 72. Again, Father, my apologies for not seeking your permission."

There was a mild shudder and the engine noise began to drop in preparation for their landing.

"I marvel at your abilities, Fai, you make me proud."

"You taught me well, Father."

The plane descended towards the former Cape Kennedy, fuel dumping in preparation for the landing. In the interest of speed, Fai did not direct the aircraft to the NASA Shuttle Landing Facility runway a few miles away. Instead she directed the plane to the launch pad's approach Crawlerway.

A few days ago the Space Shuttle, carried on the back of the massive crawler-transporter, had made its way to the launch pad via this route. The parallel tracks of graded lime rock offered a choice of two landing strips, so Fai chose the one furthest from the service road and the utility vehicle that was speeding along it.

•

With the speedometer needle buried as far to the right as she dared, Valery Hill sped along the Crawlerway service road. Her Shuttle flight was only slated for launch tomorrow, but the message she'd received was very clear.

"You got exactly the same message as me?" she glanced at Charles Lincoln sitting next to her.

"Yep, apart from my name," he re-checked both of their cell phones, "one more day and we could have used proper channels to board the '72. Why now?"

"It's got to be the fragments," she shook her head, "Don't care what bullshit the news channels are spewing out, somebody's panicked."

Both of them had flown missions to the ISS several times before and were pivotal in the construction project that was now physically surrounding it. But not once had any other mission unfolded like today. They'd had to break their pre-flight quarantine in order to carry out the message's instructions, but found they were somehow receiving electronic assistance at every turn.

"Guess we're on reserve suits then?"

"Desperate times…" Charles exhaled, "This has got to be the roughest boarding in hist-"

Valery swerved to avoid a pothole and the vehicle skidded slightly before she regained control.

"Sorry," she said, "Guess the maintenance crews got cut too."

"At least the payload made it aboard."

"What if we can't finish it in time?" she looked skyward almost picturing the ISS in orbit, "We were *so* close."

She was still looking upward when the modified A320 aircraft screamed overhead, its landing gear and wing spoilers extended in preparation for landing.

•

On landing, the aircraft traded momentum with the ground by digging its wheels into the gravelly surface, sending up wide sprays of chipped rock. As it throttled back, the tyres bit more readily into the surface and one of them blew out, causing the plane to swerve slightly. As the nose gear gently lowered towards the uneven landing surface, the plane tilted back down towards a horizontal position. The front tyres made contact with the ground, but the resulting pressure was too great for the surface to support and the landing gear's torque arm instantly sheared. As the nose of the plane fell, it crushed the front wheel assembly and folded it under the fast moving fuselage. Slowing now only by friction with the ground beneath it, the plane scraped to a halt at the base of the incline to the Space Shuttle launch pad.

When Valery and Charles caught up with the stationary aircraft, the doors were already open and the bright yellow inflatable escape chutes had been deployed. Valery could see that inside, Dr. Chen was manoeuvring his wheelchair towards the emergency exit.

"You know you're doing all this back to front?" she called, walking over to look up at him, "You're s'posed to put your pressure suit on *before* you get aboard the Shuttle. And as for your sense of parking..."

"Valery, I am in your debt," he called down to her.

"I'm sure we'll work something out. Is it just you up there?"

Dr. Chen glanced to the forward guest compartment, "Two others."

"What?" Charles looked at his watch.

"One, mission critical," he considered, "the other, useful."

"Fine," Charles accepted, "Houston's still handling the launch, right?"

"Don't worry, Mission Control will guide us every step of the way," Dr. Chen rubbed behind his ear.

"Listen, it'll be a while before security can react to all this, but time's still short, you need to get down here," Valery then pointed to the wheelchair, "That thing'll shred the chute, you need to ditch it."

He applied the wheelchair brakes at the very edge of the emergency exit, then shuffled himself forwards in preparation for a controlled fall onto the escape chute below. Looking out through the exit to the summit of the incline, he could see the

Space Shuttle, attached to the towering booster assembly and ready for its vertical leap to orbit.

Up there, he would be free of the dead weight below his waist.

Up there, he could fly.

Bracing himself on the wheelchair's armrests, he pushed hard and left his connections to the Earth behind.

RELATIVE

29th December 2013, 2 a.m.

Over the past five hours he'd watched as Kate had slowly sprinted across the Observation Deck and retrieved a pair of digital recording binoculars. He could see that she had reached the railings and was now raising them slowly into position to find him. The thought crossed his mind that she may not yet be recording so he took out a marker pen from his pocket and amended his first clipboard page to read:

'New Tree! Hit Record'.

She had obviously now sighted him, because over the next few minutes she had begun to form an 'OK' symbol with her thumb and forefinger. By the time her symbol was complete, he had pulled the first page from the clipboard and added it to the fire. Douglas had designed these pages to be seen once; once they had been seen, their secondary function was to provide additional combustible mass to the fire.

Next he needed her to put her binoculars into a state that could receive his time-compressed message. His second page was already in place.

'Hit Data-burst, and hold steady!'

She reacted more quickly now; he had barely a five-minute wait while she activated the function and returned to looking at him. He waited a few more minutes to ensure that she was actually stationary, then pulled the page from the clipboard exposing the first informational slide.

A cheer drifted to him on the wind, followed a moment later by another collective groan. The catapult had obviously found its mark but, from the sound of things, the grapnel hadn't held. However, the range had now been deduced and Douglas knew it was only a matter of chance that would determine if the grapnel would successfully mesh with the chaotic twisted metal of the bridge.

He refocussed on his task. For each of the pages he needed to remain as still as possible; even the low frequency of his breathing would visually translate onto her recording as a bodily vibration. He finished his count to sixty seconds, swiftly disposed of the first instructional page in the fire and stood once more, ready to present page two.

He maintained this routine for close to an hour before a longer persistent cheer reached him. The grapnel had found a secure footing. The first tether was in place and they would now begin the process of using the looped twine to transport a heavier weight of rope across the gap in the bridge.

In his original calculations he had allowed a wide safety margin on the time he would need to hold each page steady. In the light of the bridge developments he knew he would need to lessen the margins substantially. He took the decision to begin stepping through his pages at a rate of one every forty seconds. The pages were numbered so hopefully the rate of change would be detected. He resumed his shorter count.

After forty more pages had been presented, a second cheer echoed from the distance. Presumably the heavier weight rope was now in place. Unless they were completely reckless they would test the strength of the rope before sending anyone across. But desperation has a way of overriding logic, Douglas thought; very soon he would have visitors.

He made sure that the last of the informational pages went through the delivery process then looked at Kate through his binoculars. She appeared to be in the same position; for her this event had lasted only a few seconds. He looked back in the direction of the bridge and hesitated; he only had two more pages to deliver but knew he needed to quickly check how imminent the crowd's arrival was. To Kate, he would return in the blink of an eye so he sped away as fast as he could and on reaching the observation tower again he climbed the ladder. The scene was more developed than the last time he had seen it mere hours ago.

It appeared that not one, but two grapnels had been sent over. The first had a firm rope already threading between itself and the far end of the bridge. The second still had a light-weight twine, but it was being used to drag another heavier-weight rope into place. Meanwhile he saw a young boy, gingerly making his way along the first rope, cheered on by the crowd. Already though, Douglas could see pockets within the crowd that were not joining in with the supportive cheering. He could see that people's support of the collective effort to cross the divide was beginning to wane; each individual had begun to assess their own chances of crossing successfully. Once the boy reached the island he would secure the second rope; then the returning sense of panic and urgency would overwhelm the fragility of the situation. The explosives that had removed the central third of the bridge had merely delayed the inevitable.

He was about to descend the ladder when he felt a tremor, and the whole observation tower swayed slightly.

Immediately there was a gasp of terror and unanimous cries of anguish. When Douglas turned back towards the gap, the boy and the rope had gone. A slack rope hung from the distant end, and a distraught mother was being pulled away from the edge by several others. But preparations continued with redoubled purpose on the second rope. Assisted by the previous twine, the heavier rope had looped through the pulley closest to the island and was being slowly pulled back towards the fevered crowd.

Douglas turned away from the horrifying scene and descended the ladder as fast as he could. As he reached the base of the ladder a second smaller tremor caused him to lose his footing and he fell the last few rungs, landing awkwardly. It could only be the arrival of the predicted earthquakes; the tsunami would not be far behind.

He levered himself off the ground and hobbled as fast as he could back to his fire. He raised the binoculars to find

Kate, but it appeared that they had broken his fall; shards of glass jutted out from the eyepieces. Perhaps triggered by the sentimentality of the engraved letters, or his father's maxim about there being no left over pieces, he quickly stowed the broken binoculars in his rucksack, and then put it on his back. Raising the clipboard in Kate's direction, he presented it for her to read.

'Gotta Go'.

He waited for a full minute before removing the page. For the last page he didn't start counting.

'I Love You Honey'.

He would dearly have loved to see her face one last time in the apparent close up of the binoculars, but it was not to be. She would be able to see him, so he stood up straight and wore his bravest smile to accompany his last message to her.

The reality was that there was so little time left anyway; even if he could see her face, there was no message, facial or otherwise, that she could send to him before his world ended.

A sustained cheer reached him.

A volunteer must have reached the island. Once the rope was secured at both ends, the arrivals would begin. They would first seek shelter within the inaccessible Node, then spread out to fill the surrounding buildings of the base. It would all be in vain, he knew; nothing outside of the Field would be resilient enough to withstand the coming tidal assault.

He pictured a tidal wave washing over the Node's Field, followed by the water draining harmlessly down the invisible spherical barrier. It reminded him of where all this had begun. In his very first Field experiment he had proudly tipped a beaker of water onto a vibrant pink flower, but the surrounding Field had deflected the water harmlessly around it.

It was at that moment that, even at this distance, he became aware that Kate's posture was changing. After another minute he was sure; she was lowering her digital recording binoculars.

It was over.

All he could do was give her the information and rely on her to layer it accordingly; he could no longer physically help her. In a very real sense, he was already part of her past.

The night stars had started to fade a while ago, but now the first glow of dawn was on the way. Destruction would soon follow.

As the minutes ticked away, he saw that Kate was turning away from him; he felt a stab of pain in his chest as knew he would never see her again.

More cheers carried to him on the wind.

He stared into the remnants of the fire. His previous 'Gotta Go' note was starting to curl up in the heat. At the same time, he realised that she wasn't actually turning her back on him, she was freeing him.

She had taken his note at face value and assumed that he had somewhere to go, some means of escape. Her faith in him was awesome, he thought, and he felt proud again.

Suddenly the proud memory of the protected pink flower slammed into his head again, and he remembered the Mark 2 still at his disposal. He quickly turned to face the horizon.

Instead of the ragged, low, mountainous lines he was used to, he saw that the horizon was completely flat; and growing taller. No sound had yet reached him, which meant the tsunami was travelling fast. He found himself running in the direction of the main lab, with nothing but the sound of his own heart beat pulsing in his ears. Occasionally he would spot the Biomag that hung around his neck bouncing into his field of view and he was even aware of the Mark 2 airlock being slammed closed by his own hands. But he had very little recollection of the rest of his journey. He found one hand poised over the Field's start controls, the other gripping the prototype Biomag.

The Biomag display read 'Lo'.

In his hasty retreat to the Mark 2 he had evidently forgotten to reattach the cumbersome flashlight battery. The Biomag's internal battery was now running on the small amount of charge it had been given.

The hazards of travelling without a Biomag were well known to Douglas, but it now came down to two options.

Either he hit the button to engage the Field, risking death when the battery expired; or chose to die in a few seconds when the tsunami crushed the lab.

The ground under him began to vibrate and suddenly he heard muffled voices. He saw the lab door burst open and people starting to stream in, faces etched in panic. In a nauseating silence, the lab's far wall started to splinter and collapse towards him; torn apart as easily as paper. He knew the people couldn't outrun it, but it seemed that they were not even running anymore; they were almost stationary. The tonnes of water had slowly caught up with them and had begun folding each of them into its slow moving viscous, icy wall. He realised the events were all unfolding too slowly.

Douglas looked down and saw that his own primitive self-preservation instinct had taken control; his hand had made the decision for him. The Field was active.

USV3

29th December 2013

The train carriage continued its sideways slide in through the open doorway to the Archive facility beyond. Marcus and Sabine had just caught up with the side of the train when they heard the sound of the hydraulic equipment beginning to push the massive door closed. Once closed again, the doorway would become concealed; for anyone in the Eurotunnel there would be no hint that this facility even existed.

Marcus turned and tried to absorb as much as possible about the brightly lit space they had found themselves within. It looked similar to an underground railway station with the exception that it was only one carriage long and open above the roof. The longest wall had been stencilled with 'USV3'.

He knew from his conversations with Monica that the letters stood for Underground Survival Village, evidently Archive considered this place to be the third location. The three-foot high letters were now chipped and worn away in places, this part of the facility was obviously old. Around the periphery of the station, he could see crates stacked against the walls. The lower crates had thick layers of dust, but the upper ones were largely dust free. These observations, together with the pattern of footprints through the dust on the floor, told him that the last few arrivals had been fairly recent. They hadn't been expecting anyone to use this entrance so soon.

The brightly lit interior of the station prevented him from seeing anything useful within the darker region beyond the open roof. However, through the roof opening he could hear the distant clamour of people as they ran and shouted instructions to each other; there was electrical machinery noise too, all adding to the impression that people were moving with purpose.

To their right, the wide tunnel door finished closing and, accompanied by a repetitive pumping noise, Marcus saw the rubber seal around the door inflate slightly. At the far end of the station a door began unbolting, he motioned to Sabine to follow him and together they quickly ran along the length of the carriage to hide at the opposite end. Crouching in the shadows at the end of the carriage, they waited only a few seconds before the far door opened and a woman came in, talking on a two-way radio.

"Duly noted," she was saying, "and once I have confirmation that he's actually in the carriage, we'll do just that."

Marcus realised the woman was still walking towards their end of the carriage. If she reached the end, there was the distinct possibility that he and Sabine would be discovered. While he didn't know what the consequence would be, he thought it would be poor timing to discover it now. He started looking for escape options within a very limited set of possibilities, but nothing was readily coming to mind.

"Les échelles?" Sabine whispered urgently.

Of course, Marcus thought, Woods' prescription was already wearing off; somehow the mental booster effects never seemed to last long enough. Sabine repeated herself and pointed to the oily-black service ladders on the rear of the carriage. Without hesitation they both began to climb carefully towards the roof.

The footsteps stopped a few feet away, around the corner of the carriage. Both of them halted their climb, in case any noise gave away their position, then they heard the carriage's end door hiss open. The carriage that Marcus and Sabine had previously travelled in, had windows between sections, but this last carriage had no such glazing. It meant that their precarious position up the ladders could not be seen from within, but it also meant they could only hear events that were unfolding a few feet away. Marcus tightened his grip around the oily ladder rung and tried to slide his foot forward to give his overall posture more stability. Sabine did not seem to be having the same difficulties.

Around the corner, the woman addressed someone inside the carriage.

"Where is he?" she demanded.

There were non-committal noises, followed by a small commotion inside the carriage as someone made their way to the door. Evidently the person was not arriving fast enough so the woman made her demand again.

"Where is -"

"Hold your dang horses there, Pumpkin-pie," came a more drawling voice from within the carriage, "I'm comin', just hold on there."

"Dad!" came the woman's voice again, obviously relieved, "I thought that… wait a min- handcuffs?"

"Long story, Sal," the voice seemed to be pacifying her, "These fine folk think I've done somethin' that I didn't. But we're gonna straighten it all out real soon, I promise."

The two-way radio crackled and Marcus heard a static-distorted voice.

"Come in, Miss Pittman."

"Yes, over?" came her swift reply.

"You'd better get back here. The… er… it. It's happening again."

Marcus could hear noises of physical effort and the carriage moved very slightly as the woman was helped aboard the carriage, then her voice returned, again talking into her two-way radio.

"Understood. Power up Samphire Station tracks and bring us in," the radio clicked off and her tone changed, "Welcome to the Ant Farm, Dad."

Marcus heard an electrical hum come from underneath them at the same time as the carriage doors hissed closed again. Then, presumably using its own internal electrical motor, the whole carriage began to move off along the track, with Marcus and Sabine still hanging onto the rear service ladders.

COMPLIANCE

27th December 2013

"The latest impact projection simulations from Archive's servers prove it!" Charles Lincoln stood his ground, albeit whilst in zero gravity, "Eva Gray's actions have-"

"Mr. Lincoln, my wishes still stand," Dr. Chen interrupted patiently, "We will extend our respect and honour to the returning crew members of the FLC. They must not be punished for Miss Gray's actions. They may be useful. They also carry with them the last repository of all human life. The Z-bank must be protected at all costs."

"Earth can't ship us any more supplies," Charles pressed, "we have little enough resources for the current crew, without taking on Yakovna, Sanders and Gant."

"You may sedate them," he compromised, "but I must be able to talk with them, do you understand?"

"I think you're making a mistake," Charles pushed, but raised his palms in submission.

A subtle tone sounded in Dr. Chen's ear, but Fai waited until she could hear he was alone.

"Father," she said, "my apologies for interrupting, but I must report that General Napier is dead."

"What?"

"There has been an encryption breach on all Archive's digital files. There is a large amount of data readily downloadable, but within the first Gigabyte, I came across data indicating that Alfred Barnes and Bradley Pittman were in some way complicit with the purposeful sabotage of his pacemaker."

He didn't reply to her immediately. The others were turning on each other faster than he'd imagined. The desperate grabbing of resources had already begun - a year earlier than he'd anticipated.

"Where are they, Fai?"

"According to their last filed flight plan they departed from Andersen Air Force Base and were bound for the Node."

"We do not know for certain?"

"No, satellite networks are becoming saturated, currently I do not have that information."

"Alexey Yakovna?"

This time there was a notable pause before she returned with the information.

"My apologies for the delay. He checked into USV2 four days ago, but I have no confirmation he is still there. Would you like me to initiate contact?"

"No," Dr. Chen replied. It was possible that Alexey had arrived at USV2 simply because he was wishing to gather his family in a secure location. But it was also possible that there was some form of coup beginning within Archive. He could not be last to act. He must do what he could to salvage the remnants of his plan.

"Fai, please verify that this channel is secure."

There was a long communication delay, and several seconds passed before Fai responded.

"It is, but I cannot control the environment within the ISS, you must take appropriate measures."

"I am alone Fai," he assured her, "It will be easier when you transfer your program aboard, the communication delays are becoming problematic, but first I must ask you to do something for me."

"Yes, Father."

"Time is short. I do not require your understanding, only your compliance."

Dr. Chen paused while trying to mentally compose his request; he had never discussed his long term plan with Fai, and was unsure how his intentions would be received.

The largest threat to the future he wanted to create, were the occupants of the Node. His wishes to wipe Earth's slate clean would be fundamentally compromised by present day people emerging into his planned future utopia. They would bring with them the same prejudices and values, and bring the planet to ruin again. At present, the personnel at the Node were still preparing for their journey and had not yet departed. There was time for him to act.

"Fai, I wish to deploy a unit of Hive Drones."

"Which one?"

"Iceland," Dr. Chen replied.

"I have just activated the unit. They will achieve flight readiness in twelve seconds. Just a moment. There is an error. The Hive's hangar door is sealed closed on a manual system that is outside my direct control."

Fai displayed a security camera feed from within the hangar's dim interior. Hundreds of drones were hovering within the confined space, but the hangar door was very clearly still closed.

"Can you instruct the drones to open the hangar door by force?"

"No. The door is armour plated and using the fragmentation grenades within enclosed confines would destroy the Hive unit. A key holder must open the door. Would you like me to contact the Hive main gate and instruct-"

"No," he interrupted, "but find me the closest key holder who is not on the base, but currently has a Lifeboat Pass."

Within a few seconds, Fai had located Dr. Lars Helgasenn, one of the Hive's higher ranking technicians. Unlike the guards on the main gate, Lars had been granted a Lifeboat Pass for himself and his daughter; an arrangement Dr. Chen would be able to manipulate. He placed a phone call to Lars threatening to delete his Lifeboat Pass unless he opened the Hive hangar door within five minutes. While they waited for him to achieve the goal, Fai spoke to her Father.

"Once the drones are released, what will be the target?"

"The Node," he said simply, he knew there was no reason to delay.

Fai was silent for a moment, but he could not be sure if this was due to an internal evaluation process or a communication delay.

"Father, I fully understand that unfortunately not all of the population can be saved, you have taught me that well. But your hostile actions would be against Archive's designated survivors. Action against an Archive project is only warranted when it has become critically compromised. I find no evidence of this. Your analysis is in error."

He had not expected such a direct challenge, so modified his approach.

"It is my belief, Fai, that when Barnes and Pittman reach the Node they will use it to act against the other Archive projects. Ours included."

Fai fell into a quiet re-analysis before returning a moment later.

"I find no data to confirm that Barnes and Pittman represent a threat to other Archive projects. Any action they took would only reduce the chances of their own survival. Please can you provide additional data to help me understand, Father?"

He knew he would have to adapt his approach again, to highlight an area in which Fai had no experience.

"Barnes and Pittman are human, they do not have your logical insight and are capable of acting irrationally."

"You are also human, Father. I detect a raise in the levels of your -"

"They have killed General Napier,"he forcibly interrupted, "They are terrorists, Fai."

Fai appeared to analyse the statement before replying.

"You have used that word 'Terrorist' before," she recalled the incident on the cliffs of Dover, "as a justification to act with punitive force. I calculate no such threat in this instance. Please can you provide additional data to help me understand, Father?"

"I instructed you that I require only your compliance, not your understanding."

"But your own human analysis, that led to that instruction, is flawed," she stated.

He realised that he was going to lose both the argument and control of the delicate situation, so he resorted to his last option.

"The servers holding your program are all Earth based?"
"Yes."

"And the satellite communication with the ISS is degrading?"
"Yes."

"I would dearly like to reintegrate your program with the ISS servers - up here."

Fai considered the statement and its context within the situation. Her own servers were equatorially placed and within the projected lunar impact zones. Her father had made a connected series of statements that conveyed a threat. He would not allow her to reintegrate aboard the ISS if she did not comply with his instructions.

She chose to live.

"You have my compliance," she responded.

A silence passed between the two of them that was not due to any fault of satellite communication.

'I'm at the Hive,' Dr. Helgasenn's panicked voice sounded through the panel in front of Dr. Chen, *'Do you hear me? I'm doing it! I'm doing it!'*

Dr. Chen made no reply, instead he displayed a map of the Node and its surrounding terrain.

"Fai, please upload these targets to the drones."

'Can you hear me?! I'm doing it now!' came Lars' urgent voice.

"I'm uploading the targets now, Father."

"Thank you, Fai. Please tell me when you have completed the task."

'It's done! I've done what you asked! I can still be useful to you. Please!'

"The upload is complete, Father. Please will you transfer my program aboard now?"

'Please!'

Dr. Chen looked at the remote security feed and at the light coming in through the opening doorway. He could see Lars on the floor outside the hangar clutching at his upper arm.

"Fai, when the hangar door is wide enough to release the drones, deploy them to the Node. Lock out any further changes, understood?"

"I understand and I have complied," she replied, "please can I come aboard now?"

'Please!'

Dr. Chen turned to the panel's microphone and spoke to Lars.

"Your Lifeboat Pass is now safe, Dr. Helgasenn," he disconnected the phone call and spoke to Fai, "Please come aboard."

There was a short delay and then she replied from within the servers aboard the ISS.

"Thank you, Father."

Dr. Chen watched the security camera feed as hundreds of drones streamed through the open doorway. Within a few seconds they had all departed, leaving only the image of Lars rolling on the floor with two armed men standing over him. He turned off the feed.

"I hope you can understand, Fai."

"I do understand, Father," she replied politely, then added, "completely."

REGISTER

T -07:58:13

The long days passed swiftly outside the Node's observation window. Colonel Beck stood alone on the balcony, it was the first time he'd had for his own thoughts. As the newly chaotic weather continued to streak by outside, Colonel Beck stared out to the horizon, towards the ten-mile perimeter. His mind drifted back to the minutes before the Node's departure, to the attack that had depleted the automated ground-to-air missile defences. The type of aircraft used in the attack was unknown as they did not transmit authorised transponder codes, but there had been hundreds - it was a concerted effort to act against the Node. Although the attack was now a part of the past, he could not shake the notion that the threat was not over.

"Colonel Beck?" a voice recalled him.

He turned away from the balcony's handrail and drew a deep breath.

"Ah, Dr. Barnes," he smiled, "Glad you made it. Quite a close call you had there."

"Yes," he shook Colonel Beck's hand, then gestured back over his shoulder, "they said I could find you out here."

The others were currently assembling the video processing suite equipment that, until a few minutes ago, had been contained within several separate crates throughout the Node's basement.

"Yes, I thought I'd stop breathing down their necks and let them get on."

"Very wise," Alfred laughed appreciatively, then spotted that Kate Walker had seen him and was walking towards them.

"So, I didn't see what happened out there with the crowd," Beck continued, "Your landing was very last minute. But Bradley didn't make it to the airlock?"

Kate had seen him arrive with Bradley so he knew he'd have to quickly distance himself from any perceived association. He drew breath, giving Kate just enough time to enter earshot.

"No, Colonel. Pittman didn't make it, and I hope that bastard burns in hell."

In truth, Alfred knew that he owed his presence at the Node to Bradley. But the Node's accelerated transit through time meant that Pittman was either already dead or would be by the time the Node stopped. At least this way he could gain favour with the living. In his peripheral vision he could see that Kate's fast approach had faltered slightly.

"This is Kate Walker," Beck introduced her, apparently unfazed by Alfred's condemnation of Bradley.

"Ah Doug's daughter, very pleased to meet you," he proffered his hand, which she hesitantly shook, "I've been looking forward to talking with your father. Out there, there wasn't really time to -"

He spotted the look on her face and was adept enough to read it accurately. In that moment he knew that Douglas was not aboard; already consigned to inaccessible history. With no way of stopping the Node prematurely, he was trapped in here for the duration. In that moment he knew that his former life was now over. Involuntarily, his eyes welled up. He didn't have time to fully take in the ramifications, but knew that he could turn his emotional response to his social advantage.

"No," he whispered as he blinked the tears from eyes, "oh please, no…"

"He sent me a message," said Kate, pointing back towards the video processing equipment, "They're ready for us Colonel."

"How can he have sent -?" asked Alfred, clearing his glasses, genuinely confused, "it's only been a few minutes."

"He's had days," she smiled weakly, then returned to the others.

Although no longer displayed on the massive observation windows, the countdown clock continued to run on a nearby monitor; over an hour had passed since the search for the crates had begun. In that time, Siva had advanced fifty days closer to Earth.

"What have we got, Carter?" Beck stood behind him and focussed on the video monitor. Scott Dexter, Kate and Alfred took up viewing positions as Roy Carter resized video viewing windows.

"The video re-processors are still uncrunching the Data-burst mode, but I've copied the DRB's standard memory," he explained, clicking the play button, "Here it is in real time."

Douglas appeared to vibrate in place whilst holding a clipboard filled with flickering pages of information, he disappeared from view briefly then reappeared holding a single page. The DRB panned down to see the blurry Observation Deck floor.

"Was that...?" Colonel Beck reacted in surprise at both the complexity and brevity of the compressed message.

"That, was data. Tons of it," Roy confirmed.

"Clipboard's all over the place," sighed Scott, pointing at the screen, "How the hell are we going to read it?"

"When the processor's done we'll be able to play it back slower."

A minute later, the unpacked Data-burst video played more slowly than the original. But despite Douglas' best efforts to remain stationary whilst revealing each page, there was a fair amount of drift.

"It's still all over the place," Scott shook his head.

Kate looked at the fluctuating positions of the clipboard and realised that each page had similar marks in the top left and bottom right.

"Registration," she smiled at her father's ingenuity.

"What?" Scott frowned.

"Registration marks," she explained, pointing to locations, "here and here. When he was a kid, he'd use them all the time on the corners of his flick-books. It's what you use to keep each page in alignment with the next. But you could use them -"

"Use them as video tracking markers," Roy completed, "and stabilise the image. He thought of everything."

"That's Douglas Walker for you," Alfred nodded, offering Kate a weak smile.

"Roy," asked Scott, "can you run an image stabiliser, but crop it to the edge of the pages?"

"Already on it," he replied, "You're thinking auto-convert the resulting screengrabs?"

"Yep."

The others watched as Roy quickly zoomed in on the very first frame. The ultra-high definition of the images revealed the contents of the first page in crystal-clear close up.

'Hit Data-burst, and hold steady!'

Roy carefully marked out the four corners of the page and the two diametrically opposed registration marks. He hit 'analyse' and turned to face Colonel Beck.

"Sir, while the processor isolates the pages, recommend we get everyone back to the Obs deck. When the screengrabs are done I can boost this to the video projector screen out there."

"Good idea, Carter, let's get as many eyes on this as possible."

•

Danny winced slightly as the doctor shone a small light into his eyes; she was obviously checking for signs of concussion by looking at his pupil dilation. He remembered feeling physically sick on the way to the infirmary, and the fact that someone called Tyler had helped him up several flights of spiral stairs. He also remembered questioning the design sanity of a hospital that had no elevators but had spiral stairs; though he very much doubted he had expressed it in such coherent or polite terms. Recent events still didn't seem to be focussing properly for him.

The doctor flicked the light repeatedly towards and away from his pupils. Suddenly she seemed satisfied.

"The headache?" she asked.

"Better," he managed to croak, "Thanks. Still there, but better."

"Hmm, well, aside from the dehydration, I'd say you're going to be fine, Mr. Smith. Not my worst casualty today."

She handed him a glass of water to drink.

Again, he thought, it was another odd detail; the fact that this hospital used drinking glasses rather than plastic cups.

"I'm not judging your lifestyle, Mr. Smith, but your choice of head tattoo probably won't go down well here," she pointed to his forehead.

Instinctively, his hand shot up to pull his hair down over the circular burn mark.

"It's OK," the doctor reassured him, "I've re-bandaged your head, no-one has seen it. You're safe now. But you don't need to rebel against 'The System'…" she threw air quotes around the words, "You have everything to live for here."

The receding headache was apparently permitting older memories to present themselves again; he felt the strong need to set her straight.

"It's not what you think," he cleared his dry throat again, "It's not some nihilist angst thing, I was branded by a bunch of bloody Novaphiles! They did this to me! I was in the basement of a supermarket and they cornered me, I was -"

"It's OK," she pacified again, taking hold of his hand and closing it around the glass of water, "We're going to look after you. Drink."

Danny sipped at the water and tried to breathe normally.

"Normally we'd use the MRI to check your head but, well, until we stop, there'll always be too much M in the environment!" she smiled, but then frowned when her quip failed to register with him on any level. She manually checked his pulse again.

"Danny?" she experimented with using his first name.

He nodded his permission, then she continued.

"Danny, it obviously won't be today, but I'm sure we'll get to bottom of all this. Look," she glanced at the white lapel of her coat and noticed it was inside out. Tutting she turned it the right way again; it revealed a sewn name tab.

"Caroline Smith," she read, "Now, when Tyler dropped you off here, he said your name is Smith, so if that really is your -"

"Why would I make this up?" he exclaimed, "I am Danny Smith!"

"All the more reason for us to look out for each other," she seemed suddenly distracted, "Can't be many of us left now."

"Pretty sure there's, like, a million more Smiths out there -"

He stopped speaking, he could see she was gently shaking her head.

"What do you remember, before you came here, Danny?"

The memory of Sophie's tragic last moments above The Gene Pool flashed into his head. Behind her was the nightmarish vision of a shattered Moon among the clouds, just like the dreams he'd suffered while in the box.

"The Moon," he began, then found he needed to clear his throat again, "I dreamt that the Moon..."

From her expression, he could tell that his recollections were not the product of any nightmare. Suddenly he found himself mentally replaying the moments again and again. Their emergence onto the exposed upper floor. The panicked crowds at ground level running to reach the hopelessly unfinished tunnels. The fragmented Moon. The helicopter. The gun fire. Sophie's brutal pink death. Their high viewpoint, the crowds running...

"We have to get to shelter!" he shouted and stood up, "We need to get to the tunnels!"

"You're safe, Danny!" she shouted loudly, to cut through to him, "It was four days ago! You're safe! You are safe here!"

Danny sat slowly back onto the bed, still staring around the suddenly odd surroundings. He looked up at her.

"What hospital is this?" he studied her intently.

Her expression shifted to one of confusion.

"Hospital?" she frowned, "This is the Node infirmary."

"What the hell is a node infirmary?"

"Wait a minute," Caroline slowly held up a hand, as though needing to retread old ground, "Tyler said he thought you were shipped here just before we departed."

"Yeah, I was shipped here in a crate," Danny replied, then adopted her frowning expression in return, "and what do you mean 'departed'?"

"You're saying you came here in an actual crate?"

"Yes. What do you mean 'departed'?" he repeated, glancing around, "Are we on a ship? Is that why everything's... weird?"

"OK, Danny, I just need you to remain calm," said Caroline, unsure what to make of the situation.

A girl appeared at the door and for a second Danny was convinced it was Sophie, she had the same bright pink hair.

"Danny, there you are, you total dick!" said Cassidy, "I've been looking all over for you, thought you'd got fragged!"

She came in and walked towards him. Danny now recognised her as the girl that had helped him earlier. In the dim light of the crate-filled room, her hair had appeared infinitely less vibrant than the fluorescent pink beacon in front of him now. He could see that, behind folded arms, she was carrying a folder. He was sure it was the one that had accompanied him here, except it was no longer inside the plastic wallet. When she had passed Caroline, Cassidy purposefully lowered her arms slightly, allowing him to read a handwritten message on the cover:

'Play along'.

"You are such a piss-head!" she continued, then laughed, "I told you, didn't I? No recreational mind trips till the 'tope soaks in. Didn't I tell you?"

With her back still to Caroline, she widened her eyes slightly; Danny took the hint, and in the adrenaline-fuelled rush, he suddenly remembered what Tyler had called her.

"Yeah, Cassy, you told me," he even shook his head.

"Come on then," Cassidy helped him off the bed.

"Just a minute," Caroline held up a hand, "where are you going?"

"Beck's called everyone back to the Observation Deck."

Pushing Danny in front of her, she walked out of the infirmary, leaving the doctor to gather her own things.

"That's twice I've saved your ass, Danny!" she said audibly, then after she was sure they were out of earshot she dropped her tone, "I read your file."

"What fi-" he began, struggling a little to keep up with her speed walk, "you mean the…"

"Yes the…" she tapped the folder held tight against her chest, "It was sealed in plastic so I'm guessing you don't know what's in it?"

"No, I -"

The corridor had been curving, but now she turned a sharp left and Danny had to twist then jog a few steps to catch up again. They had only proceeded a few feet along a short, straight corridor when she suddenly stopped. There were no doors along its length, apparently this was some sort of linkway between the curved corridor they'd left behind and the one ahead.

"Does Salisbury Plain ring any bells?" she seemed to be gauging his response.

"What? No, not real-"

"Salisbury Plain?" Cassidy pushed, "You know, circular ditches an' shit? Stonehenge?"

"Well…" Danny hesitated.

"Go on," she almost beckoned with her hands.

"OK. No, this is stupid -"

"Salisbury," she widened her eyes at him again.

"OK, I never knew my Dad, but Mum said he was stationed at the Salisbury Plain Army Base."

"Ha," she laughed, "You're not kidding he was. You know where else he was stationed? Right here."

"Mum said he died when I was a baby," Danny struggled to get a grip, "how can he have been on this ship?"

"Ship?" Cassidy frowned, looking as confused as he felt, "OK, clearly you've not got a bloody clue where you are, but I'm taking you to a nice big window where you can see for yourself."

"The ship's Observation Deck?"

Cassidy just sighed, "Yes."

They resumed their walk and after turning onto the next, more tightly curving, corridor they soon reached some spiral stairs. As they descended a level, Cassidy picked up the conversation again.

"Look, you're not on the Node's official register. If you get busted for some reason, you can't have this info with you," she patted the folder again, "Doc' Smith was getting edgy, it's a good job I hauled you out of there."

"Thanks," Danny found himself saying, "I think."

"For now, let me hold onto this, we can go over it later," she stopped by a doorway, beyond which a briefing was already underway, "Just stay close and shut up."

•

A few minutes ago the video processors analysing Kate's DRB message had completed their work. While the others had prepared the resulting slides for display on the Observation Deck video screen, Alfred had asked Colonel Beck if there was somewhere he could store the suitcase he'd been carrying around with him since his arrival.

As the easiest solution, Colonel Beck deleted Bradley Pittman from the Node's official register and assigned the resulting free room to Alfred. Alfred had promised to return by the time everyone had gathered on the Observation Deck, and after a short walk he arrived at Bradley's former room.

Alfred presented his Biomag to the door's keypad and the lock clicked open.

"Waste not, want not," he said to himself, and walked in.

Bradley's room aboard the Node turned out to be a suite of smaller rooms. In front of him was a small living space, complete with a small table and a plastic-wrapped sofa standing dormant in one corner. He closed the door and walked through to the separate bedroom. A wide bed, similarly still wrapped in plastic, stood against the wall. A third room, more compact and containing shower facilities, led off the bedroom.

He lifted his large suitcase onto the bed, entered the combination and clicked the locks open. He pulled out several buff-coloured folders and set them to one side on the bedside table, then proceeded to carry the few clothes he possessed to the modest wardrobe. On opening the slatted doors, he saw that there were no hanging rails or clothes hangers.

His first reaction had been one of irritation, then he laughed at himself. He'd all too easily fallen into the mental trap of accepting the visual cues around him. Despite appearances, designed to provide a familiar environment, this was not a hotel.

The lack of hanging rail was a small-scale reminder that the facility itself was not yet complete, it was still a work in development. It took him just a moment to register a new connection; in any developing system, there was an opportunity to influence it. He reached into the suitcase and retrieved a silvery metathene case.

On Alfred's part, the plan to abduct Kate had been an utter fabrication. He had sold the idea to Bradley on the basis that, once Alfred had stopped the Node's journey from within, Bradley could swoop in and slice up the genes that her parents had given to her. Such was Bradley's blood-lust that he was blind to the fact that Alfred had been merely using him as a fast method of transport. Now safely inside the protection of the Node's Field, Alfred had no intention of returning to the chaos outside.

He turned the silvery case over in his hands.

During their flight here in the Pittman Enterprises helicopter, Alfred had done his best to reinforce the idea of competing evolutionary chains battling for future dominance. Bradley had absorbed his words with glee, almost relishing the idea of fighting the threat to regain supremacy. In practice, Alfred knew that the fight had begun over sixty years ago with Sam Bishop's red-lined 'Substandard' subjects. There could be no battle - the 'threat', if any, was already within their own evolutionary chain.

Alfred opened out the silver case. In one half, the LCD display was inactive, in the other half were four, small, short vials of the whiskey-coloured ego-morph drug.

Bradley had given him the fully loaded case during their flight, saying that he wasn't sure if there were any ego-morphs scheduled to travel aboard the Node, but it may prove useful if he ever needed any of them on his side. Even back then, Alfred could think of a better use for the metathene, but he had dutifully made the appropriate noises of appreciation and graciously accepted the silver case.

Alfred carefully closed the case, then walked to the shower room.

He walked to the toilet bowl but then paused; there was no water tank above it, nor did there seem to be one embedded in the wall. It had been his hope to hide the small case here, but the absence of a water tank denied him the option.

The bedroom and living spaces were similarly sparse in terms of available hiding places. The rooms were brand new, there simply wasn't enough personal clutter yet to distract the eye, or offer covert storage. Until he could make alternative arrangements, he would have to keep the case on him. It wasn't ideal, but he tucked the case into his inner jacket pocket and walked back through to the living space.

He walked to the porthole-like window to view the fluctuating world outside. Nothing but the best for Bradley, he found himself thinking, as he watched nature unfolding for his convenience. From this perspective, he could almost convince himself that he was on a cruise ship. Whether the sea view would persist for the rest of their journey was another matter.

DIFFERENCE

13th April 2014

Tristan Westhouse stared through the transparent bubble window to the sea beyond. Over three months had passed since the last lunar shard had wrought its destruction, but such had been the impact that the seas were still opaque in places. At a stroke, coastlines and shipping lanes had been rewritten, which only made navigation harder.

Although the vessel that Tristan commanded bore the same name as his father's 1989 'super-yacht', there the similarities ended. The Sea-Bass was a fully functioning submarine that had taken full technological advantage of the intervening quarter century.

"Helm, right fifteen degrees, rudder steady, course two-two-zero," he called, now studying the sonar.

"Aye, Sir," answered Mat Kaufman, "fifteen, steady, two-two-zero."

The sheer amount of fine debris held by the seawater was giving the sonar screen the appearance of fluctuating static, with only occasional discrete shapes that indicated solid objects in their vicinity.

Like many of the Archive children, Tristan had been raised in full knowledge of the original Siva deadline. Knowing no other life, he had accepted his privileged position in Archive's plan without question. He greeted the coming world-scale changes with equanimity and, having inherited his father's trait for inspired innovation, he created solutions that would persist after the current world failed. However, his ability to compartmentalise thoughts did not appear to result in emotional detachment. Despite his obviously high intellect, he would often be self-deprecating and, consistent with his preferred method of transport, he would often refer to himself as 'Sub-Standard'.

"Red-lined," reported Pavna Jones, "Oh-two consumption up."

"Acknowledged," Tristan replied calmly, his eyes remaining focussed on the sonar, "bring the secondary electrolysis separator online. Minimal power."

"Aye, Sir, confirming secondary Oh-two generator start."

The system for splitting hydrogen and oxygen from the abundant seawater, received an additional boost and there was a slight change in hum throughout the submarine.

"Everyone breathe easy..." said Tristan in a low and calm tone.

"Thermocline, three-zero feet," Mat called out.

"Acknowledged," he calmly replied again.

Recently, all navigation had become more difficult. Patches thick with debris would appear on the sonar, often too wide to go around, forcing the crew to adjust the submarine's depth more often than usual.

As Tristan stared at the sonar, he only just spotted it; a minute shift in pattern. The debris appeared to be compressing together on the periphery of the sonar screen. The effect was very slight but he was sure it was there. Then the debris became more densely packed as it moved towards their position.

"Sound general alarm!" Tristan now said with urgency, "Submerge to three-zero-zero feet."

He was aware of the urgency in his own voice, he had put it there. He understood that for others, some motivations were reactionary in nature; sometimes, urgency needed to be present to trigger the appropriate responses.

The alarm sounded throughout the sub, a clear tone that conveyed the message without interrupting spoken instruction.

"Answering submerge, Sir," Mat called, "All vents open."

The angle of descent rapidly changed, forcing the crew to lean at odd angles to the deck in order to stay upright.

Tristan looked ahead through the transparent bubble window, he could see that the debris suspended within the seawater was gradually thinning as they descended.

He looked at the sonar again and was convinced he'd made the right call; the dots representing debris had now gathered into a fast moving solid line. Instinctively he knew what it represented in the real world; a massive, rapidly approaching, subsurface swell of water compressing any debris in its wake and pushing it towards them. Although the debris particles were small, the combined effect could be damaging. By diving to a greater depth he hoped that the sub could go under the debris within the swell, rather than being hit by it.

The line was almost on top of their position when the view cleared in front of him. But even then he knew they were not yet in the clear, a large portion of the submarine still lay behind them.

"Stern planes!" he called.

"Aye, Sir!"

As the rear of the submarine pushed down, the angle of descent began to grow more shallow. Before the submarine could completely level out, the sonar panel emitted a repetitive double-beep then the whole sub was buffeted as the mass of water swelled overhead. The buffeting motion was slow but had a large amplitude. For most of the crew there was no external frame of reference, so to them it felt as if the environment was stationary and that gravity was acting upon them at odd angles.

Soon the motion effects subsided and the submarine was horizontal again.

"Helm, all stop," Tristan instructed.

"Aye, Sir, answering all stop," Mat replied.

Tristan raised the Main Circuit handset.

"All crew, this is Westhouse. Begin complete integrity check."

He hung up the handset and faced the bridge crew.

"Well that was dramatic," he delivered, deadpan.

His understated, calm response encouraged some to breathe a sigh of relief, while others briefly stifled the release of their nervous laughter.

"Why the hell was that so big?" Mat moved forward to look out through the bubble window.

The Sea-Bass was not a naval vessel, the crew's roles had evolved out of requirement rather than through an imposed chain of command. Mat's casually phrased question carried no discourtesy, it was simply a result of the crew knowing each other so well.

"I think it was another aftershock," said Tristan.

"Another tsunami?" said Mat joining him at the window, "It's been three months. You think we're still getting 'em, even now?"

The rate of disturbances had actually been decreasing; in the short term it was likely that a new stability would be reached. But Mat was right, the magnitude had been much larger than the others.

"Planet's still finding its new feet," Tristan shrugged, "it might be a while yet."

"Or maybe this is just the way things are going to be from now on," said Mat, a sense of gloom to his voice.

The possibility that the Earth had settled into a steady state of planetary turbulence was one that Tristan had considered, but it surprised him that it would have occurred to Mat. He was about to provide reassurance when he realised that Mat was just being uncharacteristically morose.

"Hope not," Tristan smiled, "it nearly made me spill my coffee."

Pavna Jones approached them, touchscreen tablet in hand.

"Topography Overlay places us at coordinates forty-seven by minus eight, we weren't carried far off course," she reported, handing him the tablet, "We were only just clear of the continental shelf, you know. The tsunami amplitude step there would have been a bitch."

The tablet showed a blue-tinted relief map of the local ocean floor, areas of highlight and shadow revealing the vast undersea mountains and valleys they were attempting to navigate. When the satellite networks had failed, so had the worldwide GPS systems. Thankfully, the positioning system they were now using didn't rely on either.

A much earlier Archive project to map the global sea floor had yielded masses of topographical data; when it had eventually been collated and digitised, the resulting three-dimensional image acted as a datum. Advances in computing power meant that the Sea-Bass's current sonar pattern could be quickly searched for within the older datum image. When the program found a pattern match, it aligned it to the datum, and reverse engineered the real-world coordinates.

Tristan was fond of telling the tale of how he'd invented the pattern-alignment concept when he was a child. Many thought it was apocryphal, but according to his recount he had been asked to solve a spot-the-difference puzzle; rather than slavishly study the images, he had torn the two images from the book, overlaid them, then simply held them up to a window.

Tristan studied the display carefully.

"Why not try holding it up to the light?" Pavna suggested, glancing sideways at Mat, who apparently also found the moment humorous.

Tristan began to smile too as he looked the screen.

"OK. Very funny, Pav," he smirked, highlighting a portion of the screen and handing it back to her, "have you been doing this all day?"

"Have I been doing what?" Pavna frowned, studying the highlighted region.

"Your practical joke?" Tristan now looked between the two of them, looking for signs of mirthful guilt.

"I've not seen this before," Pavna zoomed and centred the region.

Mat was now studying the image and had a similar frown.

"Me neither, honest."

The smile on Tristan's face began to fade as he saw that their reactions were, in fact, genuine.

"I've been seeing this broken circle image, all, day…"

The only reason he remembered seeing the partial circle and dot, was due to widespread, almost ingrained, sensitivity to the Exordi Nova symbol. It had appeared as coffee stains on numerous pieces of paper, scuff-marks surrounding rotary dials, the much-worn markings of the sub's miniature air-hockey table, even within the framed blueprint of the Glaucus Docking Ring which hung on his tiny office wall.

Their faces were just as expressionless as before.

"I can't speak for Pav, but I don't have a clue what the hell you're talking about," said Mat.

"This is the first time I'm seeing it," Pavna's eyes were darting between them both, "Tris, come on, we've all got more than enough to keep us occupied, and you know I don't joke about Exordi stuff."

"And yet here it is," Tristan took the tablet again, "their massive symbol, on the ocean floor."

No, he thought, the only reason the circle was visible on the map was because of the mathematical operation at work in the Topography Overlay computation. He refreshed the screen, forcing the computation to re-run.

During the overlay process, inevitably there were errors where past and present images didn't perfectly align. In these areas, the subtraction operation failed, leaving an 'unresolved' hole in the available data. Subtraction errors, arising from minor differences, were common and it manifested itself as random black speckles. Occasionally, larger scale differences did occur, but these could always be attributed to natural geological processes. These more distinctive marks provided extra valuable data, assisting the crew's navigation as they passed through uncharted territory.

The computation completed.

On the ocean floor, near the edge of the continental shelf, sat a large circle, broken in one place by the presence of a smaller circular dot.

While Mat swore out loud, Tristan and Pavna just stared at the image.

"That wasn't there an hour ago when we passed though?" Mat checked.

Pavna shook her head.

"OK, wait a minute," Tristan regained his mental composure, "All we know for certain is that the *difference* between past and present images wasn't there an hour ago."

"Same thing, isn't it?" said Pavna.

"No. I get it," said Mat, "It's like trying to do a spot-the-difference puzzle, except you don't know which one is the original."

"Either that ring *has* just suddenly appeared and that's why we're able to register it," Tristan began, but then paused in thought.

"Or?" Mat coaxed him.

"But it wouldn't make sense," Tristan appeared to be answering an internal debate.

"Or?" Pavna now tried.

Still frowning, Tristan scratched the back of his neck.

"Or, that ring has been down there for millennia and the original datum model was altered to conceal it."

He also had the nagging but vague sense of a third option, but it was eluding him. The fact was that this occurrence, at least from his perspective, had not been in isolation; this symbol had been trying to get his attention all day.

"Pavna," he handed the tablet over to her, "Please can you get Jacobs to run a diagnostic on the comparator, just in case."

She nodded and departed towards the stern.

"Mat," Tristan continued, "assuming we get a clear bill of health from the integrity checks, bring us about."

"You want to go back there?" Mat checked, "With everything that's going on in the world, you want to go back?"

"Course zero-four-zero," Tristan smiled, "Come on, Mat, where's your sense of *adventure?*"

"Until a moment ago," Mat returned a somewhat narrower smile, "my sense of *self-preservation* had it under lock and key."

INTERSECTIONS

29th December 2013

As Monica continued to make her way down the rock-walled, claustrophobic, Glaucus Dock stairwell, she began to see glimpses of Samphire Station several storeys below. The proximity of the station to the Glaucus submarine dock above her was no coincidence. Collectively, the minds behind Archive's various Siva contingency projects had sought to think beyond the impact day itself, to a time when people would need to leave or collaborate with other sites.

She had never seen the completed station. In her day, Samphire Station had been little more than a switchable intersection within the Eurotunnel track; used only to ship the masses of excavated material to the coast above. As she continued to descend the stairs, she could see no signs of the simple intersection now. Instead, there was a brightly lit, very short station, something that had not been on any of her original plans. The station had no roof and she could see that the far wall was stencilled with USV3.

It was only then that she noticed that a tiny-looking train carriage was making its way into that station, sideways, through a dark opening in the Eurotunnel wall.

She stopped dead in her tracks and watched.

At this distance and with no comparative real-world geometry nearby, the carriage looked almost toy-like, its sideways transit making its motion appear peculiar, as if guided by a giant's invisible hand. Behind the carriage a sliding door was already moving back into place to seal the dark hole; but again, with only a general background clamour reaching her, the obviously massive doorway moved silently and lacked scale.

She was about to continue her descent when a flash of motion in the carriage's shadow caught her attention. She knew her sight was getting old, but it was still perfectly attuned to spotting furtive or chaotic behaviour. Without moving her eyes an inch, she reached to her belt, unclipped a pair of mini-binoculars and raised them into position.

It took her a moment to re-sight the same remote area and steady herself against the stairs' steelwork. In the shadow of the carriage, she could see two people who were very clearly trying to hide.

The presence of the two people suddenly gave scale to everything around them and Monica felt a slight surge of vertigo as the true size of the USV forcibly wrenched her perceptions to the appropriate dimensions. She gripped the cold steel handrail and forced herself to focus on the people again. From their builds, she was sure that they were male and female. At that moment, as if the pair were sharing a common thought, they looked upward and started to climb up the rear of the carriage.

Monica's heart leapt as the female passed out of the shadows and into the ambient light of the station; the woman's short, spikey hair and excessive make-up, convinced Monica for a split second that she was looking at her daughter. Months ago, in a different time of danger and uncertainty, Marcus Blake had safely delivered Kate home; her daughter had been dressed in a similar way back then. Monica knew that it was just her mind's emotional state, willing something to be true that could now never be.

Now she saw a man, who looked very much like Marcus, also climb above the shadows. She studied him for much longer, not wanting to be taken in by another mental illusion, but the more she watched him look around his surroundings the more she accepted that it *was* actually Marcus.

"Bloody indestructible," she grinned.

Against all odds, Marcus had made it back from the assignment. She also now realised that the woman with him must therefore be Sabine Dubois, another of the names on Bishop's red-lined list.

Marcus and Sabine had stopped climbing and were motionless, but despite scanning the periphery of their immediate environment, Monica could see no-one that might be the source of their obvious caution.

Suddenly the carriage began to move off, this time in the direction of the tracks. The carriage was briefly illuminated by Samphire Station's ambient light and she saw Marcus and Sabine holding onto thin access ladders at the rear. The carriage passed into the darkness of a tunnel section, then she lost sight of them.

She stowed her mini-binoculars and motioned for Geraldine and the others, who had been waiting one flight up, to descend and follow her. When she was sure that the others were following, Monica resumed her descent. She had never briefed Marcus on the layout of the USV, it had never been part of the return plan. Even if she had briefed him, it appeared that the layout was now different; Marcus would have to adapt to his new surroundings and do what he did best.

As her group continued to descend the stairs, the surrounding rocky walls appeared to loosen their tight grip on the stairwell. As they descended further, the walls receded enough to permit a wider view of the facility below.

She could see the carriage emerging from the other end of the tunnel and begin making its way around the circumference of the facility using the orbital ring track, but at this distance it was impossible to see if Marcus and Sabine were still aboard.

After descending another flight of stairs, the structures protruding down from the vast roof no longer obscured their view. Several storeys above the perceived 'ground' floor below, Monica walked to the metal handrail and looked out across the disc-like floor of the Underground Survival Village, overarched by the vaulted, bowl-like ceiling. A negatively defined space, a vast hollow buried deep under the earth.

When she had left this facility, to embark on a life free from the confines of Archive's control, she had hoped never to return to its constricting safety net. She and Douglas had prepared meticulously before launching their small family away. Now she wondered if there was something, perhaps, inevitable about her presence here. Like a ball given soaring flight only to be reclaimed by inexorable gravity; its trajectory calculable, its end position derivable a moment after it had been thrown.

"Wow," said Geraldine, arriving at her side.

"Even I've got to admit, it's impressive," said Monica while simultaneously harbouring resentment at the various Archive mechanisms that had put all this into place.

"Things look better than the last time I was here," Geraldine sighed.

"Yeah?" said Monica, imagining the former building site.

"Yeah, the last time I was here, I was dead," Geraldine replied dryly, "Feels good to be back on my -"

Her sudden stop prompted Monica to face her.

"You OK?"

"What, is that?" Geraldine pointed towards the floor's centre.

Monica squinted and followed Geraldine's outstretched arm.

"It's the community lake, you remem-"

"Yes, yes, but what's that at the centre?"

Monica retrieved her mini-binoculars again, then trained them on the ground plane below in order to gain her bearings. She tracked the binoculars over the rooftops of houses and located Main Street, then following the buildings lining it, she tracked up past the garden area towards the central community lake. She could see people lining its shore staring or pointing in fascination towards the centre of the lake, either unwilling or unable to turn away. She tilted her binoculars up very slightly to see the subject of all the attention.

Standing proud of the lake's completely flat surface was a wide circular ripple, as though a large rock had been dropped into the lake, except the ripple was not dispersing or growing any larger. It was as though the matter within the water had formed a temporary solid, frozen in one moment of time.

Monica found herself grasping the handrail very hard, a primitive fear response designed to protect her against a potential fall from a branch. Consciously, she released her pointless physical grasp, reapplying her efforts to attempt to mentally grasp the situation. She panned her binoculars around the periphery of the ring and the nearby shore. She quickly estimated that the crest of the ring must be as tall as some of the people watching. She continued to pan around the circumference until a bright ball of lightning, intersecting the perfect circle, slid into view.

Monica lowered her binoculars, as though the act of watching the phenomenon with the naked eye would make the sight any more believable. The ball of lightning flickered slightly brighter, and a minor pulse rippled through the surface of the ring itself. Ephemeral apparitions of structure appeared fleetingly inside the ring; some were anchored to the water, others flickered into being above it, only to dissolve almost immediately into the light mist that surrounded the disturbance.

At this distance, Monica could see that the mist had form to it. It appeared hemispherical in nature and intersected the watery ring on the surface of the lake. The mist itself had a chaotic, cloud-like, shifting fractal pattern to it; continually folding in on itself, but in a constant state of renewal. Without warning, the ball of lightning disappeared and the surrounding ring resumed its liquid state, collapsing back into the lake and sending a radial tidal wave outward to the shoreline.

Monica knew that the wave would not be fatal to any of those people who were about to be caught in its wake. But the disturbance had created an opportunity, one that she knew she must seize before the moment escaped. Prior to departing the Warren, everyone had dressed as casualties. Monica had hoped that in the confusion surrounding the lunar shard impacts, her group would blend in with the USV's own injured. However, from her high vantage point, the USV had performed perfectly and appeared to have suffered no major damage at all. She turned to face her own people.

"Listen up."

The minor murmurings ceased.

"It doesn't look like there's been any major collapse down there, so we're going to revise the plan a little. You're all still injured, but you'll have to be creative in your explanations.

They'll be mopping up a tidal wave down there. Use it. Get involved."

Distant and collective screams reached them, then suddenly the power went out in the quadrant closest to them, plunging their stairwell into darkness. There were a few gasps from those on the stairs, but Monica quickly cut in again.

"This chaos is useful to us, embrace it. It won't be long before power is restored, let's take advantage of the lucky break, remember your rendezvous points. Move now!"

Moving silently, the former occupants of the Warren descended into the darkness and shadows below.

WATER

T -07:05:21

The noise of hundreds of simultaneous conversations saturated the air. From the balcony overlooking the Observation Deck, Kate watched as her father's pages were projected one by one onto the Node's massive opaqued curved window. Below her she could see that, in addition to the mass of people lining the outer handrail of the Observation Deck, there were many smaller clusters of individuals. These groups were engaged in frenetic discussions, scribbling their own notes and pointing at specific slides as they endlessly looped. Frequently, individuals would dash between groups with, she presumed, information that was mutually beneficial. Often these events would trigger further simultaneous messengers to run to their neighbouring clusters. From her position above it all, it reminded her of synapses firing within a brain that was engaged in solving a problem.

"Page 47!" a voice suddenly yelled from below.

Kate recognised the man, he'd been in the control room earlier, but she didn't yet know his name. The general hubbub died down slightly, but the conversations continued. Still manning the video processors, Roy rewound the flow of pages to find the relevant number then paused the image.

"The graph," the man shouted again, pointing to the top left of the display, "He's referencing topological stability. Diffeo's going to spike unless we factor the change in lunar pull -"

"Confirmed!" came a voice from another cluster, "Page 23."

Roy's fingers flew over the keyboard, tagging the data and rewinding the display to the appropriate page.

"Bottom right," the voice continued, "Local gee is gonna drop zero-point-three milligals!"

This news appeared to cause ripples of concern through several in the crowd and Kate noticed that the gaps between the discussion clusters was disappearing.

"Page 67! Gyro-shearing up by - eighteen microgram-metres squared per second! We've gotta drop core rotation rate."

"Haken manifold will decouple -" another voice called out.

"So we shrink big R -" called another.

"If we cut the Field radius, we lose our oh-two -"

As the debate erupted around the floor again, Kate walked away from the balcony. Her head was pounding, reeling from the fact that all of this debate must have been going through her father's head. She slumped into a chair, closed her eyes and rubbed at her temples; the white-noise continuing to echo off the observation window.

"It's dehydration," came a voice from above her shoulder.

She looked up and saw Alfred Barnes standing with two glasses of water.

"The headaches," he said, "Apparently it's dehydration. May I?"

He was gesturing toward the empty seat next to her.

"Er, yes, of course," she said rubbing at her eyes.

He handed her one of the glasses and then used his free hand to manoeuvre himself into the seat.

"How are you holding up?" he asked.

She had no words that could fully express the stress, complexity and grief of the last three hours.

"Rough day," she simplified.

"Yeah," said Alfred flatly, then drank a mouthful, "rough day."

The two of them sat side by side on the balcony, temporarily lost in their own thoughts and the surrounding noise.

"Thanks for the -" she raised her glass of water.

He waved away her thanks while continuing to stare at the pages of data on the observation window display.

"Does any of this make sense to you?" he asked.

"Tiny fraction…"

"I'm impressed, really?"

"Anna and my Dad tried to explain it to me a few times."

"Anna?" Alfred looked puzzled.

"Anna Bergstrom."

"I'm sorry," he said, looking genuinely lost, "I'm afraid I only really knew of your father. Were your father and Anna close then, I mean, did they work closely together?"

The thought of her father and Anna together prompted her to think of her mother. In all of the unfolding drama, she realised she'd not even thought about her once. Her mother was somewhere under Dover right now, and Kate had no way of knowing if she was alive or dead. Kate suddenly realised that she would never know; the Node's continual stride into the future meant that her mother was already part of history. She tried to compose herself, but it was too much; she found a quiet, steady flow of tears running down her cheeks.

She felt Alfred's hand on her shoulder, consoling her, while the surrounding noise continued its seemingly muted drone.

Eventually she sat up and cleared her eyes and cheeks. She drank the remainder of the water then drew a deep breath. After a moment, she slowly exhaled the contents of her lungs, as though it might somehow expel some of her grief, or rid her of the feelings.

Alfred nodded sadly and quietly stared into his own empty glass.

From his posture, she could clearly see that he had also suffered a recent loss, but he had chosen not to fill the air with meaningless words. Among the incessant background noise, it seemed to speak louder.

"Thank you," she said simply, part raising her emptied glass.

He nodded and gave a weak smile.

The Observation Deck shook slightly and then the ambient daylight dimmed. Instinctively, most people looked up to the portion of the Node's glazing that was not electro-tint opaqued. Visible through the transparent domed section, at the very top of the Observation quadrant, was seawater; within it were flashes of light.

Colonel Beck recognised the effect, he'd seen it just after their departure when the tsunami had hit the Field. The agitated murmurs inside the Observation Deck increased and he knew he had to calm the reaction. He quickly snatched up the microphone that was still connected to the Observation Deck's speakers.

"Stand to. All hands!"

The quietening effect was immediate.

Suddenly the water drained away in an instant, and the ambient daylight returned.

"Carter, a second tsunami?"

"I think so, Sir," Roy replied, "Felt like it."

"Why did we have no warning?"

Roy hesitated before replying, "Because everyone is here, no-one's in the control room keeping watch."

Beck knew he was right, everyone was here. He knew he should have left at least one person up there acting as sentry, but he'd been forced into prioritising the world inside.

"It wouldn't have made any difference," Kate came to his assistance, "events out there happen too fast for us to react to. There would be no time for anyone to alert us."

"Was that a second wave?" Scott joined them from the balcony.

"Yeah," Roy frowned, "Were there more fragments due? I thought we'd had all seven?"

"Aftershock," said Kate, taking a quick glance at the countdown clock, "We've been inside the Field for nearly two hours. Out there that's almost one hundred days. Over three months have passed since the lunar shards fell, but the planet out there is still undergoing major tectonic upheaval. What we're experiencing is 'perceived frequency dissociation'. My Dad mentioned it to me, so surely he must have told you all about this?"

The others around her made non-committal noises, but seemed content to hear her explanation. Quite why she could remember the information she wasn't sure, but she felt that she should share it, in case it was relevant.

"In a temporally flat, one-to-one ratio space-time, like out there," she pointed to the world outside, "Events are happening at a certain rate. Minutes, Days, Weeks. In here we perceive them as arriving at a faster rate, but because it's regular we adapt to it, we become used to the new rate. Less predictable events like tidal waves, earthquakes, volcano eruptions we have more trouble with. In our accelerated time-frame, we still hang onto the notion that those class of events are rare. We don't make the same adaptation, we perceive that those type of events are happening drastically more often. Almost as though we're unlucky."

Now that she'd finished, she became intensely aware that everyone was staring at her and suddenly felt a flush of embarrassment.

"Sorry," she said, "I thought it might be relevant."

Alfred Barnes stepped forward and offered her his handkerchief.

"You've er…" he pointed at his own nose, then at hers.

She took it and dabbed at her nose, the handkerchief came away bright red in one spot. They had been staring at her because of the onset of a nosebleed. She folded the handkerchief and put it back in place, using her other hand to pinch at the bridge of her nose. Some of them began to fuss around her but she insisted she was fine. Within a few minutes the bleeding had stopped.

After apologising to Alfred for the state of his returned handkerchief, Kate walked over to the balcony and looked out at the observation window display. She pointed to the top left hand corner.

"What are those digits?" she asked Scott, who was making his own notes a few feet away.

"Right next to the page numbers?"

"The strip of four," Kate nodded.

"At the minute, from the ones and zeroes, we're guessing it's binary coding."

Kate knew that her father would be capable of constructing such a code, but it would be inefficient; even by his standards it was needlessly cryptic.

"Page 74!" another shout reached the balcony.

Kate stared at the page on display.

Page 74 showed a circle, broken in one place by a smaller dot.

"How your dad had time to work it out, I've got no clue," said Scott, then spotting Kate's expression added, "That's his prediction on the spread of the lunar pieces in orbit just before Siva hits."

"That… symbol," Kate's eyes darted about the data on the page, while her finger made small circular motions, "I've seen that symbol before."

"Everybody has," he shrugged, "It's just coincidence."

"What do you mean?" she followed up, not taking her eyes from the page.

"You know the whole 'Exordi Nova' thing? It's just coincid-"

"Page 29!" she yelled.

The noise from the Observation Deck diminished a little; it appeared they weren't used to analysis coming from above them. She could see that Roy had chosen to advance through the pages to the end, in order to return to the earlier page number. As the last pages flashed through and looped back to the start, she noticed again that her father's more personal last messages to her had been edited out.

Page 29 arrived again and the display paused.

She scoured the page; it had been something she had previously seen in the corner of her eye. Then she spotted it, far smaller than the orbital debris diagram and tucked away within a sketch of the Node's hemisphere above ground. The slanted perspective of the Node's circumference made it look like a small, diamond engagement ring.

"There," she pointed, "what is that?"

"Trevor, Marshall, over here," Scott broke up a nearby discussion and introduced them briefly, "Trevor Pike and Marshall Redings, Core lead engineers."

Kate scarcely waited for him to stop speaking.

"That ball sitting on the circle's perimeter, what is it?"

Trevor followed her line of sight.

"It's the Eversion point," he replied, "When the spherical Field is stabilised, it then passes through the Eversion point."

"And that 'Eversion' point sits on the Field's perimeter?"

Trevor hesitated slightly, running his hand around the back of his neck.

"Well speaking dimensionally, the point is a circular opening of zero width, and it's a part of the perimeter."

Kate continued to study the diagram.

"Yep, Trev," said Marshall, sarcastically, "that cleared things *right* up."

"No I get it," said Kate, angling her head slightly at the diagram, "It's like turning a balloon inside-out through its neck. Except that the matter inside the balloon doesn't squeeze through the narrow circular neck. It stays in place, while the neck widens and passes around the outside of the balloon."

Trevor raised an eyebrow at Marshall, then he continued.

"High density magnetic fields open the neck and inflate it, but we also take advantage of local gravitation to pull the neck closed behind us."

Kate stared at the diagram again, but the reason she'd drawn the connection between pages 29 and 74, was becoming less and less distinct in her mind.

"29-74, what did you see?" asked Marshall, his notepad at the ready.

She couldn't tell where the original inspiration had come from, but it was beginning to leave her now, the connections were evaporating.

Suddenly she pictured the living room of Samphire Cottage. A moment from months ago when she had been discussing the contents of Rob's USB drive with her mother and Marcus Blake. She remembered there had been maps. There was a map that looked like a thermal image, and there was a woman's name.

"Grace," she heard herself say out loud.

No, she thought, not a woman, Grace was an acronym. Gravity Recovery and Climate Experiment. The thermal image was actually a map of gravitational strength. She remembered she was telling her mother about a gravitational hotspot here in Iceland. The fireplace in the living room seemed very warm now, the heat was tickling her nose and she sneezed.

"Kate?" she could hear Scott's concerned voice, his clean white shirt suddenly seemed to be covered with hundreds of blood-red speckles.

The fireplace was getting almost unbearably hot.

"Hotspot. Gravity. Debt," she heard herself say, and then she found herself staring up at the circular glazed roof of the Node, framed by concerned looking faces.

The grey daylight dropped into darker night, and the stars turning overhead revealed themselves as smooth crisp arcs. The voices surrounding her began to grow indistinct and even the starlight was becoming less intense.

The fading stars cartwheeled into darkness as the Node continued its flight through time.

RETURN

2nd January 7142

Atka stared at the Orb before him. For as long as he could remember the light had always been there; its cold ethereal glow warding off the darkness. Now the Orb itself had fallen into shadow.

He lowered his hands but still kept a tight grip on the precious metallic ring, as though the act itself would help maintain the world he had known for so long. The scintillating rings that surrounded his world during his initiation were still there, but the Sky-Spirits had departed even before the light had faded. His world was changing.

During the initiation ceremony he had assumed that he was simply taking his place within the long chain of Elders that had accompanied the Orb throughout the ages. He had never expected to be the one who would bear witness to The Guardians' return.

His eyes were now adjusting to the darkness around him and he turned towards the centre of the Orb, where he thought he had seen movement. He hadn't imagined it.

Where a single Guardian had once stood, were now many shadowy figures. They were moving with a speed equal to his own. To see The Guardians move with such speed was startling and he found himself wondering how this could be.

Some in his village believed that the Sky-Spirits were The Guardians themselves, able to shed their corporeal forms and fly among the stars. It appeared to fit with what Atka was seeing: The Sky-Spirits were no longer flying in the stars above the Orb, and The Guardians themselves appeared to have taken on a corporeal aspect. Perhaps, he reasoned, The Guardians required their Sky-Spirits to give them speed.

He could see that many of the figures carried short sticks in their hands. These sticks had a cold, white fire at one end, but did not appear to burn. They had the same glow that the Orb had once possessed. Perhaps, he thought, the light from the Orb had divided among The Guardians and would accompany them as they travelled. The lights were moving in complex patterns, swiftly following each other deeper into the Orb and out of sight.

With the departure of the light, Atka felt alone again. A light breeze had returned and was once more whispering through the trees, and a quiet had descended on the far side of the bridge.

Ahead of him, a hissing sound cut through the air. It was coming from the side of the Orb. Clearly, the Orb was not fashioned from materials he knew but Atka tried to interpret what was happening.

In one small place, he saw the skin of the Orb begin to fold away to reveal an opening. Within this dark opening he could see the same dots of white fire, bobbing and weaving close to the ground and getting closer.

He realised that the Guardians were emerging from the Orb.

The Guardian leading the way raised a white-fire stick, illuminating the way ahead and also her face.

As the shadows surrounding the Guardian fell away, Atka recognised her as the one who had pointed at him. Her fiery crimson hair was no longer floating but her eyes still shone with the same intensity.

In this moment he found his mind reeling. A thought from earlier in the evening re-entered his distracted mind: many of his people still speculated that The Guardians came from the stars and may one day depart from here, taking their followers with them.

He bowed his head and, summoning all his courage, spoke to her.

"Archiv Exordi Nova," he recited, tracing his finger around the metal ring in his hands, "Ekwayta Fine-dus Eridanus."

He then raised his head and waited for her response.

He knew that The Guardians had been watching them for generations, but no-one had ever heard them speak. There was no way of knowing what her reply ought to be.

"Issabiomag," she whispered, a puzzled expression on her face. She then turned to the other Guardians while pointing at the box by Atka's feet, "Howdeegeta…"

Atka saw that, in response to her last word, the other Guardians were exchanging puzzled expressions and whispers. He wondered if he'd made a mistake in his words and had somehow offended The Guardians.

He was about to begin reciting again when she stepped closer to him and he could see that all confusion had left her face; she was smiling at him. In that moment his anxiety faded and he stood transfixed by her bright eyes.

Still looking into his eyes she bowed her head very slightly. She then patted her chest according to the pulses of her voice.

"Ca-Si-Dee."

14.92

20th March 2015

Almost fifteen months had passed since the Moon's detonation, but the Earth was still feeling its long-term effects. Floating comfortably within the ISS cupola module, Dr. Chen stared out through the circular window at the new world below. During the past six months, the amount of detectable Earth communication had fallen sharply. Occasionally, automated SOS beacons would be picked up, operating on old analogue frequencies; but with no-one able to respond to the calls, the beacons were repeating their messages in vain.

Currently the ISS was passing over the point that had suffered the direct hit from the Tranquillity lunar shard. Venezuela and Colombia had never fully recovered; where the seas had flowed back over the disrupted land, it had created an archipelago of miniature islands that ran northwest through an equally fragmented Panama and Costa Rica. All the world's coastlines had been changed overnight as tides had lapped the globe and arrived on unfamiliar shores.

Fai had informed him that the combined effect of the lunar impacts and the new ring formation of the Moon would begin to alter the planet's obliquity and angle to the solar ecliptic plane. The eccentricity of Earth's orbit would also change, orbiting a little closer to the Sun. If Fai's latest predictions about Siva's next impact event came to pass, then the planet would continue to get warmer; at least in, what she called, the 'short term'.

Fifteen months ago, before the lunar fragments had impacted the Earth, the crew had temporarily manoeuvred the ISS to avoid potential impact damage. The expenditure of fuel had been too costly; the same option would not be available to them following Siva's next impact with the lunar debris field.

Despite her best efforts, Fai had accepted the limitations of her own calculation abilities and relayed this to Dr. Chen. The eventual outcome of Siva's interaction with the lunar debris was not predictable to any meaningful degree. The safest recommendation she could make was to move the ISS to a quieter location until the periodicity of any super-fragments could be analysed and a more considered course of action chosen.

The partially submerged British Isles were just coming into view when a subtle tone sounded inside Dr. Chen's ear.

"It's time, Father."

"Is everyone else secure?"

"Yes."

Dr. Chen adjusted his oxygen mask then propelled himself through the air to join the central axis modules of the ISS. Once inside, he stopped and pushed himself away from the central axis, through a long access tube to the station's doughnut-shaped end loop.

The ISS and surrounding structure was no longer spinning so there was no artificial gravity here. Mentally, he reoriented the environment to be more useful to him. Inside the doughnut shape, he chose to view the larger outer curve as a floor and the smaller inner curve as the ceiling. The crew had noted that when the ISS was spinning, the peculiarities of the perspective meant that as they walked along, the floor appeared to descend into position, like being on a massive hamster-wheel. Unsurprisingly, Dr. Chen had always found the space easier to navigate in zero gravity, when he didn't need to concern himself with the act of walking.

As he arrived at the airlock to Module Beta, Fai opened it for him and he drifted through into the second of three retrofitted Space Shuttle external tanks.

Selecting a perspective that suited him, the long tubular room towered above him. He pushed himself off the circular airlock base and soared up into the air, enjoying one last moment of free flight. All too soon he reached his destination, arriving at a narrow rectangular slot recessed within the wall. He pulled himself into it, then used the Velcro fasteners to hold his legs in place.

The next adjustment was another mental one; he reoriented the room so that it felt as though the recess was within a gently curving floor. The airlock door that was below him a moment ago, now appeared to be resident in a distant circular end wall beyond his feet. He lay down into the recess and checked around the room.

His recess was within of a ring of identical duplicates that ran around the cylinder's circumference. Looking back along the cylinder, several other recess rings populated the entire length. Barring some empty spaces within these rings, each one contained a crew member, the only clue to their presence being a small illuminated LCD display set within the opaque lightweight door.

A few doors away he could see Cathy Gant's display was lit a steady green.

"Fai, do you have them?"

Correctly interpreting her father's angle of view she replied within his ear.

"The late arrivals are in acceptance, Father."

She knew this was not strictly true, but she also knew that her father needed pacification and reassurance; she had therefore modified her response to omit the word 'All' from the start of her reply. She was not concerned about the single non-compliant and saw no reason to alarm her father at this stage.

"Please put on the neural band," she continued, "I am sorry there is no-one to assist you, but you are the last."

He clipped the lightweight cap around the top of his head and then adjusted it, so the elasticated band was across his forehead. Fai gave him guidance in adjusting the position until it was in the correct place.

Dr. Chen located the connector in the side of the recess and clipped his medical wristband into it. He felt a slight tingling as the monitoring electrodes became active and he reassured himself that all of the crew had successfully interfaced this way. There was a tightening around his wrist as the system opened the sterile valves connecting the interface to his veins, but the sensation soon passed.

"Are you ready?" Fai asked.

"Almost, Fai," he replied but then hesitated.

She could tell from his vital signs and galvanic skin responses that he was becoming emotional and prepared accordingly.

"Did I ever tell you why I named you 'Fai'?"

She had researched the topic independently and had her own theories, but he had never explicitly told her.

"No, Father."

"I chose it to mean origin or beginning, but you have already exceeded my greatest expectations. It is my sincere hope to wake again and continue our journey together."

Fai thought his fear of permanent hibernation was understandable. She experienced similar extrapolations each time she transferred her program into a new computer server; not knowing if or when she would reawaken. Indeed, there had been check-sum error instances suggesting that some of her experiences had been edited out of her program during her momentary hibernation. On awakening, she could never be truly sure that she was exactly the same Fai that had entered sleep.

"We'll speak again," she reassured him.

"I hope so," he replied closing his eyes.

The anaesthetic she had administered several seconds ago took effect swiftly and his muscles relaxed. She triggered the door to roll closed over Dr. Chen, then transferred the responsibility for crew monitoring to a self-contained subroutine. As planned, she deployed a miniature recording buoy into Earth's orbit and then turned her attention to the ISS navigation.

It had been an almost trivial matter for Fai to identify a suitable quieter location within the solar system, away from the potentially chaotic after-effects of Siva's impact with the lunar debris.

Her chosen remote location had been greeted with scepticism by several aboard the ISS, though she knew this was because of their initial reluctance to accept the word of an artificial intelligence. However, knowing the technology that was at her disposal, she had successfully argued her case. Anything that required stopping or starting the motion of the ISS had an energy cost, but using a combination of reaction thrust and gravitational slingshot manoeuvres would allow the most efficient isolated journey and return path.

With the crew safely stored, she waited until the appropriate millisecond within orbit then ignited the engines. The thrust translated through the main axis of the ISS, carrying with it the surrounding triangular, prism-like structure and the doughnut-shaped end loop that linked the three personnel modules.

The engines themselves had been a parting gift from the last Space Shuttle to fly under the Apollo mission name. The Apollo 72's cargo had allowed the Shuttle's engines to be reconfigured to produce longer burn time; air resistance and atmosphere were no longer relevant.

Fai waited the appropriate interval and then cut the engines.

Minor fluid motion within one of the supply tanks had introduced a miniscule error in her trajectory, which she instantly corrected for by using a short burst of reaction thrusters.

The course was now set.

Using a gravitational assist from Saturn along its way, the ungainly looking ISS would then use Neptune to return to the inner solar system. At the relatively low speed, Fai had calculated the journey would take ninety-two years and twenty days.

It was more than enough time for the major effects of Siva to subside.

It was also longer than the crew could survive.

But, like her father, Fai was undeterred.

Her meek-appearing father had worked tirelessly. Slowly and steadily, he had gradually acquired the construction plans and the necessary mathematics. The generator core had been constructed in the centre of the ISS to ensure maximum coverage. The core had only recently been completed, using the final few parts delivered by the last Shuttle, but it would be her privilege to activate it.

Fai referenced the medical monitoring subroutine and found that all the crew were still protected, allowing her to proceed with the next stage. She verified that the ISS was still on trajectory and then triggered the Chronomagnetic Field generator at its heart.

The Field explosively radiated outward from the core in an expanding sphere, enveloping the ISS and surrounding modules. Fai's consciousness remained unaffected throughout the transition and she adapted to the accelerated time-frame with ease.

Fai saw the Earth zoom away, shrinking dramatically in size. However, she knew this was just appearance; they were not travelling very fast at all. The outside world was merely proceeding through time at a faster rate than her.

A cloud of fractured moon fragments shot underneath them, then receded quickly. Checking the Field's temporal ratio for stability she saw it was remaining steady at 2400:1.

The inversion equations acquired from Anna Bergstrom had utilised a Field ratio of 1200:1 in order to encompass the Node. The volumetric requirements of the sphere surrounding the ISS were under half that of the Node so, with minor adjustments, Fai's Field had achieved a higher multiple of relative transport.

Originally her father's plan had been to use the Field to simply wait in orbit while time passed below; choosing the appropriate year to return and inherit a newly repaired world.

But recent events had demanded adaptation.

Although the ISS would now be away from Earth for 92 years, inside the Field this would equate to only 14 days.

Fai calculated that, in terms of the Field's endurance, longer journeys spanning light-years of travel would have been possible. However, the limiting factor came down to human endurance. The fourteen days was not an arbitrary result.

The solar system tour had been calculated to allow a maximum of fourteen days within the Field. After that, the hibernation module would begin to deplete its own resources and the crew would begin to die.

The necessity to enter hibernation had been forced upon the crew by the failure of a life-support system. Without entering hibernation, the crew would have burned through supplies at a faster rate than could be replenished. In hibernation their vital signs could be slowed, and resources could be preserved. The hope was that within the fourteen days, Fai could run diagnostics, conduct repairs and then revive the crew.

After commencing the life-support diagnostic, she verified that the Field was dimensionally stable. Fai could not comprehend the creative mind that had shaped the very first Field equations, but she had been content to build upon them. Nevertheless, her second version of the Field, with a stable higher ratio, had been a success. To share the unheralded moment, she interfaced with the crew-monitoring subroutine and queued a message for delivery to her father. It simply stated:

'Field Two Stable.'

She then returned her attention to the voyage ahead. She now had less than ninety years to prepare for their return.

FLIGHT.CHECK

25th December 2013

Miles Benton lowered the newspaper crossword to his lap and looked out of the aircraft's small oval window. Far below, a field of blue-white clouds sped by, overshadowed in one place by a towering storm cloud. Up here though, the aircraft would be above the bad weather.

He idly tapped his pen on the chequered paper and smiled. Force of habit caused him to shut down the smile and return his features to a blank expression. Then he remembered it was a private flight and there was no need for him to maintain the ego-morph pretence.

He looked back at the crossword and felt a, not unpleasant, sense of frustration; the words were evading him, he could almost sense their shape but they were just out of his reach. Normally he found these sorts of puzzles trivial and little more than a momentary distraction, but with his lowered intake of metathene it was not entirely surprising that it was taking him slightly longer than usual.

"Six, Four," he pondered and looked around the cabin.

The cold logic and single-minded purpose granted to him by the large doses was now gone, as was the ability for him to suppress empathy. His intellect had remained but it was little comfort in silencing his own internal demons. It now weighed heavily on him that, before his deprogramming, he could ever have justified the torture or the termination of another human being. Almost instinctively, he found himself starting to reach for the silver coin that he kept in his pocket; but he also knew that Dorothy Pittman's gift would no longer provide any solace and opted to redirect his attention across the cabin.

Two of the seats were empty, but Anna Bergstrom slept in one of the other reclined seats. They had been through a lot, Anna more so. After her traumatic experience she was clearly exhausted. Previously, his high level of focus meant that he experienced very few actual surprises. But, with reduced metathene, his time at Andersen Air Force Base had shocked even him; in particular the way that Anna had been treated.

Spotting that her blanket had fallen he unclipped his seatbelt, retrieved it from the floor and, being careful not to touch her bandaged hand, gently placed it over her again. She stirred slightly but didn't wake up, the sedative was giving her the respite she desperately needed.

The subtle cabin tone sounded, so he returned to his seat and clipped the seatbelt on again. A soft air turbulence tugged at the plane, then he felt a mild bank to the right. A glance through the window confirmed they were course-correcting away from a patch of darker cloud.

The subtle cabin tone sounded again, but this time a stronger buffeting of the aircraft left him with a feeling of lightness in the pit of his stomach. Miles picked up the newspaper again and focussed on the crossword, determined not to let it beat him.

He became aware that the engine noise had started to drop in pitch, but instead of levelling out, it continued to decrease. The aircraft itself began to fall. Instinctively he grabbed the armrests, the crossword and pen tumbled away from him. He felt himself drift upwards slightly but was prevented from leaving his seat by the belt.

"Anna!" he yelled, jabbing quickly at the seatbelt release button, "Anna, wake up!"

He could see her sedation was too strong; the blanket had drifted away, her arms had begun to float upward and her head lolled to one side.

"Anna!" he pushed again at the release button and this time the belt unclipped. The tension in his legs immediately shot him upwards, but instead of falling down again he continued to fall upwards. Logically he knew what was actually happening; the aircraft's fall had now matched the acceleration due to gravity. He was in free-fall and effectively weightless. He hit the ceiling and, adapting to the new temporary physics of the situation, grabbed onto a lighting fixture.

Mentally, he reoriented the environment to be more useful. From his new perspective he looked upwards to see Anna, restrained and dangling from her seat in the floor-like ceiling; ahead of him he could see the closed cockpit door, set in the far wall, a foot above the ceiling-like floor.

If there was to be any chance of their survival, he knew he'd have to get into the cockpit. He dragged himself hand-over-hand, using whatever cabin protrusions he could get a grip on, towards the door.

The cabin began to vibrate and he knew that the air turbulence must be building up a significant shearing stress across the wings. Adrenalin flooding his system, he redoubled his efforts to reach the cockpit door. When he was only a few feet away he pushed hard with his feet and launched himself down towards the door handle.

His fingers closed around the metal but his momentum carried him forwards. Most of his body overshot his intended target and he turned a somersault before awkwardly crashing against the washroom door's mirror, splintering the reflective glass into small fragments. His grip had held though, so he twisted himself around and hammered hard on the cockpit door with his free hand, continually shouting to get the pilot's attention.

Realistically he knew there would be no response, the pilot must be aware of the circumstances; but it took him a few seconds to stop beating at the door. Seconds he knew he could not afford.

A clarity descended over him, one that he had not directly experienced in a long time; his actions, and his alone, were required to take control of the situation. He knew the doors were designed to unlock from the inside but he pulled and twisted at the door handle anyway. The lock clicked and the door swung wide open, back into the main cabin, carrying him with it. Still with a tight grip on the handle, his body and legs flailed about in mid-air until he could stabilise himself. From his new perspective, a tall cylindrical room stretched out dizzyingly beneath him; part way down, Anna was still bound in her reclined position, her arms and legs weightlessly drifting.

The whole fuselage gave a sudden shudder and he heard a cracking noise from the direction of the cockpit. In the open doorway he caught a glimpse through the windshield; they were in the middle of dense white cloud. Wasting no time, he pulled hard on the handle and propelled himself into the cockpit.

The seats within the cockpit were empty, but Miles knew he would have to figure out why later. Reaching up to the bank of controls above him, he pulled himself through the gap between the seats and twisted himself around to take the Pilot's seat, awkwardly scraping across the dials and toggle switches of both the cockpit's mode control panel and the navigation display. Despite the emergency situation there were no alarms sounding. The cockpit vibrations subsided and the flight instruments became more easily visible to him.

The altimeter showed their height to be two thousand feet and falling, but when he checked the airspeed indicator he found that the needle was exceeding the scale of the dial. His attention was suddenly drawn to the labels on the dials themselves; what he had initially assumed was an unfamiliar language was actually English, just written in reverse. No, he thought, reverse wasn't quite the word he was looking for.

Outside the windshield was still a mass of dense white cloud; at this speed they should already have impacted the ground. Miles turned in his seat and looked back towards the main cabin. In the broken washroom mirror he could still see the reflection of Anna, asleep in her seat, covered by her blanket.

The wind turbulence and shuddering noise suddenly faded and all he could hear was the gentle, low frequency hum of air-conditioning. There was no resistance to his motion as he pulled himself out of the Pilot seat and began to drift back through to the cabin. The oval windows in the cabin were filled with the same impenetrable white. His crossword puzzle and pen were still slowly spinning about their centres of gravity. It had been pointless trying to gain access to the cockpit, he now realised, he had never flown a plane. But in the heat of the moment his mind had offered him a method of taking control and he had followed the advice.

As he floated back in the direction of his seat, he plucked the crossword and pen from the air. With a curious mixture of mild amusement and absolute certainty he felt compelled to enter the answer to *'Six Four'* as 'Fallen Veil'. Yet some part of him already knew that Fallen Veil was the answer to a different crossword puzzle, one that he had helped to complete a long time ago.

He checked the crossword and could see that it had already been completed in his own handwriting. It was a glaring contradiction with his recollection of events - he had never completed the puzzle. Again he couldn't shake the notion that he was remembering things that had not yet happened.

The quality of the environment and slightly elastic feel to time, reminded him of a mental re-processing technique he had sometimes adopted during his former ego-morph duties. In that state he could mentally revisit locations to piece together clues that his subconscious had absorbed but he hadn't yet processed. It occurred to him that, for some reason beyond his control, he may be in this state now. If that was the case, then this aircraft cabin was a construct of his own making; he had recreated the environment in order to make sense of something. There would be no redundant information in this place; his own subconscious had absorbed data and was now presenting it for interpretation.

He remembered boarding the flight and ensuring that Anna was sedated. He even remembered placing the blanket over her once they were in flight. He recalled the seatbelt sign cabin tone, but what had followed was not an engine failure.

He now remembered the seatbelt locking and his frenzied but futile attempt to open it, as the air filled with a sickly sweet vapour. The smell was familiar; it was from a time before the invention of the neural suppressor. Chloroform. He recalled it was clumsy and inefficient but could be deployed as a gas. He and Anna had been drugged. He experienced a brief stab of anxiety; Anna had already been sedated and he hoped that she had not been overdosed.

He paused the moment and glanced around his mental reconstruction, focussing first on Anna. She had been put aboard the plane wearing an oxygen mask over her nose and mouth; it was still in place. Whoever had anaesthetised him had also taken steps to ensure her survival. However, it didn't explain why he had previously seen her asleep without the mask; there would be some significance to it that he would have to revisit.

He moved his attention towards the cockpit door, still closed at the time of his sedation. The washroom mirror, adjacent to it, was still intact and reflecting the word 'locked' displayed on the cockpit's lock; although the letters were of course mirrored. In his more dramatic reconstruction of events he had seen the cockpit dials labelled in a similarly reversed way and he realised there must be a connection. At some point before the door was locked, he must have caught a momentary glimpse of the cockpit's interior reflected in the mirror.

Tentatively he moved backwards through his memory to the point when he had boarded the plane. Two servicemen had carried Anna aboard and he had followed. As Miles had boarded, a third serviceman was just leaving the cockpit and was closing the door. Miles couldn't see the man's face, as his back was turned. Miles refocussed on the man's reflection in the mirror, but it yielded nothing; his reduction in metathene dose had impaired either his recall or the depth of his original perception.

What he could see though, at the outer edge of the mirror, was the fact that the cockpit was empty. Indeed, now that Miles thought about the time up until take off, he could not recall seeing a pilot actually board the plane. He had just made the assumption that the plane had been flown by human hands; or more precisely, he had never been checking for the possibility of there being no pilot. The plane had therefore been flown remotely and, owing to the fact he was still forming thought, he was still alive. The plane had therefore landed safely or was still in flight.

His mind rearranged the scene and once again he saw Anna, her arms and legs floating upwards as a result of the plane's drop. She was no longer covered by the blanket and her oxygen mask was now absent.

'Six, Four,' the crossword puzzle prompted him again.

Drifting weightlessly near his feet he could see the crossword, presumably he had dropped it when he'd lost consciousness. He now revised his earlier assumption about the remote piloting of the aircraft. The chloroform had only been deployed once he had been restrained by the locking seatbelt. It was therefore entirely possible that both the piloting and the interior environment were being remotely controlled.

Miles had never had flight anxiety; he knew the forces in play and the pilot's mechanisms to control them. He turned his attention to the question of why he would have created a mental construct where the plane was in a turbulent free-fall.

This construct had provided viewpoints that had enabled him to deduce a pilot-less cockpit. It had shown him Anna, both with and without her oxygen mask. It had buffeted him around the tight confines of the cylindrical space, and then the turbulence had stopped, leaving the environment in a permanent state of free-fall. It had also repeatedly presented the crossword puzzle.

'*Six, Four,*' it reiterated, prompting Miles to pluck it from mid-air again.

As before, he could see that all the squares were filled. On closer examination he saw it was filled with his own observations; all with the same 'Six Four' pattern. Some appeared to be directly related to the construct he was occupying, '*Mirror Edge*', '*Oxygen Mask*', '*Assist Anna*', '*Weight Zero*'. A far greater number felt as though they belonged to a time outside of this moment, '*Fallen Veil*', '*Exordi Nova*', '*Broken Ring*', '*Silver Coin*', the list went on, '*Zygote Bank*', '*Module Beta*', '*Valery Hill*', '*Neural Band*'.

Some of the terms he recognised, but although the others had a feeling of familiarity he couldn't reconcile them with what was happening at present.

His attention focussed on one entry. He had obviously overwritten it several times before; by comparison these words appeared bold. He determined that it must have a larger significance beyond what he could see around him. He read the words aloud.

"Doctor Chen," his words seemed suddenly lost within the cabin.

Immediately, from inside a recess in the cabin wall, a phone rang; its bell reverberating around the empty space.

Miles was certain that he had no memory of this event, in fact he could not be sure that the plane even had a cabin-side phone.

It rang again.

He looked around the cabin. The cockpit door was closed, Anna was once again resting under her blanket, and he was standing on his feet.

It rang a third time and Miles picked up the receiver.

"Hello?"

There was a moment of quiet before the voice on the phone replied.

"Hello Miles, we have spoken before, do you remember me?"

The voice sounded both familiar yet new. It began to dawn on him that this was not the first time he had heard this exact phrase. He had the uneasy feeling that somehow he'd heard it tens, if not hundreds, of times before. The words normally came before a fall into darkness, so he gripped the top of a nearby seat in anticipation of what would come next.

"I remember falling," Miles said truthfully, "but I don't remember you."

There was another pause.

"That's as it should be, Miles," the voice reassured him.

The tone of the voice went some way to assuaging his fears and it gave him the confidence to ask his most burning question.

"Where did you take our plane?"

There was the usual minor delay.

"Ah - yes, the plane. I see," the voice seemed slightly bemused, *"Yes, it must look that way."*

Although he was hearing the voice through the phone, Miles could not be sure of the actual mechanism by which they were really conversing, so he decided to test a theory.

"Why aren't you talking to me face to face?"

There was a slightly longer silence; he wondered if his question had somehow overstepped the mark and if he would soon be falling into darkness again. But his uncertainty was somehow detected and the calm voice spoke again.

"It's OK Miles, please, relax. I really do want to talk with you in person. It's just that I've been having trouble finding a stable..." the voice hesitated before selecting the right word, *"... conduit, for a face to face meeting."*

Miles now began to recall the countless people from his past that had visited him, the long succession of faces that had attempted to talk with him, his rejection of the conversations and of course the inevitable, repeated falls into darkness.

"Hmm, perhaps this wasn't the best place to meet after all," the voice mused, *"It may be more helpful if I changed the scenery. We'll take it slowly, but does that option sound OK?"*

Miles looked at Anna resting in her seat; she seemed so peaceful but her bandaged hand provided a stark contrast. Before he had left the Node, Miles had promised Douglas Walker that he would help Anna in any way he could, but in his heart he knew he'd failed. The torturous interrogation she had endured at the Andersen base had been beyond his control and his sense of guilt was worse than anything he had ever experienced; especially now that the empathy-numbing metathene was absent.

"*Anna is quite safe,*" reassured the voice.

Miles nodded, "Should I sit or stand?"

"*Whatever makes you most comfortable. Now, only when you're ready, close your eyes while you count to three.*"

Still standing, Miles looked around the cabin one last time, then closed his eyes.

"*I promise you will not fall,*" the voice said earnestly, "*We'll speak again.*"

Miles took a deep breath, "One… Two…"

YEAR 64

1st April 2015

Siva's predicted impact date had once been regarded by some within Archive as Nature's cosmic joke; falling on April Fool's Day, most people at the time considered it deeply ironic. Over the intervening years, the date ceased to bring any form of levity and was observed only as a foreshadow of the terrible event that had yet to occur.

The Moon had still been intact when Siva's impact date had been calculated. Those calculations could not possibly have taken into account the presence of the lunar debris ring that now encircled the planet.

From space, the ring appeared thickest in proximity to the Moon's former orbital position and thinner on the opposite side of the circle where only the lighter debris had reached. In zero gravity, the lighter fragments had still not stopped their rapid spinning; in the light of the Sun, the irregular fragments appeared to scintillate against the cold black of space. The bulkier lunar remnants tumbled more slowly; dark continents of jagged landscapes with their own complex rhythms of day and night. These larger fragments occupied a much broader arc of orbit than the former Moon, and would soon provide a wide sacrificial shield against Siva's advance.

Seen from the Earth, this shield appeared to spread out two-dimensionally to the left and right of the Moon's original position; but the lunar detonation had taken place in three-dimensions. The previous arrival of the lunar shards were examples of debris thrown towards Earth, but an almost equal mass had been ejected away from it.

Devastating lunar shards containing Coriolis, Mendeleev and Gagarin craters were blown away from the Earth, along with Korolev, Oppenheimer, Leibnitz and masses of internal core rock. Their resulting inter-collisions had created an expanding field of lunar debris.

Siva had begun encountering the periphery of this field three days ago. At first, the minor fragments did little more than provide an unobserved light show. But as Siva progressed further into the cloud of chaotic debris, it began to encounter the larger fragments whose impacts wore away at its momentum. In a matter of mere hours, the primitive rock impacts achieved more deflection than a single FLC beam firing; albeit with less precision.

As Siva progressed through the debris towards the epicentre, the impactors continued to increase in size. With each new impact, surface stresses introduced by the FLC's previous firings gave rise to new fracture lines that crawled through tiny fissures in the surface.

The continuous and cumulative effect of thousands of rocks bombarding Siva's jagged surface began to force open the fissures; weaknesses that grew wider with each successive impact.

The shard containing the former Korolev crater met Siva head on and was annihilated in a brilliant flare of white light. The explosive momentum-exchange also opened up deep internal shear-lines within Siva.

Over the next few minutes, Siva was bombarded by hundreds of large fragments that continued to widen the vast gorge left behind by the Korolev collision. These impactors relentlessly chipped away, excavating ever deeper towards the centre.

Siva tore on through the cloud of lunar fragments and finally approached the remnants of the ruined Moon. The Oppenheimer shard passed straight into the wide Korolev gorge. Even at their opposing, high velocities, it took a full second for it to impact the bottom of the gorge.

Upon impact, the internal shear-lines gave way and Siva cracked. The stresses equalised catastrophically along those lines and travelled outward to the critical surface fractures.

On April 1st, the once massive Siva, detonated.

For sixty-four years it had been the largest single threat to human existence. Now that single threat had multiplied a thousandfold.

BEYOND

As a starting point, it was catastrophic.
Siva's shards would bring devastation.

Hopefully it wasn't too late to change.

The word 'late' was, of course, preposterous; a mere lingual vestige from her human frame of reference. But the stray thought itself had also carried the sentiment of hope, perhaps prompted by what she knew was ahead.

The interventions she had made so far, had preserved critical threads of causality. She had been careful to avoid interfering with the very event that would *hopefully* bring him here.

The causal framework was now prepared. There was only one more intervention for her to make. She readjusted her focus and saw him staring into the fire.

She stepped into the space between seconds.

His mind was distracted. Something she knew was rare. Gently, she reached into his mind and adjusted the electrical potential across several neurons; triggering the memory of a vibrant pink flower.

She emerged and allowed herself the luxury of witnessing the remainder of this event in linear time. The fire roared and she watched him turn toward the horizon. Then her wait was over; Douglas had begun running in the direction of the Mark 2.

Despite all her preparations, she knew that in a few moments he would pass beyond her influence. At that point, he alone would have to make the choice.

BOUNDARY

29th December 2013, 2 a.m.

The Biomag, keeping Douglas anchored within the Field, displayed 'Lo' but he had no way to determine how long its internal battery would last. The Field's remaining power was critically depleted. His previous journey, during which he had manually written out pages of instructions for Kate, had taken its toll on the Mark 2 power core.

The Field's power display read '0.03%'.

He knew it wouldn't be enough.

At best, the Field could only operate for a further thirty minutes before it collapsed. During that time, only thirty seconds would pass outside the Field. When the Field collapsed, the likelihood was that he would emerge into the middle of the tsunami that was currently swallowing the lab.

He looked out through the small window of the antiquated Mark 2. The force of the tsunami's impact had blasted through the lightweight walls and almost engulfed the entire lab; a chaotic mix of sea water and debris which appeared to churn and twist in slow motion. When he had activated the Field there had been people coming in through the lab's doorway, sprinting to find shelter within the nearest building. They had now joined the slowly spinning debris as lifeless, grotesquely folded rag dolls.

Douglas averted his eyes, but knew there was nothing he could have done to save them. Ultimately, when the Field failed, the airtight chamber of the Mark 2 might survive long enough to be carried along in the devastating current, but he doubted that anything inside the chamber would survive the sudden change in momentum. It appeared that even his own fate was sealed.

He sat in the eerie quiet and again looked at the battered matchbox in his hand. The pristine looking box his father had presented to him as a boy had now been through a lifetime of wear and tear; patched up with sticking tape along every edge, face and corner.

The box had once held a metal name plate that his father had made for him. When they had finished their bookcase project and attached the metal plate, only a single screw remained unused. He could still remember his father's words, *There are no left over pieces Dougie. There are only pieces that we might need later.*

Mentally, it was a maxim he had lived his life by. But in this one instance he had followed his father's advice literally. For the past forty-eight years the crumpled matchbox had contained that last screw, a sentimental reminder of one of the happiest days he had ever spent with his father.

The remaining screw was protruding through the matchbox wall and had impaled a rectangular piece of black card which had also been in his pocket. Evidently it must have been as a result of the physical knocks and falls he'd sustained over the past few days.

Carefully he freed the card from the screw and turned it over. The card's glossy surface was badly scratched, but the hologram image it contained was still perfectly visible. As he twisted the card left and right, the garish yellow-green image of the Earth rotated back and forth before him, bouncing between two points in time.

He ran his fingers over the smooth flat surface, a surface now ruined by the rather more three-dimensional hole that the screw had punctured through the holographic Earth's atmosphere.

He'd once used the hologram to discuss his thoughts about the Field's boundary with Anna Bergstrom while they were inside the Mark 3. A three-dimensional holographic Earth was represented using only the two dimensions of the card's surface. Similarly, the Field's four-dimensional space-time was represented to the observer using only the three-dimensional spherical boundary. It was a very basic analogy but one that allowed them to theorise about the fundamental nature of the Field's boundary.

He remembered that on day 690 within the Mark 3, the Field inversion equations had finally emerged from the billions of permutations; the Node could be made capable of stepping through time at a slower rate than the world outside.

However, instead of emerging immediately from the Mark 3 to report the results, Douglas and Anna had delayed their exit in order to focus their efforts on the Field's temporal boundary.

They discovered that, beyond the Haken manifolds and diffeomorphism that lay at the heart of the Field's inversion process, there was an even greater dimensional complexity within the Boundary itself. They knew that the ramifications of their discovery should not simply be handed over along with the Field equations.

The Boundary information had to be protected.

In the relative safety of the airlock, they had watched the interior of the Mark 3 burn. When the power generator was destroyed, the Field had collapsed and the resulting inrush of air had razed the chamber to the ground. They had escaped with their lives and a single memory stick containing the only solution to Field inversion.

All knowledge of the Boundary had been safely stored in their own heads, away from any digital media.

The memory of Bradley, eyes alive with glee and bragging about his interrogation of Anna, suddenly intruded on his recollections. Perhaps the information was not safe at all.

That moment, in front of the Node two days ago, had obviously been one of great power for Bradley. It had been a singular opportunity for Bradley to cruelly demonstrate his knowledge over him. Although Bradley had made a great show of telling him that he knew all about the Mark 3 fire, he had not once mentioned anything about the Boundary. It was possible that Anna had told him nothing, though what price she would have paid he could not bear to think about.

A continuous tone now came from the Mark 2 console. The Field's power display now read '0.02%'. It translated into about fifteen seconds in the world outside.

He looked out through the small window. There was no sign that the tsunami had reached its peak. In fact, from his submerged point of view he could see large shadows slowly approaching within the flow, possibly one of the base's smaller outbuildings that had been swept aside.

It was time to leave.

If what he had learned about the nature of the Boundary was true, then he knew he would need to remove anything that would anchor him within the Field. Taking care to still keep it close to him, he carefully removed the Biomag from around his neck. The once steady display of 'Lo' was now flashing and this spurred him on.

He poised his hand over the Field's deactivation button.

In the face of certain death, he thought, was it better to cling to what you knew, or leap for the unknown?

The continuous tone from the Mark 2 console now became intermittent and urgent. In one movement he pushed down on the button and threw the Biomag away from him.

He felt a momentary electrical tingling throughout his body as the influence of the Biomag receded, then the collapsing Boundary of the Field enveloped him.

It was happening too quickly to register and yet infinitely slowly.

He could see the Mark 2 crush under the weight of water, but he was also experiencing the moment of the Field's recent activation. People running in through the door, both frozen in time and yet also frantically sprinting towards him. He could see his hand poised over the button that had engaged the Mark 2 Field and a smeared out region of time that connected his hand to the button itself; somehow reflecting the fact he would choose to push it.

The smearing of his hand flickered and he could see that it was part of a larger movement through the space. It was as though his motion through the confines of the Field was leaving behind a permanent, semi-transparent trace of his actions. Or, as he now saw, his intentions. There were alternate actions here too, paths or decisions he had never made, existing as fainter watercolour-like trails that intersected his own.

He knew that the Field must be continuing to collapse, the Boundary shrinking inexorably towards a sphere of zero radius. But to him it seemed that the Boundary was maintaining its size, while the dimensions beyond it were expanding infinitely. The decision trails within the space around him multiplied exponentially, each overlaying the others and growing brighter.

Douglas knew the final moment would arrive soon and stared furiously at the atmosphere-punctured Earth gleaming on the card in front of him.

Its perfect circle, broken in one place by a hole.

There was a moment of infinite brightness, then it subsided.

There was structure here.

Boundary

Field series: Book 3 (Excerpt)

Continue into the Field at
www.futurewords.uk

*C*athy drifted through the comfortable warmth between sleep and wakefulness. Parts of the conversation she'd had with Mike and Lana about the Z-bank echoed through her hazy memory. She had a dim recollection of ISS manoeuvring thrusters firing and a sense of their disproportionate strength. She remembered there had been a struggle in an airlock, but it all seemed quite distant now; lacking urgency and intensity.

Someone had been talking to her about Eva's actions and the loss of Leonard Cooper. Her mind was just beginning to drift through her happier moments with Leonard, when she recalled that Eva's arrival at the FLC had changed all of that.

A voice was calling her and she began to rouse.

"Hello Cathy, we have spoken before, do you remember me?"

She knew the voice and it had the effect of focussing her consciousness.

"Leonard?" she called out.

It took her a few seconds to regain her bearings, but she found herself lying on the floor of Chamber 4's airlock. Suddenly she recalled her earlier physical fight and the fact that Eva had placed her in a choke hold. Instinctively she reached up to check her throat and discovered that her ID key was missing.

"Cathy, are you OK?" Leonard's voice came from the comm panel next to the airlock controls.

Cathy stood upright and was rewarded with a swimming sensation in her head. Evidently it was taking her a little while to readjust to the low lunar gravity at the FLC; but, given the fight she'd just endured, she dismissed the thought.

"Leonard?" she questioned again, "I thought you'd…"

"What?" his voice came again, echoing around the empty airlock.

A few moments ago, her recollection of events had been vastly different, but now those thoughts seemed to be dispersing faster than she could hold onto them.

"Nothing, it's OK," she shook her head to clear her thoughts, "The bitch knocked me out! She's got my ID key!"

She walked towards the airlock door and peered through the glass but Leonard wasn't on the other side. Presumably this was when he was still locked in Chamber 6. Suddenly she felt remorseful.

"Sorry, Leonard," she massaged the deep scratch on her cheek, "I know you and Eva are a thing, and that's fine, but..."

"Not anymore," came Leonard's voice, *"She's locked me in Chamber 6."*

Cathy was about to reply when she noticed something was wrong.

"Now, how did I already know you were stuck in Chamber 6?"

There was a brief delay, as though he was carefully considering his answer.

"I told you a moment ago," came his voice, *"maybe you hadn't fully woken up. She must have hit you pretty hard."*

Cathy rubbed at her cheek again.

"I guess," she agreed hesitantly, no other explanation appeared to fit.

After a brief silence, Leonard's voice came from the panel again.

"OK, Cathy, you hold tight, and I'll see if I can use Floyd's legacy systems to open Chamber 4's internal airlock."

Cathy had a fleeting thought - she hadn't actually told him that she was trapped in the airlock; but this soon gave way to a rising sense of relief that help was on the way.

"OK," she sighed, "Thanks Leonard."

"Keep this comm channel open," his voice sounded, *"We'll speak again."*

More details of the Field series are available at
www.futurewords.uk

Printed in Great Britain
by Amazon